"There's a blacksmith, all right, m'lord," the groom said, removing his hat and wiping his hand across his grizzled and sweaty head. "Only he's dead."

Ottilia saw renewed vexation leap quickly into her husband's eyes, and made an immediate effort to deflect his attention. "Recently, Ryde?"

"Last night, m'lady."

"What happened to him?" Ottilia asked.

"Seems the roof caved in on him, m'lady. And they're saying he had his head bashed in."

"Good God," uttered Francis, startled.

"Was it the storm, Ryde?"

A faint twitch attacked the groom's mouth and his eye gleamed. Noting these rare signs of amusement, Ottilia waited with burgeoning interest.

"The storm, m'lady, or a witch's curse, if the villagers are to be believed."

A spurt of laughter was surprised out of Francis, but Ottilia was intrigued.

"Don't dismiss it so lightly, Francis," she said. "Perhaps the woman has second sight."

"Tillie, I will not have you embroil yourself in this business."

"I promise you I only mean to satisfy my curiosity."

"Promise forsooth! Do you take me for a fl___ ___ w you to set foot in the place, as sure as check ___ nobbing with all and sundry and hunti___

"Not necessarily," objected O___ "Merely because the villagers ar___ ___ot of superstitious nonsense does ___ ___uilty."

Berkley Prime Crime titles by Elizabeth Bailey

THE GILDED SHROUD
THE DEATHLY PORTENT

THE
DEATHLY
PORTENT

Elizabeth Bailey

BERKLEY PRIME CRIME, NEW YORK

THE BERKLEY PUBLISHING GROUP
Published by the Penguin Group
Penguin Group (USA) Inc.
375 Hudson Street, New York, New York 10014, USA

Penguin Group (Canada), 90 Eglinton Avenue East, Suite 700, Toronto, Ontario M4P 2Y3, Canada (a division of Pearson Penguin Canada Inc.) • Penguin Books Ltd., 80 Strand, London WC2R 0RL, England • Penguin Group Ireland, 25 St. Stephen's Green, Dublin 2, Ireland (a division of Penguin Books Ltd.) • Penguin Group (Australia), 250 Camberwell Road, Camberwell, Victoria 3124, Australia (a division of Pearson Australia Group Pty. Ltd.) • Penguin Books India Pvt. Ltd., 11 Community Centre, Panchsheel Park, New Delhi—110 017, India • Penguin Group (NZ), 67 Apollo Drive, Rosedale, Auckland 0632, New Zealand (a division of Pearson New Zealand Ltd.) • Penguin Books (South Africa) (Pty.) Ltd., 24 Sturdee Avenue, Rosebank, Johannesburg 2196, South Africa

Penguin Books Ltd., Registered Offices: 80 Strand, London WC2R 0RL, England

This book is an original publication of The Berkley Publishing Group.

PUBLISHING HISTORY
Berkley Prime Crime trade edition / April 2012

Library of Congress Cataloging-in-Publication Data

Bailey, Elizabeth.
The deathly portent / Elizabeth Bailey. — 1st ed.
p. cm. — (A Lady Fan mystery ; 2)
ISBN 978-0-425-24567-5 (pbk.)
I. Title.
PR6052.A31857D43 2012
823'.914—dc23
2011037239

PRINTED IN THE UNITED STATES OF AMERICA

10 9 8 7 6 5 4 3 2 1

ALWAYS LEARNING   PEARSON

To my mother,
Shula Bailey,
for her unfailing support and inspiration.

THE
DEATHLY
PORTENT

Chapter 1

It was an ill night to be abroad. The shouts of men, one to another, echoed into the dark, along with the stamp of heavy feet over ground sodden with the droning rain. Here and there, a remnant flicker of the dying fire and the gleam from a shuttered lantern pierced the relentless black, and a distant rumble promised worse to come.

Out of the troubled voices rose a chorus of youthful jeers, closing on running feet as they hastened away from the commotion. Huddled in her cloak, with Tabitha's strong arm about her shoulders urging her on, the young woman raced for shelter. Not from the storm, although its unkind advent had precipitated just the outcome she dreaded. Rather, from the familiar appellation burning in her ears and the sting of the stones thrown by the village boys.

She knew not whither they were headed, except that it lay in an opposite direction from the little cottage she now called home. What with the darkness and the snarling wind, the wetness falling on her face and flattening the hair to her head, and the cries behind ringing in her brain, she could scarcely see to set one foot before the other. Not that it mattered. Not if fate's decree had set a man's life to her account.

Of a sudden the world around her slashed into view as the skies were cut asunder. In the sheet of white, poised for a brief instant while the lightning struck, she saw the spire above the rooftops.

The flash lit up the bleak interior of the parlour, throwing into high relief the boxes in the centre, half unpacked, and the stark outline of the wooden settle, bare of cushions.

The Reverend Aidan Kinnerton, on his knees beside the growing pile of books, glanced up at the window, as yet uncurtained, just as the rolling thunder crashed overhead. He blinked in the dim shadows left behind after the massive glare, the candles struggling to do adequate duty in its stead.

The rain gained momentum, and for an instant Aidan imagined himself back in Africa, with one of its swift and violent storms raging over the crude thatched hut where he had lain, helpless and weak with fever, while his pathetic little flock of converts reverted to their heathen gods and the insane mutterings of the witch doctor.

A second crack of light startled him out of remembrance, and the instant rumble that followed reverberated in his head. Sighing, he turned back to his task of sorting the books, struggling to read their spines by the light of a candelabrum he had set upon the floor. He would undoubtedly do better to leave it until morning and go instead to his bed, but Aidan knew he would not sleep with the intermittent thunder and the persistent dinning rain. And if he did by chance drop off, the raging skies must inevitably bring on his dreaded nightmares. Those lurid dreams of dancing black warriors armed with spears and the call of the tom-toms beating into the night.

The sounds of the storm were abruptly superseded by a violent knocking that seemed to come almost out of his thoughts. For an instant he lost sight of his present situation, and it took a moment to realise that the noise was penetrating through the hall from the front door.

Aidan leapt to his feet, obeying the impulse of shocked question. His footsteps echoed on the bare boards as he crossed hastily through the dimness of the big square hall. Beyond the front door he could hear shouts, and in quick succession there came two thuds against the wooden barrier just as he reached it. Instinct told him these were not made by fists hitting the door. Someone was throwing missiles.

His fingers were numb with cold, he realised, as he fumbled in his hasty effort to turn the large key, and the fleeting thought passed through his mind that he should have kept the fire going in the parlour. Throwing back the bolts, Aidan wrenched open the door.

Two bedraggled figures stood without, one huddled in the protective arms of the other, who looked a trifle more robust. Both were drenched. The larger of the two let out a thankful gasp as she caught sight of Aidan.

"Sanctuary, good sir, for my mistress, else the little beasts will stone her to death."

Aidan's gaze turned automatically to the woman she held, whose head lifted just as another fork of lightning lit up the sky, revealing a brief image of a ravaged face, streaked dirty and wet, with hollow cheeks and wounded eyes, and long hair plastered to her head.

"Come in, come in," Aidan uttered as the dark enveloped them again and the thunder rattled above them.

He swiftly pulled the two women through the door and then thrust outside, putting up a hand to keep the wet out of his eyes as he sought for the perpetrators of this vicious assault.

"Who are you? Show yourselves!"

He could just make out a coterie of figures inside the gate. From their stature, Aidan took them for boys. He raised his voice.

"I see you there. Who are you? Be sure this will not go unpunished!"

At this a hoarse crack of laughter emanated from one of the group.

"It be her as'll be punished," came in retort.

"You watch yourself, Reverend," shouted another. "You don't want nowt to do with her. A witch her be."

Before Aidan could respond, a chorus of mocking laughter echoed into the darkness. And then the boys were off, running back in the direction of the village green.

Aidan watched them disappear into the gloom until discomfort reminded him that he was standing in the driving rain. Hastening back into the house, he shut the door and shot the bolts, shaking off the damp. Then he turned to find the fugitive leaning into the wall, her breath coming short and fast.

"Softly, ma'am. You are safe now."

He spoke without thought, and the dimly seen outline of the woman turned towards him. But if she was about to speak, she was forestalled by the maid who accompanied her.

"Safe, is it? She'll not be safe, Reverend, if she goes back to the cottage. They'll come after her there, sure as check, if that fellow is dead."

Low-voiced, at last the other spoke. "I should not have told him."

"Hush now, Miss Cassie. It ain't no use repining."

In the gloom, Aidan saw the woman sway. The maid caught at her before he could step forward.

"Begging your pardon, Reverend, my mistress is like to fall down if I don't get her sat down quick."

"Yes, of course. Forgive me, ma'am. Will you come into the parlour, both of you?"

Darting ahead, Aidan held the door open, thankful that his two candelabra spilled a modicum of light into the hall to show the way.

"Take care as you enter. I am but half unpacked as yet, and the floor is strewn with belongings."

"Never you fret, sir," said the maid. "I'll see to her."

Aidan took up the candelabrum from the floor and watched the maid shepherd her mistress towards the wooden settle.

"Sit you down, Miss Cassie."

Obedient, the woman sank into the seat, and then she looked up, directly into his face. The candlelight gentled the harsh planes of her dampened features into a softer glow, and Aidan realised she was barely a woman yet. A girl—aged by suffering?

"You befriend me at your peril."

Struck by the vibrant note in her husky voice, Aidan held her gaze, speaking with gentleness.

"As a man of God, it is my duty to befriend anyone who calls upon my charity. Where is the peril in that?"

He watched her fingers curl into claws. "They will revile you. They will tell you I am in league with the devil and you must shun me."

"Then they will find themselves mightily at fault."

She stared at him, her eyes dark with a species of pain that cut Aidan to the heart. "I should not have told him."

The maid clicked her tongue at this repetition, and Aidan glanced at her.

"Pray sit by your mistress and take care of her while I fetch my housekeeper, who will find towels and prepare a bedchamber."

"A bedchamber?"

Aidan smiled at the shock in the maid's voice. "You asked for sanctuary, did you not? I cannot think it wise for your mistress to venture out again tonight."

The girl shuddered, pulling her cloak more tightly about her. Aidan moved a step closer and set his hand palm up. She looked at the hand, then up into his face.

"You are a gentle man, sir."

Then, like a child, she lifted her hand, fingers outstretched and trembling, and set it upon his. Hers was a slim, cold hand, colder than his, and Aidan held it strongly.

"Let me but set all in motion, and then you may tell me everything."

The overnight storm had given way to a fresh summer day, with a rapidly rising temperature. But it had left the roads a quagmire.

Lord Francis Fanshawe was hot, sticky, and decidedly out of temper. He unbent his body from useless contemplation of the axletree, in the vain hope that Ryde was mistaken in saying it was broken. He shifted to flex the ache in his back from bending too long and regarded the muddy road with acute disfavour. The coach wheels were stuck fast, and his boots were caked. They were probably ruined forever—or would be, once he put them in the hands of the boots at a wayside inn. Why in Hades had he come away without his valet?

As if in sympathy, his stomach growled, protesting the hours since breakfast. Francis glanced over to where the three remaining horses, released from their traces and temporarily tethered to a nearby tree, were grazing, ready to eat themselves into a stupor while Francis starved.

At that instant, his gaze fell upon his bride, and his vexation intensified. Tillie was palpably to blame for these evils, but instead of decently railing at an unhappy fate, she could think of nothing better to do than to wander along the roadside admiring wildflowers and humming.

"Ottilia!"

His wife of a few short weeks merely turned her head and waved before continuing on her way. Francis cursed and strode in her direction.

"For pity's sake, come and wait in the coach," he called. "You will exhaust yourself wandering about in this heat."

Tillie checked and turned her clear gaze upon him, raising her brows.

"I am more like to faint from being shut up in that stuffy coach, do you not think?"

"No, I do not. It may be hours before Ryde or Williams gets back."

His groom, despatched to locate the nearest smithy, had gone off in one direction across country, while the coachman, riding the post-horse, had gone back along the main road towards Atherstone, through which they had passed a little before the breakdown, in a bid to locate a decent hostelry where some form of transport might be hired to enable the stranded travellers to seek shelter.

"Surely not," objected Tillie. "That kindly yokel spoke of a village a mere half mile or so from here."

Francis all but snorted. "Do you know no better than to take a country fellow's estimate for gospel? I daresay it is five miles or more to this Witherley place, if we only knew."

For a moment, he received no reply other than his wife's measured regard. Francis knew that look.

"If you are about to try your cajolery on me, Tillie, let me warn you I am not in the mood."

Tillie's characteristic laugh escaped her lips, and his ill temper lightened briefly. "I can see that, my dearest."

She stepped gently off the grass verge and picked a path across the muddy road, holding up her skirts. Having wisely left her travelling greatcoat in the coach, she was clad only in a gown of soft green muslin that emphasised her curves, a mere wisp of lace tucker covering the swell of her bosom. Below her chip straw bonnet, tendrils of her banded hair escaped confinement under a cap and her high-boned cheeks seemed unaffected by the heat that was adding to Francis's frustrations. For an instant he softened, reflecting on the pleasure the mere sight of her gave him, transformed—thanks to his mother's insistence and his own open purse—from the dowdy companion he had first encountered. Then his eye caught on the clutch of coloured stems tucked in her fingers, and his irritation flared anew.

"You are the most maddening female, Tillie," he told her as she came up.

She looked rueful. "Dear me. Am I still in disgrace?"

Francis almost relented, but for the lurking twinkle in his wife's eye. "You know very well we should not have been in this mess had you not insisted on leaving your godmother's this morning. Anyone with a modicum of common sense must have known what the outcome would be after such a storm as we had last night."

To his intense satisfaction, his wife's patience cracked.

"For heaven's sake, Fan, don't start again! All well for you, able to leave the room the moment you could no longer endure it, but I was obliged to answer again and again to the same set of questions and comment. I tell you, if we had not escaped, I would have been ready to stab her with the carving knife."

"Thus ensuring you don't receive a farthing when she is finally gathered to her forefathers."

"Just so," Ottilia said, disregarding his sarcasm. "Far safer to leave at once."

The duty visit to Lady Edingale had indeed been trying, as Francis was obliged to concede. Tillie's ancient benefactor, a schoolfriend of her deceased grandmother, was both deaf and forgetful. She had signally failed to grasp the fact of Ottilia's marriage, despite endless repetitions by both parties and the old lady's long-suffering companion. Or if she had grasped it, she had forgotten it within minutes, enlivening every attempt at conversation with a refrain that at last alienated even his wife's wide tolerance.

"You should think of getting married again, Ottilia. You cannot be mourning your lost love forever."

In vain had his poor Tillie, virtually shouting into the old lady's ear trumpet, protested her new state. It proved of no avail to point Francis out as her husband, for whenever he walked into a room where she was, Lady Edingale invariably took immediate exception to his presence.

"Who is this? What's that? Francis, you say? Know him? Of course I don't know him. Never seen the fellow before in my life."

Nevertheless, it had been foolhardy to set out in these conditions, despite the early promise of the sun. Annoyed with himself for giving in to Tillie's insistence against his better judgement, Francis was aware of being driven to vent his spleen unfairly. He moderated his tone.

"Tillie, I'm hungry and hot and frustrated."

A faint smile flickered on her lips. "And sadly out of temper." She lifted the gloved hand in which her collection of wildflowers was still clutched and rested it lightly against his chest. "Could you truly have endured another such night of creeping about in the dark?"

Francis felt his irritation melting away. Lady Edingale's steadfast refusal to acknowledge their marriage had resulted in furtive assignations in either one of their allotted separate bedchambers. His fingers came up to grasp her hand as he lifted a teasing eyebrow.

"To tell you the truth, I was rather enjoying the romance of it all."

He was rewarded with the gurgle that never failed to affect him.

"You should have mentioned that at the outset," said Tillie. "Such an argument might well have persuaded me to remain."

"What, and miss this adventure?"

"How well you know me!"

He had to laugh. "Wretch!"

Tillie leaned up, and Francis obligingly kissed her on the lips.

"Am I forgiven?"

He gave an elaborate sigh. "I suppose I must be magnanimous."

"Especially considering I am the newest of brides and entitled to a deal more latitude than might normally be the case."

"Latitude? I am more like to end by locking you up and forbidding you to leave the house under any circumstances."

"I should call on your friend George to throw a rope ladder up to my window," returned his wife with scarcely a tremor in her voice. But the mischief in her eyes drove away the last of his irritation.

"Is that the best you can do?" he scoffed. "For shame, Tillie. And here I thought I would provide you with puzzle enough to tax your ingenuity to the utmost."

Before she could retaliate, a hail from behind drew Francis's attention. Releasing his wife, he turned to see his groom reentering the main road from the little lane into which Ryde's steps had been directed by the local whom Francis had earlier accosted.

"Ah, there you are at last."

As Ryde crossed the road towards them, Ottilia noted a look of perturbation in the man's face.

"All is not well, I think," she murmured.

Her husband cast her a frowning look but made no comment, instead turning his attention back to the groom. "Had you no success? Don't say there is no blacksmith at this village after all."

A faint smile twisted Ryde's lips as he came up. It struck Ottilia as grim. A dour fellow at the best of times, the groom was nevertheless, so Francis assured her, one of his household's greatest assets. He had served his master from Lord Francis Fanshawe's earliest years and, like his valet Diplock, had followed him through his soldiering adventures. Ottilia had learned already to trust the man's judgement.

"There's a blacksmith, all right, m'lord," he responded, removing his hat and wiping his hand across his grizzled and sweaty head. "Only he's dead."

Ottilia saw renewed vexation leap quickly into Francis's eyes, and she made an immediate effort to deflect his attention. "Recently, Ryde?"

"Last night, m'lady."

"Last night?" Francis echoed. "If that isn't the devil's own luck."

"For Duggleby, m'lord, as I hear is the man's name."

From no other servant would her husband have accepted the implied rebuke, Ottilia knew. She intervened swiftly, knowing his temper to be exacerbated already.

"What happened to him, Ryde?"

"Seems the roof caved in on him, m'lady."

"Good God," uttered Francis, startled. "Then the poor fellow was crushed to death?"

"Was it the storm, Ryde?"

A faint twitch attacked the groom's mouth, and his eye gleamed. Noting these rare signs of amusement, Ottilia waited with burgeoning interest.

"The storm, m'lady, or a witch's curse, if the villagers are to be believed."

A spurt of laughter was surprised out of Francis, but Ottilia was intrigued.

"How could that be?"

Ryde shrugged. "I couldn't make much sense of it, m'lady. Seems this witch claims she saw the roof come down in a vision."

"Wise after the event, eh?"

"Before, m'lord. By all accounts, this Mrs. Dale gave warning to this Duggleby a couple of days back."

"And it happened as she said? Sheer luck, no doubt."

Ottilia put up a finger. "Don't dismiss it so lightly, Francis. Perhaps the woman has second sight."

The groom was nodding. "That's what they say, m'lady. It ain't the first time as she's been right."

"And I daresay the villagers don't like it?"

"No, m'lady. They say she caused the roof to fall in."

"Yes," Ottilia mused, "people are apt to attack what they fear or do not understand."

"That's why you spoke of a witch's curse, Ryde?"

"Yes, m'lord. Only it's worse than that. Seems the place was set afire. And rumour has it the doctor weren't satisfied as it was the cave-in as killed the blacksmith. They're saying he had his head bashed in."

"But his head must have been damaged by the falling masonry," objected Francis.

Ottilia's mind was buzzing. "Do you say someone administered a blow to the man's head before the roof fell in on him?"

Ryde grimaced. "It's what the tapster in the tavern told me. Only the constable can't go arresting the witch because she's took sanctuary in the vicar's house."

A ripple of unholy delight ran through Ottilia. "It sounds the most glorious muddle."

But her husband's attention had reverted to their own difficulties. "What the devil are we to do now?"

"Nothing for it but to wait for Williams, m'lord."

Ottilia ignored her husband's fluent curses and once more claimed the groom's attention. "Is there a decent hostelry in this village, Ryde?"

"In Witherley, m'lady? But there ain't no point in going there."

"Is it a pretty place?" pursued Ottilia, wholly ignoring this rider.

"Tillie, what are you about?"

She heard the suspicious note in Francis's voice, but she did not answer, merely putting out a hand to enjoin his silence.

The groom looked both puzzled and suspicious, and his answer was brief. "It's well enough, m'lady."

"And does it have a decent hostelry?"

The repetition made Ryde frown and cast a glance at his master. Ottilia turned to smile blindingly at her husband. His gaze narrowed a little, but he did not fail her.

"Answer, man."

Ryde's patent disapproval increased, but he did as he was bid. "I did see a likely place across the green from the Cock and Bottle."

"Excellent," said Ottilia. "Francis, why should we not rest there for a while? You may satisfy your hunger, and I can—"

"Ryde, go and check on the horses," said Francis, cutting in without apology.

Ottilia gathered her forces while Francis waited until the groom was out of earshot. The moment he turned on her, she caught his hand.

"I know what you are going to say, Fan, but—"

"Tillie, no!"

"—it will be only for an hour or two, and I am excessively thirsty—"

"An hour or two? I know you better than that, my love. And pray don't give me any fiddle-faddle about thirst and hunger."

Ottilia released his hand. "Well, but you said you were starving, and I could kill for a cup of coffee."

"And there you have uttered the operative word. Tillie, I will not have you embroil yourself in this business."

Ottilia could not suppress a giggle. "Well, I will admit to being intrigued, but I promise you I only mean to satisfy my curiosity."

"Promise forsooth! Do you take me for a flat? If I allow you to set foot in the place, as sure as check you will be hobnobbing with all and sundry and hunting down this witch."

"Not necessarily," objected Ottilia without thinking. "Merely because the villagers are silly enough to fall for a lot of superstitious nonsense does not make the woman guilty."

Francis threw up his hands. "I knew it! You are going nowhere near the place. Besides, how will you get there?"

"On foot, of course."

"You'll walk half a mile or more?"

"I am not made of china, Fan. I was bred in the country, you know."

"That is all very well, but we are due at Polbrook in a matter of days."

"Who said anything about days?" said Ottilia mildly. "I was only thinking of remaining there until Williams has found somewhere more suitable."

"Yes, and when Williams arrives to fetch us, I suppose you will meekly get into the carriage and allow yourself to be driven away just when you have uncovered half a dozen clues to set you on the trail of the murderer? No, Tillie. I know you too well."

Ottilia smiled at him. "But are you not the teeniest bit curious?"

Her husband's eyes narrowed, the beloved features growing ever more suspicious. "Don't waste your cajolery, Tillie, for I am adamant."

Ottilia blinked rapidly and fetched an elaborate sigh. "I did promise obedience."

Francis was almost betrayed into a laugh, but he managed to suppress it. "You did. And if I remember rightly, you declared after the business with my family last year that one murder was quite enough for you."

Mischief flitted across her face, and he could feel his resolve weakening.

"Astonishing, is it not, how one can be mistaken? But although it was all perfectly horrid in the end, you must recall that at the outset I was highly entertained."

Which was perfectly true, Francis was bound to admit. At the time, his world turned upside down by the discovery of his sister-in-law's death and his brother's subsequent disappearance, he had been too upset to think beyond the immediate necessity to handle the aftermath. That very day he had met his future wife, and been grateful thereafter for her calm good sense as she set about uncovering the culprit, and indeed for the playful manner that had done much to lighten those dark days. His heart softened despite himself.

Abruptly, he turned to call to his groom. "Ryde, exactly how far is this Witherley?"

A hand stole into his and squeezed. "An hour or two, no more."

Francis looked down at his wife. He knew that smile. He groaned inwardly. Let Tillie but get her teeth into this and nothing would serve to bring her away until it was all over. All he could hope was that it would prove but a storm in a teacup.

S tepping into the village tavern for the second time, Aidan was a trifle wary. Last night, led thither by the maid Tabitha once his visitor had been delivered into the hands of his housekeeper, he had done little more than introduce himself, give his condolences to the bereaved family, and say his piece over the body of the dead man.

He had found the doctor in attendance, the blacksmith's corpse having been brought in and laid upon a long table in the taproom of the Cock and Bottle, an establishment of cheerful aspect at odds with the night's dismal events. Brasses and copper gleamed off the wooden beams in the candlelight, which was mostly concentrated around the table. There was a wide fireplace, innocent of flame to its piled up logs despite the chill left by the storm, and a collection of wooden settles, in one of which sat a huddle of weeping women and children.

None had questioned Aidan's presence, but he had sensed a mood of surly suspicion, particularly from the landlord Tisbury and his wife. Nothing was said, but he caught a number of alien looks, the reason for which he very soon found out.

As he had turned for the door, he was accosted by the doctor, who had made himself known by the name of Meldreth.

"Are you for the vicarage, Mr. Kinnerton? My house is in your way. Allow me to accompany you."

Aidan accepted gracefully and waited by the door while the doctor lingered.

"Have Duggleby's body conveyed to another room, Tisbury. One with an adequate window, if you please. I must examine him again by daylight on the morrow."

They left together, and once outside, the doctor paused, his keen glance appraising Aidan from under a grizzled wig. "A word of caution, Mr. Kinnerton."

Turning, Aidan surveyed him, stiffening a little. "Which is, sir?"

A faint smile tugged at the corners of the doctor's mouth. "No need to poker up. It is not I who would censure you."

Relaxing, Aidan returned the smile. "The villagers, you mean? There was a degree of sullenness in my reception, I noticed."

"Yes, they are not pleased. Mrs. Dale was seen to enter your house, you see."

Aidan frowned. "Mrs. Dale?"

"The young female they believe to be a witch."

Recalling the maid's "Miss Cassie," Aidan was surprised, but he let it go for the moment. "Ah, yes. She warned me there would be repercussions."

"Worse than she supposes, I'm afraid."

An interrupted rhythm disturbed Aidan's pulses. "What do you mean, sir?"

"There is already a move towards blaming Mrs. Dale for Duggleby's death, but that is merely due to her having seen a vision of the roof coming down."

"So I understand. But then?"

The doctor hesitated, drawing a sighing breath. "There can be little doubt that Duggleby received a blow to the head before the roof fell in on him."

A sense of deep foreboding entered Aidan's breast. "You are saying he was murdered?"

The doctor nodded. "I believe so. I have no choice but to fetch the justice of the peace and call in the constable in the morning."

"But do you tell me these people will suppose Mrs. Dale to be guilty of striking the man? They cannot be so prejudiced."

"Yes, but I'm afraid they are, Kinnerton."

"Then I must scotch such thinking without delay."

"I should leave it for the morning, if I were you," suggested Meldreth. "The mood is ugly, and I suspect a drowning of sorrows tonight may make it worse."

This advice seemed sound to Aidan. Now, in the new day, having swallowed his breakfast and ascertained from his housekeeper that Mrs. Dale—or "Miss Cassie," as the maid addressed her—was still sleeping, he lost no time in bearding the lions in their den.

The landlord fairly glared as Aidan walked into the taproom. "What be you wanting, Reverend?"

Unsurprised by the bitter note, Aidan regarded the man's bloated countenance, the red-veined nose and cheeks arguing an unhealthy addiction to the fleshpots and the bottle. The sleeves of his frock coat clung to thick arms, and his waistcoat and breeches slumped over a protruding belly.

Aidan gathered his forces and fired the first broadside. "I have come, Tisbury, to do what I may by way of making peace in an unnecessary war."

The landlord's brows drew together in puzzlement. "What be your meaning?"

Holding the man's bloodshot eyes, Aidan pursued a forthright course. "I understand there is talk against Mrs. Dale."

Tisbury looked taken aback for a moment and then rallied, coming back with vigour. "Aye, that there be. Mighty ill it be to see Duggleby brought down for the spite of that devil's daughter."

"Devil's daughter? You speak of such before me, Tisbury, a man of the cloth?"

"And why wouldn't he?" came from behind Aidan in a snapping tone.

He turned to confront the female he recalled as the landlord's wife. "Ah, Mrs. Tisbury, yes."

She was a small scarecrow of a woman, with a mean mouth and piggy little eyes which sparked up at him as she spoke. "Aye, and I'd like fine to know as why you bain't damned that witch, seeing as you be parson round these parts."

"My dear woman," Aidan retorted, dangerously quiet, "we are not living in the Middle Ages. Exorcising evil spirits forms no part of my function here."

"No, for you takes and hides 'em in your house instead."

A young fellow in homespuns, whom Aidan recalled as the tapster, intervened at this point. "Bain't no spirit, Mistress. The witch it be, for as Farmer Staxton's boys said last night. Her've run away to the vicarage."

"If'n she bain't flown there on a broomstick," cackled an elderly individual from the corner, removing a clay pipe from his mouth.

"Aye, you be free enough with your jesting, Pa," snapped the landlord's wife, "but she've gone too far this time."

"She bain't got no broomstick, Mr. Wagstaff," asserted the tapster, who had apparently no ear for wit.

The landlord stepped in again. "Broomstick or no, I'll see to her personal if'n she bain't thrown in the lock-up."

An uneven ripple disturbed Aidan's heartbeat, but he was buoyed by the familiar rush of iron that entered his backbone. He had not faced a tribe of spear-wielding savages without learning a trick or two. He allowed his voice to fall into the round, authoritative tones of the pulpit.

"That will do!"

The tavern fell silent. Both Tisbury and his wife looked thoroughly astonished, and the tapster's mouth fell open. Before they could recover themselves, Aidan swept on.

"The facts, it appears, have so far escaped your attention, but know this. Last night I gave shelter to a lady who was being treated in as barbaric a fashion as I have encountered. I have been out of England for some little time until recently, so I must plead ignorance to any possible changes in manners or custom. Yet it hardly seems possible that pelting a woman with stones has become common accepted practise."

Tisbury had the grace to look shamefaced, and the tapster reddened. Aidan looked from one to the other and then allowed his gaze to encompass the rest of the villagers present. They were few this morning, most presumably already at their work, but as Aidan's gaze shifted from face to face, each dropped his eyes. At length, the aged jokesmith broke the tension.

"That's right, Reverend. Give 'em pepper. And if'n they won't see sense, take and knock their heads together."

"You shut it, Pa."

Alone in the assembly, the landlord's wife remained undeterred. Confronting Aidan, she thrust up her chin and her eyes snapped.

"No one bain't saying as them boys had ought to throw stones, Reverend. But that there Mrs. Dale bain't no ordinary female. Dangerous her be. And if'n her bain't gone and killed poor Duggleby, then my name bain't Tisbury, neither."

A surrounding murmur, possibly of agreement, was backed up by the woman's husband, although his belligerence had lessened. "It bain't nowise nothing but the truth, Reverend. Mrs. Dale done it, and if'n I had my way, I'd send Will here for to fetch Constable Pilton to lock her up straight."

He flicked a hand at his tapster as he spoke, and the young fellow, recovering his countenance, perked up and nodded assent, yet looking ridiculously scared. "Bain't the first time as her've said as her seen things, and then they happens. Her done it, Reverend, bain't no doubt of that."

For a moment Aidan weighed what he might say. How much did they know? Was it common knowledge yet that

Meldreth believed the blacksmith had been murdered? He tested it out, keeping his tone even.

"And how, may I ask, did she perform this feat? Did she climb up onto the smithy roof? Or are you supposing she recited incantations to bring on the storm?"

His sarcasm was rewarded by a fit of high-pitched laughter from Mr. Wagstaff, but his daughter stood her ground, directing a venomous glare up at Aidan.

"Her bain't got no need to climb up no roof, Reverend. A witch, bain't her? Her'd only to call up her devil master and ask him to throw the roof down on Duggleby."

"After her've done for him with a hammer to his head," said Tisbury.

This time the chorus of assent was louder, as if the villagers, having dared so far, grew the braver now it was said. They knew, then. And yet were prepared to add this prosaic fact to their absurd suppositions of witchcraft. Shock was uppermost with Aidan. He had not truly believed until this moment that there could be such ignorance rife in the village. How it was to be countered, he had no notion, but on one thing he was determined. No witch hunt would succeed in Witherley, if he had to stand personal guard to the young woman at present safely in his house.

He drew himself up, took time to run his gaze across the expectant faces, and allowed disgust to sound in his voice.

"I thought I had left savagery and superstition behind me when I departed the shores of Africa. I little thought I should rediscover them in a quiet backwater of England."

With which, he turned from the company without another glance and walked calmly out of the tavern. The battle lines were drawn, and he felt oddly uplifted by the first skirmish. Until he reached the vicarage and discovered the bird had flown.

Chapter 2

The smithy was a sodden, blackened ruin. Ottilia's curiosity had begun to dissipate after trudging a good mile along a winding and muddy road. But she perked up instantly as they entered the village via a signposted lane. The first sight of Witherley presented a row of cottages to one side and a gleam of water beyond where a tributary stream from the Anker ran through. Once past the cottages, a turn brought them within immediate sight of the scene of last night's disaster.

The blacksmith's forge was situated just before a stone bridge, over which the lane led to a spacious green with what appeared to be the main part of the village set prettily around it. Ottilia gave it but a brief glance, her attention focused upon the wreck of the smithy.

"One cannot be much surprised the poor man did not come out of there alive."

Her spouse was similarly struck, his frowning glance travelling over the relatively undamaged façade and the surrounding walls which were partially standing. A part of the roof towards the front appeared intact, but the gaping hole beyond told its own tale.

"Take care, Tillie," Francis warned as Ottilia headed for the slatted wooden double doors, which were standing open. "The place is clearly unsafe. You had better let me go first."

Ottilia made no demur but waited for him to enter ahead, taking time to survey what she could see of the stabling area immediately inside the big doors, which was not much. It was small and relatively empty but for harnesses hanging on the walls. Francis had disappeared from sight in the direction of the big chimney at the far end of the building, but she could hear his footsteps.

"You had best come through here where most of the roof is already down," came his voice, echoing eerily in the dark interior. "There is less chance of collapse, I think."

Ottilia cast her eyes upward as she passed through and found the roof above her to be more or less intact, although the beams hung zigzag where they levelled with the main part of the coverless forge. The light was better here, and it looked to Ottilia's critical eye as if the conflagration had been of short duration.

"The storm must have put out the fire," she said reflectively, gazing at the partially burnt timbers, stark skeletons protruding from the rubble.

Francis had gone forward and was standing in a relatively empty space, looking up towards the open sky. "They were lucky. Others might well have been injured if the flames had not been doused."

"And there would have been nothing left of this place or the blacksmith," said Ottilia, lifting up her petticoats—the hems already a trifle mired from the road—to keep them off the filthy floor as she moved to join him. "And nothing to suggest his death was anything but an accident."

Her husband's keen glance found hers. "You are thinking someone set the place on fire deliberately?"

"Would not you, if you had a worse crime to conceal?" suggested Ottilia, as she looked around the ruined structure.

The accoutrements of the blacksmith's trade were largely destroyed, apart from the heavy anvil near the ash-filled pit in the deadened forge at the far end and the huge bellows behind, which had miraculously escaped damage. This area was yet under a modicum of cover, for the chimney had not caught alight and the roof damage was not so extensive.

Ottilia glanced along the mechanism that permitted the blacksmith to pull on the bellows to keep the fire going while he worked.

"How long might the forge continue burning, do you suppose, once the smith was down and no longer able to work the bellows?"

Her spouse glanced across at the forge. "Half an hour perhaps, no more."

"I wonder if the killer knew that."

Francis did not appear to hear her, his attention apparently caught by the comprehensive damage to the roof. Ottilia traced a metallic gleam to a rack of soot-coated rods, and then again to a variety of half-wrecked implements still hanging on hooks on the discoloured walls. She made out horseshoes and a wide-bladed scythe. Below there rested a large rusting wheel and several farming tools which had presumably been awaiting service. Whatever else might be left was concealed under the layer of broken struts, smashed tiles, and the muddy residue from many pairs of boots.

Moving to one side, she examined the blacksmith's table, a long wooden affair plated across the top with a sheet of metal. A deal of debris had fallen across the implements laid there, the whole blackened with a layer of soot and grime, but Ottilia thought she could recognise a collection of hammers, pincers, axes, and thick metal rods. Had one of these objects been used to bludgeon the blacksmith? Unlikely, for would not the killer have sought to conceal his weapon? Or dispose of it in some fashion?

Time would have been of the essence. Could he afford to carry the thing away and risk being seen? A thought occurred, and Ottilia took a precarious path towards the forge, stepping between a couple of massive empty buckets on the floor and slipping past the anvil. But before she could look more closely at the ashes of the fire, Francis's voice interrupted her.

"This is where the body lay."

Turning, Ottilia found her husband's gaze had dropped to the ground, where the labours of the blacksmith's rescuers were evidenced in unnatural piles of debris around the cleared area. He glanced up, his gaze piercing across at her.

"If the perpetrator knew the roof would fall, why bother to start a fire?"

"Assuming the doctor in the case is right, to conceal the blow to the head?" Ottilia offered, moving back towards where he stood. "He was taking no chances."

"That, my love, is exactly my thought."

Ottilia put up a finger. "But according to Ryde, it was the witch who had foreknowledge of the roof coming down."

Unexpectedly, Francis grinned. "Then she was not the only one. Unless the woman is a skilled woodsman."

In some surprise, Ottilia watched him pick his way through the piles of debris to one side of the smithy. He pointed upwards.

"See the remains of the crossbeam? Look at the foreshort-ened end."

Ottilia squinted up at a short projection of wood which was relatively free of soot, training her eyes upon the blunted end. It struck her as unnatural, but she could not immedi-ately see why.

"Now look at what is left of the thinner beams," in-structed Francis.

Ottilia did so, and instant comprehension struck her. Ev-erywhere but on that crossbeam the stub ends were jagged.

"It was severed."

"Precisely. And not by supernatural means. Either the

beam was sawed through or hacked, perhaps with an axe. We need a ladder. Unless we can find the other end of that beam somewhere in this shambles."

A sliver of excitement shot through Ottilia. "Fan, you are a genius!"

His lips quirked. "With such a tutor, how could I avoid learning?"

She let out a ripple of laughter. "You are an apt pupil, my dearest." Then a new thought crept into her mind. "Would the storm have been forceful enough to bring the roof down, do you think, once the beam was cut through?"

Francis's eyes narrowed. "A good question." He cast a glance about the surrounding debris. "A stout rope tied off around the beam perhaps. Unless it burned."

Ottilia's pulse pattered unevenly. "Or not entirely. Nothing appears to have burned altogether. Should we not try to search for a fragment or two?"

"Futile, I fear. And much as I love you, I am not minded to get up a sweat heaving this filthy debris about, besides ruining a perfectly good pair of gloves."

A chuckle escaped her. "I would not dare ask it of you. It can very well wait until we can engage the services of a likely local."

"Within your allotted two hours?"

She had begun an unconscious hunt, casting her eyes here and there among the fallen timbers, but at this Ottilia looked quickly at her spouse and was relieved to discover the familiar teasing look. A laugh escaped her.

"I think we had best go and find this inn Ryde spoke of and get some food inside you."

With Francis applauding this suggestion in no uncertain terms, Ottilia turned to step inside the relative dark of the roofed stable end just as a figure loomed upon the threshold. Ottilia gasped in surprise and fell back.

The outline of a woman stood there, half in silhouette but for a stark white countenance illumined in a freak shaft of light from the roofless area. A slim, cloaked creature, with tragic eyes.

For a moment Ottilia could not speak, struck by an air of haunting agony in the girl's pose as she allowed her gaze to flick here and there about the wreck of the smithy. She was young, Ottilia judged, but the hollows and planes of her pallid features made her appear older. At length, the eyes fell upon Ottilia and widened. Her mouth formed an O of surprise, and she frowned.

"Who are you? I have not seen you before. We do not have strangers in Witherley."

She spoke with rapidity, and her voice, which had a husky quality, was a meld of suspicion and fear. Ottilia pulled herself together and moved forward, catching her upheld petticoats into one hand so that she might hold out the other.

"I do beg your pardon. We must have startled you. We are indeed strangers. Our coach broke down on the post road, and we have come in search of rest and refreshment."

The girl made no move to take the proffered hand, although she glanced at it briefly.

"A man died here last night."

Ottilia weighed a lie in the balance and decided against it. "Yes, so we have been led to believe. Our groom came here seeking the blacksmith, you see."

The frown intensified, and a sickened look crept into the woman's face. "Are you ghouls, then, that you come to gawp at a man's misfortune?"

From the corner of her eye, Ottilia saw Francis stiffen and quickly put out a hand to prevent him from speech. She spoke with gentleness, feeling instinctively this creature would recoil from confrontation.

"We are here rather to help, if we can." A wild thought flitted through her mind, and she acted upon it without conscious decision. "Forgive me, but are you—now what was the name?—a Mrs. Dale, I think? Yes, that is it. Are you Mrs. Dale?"

Ottilia saw from the girl's expressive eyes that she had hit the mark. The "witch" put the back of her hand to her mouth in a gesture suggestive of nerves strung taut. Her voice became vibrant and low.

"How could you know that? Did you see it? I saw nothing of your coming."

"Perhaps you don't see everything," Ottilia suggested gently. "And no, I do not have your skill."

A laugh escaped the girl, cracking in the middle. "Skill? It is a curse, not a talent."

"But why? It cannot always result in such grave consequences as this."

Mrs. Dale sighed deeply. "They are saying I killed him."

Ottilia moved swiftly, forgetting the danger to her petticoats as she dropped them and caught at the woman's unquiet hands, holding them firm. "They, whoever they are, are mistaken, my dear Mrs. Dale. I will so prove it, I promise you."

The girl stared at her, a bewildered look in her dark eyes. "You? How can you do so? Who are you?"

"My name is not important, but you may call me Lady Fan."

Mrs. Dale did not immediately avail herself of this permission. She continued to study Ottilia, the crease deepening between her brows.

"You have seen evil," she said slowly. "The images are cloudy, but there is blackness underneath."

Ottilia did not speak. She was aware of Francis behind her, and a certain quality in his intake of breath told her this was dangerous ground. Rather to her relief, they suffered an interruption.

"Miss Cassie? Are you in there? I do wish as you wouldn't run off like that. You know I can't keep up."

The scolding note was pronounced, and Ottilia was not much surprised to see the bustling figure of a woman peering in at the wide doors. Mrs. Dale glanced back but did not answer.

"Cassie?" Ottilia said quickly. "Is that for Cassandra? How apt."

"I have my family to thank for my name," returned Mrs. Dale in a tone that sounded immediately more normal than hitherto and showed a hint of childish irritation. "It amused them so to dub me. But I am Charis."

"But how charming," said Ottilia at once. "Perhaps you should insist upon others employing your given name."

"It makes no matter," said the girl, with a return to the darkness that seemed habitual to her.

"Miss Cassie, come out of there, I beg of you."

Mrs. Dale looked back. "I am coming, Tabby." Then she turned back to Ottilia, and the ghost of a smile crossed her lips. "You have been kind. I will not forget."

With that, she flitted away and was instantly enveloped in a strong arm that tugged her out into the daylight. Ottilia found Francis at her elbow.

"You believe her innocent then?"

"Oh yes. Unless I miss my guess, the girl is too fey for the precision this murder seems to have needed."

"Well, I can't say I'm surprised she is stigmatised a witch. A stranger creature you could scarcely hope to meet."

Ottilia nodded. "She reminds me of your mother's maid."

"Venner? Yes, I remember you said you thought she was half mad."

"But I don't think Mrs. Dale is in the least mad. She is rather of that ilk of person who feels things too deeply and who lacks the social veneer that we commonly use to hide our feelings from others."

Francis looked sceptical. "Which is as much as to say that she is out of the common way and does not behave as others do, and is therefore half mad."

"Or merely eccentric, like my godmother."

"No one is like your godmother," returned her husband feelingly.

Ottilia laughed. "You cannot have lived in a village, my dearest. I defy you not to discover a veritable hotbed of eccentrics in a place of this kind, and at least one to prove a copy of my Lady Edingale."

As if to underline this statement, when they had walked not ten yards from the smithy and were about to cross the bridge, they ran into a pair of middle-aged women coming the other way. Either of whom, Ottilia instantly decided, could have walked into a roomful of eccentrics and no questions asked.

The taller of the two, clad plainly in a greatcoat dress of brown linen and an unadorned beaver hat, walked with a mannish stride, while the other, despite her obvious span of years, was the picture of femininity in a sprigged gown, a beribboned straw bonnet, and a voluminous shawl of some diaphanous fabric clustered about her shoulders. They had clearly espied the strangers, and Ottilia took immediate advantage of the situation.

"Pardon me, if you please," she said in a friendly way, going towards them, "but could you direct us to a suitable hostelry?"

She was treated to a frowning stare from the taller female, but the other's glance went from Ottilia to Francis and back again.

"Goodness, how did you come here?" she uttered in a manner that betrayed an avid curiosity.

"Only one decent inn," said the other, turning to point across the green. "That's it over there. Take the right fork."

"Thank you," Ottilia said pleasantly and turned to the one more frivolously dressed. "We came on foot. Our carriage broke down on the post road."

At this, the first woman addressed herself to Francis.

"What happened? Wheel off? Or a broken trace?"

If Ottilia was surprised, it was plain her spouse was astonished. He concealed it well, however, merely replying, "My groom believes it is the axletree."

"You'll be wanting a blacksmith, then." She waved a hand towards the ruined forge. "No use hoping for ours, as you can see. Fellow was killed last night."

"So we have been informed," said Francis.

"Gracious, who told you? I thought you must have been looking at the smithy, but I could not conceive—"

"Evelina!"

The sharp tone had the effect of making the other woman colour up, and Ottilia felt her sympathies stirred. She smiled and played her trump card.

"You are perfectly right, ma'am. But do forgive me. So rude of us not to make ourselves known to you. Allow me to present my husband, Lord Francis Fanshawe."

Ottilia had already noted the appreciative look cast upon her personable and lean-figured spouse by the more feminine member of the duo. She could not blame the woman, for she had herself been somewhat bowled over at first sight of his strong countenance with its aquiline nose and high-planed cheeks, his deep dark eyes, and the rich brown hair tied in the nape of his neck. But the name, as she had confidently expected, exercised an even more powerful effect.

"Fanshawe? Gracious! I do believe—or no, perhaps I should not—"

"Evelina, do be quiet," snapped her mentor. She tapped herself on the chest. "I am Miss Beeleigh. My friend here is Mrs. Radlett."

Ottilia replied suitably and watched Francis make his bow. There could be no doubt that the story of last year's events had penetrated even this backwater. The name of Fanshawe had appeared alongside that of Polbrook in more than one newspaper column. Only initials had been used, of course, but the scandal that had rocked the family had been widespread, and anyone who paid attention to such things would have known immediately who was meant by Lord F— F—.

Her new acquaintances were exactly what Ottilia needed, and she lost no time in consolidating her advantage.

"I hope we may meet again. I fear it will be a tedious wait until our coach can be repaired."

"Won't matter," said Miss Beeleigh. "Hannah Pakefield will be only too delighted to put you up. She can do with the custom, poor woman."

"Oh yes," agreed Mrs. Radlett, "for there are few travellers through Witherley. We take coffee at the Blue Pig nearly every day. To help poor Hannah, you must know."

"Then perhaps you will take coffee with me a little later on?" said Ottilia, seizing her cue.

If she'd had qualms, Mrs. Radlett's effusive acceptance would have reassured her. But Ottilia had taken her measure and was confident of having found one of the more prolific of the village gossips. Any doubts would have concerned Miss Beeleigh. It was plain, however, that she was in the habit of indulging her unlikely friend, even if she did not share a passion for tidbits about others.

Having made their assignation, the two ladies passed on, and Ottilia guessed they were making for the smithy on their own account. She was drawn back from contemplation by her husband's dry tone.

"The Blue Pig?"

Ottilia stifled a giggle. "Well, we are in the vicinity of Bosworth Field."

"This is in compliment to the villainous Richard, then?"

"An omen, Fan, can you doubt it?"

"Heaven help me!" He offered his arm, and Ottilia tucked her hand within it and began to walk with him across the bridge. "I trust there will be pork on the menu."

Ottilia bubbled over. "A vast platter of ham, I make no doubt."

"At this present, however, I have a more than passing interest in a tankard of ale."

"It shall be forthcoming," said Ottilia demurely.

* * *

Cassie eyed her visitor with rebellion in her heart. Was it not enough to be riven with remorse and despair on the blacksmith's account? Must she also be taken at fault for accepting the vicar's hospitality? She owed much to Lady Ferrensby. Yet it hurt to know she was so little understood.

"I realise you were a trifle distraught, my dear," pursued her ladyship in her low-pitched musical voice, "but this should have been thought of."

"I was in no condition to be thinking of the proprieties," Cassie said tightly.

"That I appreciate."

"And Mr. Kinnerton was kindness itself."

"His kindness does not excuse your remaining in his house overnight. If you do not care for your own reputation, you might at least think of his."

Silenced, Cassie stared at her. Suspicion nagged at the edges of her mind, for she knew Lady Ferrensby too well. Yet if she had brought Mr. Kinnerton to Witherley with the object of securing a sacrifice at the altar, however unwilling, she ought rather to have been pleased. Cassie's eyes ran over her, and immediately she felt, as ever, the stark contrast of condition.

The great lady of the village was stylishly if simply dressed for the country, in a gown of Canterbury muslin worked in coloured sprigs and a pretty beribboned bonnet with a neat little brim. She wore her years with elegance, the grey wings to her temples adding distinction to a countenance invariably stigmatised, not undeservedly, as handsome.

Cassie's old cotton chemise gown, with its pleated skirts buttoned from bosom to hem and its tight long sleeves, was outmoded, a relic of happier years. Not that she cared for fashion, although it was a relief to have been able to put off the disguise of her blacks.

Lady Ferrensby's cool gaze was running over her, and Cassie put up her chin as she met it head-on.

"Tabitha says you are bruised."

Cassie shrugged. "Tabby is exaggerating. It's nothing very much."

A kinder note crept into her patroness's voice. "I gather a number of stones found their mark. I am sorry you suffered that."

It was nothing compared to the suffering of her conscience, but Cassie held her tongue. Lady Ferrensby was ever impatient of the distresses that accompanied the curse of Cassie's visions.

"Still, you got off lighter than Duggleby," pronounced her ladyship.

Cassie's resolution failed, and she hit out. "You mean I deserve it more."

"Don't be silly."

"Silly? To regret having spoken? Having seen?" Cassie shivered at the memories. "I knew what must happen. I warned him. He would not believe me. He became surly with me, as they all do." In her mind she heard again the rough words, the hatred in his voice, and saw again the contempt in Duggleby's eyes. "But now he's dead, and I am to blame. And you tell me not to be silly!"

She threw her hands over her face, as shudders racked her. A hand reached to grasp her fingers and pull them down. Lady Ferrensby's eyes were kinder, and her voice had softened. Cassie gripped her fingers, fighting back the threatening tears that tore at her throat.

"Calm yourself, my child. There is nothing to be gained by falling into a passion. That will not mend matters."

Cassie shook her hair away. "I know, but I cannot help it."

"You must help it, Cassie. You must learn to control yourself."

A heavy sigh escaped Cassie's lips. "I try. But it is so very hard."

The gentler look from the other warmed her heart a little, and she tried to smile.

Lady Ferrensby released her fingers. "There now; that is better."

Cassie did not speak, afraid she could not maintain the spurious air of calm that seemed to satisfy her patroness. She was anything but quiescent inside, but she knew Lady Ferrensby disapproved of "Cassie's wild ways," as she chose to think of them.

"Besides, your visions notwithstanding," went on her patroness, "it is no use anyone blaming you. Everyone has been telling that fool of a man forever that his roof was in need of repair, but he would do nothing about it. If he had been one of my tenants instead of holding the freehold, I'd have given him snuff."

Remembering the woman in the smithy, Cassie spoke without thought. "If he did not die from the roof coming down, then I did not kill him."

Lady Ferrensby's brows rose. "You are speaking of Meldreth's suspicion? Oh, he must be mistaken. I cannot suppose anyone in the village would deliberately set out to kill the fellow, brute though he was."

Cassie stared at her. "Yet everyone in the village thinks I would do so."

Her patroness tutted. "You are being quite absurd, my dear. If one or two persons are foolish enough to—"

"One or two?"

Was she blind? Or merely refusing to see? Cassie knew the village to be Lady Ferrensby's especial concern, for her son was rarely to be seen in the place, young Lord Ferrensby declaring life at his country seat to be sadly flat. Cassie thought him remarkably selfish, to be leaving the running of his affairs in his mother's hands. But she knew Lady Ferrensby cared deeply for the welfare of those who dwelled in the Ferrensby estates, whether tenants or no. More deeply than she cared for Cassie! No, that was unfair. A flood of contrition enveloped Cassie, and she reached out to seize one of the lady's hands.

"I never remember to thank you. You've given me a future."

A sigh was drawn from her patroness. "I wish I had, Cassie. Sometimes it seems all I've given you is a burden too great to bear."

Cassie's throat tightened. "It's not your fault I am cursed."

"No." There was regret in the tone. "But I have made it impossible to protect you as I ought. I never thought at the time. It seemed the best solution to keep our secret."

"You couldn't have known I might see so much. I know you don't believe in it."

"Unfortunately, others do."

Anguish clutched at Cassie's heart, and the words wrenched from deep inside. "I wish you were right to disbelieve me. I wish I saw nothing. I wish I had ordinary dreams like an ordinary person."

Her eyes were closed, but Cassie felt the arms that went around her and briefly held her close. A momentary comfort.

"Your charm, my child, lies in being extraordinary."

Cassie would have refuted this, but she was distracted by a knock at the front door, which opened directly onto the lane. Rising, she went to answer it. The Reverend Kinnerton stood without.

"You are here," he uttered, a little out of breath. "Thank the Lord! I was concerned when I returned to the house and found you gone."

Cassie could not speak for a moment. Her hazy recollection of last night's rescue had not prepared her for the vicar's appearance in the full light of day.

His cheeks were lean, throwing his nose into sharp distinction. She judged him young despite etched lines that spoke of recent suffering. A flashing picture formed in her mind, of this same face, its leanness near skeletal, its pallor grey and cold.

"You have been ill."

A pair of dark brows rose above eyes as blue as the sky. Cassie had not seen them in the candlelight, but now their clean colour made a mockery of the image that had entered her mind.

"Yes," he said, a tiny smile hovering at the corners of his mouth, "but I am very much recovered. And at present, I am the more concerned for your welfare. How are you this morning?" His eyes shifted past her, as if he would look into the room beyond. "Are you well guarded?"

Cassie's heart skipped a beat. "Guarded?"

"Your maid is with you?"

He sounded a trifle impatient, and Cassie hastened to reassure him. "Tabitha is in the kitchen. And Sam is here, too."

"Sam?"

"Tabby's husband, Sam Hawes."

Relief showed in his bright eyes. "You have a man on the premises? That is excellent news."

From within, Lady Ferrensby's voice called out. "Why do you not invite the gentleman inside, Cassie?"

Cassie felt warmth rise to her cheeks. She had forgotten the presence of her patroness. She hesitated, recalling the earlier reprimand she had endured. Did Lady Ferrensby mean to ring a peal over the pastor?

"Well, don't keep the fellow standing about on the doorstep."

Thus adjured, Cassie retreated back into her parlour, for want of a better name, and the vicar followed her in, closing the door behind him. Lady Ferrensby had risen from one of the straight-backed chairs about the table, which comprised the only seating accommodation Cassie's meagre dwelling afforded. The reverend's additional presence immediately dwarfed the place.

"Good morning, Kinnerton," said Lady Ferrensby. "Still ministering to the village outcast, I perceive."

The burn at Cassie's cheek intensified, but before she

could protest, the vicar spoke. His tone was even, but Cassie thought she detected an edge to it.

"Indeed, ma'am. No doubt you are here on the self-same errand."

Lady Ferrensby looked a little taken aback, and Cassie noted, with relief, an amused glint in her eye. "Touché, sir. Though I suspect the need for such caution as you indulged in last night has been exaggerated."

"How can you, ma'am?" uttered Cassie, distressed. "Mr. Kinnerton did not—"

"Allow me to reassure you, Lady Ferrensby," cut in the vicar, his lean cheeks taut and a spark in his eye. "Mrs. Dale slept in a room adjoining that of my housekeeper, Mrs. Winkleigh, and the door between remained open. I did not set foot in the chamber."

"Let us hope the members of our little community may be induced to believe as much."

Cassie gasped, but the vicar came back strongly. "Your 'little community,' ma'am, is concentrated upon the far more serious matter of accusing Mrs. Dale of witchcraft. I doubt it will worry about a trifling issue of potential impropriety."

"Trifling?"

"I trust you are not suggesting Mrs. Dale has been compromised. As a man of the cloth—"

"A very young and personable man of the cloth, Mr. Kinnerton, and one who is a bachelor. However, as you pointed out, I think we may escape censure on this occasion. I daresay the village has enough distraction today."

Cassie leapt on this. "How can you talk of it so dismissively? Duggleby is dead! And they blame me for it."

"Fiddle," came briskly from her ladyship.

"You are too sanguine, ma'am," said Mr. Kinnerton, on something of a snap. "I have already been to the tavern this morning, and the mood is ugly."

Lady Ferrensby laughed. "I can readily believe it. They

have lost a friend and colleague. I have no doubt they will return to their senses in a day or two."

Despairing, Cassie glanced at the vicar, but he had closed his lips, and his eyes were narrowed.

"Which puts me in mind of my duty," pursued her ladyship. "I must see Bertha Duggleby and her children. And then I shall make the rounds and sympathise. If that does not serve, then whatever you may do in the direction of turning their minds from these silly superstitions, Kinnerton, will be of more practical value than acts of misplaced chivalry."

To Cassie's astonishment, the pastor laughed out at that. "Useless to tell you that I acted purely on instinct, I daresay."

"Like Cassie," said Lady Ferrensby with a smile. "I don't doubt that."

The vicar dipped his head. "You may rest assured, ma'am, that no witch hunt will be permitted to run free while I am vicar of this parish. I have made my views known. What is more, I intend to find and reprimand the boys responsible for attacking Mrs. Dale."

"Excellent. My dependence is all upon you, sir. Good day." She moved to the door, turning to look at Cassie. "Do try to keep up a modicum of common sense, Cassie. And don't let the vicar stay too long."

With which admonishment, she opened the door and swept out of the cottage, leaving Cassie with a burning resentment that found instant expression.

"She does not believe me. She thinks it is all in my mind. And she will not credit how much they hate me! Not that I blame them."

"Well, I do," came from the vicar. He moved a little towards her. "I cannot, like Lady Ferrensby, dismiss what I have heard. Nor will I minimise the danger in a bid to spare you pain. You need to know it, so that you will take the greatest care."

Oddly, Cassie immediately felt less endangered. She was

so much accustomed to being contradicted upon the findings of her senses by those who had her best interests at heart. Acceptance was a novel feeling.

"You are an unexpected man, Mr. Kinnerton."

His lips quivered, and amusement crept into his eyes. "Such an encomium from one with your gifts is equally so."

Cassie's world lightened suddenly, and she laughed. "But I don't see character in people. Only images."

"Then in that I have the advantage of you. In my profession it is a necessary skill." He stood back. "I must not stay. Little though I relished her comments, Lady Ferrensby's reprimand was just."

He went to the door, and Cassie was conscious of the onset of disappointment. And a resurgence of her earlier suspicions. She obeyed an impulse to delay him.

"Mr. Kinnerton."

He turned. "My name is Aidan."

She took it in without pausing for thought. "How was it Lady Ferrensby engaged you?"

Puzzlement showed in his eyes. "It happened she was visiting in the vicinity of my family's estate. A fortuitous meeting."

Cassie did not pause to consider her words. "You are unmarried?"

She saw the frown in his eyes, but her need was too urgent for caution.

"Yes. Does it show?"

Cassie gave an impatient shake of her head. "No. How should I see such a thing? But of what degree is your family? Who are they?"

A brittle laugh escaped him. "Why the interrogation, Mrs. Dale?"

The question stopped her tongue. She could not tell him the truth. Nor did she know how to prevaricate. She had never been adept with social rules. Indeed, she'd flouted them so badly it had landed her in this sorry condition, leading a life of lies and deceit. She sought in vain for a way out, blank of mind as she stared at him.

Mr. Kinnerton's features softened, and a smile came. "You look like an infant caught out in mischief."

Warmth raced into Cassie's cheeks. She looked away. "I have no graces. I should not have questioned you."

He took a hasty step towards her, throwing out a hand. "Don't look so. It was not meant for a reproach, I assure you."

At that, a sharp sliver cut at her from the well of guilt, and her gaze flew back to meet his. "Then it should have been. I am fit for nothing less."

She watched in fascination a series of rapid changes in the blue eyes. She could not read them all, but the last struck her strongly. Compassion. His gaze did not leave hers as he came closer. He put out his palm in that odd gesture she recalled from last night, and Cassie automatically gave her hand into his keeping. The clasp was strong.

"I will not take you up on that today, but one day we will talk of it."

"As a member of your flock?"

He did not flinch. "Yes, if you will. Or as a friend."

He bent, lightly kissed her hand, and turned again for the door. He opened it and looked back. "Don't go out without your maid for company, I charge you. And have this fellow Hawes remain within hailing distance at all times."

Then he was gone, and Cassie was left to contemplate the closed door, all the confusions of the previous night rolling back to haunt her.

Chapter 3

Having made a circuit of the green, the Fanshawes arrived at the sizeable establishment to the right, which lay more or less opposite a tavern, where, as Francis surmised, Ryde must have gathered his information.

The Blue Pig was set back from the lane with a cobbled frontage and a drive leading through an archway at the side towards the back, presumably to adjoining stables. Francis led the way along a pathway in the cobbles, and a battered inn sign came into view, indeed depicting a crude blue boar which resembled the homely pig more than a little.

Francis pushed open the heavy wooden entrance door, and Ottilia passed into the shadowy darkness of a substantial hall. It was eerily silent, and her glance took in more stout doors and stalwart wooden posts between the lath walls as Francis shut the main door and moved into the musty space.

"House, ho! What, is no one home?"

His shout echoed crazily into the oak beams above, and Ottilia had the oddest prescience of impending doom. She shivered a little.

"Cold?"

She turned and met concern in her husband's eyes. Ottilia shook her head.

"A little disconcerted, that is all."

His arm came about her shoulders for a moment. "That is not like you, my love."

She gave him a quick smile. "It's nothing. A silly fancy, no more."

"Not, I trust, concerning ghosts of smothered little princes or a butt of malmsey wine?"

Feeling a degree lighter, Ottilia dutifully laughed. "Nothing so definite."

Francis released her, his tone sharpening. "You may be pardoned. The place is like a morgue."

Again, a tiny riffle of unease disturbed Ottilia's senses, and she remembered the words of Cassie Dale. *A man died here last night.*

Francis crossed to one of the doors and beat a rapid tattoo upon the wood. "Confound it, where the devil is everybody?"

Ottilia's ears caught the sound of footsteps somewhere in the recesses behind the walls. "Listen!"

In the silence, the patter of feet grew louder. Ottilia saw Francis turn towards a door at the back. It opened, and a matronly figure bustled into the hall.

"Oh dear, I'm that sorry to have kept you waiting, sir," said the woman, sounding out of breath, "only we're all in a pother today."

She came to a halt before them and dropped a curtsy, peering up at them through the gloom. Her head bobbed towards Ottilia.

"Beg pardon, ma'am, I'm sure. How may I serve you?"

Ottilia forestalled Francis as he opened his mouth to answer. Moving forward, she held out her hand and smiled at the woman.

"I'm afraid we are stranded. Our carriage is broken, and

we have no means of continuing our journey. Will you take pity upon us—Mrs. Pakefield, isn't it?"

The woman looked astonished as she took the proffered hand. "Yes, it is, ma'am, but it beats me how you knew it."

"We had the pleasure of meeting Miss Beeleigh and Mrs. Radlett on our way here. They kindly directed us to your house."

Mrs. Pakefield looked gratified. "They're good souls, both of 'em. But do you say you walked from the post road?"

"Oh, it was no hardship, Mrs. Pakefield. Only I would very much appreciate a glass of lemonade. And then perhaps a cup of coffee." She interrupted the woman's murmured assent with a gesture towards Francis. "And my husband—oh, this is my husband, Lord Francis Fanshawe." Her eyes had become accustomed to the gloom, and she was able to note with satisfaction the instant startled lift to the woman's head. "My husband would much appreciate a tankard of ale to begin with, but he is excessively hungry."

"Yes, of course, ma'am—my lady, I should say—I'll have Cook rustle up a repast in no time."

"Some ham, perhaps," said Ottilia, unable to resist throwing a mischievous glance at Francis. His lips quirked, but he said nothing.

Mrs. Pakefield at once launched into a recital of the range of viands at her disposal, ushering the visitors meanwhile through the door on which Francis had previously knocked. The atmosphere at once brightened, and Ottilia looked approvingly around a roomy apartment whose windows let onto the frontage, presenting an excellent view of the green and its environs. The sun streamed in, throwing latticed shadows onto a large round table. There was another long table near the opposite wall beyond the empty hearth, with a bench behind.

"What a pleasant room," Ottilia said effusively, crossing to look out.

A swift glance took in the tavern opposite, flanked at a

little distance by several buildings on each side, a round little grey structure in the middle of the green—a lock-up?—and a row of houses at the far end, at either side of which the divided lane led away. Behind them at a little distance rose a tower that pointed the location of the church. Ottilia could not have hoped for better.

"This is so pretty, with the view and the sun coming in."

She turned as she spoke to examine the landlady in the better light and was pleased to note the flush of pleasure rising into Mrs. Pakefield's cheeks.

"Thank you kindly, ma'am." Crossing to the table, she took hold of a large brass handbell set there and rang it violently, bobbing a curtsy towards Francis. "I'll fetch Pakefield to you, my lord, for the ale."

"That will be most welcome," he said, setting a chair for Ottilia at the round table.

She did not immediately take advantage of the opportunity to sit down, instead fixing her attention on Mrs. Pakefield. There was an anxious look in the woman's eyes, which Ottilia suspected was not entirely due to the presence of her unexpected guests.

"You look a little dismayed, Mrs. Pakefield," she ventured.

The landlady visibly pulled herself together. "No, my lady, it's only . . . Well, I was wondering . . . You see, we don't run to a parlour. But if you'll make shift with this room, I can see to it that you're private. We've none but the local gentryfolk at this present who come in for coffee each day. Leastways, the ladies do, and Mr. Netherburn if he don't go across to the Cock. They won't mind giving it up for once."

But this would not suit Ottilia in the least. She smiled as she at last took her seat. "Do you mean Mrs. Radlett and Miss Beeleigh? I should not dream of depriving them, Mrs. Pakefield. Besides, I like company, and what in the world should we do with ourselves all alone here until such time as our carriage can be mended?"

Relief flooded the woman's features. "It's good of you to say so, my lady. And today of all days. I can't think as the ladies won't come in."

Ottilia caught her husband's eye briefly as he pulled out a chair for himself and sat down. She allowed her eyelids to flicker a message, and one of his brows went up.

"Yes, we understand this is a difficult day for you all," he said pleasantly.

Ottilia sighed thankfully and threw him a look meant to convey that she would reward him for this indulgence presently.

Mrs. Pakefield immediately began to look flustered again. "Oh dear, you've heard, then? I wouldn't have spoke of it, sir, only—I mean, my lord—"

"Pray don't stand upon ceremony," Ottilia interjected. "So tedious to be forever having to remember such things, do you not find?"

The landlady looked relieved. "Thank you, ma'am. Though I ought to be able to remember, for there's Lady Ferrensby as is the great lady hereabouts, and Lord Henbury as is justice of the peace, but he's rickety these days and don't come into the village that frequent." Her shoulders jerked suddenly. "Though like as not he'll be sent for if so be it's true as Duggleby were killed unlawful-like."

Mrs. Pakefield then gasped, snatching a hand to her mouth as if she sought to thrust the words back in. Before Ottilia could seize on this cue, the door opened to admit a tall and rather skinny individual with a long face which struck Ottilia as appropriately lugubrious.

The landlady turned with obvious relief. "Pakefield, here's visitors as has had their coach broke. This here's my husband, my lady."

In the act of approaching, the landlord halted, his jaw dropping. "My lady?"

"It's Lord Francis Fanshawe and his good lady, Pakefield."

The man's eyes went from one to the other, but his jaw remained slack. Ottilia cast a look at her husband, and he at once rose to the occasion.

"Ah, Pakefield, in good time. I will be obliged if you can furnish my wife with a glass of lemonade and a tankard of your finest ale for myself."

The landlord looked once more at the visitors and then stared blankly at his wife. Ottilia saw the woman dig an elbow roughly into the fellow's ribs, and he winced.

"Get you gone, Pakefield," she prompted in an audible undertone. "Ale for the gentleman and lemonade for the lady. Be quick now."

His wife's urging seemed to affect the landlord, for he nodded several times, still apparently bemused, and then turned for the door. Mrs. Pakefield's manner became apologetic.

"He's that put about, ma'am, what with all the excitement. I hope you'll forgive it."

Ottilia leapt on the refreshed opportunity. "By all means. You are speaking of your blacksmith, I daresay. I gather there are suspicions that the poor fellow was murdered?"

The word acted powerfully upon the landlady. Her face went white, and she swayed alarmingly. Ottilia rose, but Francis was before her, seizing a chair and thrusting it behind the woman in time for her to sit down plump upon its caned seat.

"I am so very sorry," said Ottilia, leaning over the woman and taking up one of her slack hands. "I shocked you, Mrs. Pakefield."

The landlady shook her head numbly. "I never thought of it 'til you said it. To think of such a happening in our village. Murder!"

"It is a horrid word," Ottilia agreed gently, chafing the woman's hand. Out of the corner of her eye, she noted Francis slipping quietly out of the room into the hall and interpreted his departure as tacit permission for her to pursue her investigations. Or else he placed little trust in the reliability of the landlord to fulfil his needs without prompting, which seemed only too likely.

She released Mrs. Pakefield's hand and drew her chair closer, with the intention of creating an atmosphere of intimacy.

"Come, Mrs. Pakefield, I wish you will unburden yourself. You may speak freely to me, I promise you."

The tone had its effect. A little colour returned to the woman's cheeks, and she sat up straighter in the chair.

"It's a dreadful business, my lady, what with Duggleby buried in the wreckage and all the men digging to fetch him out."

"It seems there is a neighbourly spirit in your village, Mrs. Pakefield."

The landlady seemed dubious. "What else could anyone do? Not but what half of them hadn't had their differences with Duggleby. A surly, disobliging man he was, and I don't care who hears me say so. But I'd take my oath no one in the village were that much his enemy as to take a hammer to his head."

"Yet it appears someone did so."

"So Molly Tisbury says. Not that I'd believe nothing she said, for a worse fibster you couldn't hope to meet."

Ottilia's mind was already afire. There was enmity enough to be sought for, it would seem. But she wasted no time in idle comment. At any moment, Mrs. Pakefield might recollect her place and clam up.

"Who is Molly Tisbury?"

The woman's head came up at that, and there was malice in her eyes. "Runs the tavern over yonder, where they took and brought Duggleby last night. Not that there's need for her to crow over that, for I'd not have had the brute on no table in my coffee room, that I can swear to. And if she thought to make me jealous by such a boast, she knows by now she's disappointed."

It was evident to Ottilia that a lively rivalry existed between the two public houses, despite their different functions in the area. It was not hard to seek a reason, for it was obvious that while the Blue Pig catered for the genteel part of the population, the greater part must of necessity patronise the Cock and Bottle. It did not take much imagination to perceive how jealousies might arise in either bosom. Ottilia made a mental note to send her husband off as soon as she could to glean what he might at the more common tavern. And to find out where the body was now.

"Was Duggleby found dead where he lay, do you know, or did he die later?"

"He were dead in the forge," sighed the landlady. "The wonder is the whole place weren't burnt to a cinder." She drew in a sharp breath. "Which is as well, for I daresay it wouldn't have took much for them devils to fling poor Mrs. Dale into the flames instead of setting the boys on to stoning her."

"Dear me," said Ottilia. "I had not heard about the stoning. I must say she did not look very much like a witch to me."

Bewilderment wreathed Mrs. Pakefield's features. "You've seen her?"

"I met her at the smithy a little while ago."

"She went in there, did she?" Shaking her head, the landlady tutted. "She'd have done better to have stayed away."

Ottilia brought her ruthlessly back to the point. "How widespread is this belief that the poor creature is a witch, Mrs. Pakefield?"

The landlady's features formed into a glare. "Ignorance, that's what it is. Not that I'd expect nothing less from as silly a female as you could hope to meet."

"Molly Tisbury?" Ottilia guessed.

"Yes, and if it don't show how fitted she is for her station, I don't know what does. She's the ringleader."

"Indeed? And how many is she leading?" asked Ottilia, unfailingly persistent.

"All of 'em, far as I can see," snapped the landlady. "Can the girl help it if she's got the sight? To think that creature dared to dictate to me in my own home, saying as I should turn the poor young thing away from my door and refuse to serve her. As if I would!"

Ottilia played an ace. "How fortunate you are not among those who choose to persecute her. She must be glad of your sympathy."

Mrs. Pakefield looked a little uncomfortable at this. "Well, she don't come in often. She ain't what you'd call one of them as seek society, Mrs. Dale ain't. A bit of a loner, she is."

"Well, if she is shunned by half the countryside, that is scarcely surprising," said Ottilia tartly before she could stop herself.

The landlady flushed, and her tone sharpened. "I've said as I ain't one of them, ma'am."

"Good gracious, of course not," Ottilia said at once in a conciliatory tone, trying to retrieve her slip. "I was rather thinking of such persons as Molly Tisbury and her ilk."

The glare returned to the landlady's face. "Yes, well, she may change her tune soon enough. Seems the Almighty has produced a new champion in Reverend Kinnerton, and by all accounts he ain't best pleased. I hope he thunders at 'em from the pulpit come Sunday."

This was intriguing, to say the least, but Ottilia let it alone for the moment. She was anxious to learn more of Cassie Dale.

"What of Mrs. Dale's husband?"

"Dead. Leastways, she came here a widow. Tragic it is, for she can't be much more than eighteen. Though it don't show in her manner, for she's one as talks as if an old head were on her shoulders. And she's prickly, if you know what I mean."

With which Ottilia could not but agree, though she refrained from saying so. "If she is regarded in such an unfriendly light, that is natural, do you not think?"

Mrs. Pakefield frowned. "Yes, but that's not it, ma'am. You can't pass the time of day with her like most folks. She's apt to go off random-like in the midst of talking, as if her thoughts are out of tune with her speaking."

Which did not come as much of a surprise. Small wonder the villagers found her out of place. Oddities of conduct combined with second sight? A recipe for disaster. Ottilia was conscious of a lively desire to see more of Cassie Dale.

"Where does Mrs. Dale live?"

Mrs. Pakefield sighed. "She's in the last of the cottages up by the river."

"You mean the ones we passed as we came into the village?"

"That's right, ma'am."

Satisfied, Ottilia sought another point of information. Rising, she crossed to the window. "Is that a lock-up in the middle of the green, Mrs. Pakefield?"

Mrs. Pakefield shivered. "A nasty old place it is. Not much used, thank goodness. To my mind, it had ought to be demolished. It's like a well in there after the rain, damp and smelly, not to speak of the rats."

"Though your village is otherwise very pretty, Mrs. Pakefield," soothed Ottilia. "And you appear to have everything you need. Is that a shop?" She pointed to the building nearest to the Cock and Bottle.

"Uddington's, that is."

"Might one obtain such items as soap and tooth powder there, do you think?" She saw a hopeful look creep into the landlady's eyes and hastened to build it up. "There is no saying how long it may take our coachman to find someone to effect a repair, and our groom cannot leave the carriage unattended to bring our luggage here."

Mrs. Pakefield was rubbing her hands. "Never you fret, my lady. If so be as you need anything, you've only to ask. And you'll find all such necessities at Uddington's. He's an odd one is Uddington. Keeps himself to himself, so to speak. Getting on in years he is now, but he's a good sort of man in his way and does the best he can."

Devoutly trusting that Francis would raise no serious objections to remaining overnight, Ottilia thanked the woman, making a mental note to pay a visit to the village shop before the day was out. Although no doubt she might trust Mrs. Pakefield's servants to clean off the dirt adhering to the hems of her petticoats and to clean her husband's boots.

The door opened, and Francis himself came in, bearing a tray upon which reposed a tankard, a jug, and a large tumbler. Mrs. Pakefield, reminded of her duties, exclaimed, moving swiftly to relieve him of his burden.

"Beg pardon, my lord. You should've let Pakefield bring it."

Ottilia watched her husband's practised smile appear. "I fear your spouse is still a trifle overcome by these sad events."

The landlady set the tray down and lifted the jug. "It's upset the whole village, my lord." And to Ottilia, "Beg pardon, my lady. I should have seen to your needs instead of standing here gossiping."

"I cannot accuse you of that, Mrs. Pakefield," Ottilia said gently. "In your place, I should have been as much discomposed."

The woman dropped a curtsy. "It's kind of you to say so, my lady. But I'd best go and see to finding something to satisfy his lordship's hunger. I'm that put about to have kept you waiting, my lord. It shan't be long."

With which, she hurried to the door and disappeared through it. Ottilia took a sip of her lemonade and realised she was excessively thirsty. For several moments, her whole attention was concentrated upon downing the contents of the tumbler. When she emerged, she found Francis's amused eye on her and laughed.

"There is no need to look at me like that. I daresay you did much the same with your first tankard."

He grinned. "Wretch. How came you to guess that this is my second?"

"You've been gone too long." She reached out her hand, and his fingers curled around it. "Not that I object, for I have been most usefully employed, pumping Mrs. Pakefield. How did you fare with the husband?"

Francis lifted her hand to his lips and kissed it before releasing her. "Not as well as you, I suspect. The fellow seems to have been knocked sideways. Besides having a disposition to regard everything he discloses in the most pessimistic light."

She laughed. "I rather gathered as much from his aspect. What had he to say about this business?"

As she sipped at her second glass, she listened to Francis's unvarnished account of the accident, if it was one. None had doubted as much to begin with, the landlord had told him, until the doctor had expressed his dissatisfaction.

"However, the doctor was merely overheard last night telling the vicar of his suspicion, and you know how village gossip spreads. It may prove a complete fabrication."

Ottilia eyed him. "Are you saying that only to put me off?"

Francis raised his brows at her. "After my feat at the smithy? I am resigned to allowing you a few more hours."

Relieved, she laughed. "I shall need them, I fear. But that is excellent, for I have a task for you."

He groaned. "Don't tell me. I utterly refuse to go on any wild-goose chase on an empty stomach."

"As if I would ask it of you."

"Indeed? My experience of you in the mode of hunting down a murderer leads me to expect the worst."

Ottilia took refuge in her lemonade. His tone was teasing, but she was guiltily aware of having already planned to impose upon him unmercifully. This was hardly the moment to disclose that she believed they might be obliged to stay the night. With the hope of distracting him, she seized upon an item in his narrative that niggled at the back of her mind.

"Did Mr. Pakefield say anything else about the vicar?"

Francis frowned. "No. Why?"

"Because I suspect he may be pertinent. Mrs. Pakefield spoke of him as a champion sent by the Almighty."

"A champion of whom?"

"The witch."

Light dawned in his features. "Ah, that explains it. I thought the fellow muttered something along those lines."

"What, pray?"

"The witch took sanctuary in the vicarage, as we heard, but did not come out until morning, although her maid did. The village, according to Pakefield, feels this to be the devil at work again, tempting a man of God to evil."

With his hunger satisfied by the consumption of several large slices of an excellent pigeon pie in addition to the promised ham, the jaundiced view Francis had taken of events proved evanescent, and he was fully able to appreciate the necessity—expressed, to his amusement, with an excessive amount of charm by his darling wife—to gauge the temper of the local populace. Nor, since Tillie could not with decorum frequent the taproom of the local tavern, had it taken much persuasion for him to agree to do his part. The quicker the facts were uncovered, the sooner Francis might get her away from the place.

His ingenuity had not been to any degree tested. He had pointedly ignored the curious looks which must be accorded to any stranger in such an out-of-the-way place, merely ordering a tankard and taking an opportunity to engage the tapster in conversation.

"You've had a deal of excitement here, I take it."

"Aye, we have that, sir," the man responded, and then he frowned a little. "But how you got to know it has me beat."

"I am staying with my wife at the Blue Pig," Francis informed him pleasantly. "My carriage broke down."

This piece of news appeared to interest the tapster unduly. "Broke a wheel, sir?"

"The axletree."

"Ah. 'Tis a pity as poor Mr. Duggleby been and took dead, then, for he'd have had it put together in no time."

A heavy sigh accompanied this pronouncement. Recognising his cue, Francis bethought him of his wife and did his duty.

"The blacksmith, do you mean? I hear the roof fell in on him."

"Aye, it did that, sir. And the devil's own job it be to dig him out."

"I imagine so," Francis agreed. "From what I saw at the smithy, it must have taken a deal of work and many hands."

The tapster blinked. "You seen it, then, sir?"

"On the way in. There seems to have been something of a fire, too."

"Aye, blazing it be when we brung him out, only the storm done for that soon enough."

Francis kept his tone carefully casual. "I daresay it was inevitable, what with the fire going in the forge."

A puzzled look crept into the tapster's features, and he leaned confidentially across the counter. "That be the funny thing, sir. The fire be over where Duggleby lay, but there bain't no path of flame to the forge which be out already, the bellows being still. Master Tisbury says as how the flames must've jumped by the roof afore it come down."

Or perhaps, as Tillie had surmised, someone had taken a burning piece of tinder and deliberately set alight the area around the body. Which thought reminded Francis of his second task.

"Pakefield said your Master Tisbury had the smith brought here last night."

"In this very taproom, aye. Master thought as it bain't right to leave Duggleby lying in the smithy, with the roof down and all."

"That was well thought of. Though I confess I am relieved the body has been removed."

This produced a snigger, and the tapster went so far as to wink. "It be old Pa Wagstaff as said he hoped as he bain't expected to take his drink along o' the dead, seeing as he bain't minded yet to join Duggleby in the next world."

"One can scarcely blame him," said Francis with a smile, noting the nod in the direction of an ancient sitting on a bench near the fireplace. He looked to be a fixture, and his aged gaze, still keen, had more than once flickered in Francis's direction.

"Aye, but it be nowt to do with old Pa as made Master set the body over to back of the house."

"This house?"

The tapster nodded. "Have him took to another room, says the doctor, for as he'd to look at Duggleby by daylight."

Francis caught the whiff of gossip in the fellow's voice and looked a question. The tapster cast a glance around the watching patrons, leaned over the counter, and lowered his voice.

"I heard the doc say as how he bain't satisfied as to how Duggleby died."

"You heard it?" repeated Francis, rejoiced to have discovered so readily the source of the rumour.

The tapster nodded, his eyes alight. "I heard him say as it be a hammer to Duggleby's head afore the roof come down. He be talking to the new reverend."

The door to the hallway opened, and Francis looked round as the tapster glanced up.

"Here be the reverend now, sir."

The fellow began to move away, but Francis held up a hand. "One moment. Has the doctor been here today to look at the body?"

If the tapster was surprised at the question, he did not show it, but nodded, his attention focused on the newcomer, who was coming towards the counter.

"He come early, but told Master to leave Duggleby where he be. He've gone off to fetch Lord Henbury as be justice of the peace, and Pilton, which be constable hereabout."

With which, the fellow moved to where the parson now

stood, and Francis shifted his position, eyeing the man even as he racked his brains for a means to introduce Tillie into the room where the corpse lay.

The vicar was a slim-featured gentleman with a serious expression and a pair of startlingly blue eyes. The black garb and clerical collar proclaimed his calling, and he spoke with a quiet assurance that instantly drew Francis's interest.

"Will? Is Tisbury here?"

"In the back, Reverend. Shall I fetch him to you?"

"If you please."

The tapster disappeared through a doorway behind the counter, and the vicar stood back, glancing around the taproom. He met Francis's eye briefly but made no comment, instead focusing his gaze upon a bench flanking the fireplace.

"What you done with that there witch, Reverend? Time to set up the faggots, be it?"

A high-pitched cackle accompanied this challenge, and Francis turned to find the comment emanated from the old country fellow stigmatised as Pa Wagstaff. A smoking clay pipe was in his fingers, and he sported a greasy smock and a battered hat.

The vicar nodded towards him. "I'll thank you not to jest upon such a subject, Mr. Wagstaff."

The ancient sniggered the more and waved his pipe. "And I'll thankee if'n you be minded to take a stick to my fool daughter, Reverend."

Before the parson had a chance to respond, the tapster returned with a portly individual whose unprepossessing countenance took on a discontented expression the instant his eyes fell on the vicar.

"Oh, it be you, Reverend. What be you wanting this time?"

A slight edge entered the vicar's voice. "I shall be obliged, Tisbury, if you will furnish me with the names of the village boys."

The landlord scowled. "What, all on 'em?"

"All who may answer to the charge of stoning Mrs. Dale."

The fellow Tisbury looked recalcitrant. "How's I to know which on 'em done it?"

Francis watched the blue eyes set steady upon the landlord's face. "Yet I am certain you do know."

No response being forthcoming, the vicar glanced again around the tavern. Francis saw a swift shifting among the assembled men, all but the aged Wagstaff refusing to meet the vicar's eyes.

"They won't none on 'em tell you, Reverend," said this worthy, who seemed to find every one of his own utterances matter for mirth. "What'll you do, dust they jackets for 'em?"

The parson ignored him, turning back instead to the landlord. "Have you boys of your own, Tisbury?"

"Mine's growed," returned the man, his tone sullen.

"And are they good citizens?"

"Only be one, and he be 'prenticed."

"Excellent. Now, which boys do I look for on this occasion?"

Tisbury scowled the more. "If'n you want the ringleaders, you best try Staxton's boys. Lawless little varmints they be."

"I thank you."

The vicar turned to go, but at that moment, the door opened again and a burly fellow came in, attired in rough homespuns.

"Here be Staxton himself," pronounced the landlord.

The man who had entered halted abruptly, his glance going from the landlord behind the counter to the vicar, who was facing him. Francis heard a collective intake of breath and looked more closely at the fellow Staxton, taking in the raw and ruddy cheeks and a look of fierce defiance in a pair of bloodshot eyes. It struck him the village was chock-full of bad-tempered men. Or was it due to the happenings of the hour?

"Farmer Staxton?"

The man stood his ground, his frowning gaze fixed on the vicar. "Reverend?"

The parson unexpectedly held out his hand. "We have not met. I am Kinnerton."

The farmer looked at the hand, wiped his own against his breeches in a gesture Francis took to be both habitual and unconscious, and shook it.

"Saw you last night, Reverend," said Staxton, his voice a low growl.

Kinnerton smiled. "Indeed? I regret I could not take in all the faces."

A faint twitch of the man's lips might be taken for an attempt at a smile. "It 'ud take a tidy good memory."

"True." The vicar fell back a step. "Staxton, I need your help."

"Aye?"

"Do you know any of the boys who threw stones at Mrs. Dale last night?"

There was a perceptible pause. Francis saw the man's eyes flicker. Deciding whether to lie? Then he nodded briefly.

"Aye."

"Will you furnish me with their names, if you please?"

This time the man's chin came up, but he did not hesitate. "Bart, Josh, and Abe. T'other two be only followers."

Francis watched Kinnerton's face with intense concentration. Not a muscle shifted, and the blue eyes remained steady on Staxton's own.

"I thank you. Where may I find them?"

"Over to the farm. My boys they be."

"I see."

For a moment neither spoke, and Francis found he was holding his breath. Then Kinnerton opened fire.

"Do I take it you condone the behaviour of your sons, Staxton?"

Now the farmer's eyes narrowed. "What if'n I do?"

"Will you tell me why?" asked the vicar unexpectedly.

The fellow's jaw dropped open. "Why?"

"Yes, why would a sensible man condone such conduct?"

Francis heard the edge to the parson's voice and realised the man was very angry indeed. He doubted he would remain similarly cool in Kinnerton's position.

Staxton appeared nonplussed. His jaw worked, and he blinked several times in quick succession. Then he threw up his head and puffed out his chest, the growl pronounced.

"Be you telling me how I'm to raise my own flesh and blood, Reverend?"

"I might well do so," said Kinnerton, his tone steely, "since that forms part of my ministry. But at this present I am merely asking you a question. Why," he repeated, "do you condone your sons throwing stones at a defenceless woman?"

The farmer let out a roar, like a cornered animal. His voice rose.

"A witch, bain't her? Stones be too good for the likes of her. Bain't enough as her've killed Duggleby. Who be next? If you've a mite of sense, Reverend, you'll have nowt to do with her, or you be a-going to end up same as Duggleby."

"Is that a threat?"

The deadly quiet of the question did nothing to lessen the force of its impact. The entire taproom went still, every eye turning upon Farmer Staxton. Francis felt momentarily in awe of the slight figure standing firm before the onslaught of the farmer's wrath.

It took several seconds, but the vicar won. Staxton fell back, dropping his gaze.

"Bain't no threat," he mumbled. "Didn't mean nowt by it."

"Very well," came the quiet response. "Bring your boys to see me at the church, if you please. At three o'clock."

Staxton glanced up once and then back down. "Aye, Reverend."

"Don't fail."

The farmer mumbled something that might have been assent. Without another word, the vicar passed him and quietly left the taproom. An idea leapt into Francis's head. If this Kinnerton could be of use to Tillie, he was a fellow eminently worthy of cultivating.

Chapter 4

A less likely friendship Ottilia could scarcely have imagined. The two ladies were so very different in both style
and manner, it was hard to fathom what quality each found
in the other to admire.

She was not much surprised, though indeed gratified, to
find her casual invitation taken up with more speed than
etiquette, and she suspected it was Mrs. Radlett who had
instigated the visit. Francis had only just been despatched
on his mission when the two ladies arrived in the coffee
room.

Ottilia had noticed the difference upon first meeting, but
it was intensified close to. Miss Beeleigh's rough manner was
utterly in contrast to the genteel Mrs. Radlett. Both looked
to be on the shady side of five and fifty, although the spinster
had a look of rugged strength which was emphasised by the
severity of her greying locks pulled sharply back and strictly
confined. Wholly in contrast, a quantity of improbable gold
curls frizzed out beneath Mrs. Radlett's frivolous bonnet,

which framed a face liberally decorated with paint and powder that did not quite conceal a collection of betraying wrinkles and a pasty look behind the rouge.

Miss Beeleigh evidently employed no aids to beauty and wore her years with pride. Or was it defiance? Of the two, Ottilia thought her the more handsome, with eyes fiercely dark and strong features that hinted at foreign ancestry.

The widow Radlett lost no time in ensuring she had gauged her hostess's identity with accuracy.

"Forgive me, Lady Francis, but is not your husband related to the Marquis of Polbrook?"

The hushed expectancy in the question was not lost on Ottilia, and she met the menace head-on. "Indeed, yes. His brother."

A sigh of exquisite satisfaction from the widow caused her friend to cast her a look of vexation, but Ottilia fluttered a hand and sighed on her own account.

"Pray do not trouble to conceal your knowledge of that terrible business last year. I daresay it is everywhere talked of still."

The Radlett woman's nod was all too eager. "Oh yes, even here."

"Evelina!"

The sharp remonstrance from her companion made the widow snatch a hand to her mouth. "Oh, dear, but I only meant . . ."

Ottilia smiled with exaggerated friendliness. "Think nothing of it, Mrs. Radlett. It was I who mentioned it, after all. It is so very trying, is it not, to be obliged to keep mum when one is bursting to know? I confess curiosity is my besetting sin."

"Well but one could not help thinking of it," Mrs. Radlett confided, "particularly at present."

"You mean because of your blacksmith having been murdered?" said Ottilia, taking the bull by the horns.

A snort came from Miss Beeleigh as she tugged out a chair with unnecessary vigour. "Village gossip. I'll not believe it until I hear it from Meldreth himself."

She gestured her friend to take the chair, and dragging out a second, threw herself into it, stretching out long legs and crossing them at the ankles.

"But it was Meldreth who said so," protested the other as she settled herself into the chair provided for her use, not without a good deal of fidgeting to arrange her petticoats suitably.

"By report only," snapped Miss Beeleigh. "None but a nodcock could expect Duggleby to come out alive, especially once you had seen how much debris came down."

Mrs. Radlett nodded at Ottilia, setting the ribbons on her bonnet dancing. "A shocking thing, Lady Francis. Why, I should think half the roof had fallen in."

Ottilia concealed a burgeoning amusement. "Indeed, yes."

"Place is a shambles," said Miss Beeleigh. "It will have to come down altogether, no doubt of that."

"It is certainly severely damaged by the fire," Ottilia agreed. She put a tentative toe in the water. "I suppose it is not impossible that the roof did not come down by accident."

The widow blinked out of eyes a trifle puffy, the skin faintly blue beneath them. "You did not see the storm. It was positively raging, you know."

"Still, someone might have helped it along perhaps."

Ottilia came under a gimlet beam from Miss Beeleigh's extraordinary eyes. "You're saying someone tampered with the roof beforehand?"

Mrs. Radlett's eyes grew round, dissipating a little the oddly heavy look about them. "Oh no, surely not. Who could be so wicked?"

Ottilia smiled. "Well, murderers are not renowned for kindness, you know, Mrs. Radlett."

"But it seems so horrid."

"Yes," agreed Ottilia gently. "Particularly for those who are left behind to mourn."

The widow's orbs rimmed liquid at this. "Poor Bertha Duggleby. We went afterwards to see her and the children. I daresay there is nothing to be done, but one had to ask."

"Just so," agreed Ottilia. "Will the poor woman be able to survive, do you suppose?"

"I believe so, yes, poor thing. And dear Mr. Uddington— our shopkeeper, you must know—is already taking up a collection."

Miss Beeleigh snorted again. "Collection! If Duggleby had not a fortune stashed away, you may call me a dunderhead."

"We don't know that, Alethea."

"What, when he'd had the business from the whole area for miles around for years?"

"Is there no other blacksmith in the vicinity?" Ottilia asked, her mind flying to Williams, who might have to hunt further afield to get the coach mended.

"The nearest is at Nuneaton," Miss Beeleigh responded. "A fellow started up at Atherstone a year or two back, but Duggleby, as selfish a brute as you could hope to meet, made sure he didn't prosper."

Mrs. Radlett was moved to pout. "That is too bad of you, Alethea, when you have just remonstrated with me. You can't say for certain Duggleby interfered with the fellow at Atherstone."

"I don't need certain knowledge," stated Miss Beeleigh, with a supreme confidence Ottilia could not but admire. "I know the type of man Duggleby was. Moreover, I'm surprised to hear you speaking for him after all that has passed."

Ottilia seized the cue. "It does not appear the man was very well liked, from what I have gathered."

She received a sharp glance from eyes tending to almond in shape. "Hannah Pakefield? She's hardly likely to speak well of the man. He was thick as thieves with the Tisburys, and Hannah can't abide Molly Tisbury."

"Yes, I rather caught that impression."

"Poor Hannah," mourned Mrs. Radlett, sighing deeply. "It's hard for her to see the Tisburys prosper. We do our best, you know, coming to drink coffee nearly every day. If only Witherley were closer to the post road, I daresay the Blue Pig would very soon become a profitable house."

Miss Beeleigh nodded at Ottilia. "I said Hannah would be over the moon to see you, Lady Francis. You planning to stay the night?"

Several, by the look of things. But Ottilia did not say as much.

"I'm afraid we have little choice."

Miss Beeleigh's brows lowered. "An axletree is serious. You'll need a highly competent smith to make a half-decent job of it. Good thing you don't have to rely on Duggleby. He'd have botched it so badly, you'd have found yourself stranded again within ten miles. If you take my advice, you'll send to the coachmakers at Coventry. It'll take longer, but at least you'll stand a chance of making it to journey's end."

Thoroughly taken aback, and not a little dismayed, Ottilia blinked at the woman. "Dear me. You had better have a word with my husband, Miss Beeleigh. It begins to look as if we might be here some days."

The other nodded, as if this was a matter of course. "Where is your coach? I could take a look at it."

Ottilia was half aware of showing her astonishment but was unprepared for the other's swift comprehension.

"You are surprised. Merely because one is a woman, ma'am, it don't mean one can't understand such things. I'd not trust myself to effect a repair to an axletree, but I've reset a wheel to a carriage before now."

Mrs. Radlett was nodding with vigour. "It's true. Alethea

is excessively handy with all manner of things of that nature. And it is a fact Duggleby was careless. He hated doing anything for us because he thought Alethea was too exacting."

"Certainly wouldn't tolerate his usual slapdash way of going about things. Lazy, that was Duggleby. He'd do just enough to get the job done. Soon learned who called the tune when I was paying the piper."

Ottilia did not doubt it. "Did not others also complain if his workmanship was shoddy?"

"Most wouldn't dare, for fear of having to trek for miles to get their needs seen to. Besides, Duggleby knew which side his bread was buttered. He'd not serve the likes of Lady Ferrensby so, nor Tisbury—though he's another rogue."

Mrs. Radlett's cheeks showed red through the white paint. "Now, Alethea, you promised never again to make mention of that wretched watered wine."

"I didn't. You did."

"Well, because you said he was a rogue and you've no other reason to say so. In any event, it didn't taste watered to me."

"That's because you have no palate. If you'd bought it here as I told you, it wouldn't have happened."

"And you'd have had no call to stigmatise poor Tisbury a rogue. Not that he isn't, for I've heard Mrs. Dale's Tabitha say he tried to shortchange Sam Hawes once, and Sam threatened to send for Pilton."

"More like it was that fool of a tapster who couldn't count correctly if he were to be hanged for it."

For all her acuteness, Ottilia's brain was whirling. "Pardon me, but I am a little lost. I had the good fortune to meet Mrs. Dale and—Tabitha, was it?"

"Her maid, that's right. And Sam is Tabitha's husband," supplied Mrs. Radlett.

"Pilton is our constable, for all the use he is," said Miss Beeleigh.

"Now that is unfair, Alethea. To my way of thinking Pilton is a sensible young man. But you could not expect him to do well when the poor fellow has Lord Henbury to contend with."

"Ah, I think Mrs. Pakefield mentioned him," cut in Ottilia, committing all this information to memory. "But you mentioned Mrs. Dale. I must say she did not seem much like a witch to me."

Miss Beeleigh threw Ottilia a frown. "Witch! Piece of nonsense."

Mrs. Radlett was moved to protest. "Well, but she does see things, Alethea, you know she does."

"I know she says she does."

"But everyone knows she has been right time and again," objected her friend, not a little indignant.

"A few lucky guesses prove nothing." Miss Beeleigh threw up a hand as the other opened her mouth to argue. "No use going on, Evelina. You'll not convince me."

The widow sighed. "I wish you were not so stubborn, Alethea." No response being forthcoming beyond an enigmatic stare, she turned back to Ottilia. "I am excessively sorry for the girl, you must know, even if it were true. Anyone would suppose with Sam and Tabitha to look after her, dear Cassie Dale could come to no harm, but it isn't so. She's a slip of a thing, too, poor soul. I hear those horrid boys chased her last night, all the way to the vicarage. They were throwing stones. So horrid and cruel."

"Very nasty," Ottilia agreed.

"Expect the little beasts were egged onto it by their seniors," stated Miss Beeleigh in a tone so matter-of-fact that Ottilia was startled.

Where Mrs. Radlett's eyes had begun to water when speaking of this particularly savage proceeding, the spinster evinced no vestige of sympathy. Ottilia was moved to probe.

"What a disagreeable notion. Do you truly think so ill of your neighbours, Miss Beeleigh?"

Ottilia was treated to a stony look, but there was no trace of annoyance in the woman's voice.

"Stupidity and ignorance may be found anywhere, Lady Francis. The most civilised persons can be brought to savagery by mob rule."

"Very true. And the young are apt to ape their elders."

"The boys? That is nothing to the purpose. Mrs. Dale's manifestations are insufficient to give children such a false idea of her state. Be sure these notions originated in the heads of such persons as the Tisburys, Farmer Staxton, and Duggleby himself."

"Oh, I would believe anything of Duggleby," said Mrs. Radlett, reentering the lists. "You could teach that horrid man nothing of cruelty, and I should know." Her eyes brimmed. "He killed my dog!"

Ottilia blinked at this unexpected turn. "Killed your dog?"

The ribbons on her bonnet rippled as she nodded, large tears squeezing out of her eyes. "Indeed he did."

"Evelina, my dear, you don't know that."

For the first time, Miss Beeleigh's tone held a measure of gentleness, and Ottilia cast her a swift appraising glance. There was a hard glow in the dark eyes, but the lips were oddly pinched.

"He did," came in tearful protest from the other woman. "He beat the poor thing half to death."

"Someone did, yes," returned Miss Beeleigh, still in the same tone, as if the gentleness were enforced.

Ottilia had the impression this identical discussion had been gone over many times. She caught Miss Beeleigh's glance, and the woman grimaced.

"He had to be shot."

"How very dreadful," Ottilia said automatically. "But why would the blacksmith do such a thing?"

"Because he was a horrid, evil-tempered man," the widow said, dragging a handkerchief from her sleeve, "and I'm glad he's dead."

"Evelina, for heaven's sake, don't let anyone hear you say

so!" And to Ottilia. "Toby was a roamer. Apt to run amok in the village on occasion. Duggleby wasn't the only one to complain of him."

"He was a good dog," insisted Mrs. Radlett, sniffing as she wiped at her tears. "He only barked at the horses because that beastly man cursed at him and threatened him with his whip. It was Duggleby he was attacking, not the horses. It was self-defence."

"Stuff and nonsense. Dog was a menace. I don't say the blacksmith was within his rights if he did beat Toby, but his annoyance was perfectly understandable."

Mrs. Radlett positively glared at her friend. "Next you will say you were glad to shoot poor Toby."

"No such thing. But I'd more pity than to leave the poor creature to suffer in that condition."

"I nursed him through the night, you know," disclosed the widow, dissolving into tears again. "He whimpered so, it broke my heart."

"No point in raking it all up, Evelina," came gruffly from the other. "It is best forgotten."

But it had not been forgotten, Ottilia decided. As she watched the widow dry her eyes and gulp down her tears, she noted the spinster's hand shift to lay protectively upon the other's muslin-clad thigh for a moment. A curiously intimate gesture.

Ottilia glanced quickly away, and her gaze fell upon a figure beyond the window coming down the lane from the direction of the church. As Ottilia watched, he turned into the path through the cobbled yard of the Blue Pig. She seized the opportunity to change the subject.

"Who is that coming in, I wonder?"

Both women turned to look out of the window. Mrs. Radlett exclaimed.

"It is Mr. Netherburn. Oh, I am so glad. We have not had an opportunity to talk with him yet about what happened, and I believe he was there last night."

Miss Beeleigh turned an overbright glance on Ottilia. "A good man, Horace Netherburn. If only he would cease making a cake of himself over Mrs. Dale."

The widow had been all smiles, her woes forgotten, but at this she pouted. "That is so unfair, Alethea. If poor Horace has been kind enough to befriend Cassie Dale, it is monstrous to be supposing he has an ulterior motive."

"The man's besotted."

"He is no such thing. Why, only the other day he was telling me how sorry he is for her with the horrid way the villagers go on."

"Sorry enough to put a ring on her finger, I don't doubt."

Mrs. Radlett's cheeks suffused once more under the concealing paint, and the suspicion could not but obtrude that there was more than one jealous heart at work in this scenario. Mr. Netherburn had passed out of sight, and Ottilia eagerly awaited his arrival in the coffee room.

F rancis downed the remainder of his tankard and slipped quickly out. He caught the parson up as the man started across the green.

"Reverend Kinnerton!"

The vicar halted and turned, a faint frown between his brows. As he came up to the man, Francis saw in the full daylight that his features were pallid and taut. Francis held out his hand.

"Bravo, sir! I have seldom seen a more telling performance."

A tiny smile flickered in Kinnerton's eyes as they shook hands. He looked a trifle bemused.

"I have not the pleasure of your acquaintance, sir. Are you of the village?"

Francis smiled. "I'm a stranger to the place. But I gather you are newly arrived yourself?"

"Indeed. I took office only yesterday."

"Baptism by fire?"

Kinnerton laughed, and the dark that had been in his face was swept away.

"You may well say so. But, forgive me. Your name, if you please?"

"I am Fanshawe. Lord Francis Fanshawe, to be precise. And I am here by the veriest accident."

He related the story of the breakdown of his coach, reflecting that it was not perhaps the moment for the exact truth. Besides, how in the world did one explain the extreme oddity of Tillie's insatiable curiosity in affairs of this kind?

"Unfortunate," commented the vicar. "I hope you may not be seriously incommoded by recent events."

Francis refrained from pointing out that it was his wife's antics that would incommode him rather than the peculiar circumstances in the village.

"Tell me, if you do not object," he said instead, gesturing ahead and turning to walk at Kinnerton's side, "a little more of this female who has been so badly treated. Do they really believe she is a witch?"

"Mrs. Dale is her name. I have little knowledge of her beyond the fact that she sought sanctuary at the vicarage last night. I am glad her maid saw fit to bring her to me. The mood was ugly, and I dread to think what may have happened."

"You believe the villagers might have harmed her?"

Kinnerton halted abruptly. "Did you not hear that fellow? I wish the villagers had not the habit of indulgence in the tavern. There is nothing like a meeting of like minds to whip up this sort of dangerous frenzy."

It was plain the man's mind was too strongly on the potential fate of Mrs. Dale to be readily shifted to Francis's whim— to wit, the blacksmith's corpse. He bided his moment.

"I rather think we ran into your protégée this morning."

Kinnerton's blue gaze settled on Francis with a disconcerting suddenness. "Where?"

"In the smithy."

The vicar's lips tightened. "I wish she had not gone there. Indeed, I would have much preferred her to remain safely in my house."

Francis wished fervently for his wife's intuitive powers, having no idea himself of how to direct the conversation into channels which might prove helpful. If forthrightness could serve him, he had best use it.

"I gathered from Pakefield, our landlord at the Blue Pig there, that general opinion did not favour such a course."

He received another penetrating stare as Kinnerton frowned. "What does that mean? Be plain with me, if you please, sir." As Francis hesitated, the parson reached out a hand, palm up in an oddly inviting gesture. "We are unacquainted, my lord, but these circumstances are unusual, to say the least. Besides, it is the burden of my profession that I must frequently dispense with formality."

Only faintly aware of an inner impulse, Francis gave his hand to the man and felt it shaken strongly. He nodded.

"It is a bargain, sir."

"Then?"

Despite his consent, Francis gave way with reluctance. "Not to put too fine a point on it, Pakefield says the villagers think it is the devil's work in tempting a man of God from the path of virtue."

To his surprise, this caused an unexpected change in Kinnerton's features. He grinned, and his whole countenance lightened.

"Do you say so indeed? How very edifying to be freed from blame! It must amuse me if it were not an obvious excuse to heap up the evidence in Mrs. Dale's disfavour." Abruptly he frowned again. "What did you think of her?"

Acutely assailable, Francis found himself in a quandary. It was evident the vicar had espoused the cause of the village witch. But was it wholly a matter of the compassion of his calling? A red-blooded male himself, Francis could not but suspect there might be another aspect involved. In which case, discretion dictated he moderate his real views on the subject of Mrs. Dale.

"She seemed a trifle distraught," he temporised. "Unsurprising, I would guess."

Kinnerton's eyes darkened a little. "Yes. She blames herself, poor tortured soul."

Francis noted tautness about the man's cheeks. He tried for a lighter note. "She is fortunate, perhaps, in your friendship. I am told Mrs. Pakefield heartily approves of you in the role of champion."

A faint smile touched the vicar's lips. "I am glad. This persecution must cease. Not least because I suspect it deepens already livid scars."

Light dawned in Francis's mind. "That is what you mean by saying she is tortured?"

"Oh yes. I do not know if I am capable of the necessary succour, but such demons I can understand."

Francis could readily believe it. There was that in Kinnerton's personality that hinted at unspoken sorrows. He wished fervently for Tillie's insight.

"Well, at least you may scotch these rumours of witchery," he said, feeling the words to be of little value.

The vicar's eyes flashed. "I will do my damnedest, believe me. By God, I thought I had left such superstition behind me in darkest Africa!"

Francis was struck by a sudden access of shadow in the fellow's face, and he realised that despite his own lack, he had inadvertently stumbled upon a depth hitherto concealed. Intrigued, he prompted for more.

"Africa?"

Kinnerton nodded. "I chose to do God's mission work, but my flesh proved unequal to the task."

"How so?"

"I fell victim to a local disease, a form of fever."

Both amazed and shocked, Francis stared at him. "You appear to be remarkably brave, Mr. Kinnerton."

The parson laughed, a hollow sound. "I wish I were. I fear I am at heart a sad coward."

"That seems hardly credible."

"I assure you. When I recovered, I was too weak to remain in that continent and had perforce to return to England. But I am strong again, and I cannot find the courage to go back."

Thoroughly caught by these extraordinary revelations of the fellow's character, Francis was conscious of a wave of sympathy. "Why should you feel it incumbent upon you to do so?"

Kinnerton sighed. "Because my flock became lost to me while I lay helpless in my sickness. I would have had to begin all over again, and I could not face that."

"I understand you, I believe."

Kinnerton looked keenly at him. "Do you?"

Francis smiled. "I think so. We all have our demons, Mr. Kinnerton. I am fortunate in my wife, who has laid most of mine to rest."

The vicar's blue gaze rested on Francis, and he bore the scrutiny without comment. It was an odd encounter, and despite his inadequacies, he felt as if something of Tillie's art had insinuated itself into him. She was the one with the knack of dropping into intimacy with strangers.

Kinnerton smiled. "I should like to meet your wife."

Francis seized opportunity. "Have you time now? She is waiting for me in the Blue Pig."

The arrival of Horace Netherburn in the coffee room was rapidly productive of a mood of frivolity in Ottilia that she found hard to contain. It was not so much his air of old-world gallantry, which she found quite touching, but rather the reactions he produced in the two women already present.

He began by holding the door for Mrs. Pakefield as she came in with a laden tray, meanwhile doffing his hat and waving it expansively at the inhabitants of the parlour.

"Ladies, dear ladies, forgive my unmannerly conduct and allow me to make my bow presently. But I could not reconcile it with my conscience to allow poor dear Hannah to struggle with the door while I paid my compliments to you."

An instant change in demeanour overcame Mrs. Radlett. Wreathed in smiles, she fluttered expressive hands.

"Dear Mr. Netherburn, you need never stand on ceremony with us, as you know too well." Then, to the landlady, waving a hand towards the table. "There now, Hannah, put it down, dear. Here, let me help you set it all out."

Rising, the widow proceeded to set the cups on saucers and place them appropriately, what time Mr. Netherburn busily closed the door and began his approach towards the table. Miss Beeleigh, who made no move to rise or to assist with the operation of setting out the accoutrements for the coffee, held up her hand to halt him.

"Stay, Horace. Best make your bow to Lady Francis Fanshawe before you do the pretty to us."

A pair of pale eyes goggled at Ottilia out of features unremarkable save for sagging jowls and the stamp of years cutting deep creases into sallow skin.

"Lady Francis Fanshawe? My dear ma'am, forgive me, pray. My manners, alas. I did not see you there."

An elegant leg accompanied this effusion, and Ottilia had the opportunity to take in the bagginess of the fellow's very correct attire that signalled the wastage of flesh in the onset of age. At first glance, she had taken him for close on sixty, but she rapidly revised this estimate, placing him a good ten years beyond it. Which, if he was indeed hankering after the youthful Mrs. Dale, must set him in his dotage. She held out her hand as he rose from his bow.

"How do you do, Mr. Netherburn?"

Not much to Ottilia's surprise, he bent again from the waist and kissed her hand.

"Too kind, my lady, I am in excellent health. But to

what," he continued, releasing her, "do we owe the pleasure? A rare event in our uneventful lives."

"They seem to be excessively eventful today," remarked Ottilia drily.

"Yes, Horace, don't be more of a fool than you can help," snapped Miss Beeleigh. "Sit down, man."

"Alethea!" The widow threw a frown at her friend and immediately turned on smiles as she addressed the gentleman. "Sit by me, Mr. Netherburn, do. You must not take it amiss."

Mr. Netherburn had looked a trifle disconcerted, but he recovered swiftly as he manoeuvred himself around the back of Mrs. Radlett's chair.

"I think I know Miss Beeleigh well enough not to take offence." He glanced at Ottilia. "You will find us very free, ma'am. Oh yes, very free. One cannot be standing upon one's dignity in a village, you know. And my dependency is all upon my two dear friends, for we are few, so very few."

"True enough," commented Miss Beeleigh. "Once you've counted Lady Ferrensby and Henbury, there's only Meldreth. That's the lot."

Mr. Netherburn threw up a hand. "How can you say so, dear Miss Beeleigh? Are you forgetting poor Mrs. Dale?"

"I don't count Cassie Dale," returned the other. "She don't add to the social round. Girl's a recluse."

"No, no, I will not have you say so," protested Mr. Netherburn. "She mourns still, poor creature. Mark my words, she will come out of her shell in due time."

"Not if the whole village insists she's responsible for Duggleby's death."

Mrs. Radlett, who had busied herself pouring the coffee, looked up at this.

"Oh dear, Alethea, I had near forgot all the upset. Cannot we talk of something else?"

"Dear Mrs. Radlett," broke in Mr. Netherburn, seizing

her free hand and giving it a squeeze. "Always so sensitive, so sympathetic."

Ottilia did not miss the glance that flickered from the pale eyes towards Miss Beeleigh, as if to emphasise the lack of sensitivity in that quarter. Trusting she would not be similarly stigmatised, she thrust the talk back in the direction that suited her.

"Have you any opinion on this business, Mr. Netherburn?"

He looked flattered and preened a little. "Who has not, Lady Francis? I cannot remember a blacker day in the village, not even when poor Mr. Uddington lost his wife."

"She died?"

"Ran away," said Miss Beeleigh succinctly. "And took the boy with her."

Mrs. Radlett's evident love of gossip overcame her, and she set down her cup, leaning eagerly towards Ottilia.

"It was years ago. Five or six at least."

"Seven," stated Miss Beeleigh.

"Is it so long? I remember it was just after I came here, when dear Alethea took me in. A shocking thing!"

Ottilia could not resist. "What, that Miss Beeleigh took you in? It sounds a most charitable proceeding."

"No, no, I don't mean that."

"Nothing in it," said Miss Beeleigh in a flat tone that gave the lie to an odd expression of intensity in the almond eyes. "We were schoolfellows. When I heard how things had been left when Radlett died, seemed sense to pool our resources. We deal well together."

"Indeed we do," agreed the widow, but with a darting look of doubt at Mr. Netherburn that caught Ottilia's attention.

"I understand," she said, "but what of this Mrs. Uddington? Why did she run away?"

Although Miss Beeleigh threw in another of her habitual

snorts and Mr. Netherburn shook a grave head, Mrs. Radlett's attention focused instantly.

"It was said she'd betrayed her husband. And who do you think was the culprit?" Ottilia guessed from the portentous pause just what was coming but forbore from stealing the woman's thunder. "Duggleby."

Chapter 5

Mrs. Radlett sat back with an air of satisfaction. Ottilia knew her duty.

"Dear me, you don't say so? The blacksmith himself?"

"Pah! None knows the truth of it, of course." Thus Miss Beeleigh.

Mr. Netherburn leaned in, excitement throwing pink into his cheeks.

"I had forgot it. But don't you see how this changes everything? How may anyone blame poor Mrs. Dale when there is Uddington with the strongest of grudges against the dead man?"

"But why should he wait seven years to take his revenge?" objected Ottilia.

Her auditors looked struck; all but Miss Beeleigh, who nodded.

"True. Don't make sense."

"It is a consideration," agreed Mr. Netherburn, sitting back again, but with disappointment in his face.

"Well, but he might bide his time, waiting for an opportunity," offered the widow, patently unwilling to relinquish this promising avenue.

Ottilia smiled. "Perhaps Mr. Uddington is not the only man to hold a grudge against this Duggleby. He does not seem to have been a popular fellow. Who were his friends, do you know?"

"Always been thick as thieves with Tisbury," stated Miss Beeleigh.

"Not forgetting Staxton," put in Mr. Netherburn. "One could not take oneself into the Cock without finding the three together."

"Yes, and Bertha Duggleby said she'd had comfort from Molly Tisbury last night," added Mrs. Radlett.

Ottilia put up a finger. "I would not set too much store by settled friendships. I have had occasion to observe that broken friendships produce the greatest enmity."

Miss Beeleigh was nodding. "You are very right, Lady Francis. Horace, had you noticed of late any reduction in amity among those three men?"

Mr. Netherburn sipped his coffee, evidently subjecting the question to examination. At last he shook his head.

"I cannot say I have noticed anything of the kind. But I am bound to state that all three were apt to exhibit an ill-tempered manner on occasion."

"It would be unlikely to manifest at this present," Ottilia said, "for people tend to band together in times of trouble, do you not think?"

"They are certainly banding together against poor Mrs. Dale," said Mr. Netherburn, a peevish note entering his voice.

"Indeed yes," agreed Mrs. Radlett. "Had the vicar not intervened last night, I must say I dread to think of the consequences."

Miss Beeleigh set down her cup with a snap. "I'd forgot the new vicar. His arrival should content you, Horace. Another face to add to the social circle. Young, too. Daresay he might winkle Cassie Dale out of her shell."

Ottilia watched Horace Netherburn colour up and noted the dagger look cast upon her friend by Mrs. Radlett. By good fortune, she caught motion through the window in the periphery of her vision and looked out.

"Oh, there is my husband. Dear me, is that perhaps the vicar with him?"

As one, the three visitors turned to look out of the window.

"Is it?"

"Not met the fellow yet, so we can't know."

"Ah yes," came from Netherburn. "He's the fellow on the right. I caught a sight of him earlier and thought it must be Kinnerton."

This was enough for Ottilia. She rose swiftly. "Pray excuse me for a moment. I must speak to my husband."

Without pausing for a response, she darted to the door and was into the hall and outside before any could think of accompanying her. She had no wish to make the vicar's acquaintance in the company of the village gossips, who would undoubtedly hamper her in a bid to discover all she might of the witch's champion.

She waved to Francis as she sped down the path through the cobbles and was relieved to see him halt on the green to wait for her.

"We were just on our way in to find you, my love," he said and turned to his companion. "Allow me to present my wife, Lady Francis Fanshawe. This is the Reverend Mr. Kinnerton, who has only just taken up his living at the vicarage."

As Ottilia held out her hand, she took stock of the young man. She liked what she saw. He was personable, without being handsome, but the clarity of his blue gaze sat well with her.

"My dear sir, I am enchanted. I have heard how you aided the young creature who has been so unfortunate as to incur the enmity of the village."

The severity of Mr. Kinnerton's expression disappeared,

and Ottilia was treated to an appraising look. Her hand was taken in a firm clasp, warm to the touch.

"I thank you, but anyone would have done the same."

"You are too modest, sir. I have already heard of several persons who, by all accounts, would indeed have done otherwise."

A frown appeared. "You are very well informed, ma'am."

Ottilia laughed. "I have been in conversation with Miss Beeleigh and Mrs. Radlett, whom I believe you have not yet met."

A gleam appeared in his eye. "Ah. Yes, I was warned—er—advised as to the identities of the gentry hereabouts."

"But not about Mrs. Dale, I take it?"

The gleam vanished, and a faint look of steel entered those intense eyes. "Astute of you, Lady Francis."

"My wife is renowned for her keen mind, sir." Ottilia could not help but feel a flush of pleasure at the bristle in her husband's voice. "Witherley may yet have cause to be grateful for her presence."

Now the vicar looked merely puzzled. His glance went from Francis to Ottilia and back again. A faint ripple of irritation crossed his face.

"Would you care to explain your meaning, my lord?"

"By all means," said Francis, with a promptness that caused Ottilia to set a warning hand upon his arm. He glanced at her, but the steel in his voice did not abate. "I don't know if you are familiar with the scandal that overtook my family last year?"

The vicar shook his head. "I was in no condition to take in very much at that time."

Ottilia saw Francis relax and threw him a questioning glance. He caught it and gestured towards the parson.

"Mr. Kinnerton had the misfortune to be ill for some little time. Briefly then, sir, an intimate relation was murdered. It is entirely due to my wife's tireless investigations and her ingenious mind that the perpetrator was discovered. She saved my family's reputation and our sanity."

The vicar looked thunderstruck, as well he might. Ottilia thought it well to lessen the impact.

"My husband exaggerates," she said cheerfully. "If I have a knack, it is in noticing what others might not. And those persons nearly concerned in events are apt to be a trifle blinded, do you not think?"

All at once the Reverend Kinnerton smiled and his whole countenance underwent a change. "It appears we are fortunate in your misfortune. Would it be selfish of me to hope that your carriage is not mended too quickly? Any aid you can offer in diverting suspicion from Mrs. Dale will be only too welcome, I assure you."

Ottilia held out her hand, and the vicar clasped it with both his own. She smiled at him. "I had best confess, lest the heavens strike me down. Our groom came here in search of a blacksmith, and when he brought news of the storm, the smith's murder, and a hunt for the local witch, I'm afraid curiosity overtook me."

Kinnerton laughed. "Lady Francis, I am not your confessor. What will you do?"

Francis intervened. "I have been hoping you may be able to help. The tapster tells me the blacksmith's body is still housed in a back room at the Cock and Bottle. It is imperative my wife has a sight of it."

The vicar looked startled, his glance flying back to Ottilia's face. "My dear ma'am, surely you cannot intend to subject yourself to such a spectacle?"

Ottilia saw Francis bristle again and cut in swiftly. "I am a hardy spirit, Mr. Kinnerton, and have confronted several such spectacles." She saw disbelief in his face and could not forbear a laugh. "Perhaps I should explain that my brother is a doctor. Until recently, I lived in his house and had opportunity to partake of his activities."

"Believe me, I was quite as shocked as I can see you are, Kinnerton," Francis put in, "but she is speaking the truth. I can vouch for it that she will not flinch."

The vicar spread his hands. "You leave me with nothing to say."

"But can you help?" Francis pursued, with an impatience Ottilia could not but deprecate. She said nothing, however, merely waiting upon Mr. Kinnerton's pleasure.

He frowned. "You wish me to insinuate Lady Francis into the house? I'm not sure my word will carry much weight with Tisbury."

"Nonsense," scoffed Francis. "You have sufficiently demonstrated your authority in that quarter."

Ottilia watched in fascination as this idea appeared to penetrate the vicar's mind. A slow smile crept into his face.

"I cannot deny that the notion of spiking the fellow's guns appeals to me. Shall we essay it?"

Francis looked taken aback. "Now?"

Just then a clock began to strike somewhere nearby. The parson looked towards the church. "Two and thirty. We have time yet. If you are ready, ma'am?"

The covered corpse lay on a wooden bedstead near an open window, for which Ottilia gave thanks. The natural aromas accompanying death were muted, but the heat of the day had undoubtedly worsened the body's condition, drawing flies like a magnet and pervading the atmosphere with the faint tang of rotting meat. The insects buzzed around the area and dotted the sheet with resting spots of black.

It had not taxed the vicar's ingenuity unduly to effect an entrance through the back premises of the Cock and Bottle. Tisbury, it appeared, was absent, and the tapster proved no match for Mr. Kinnerton. Within a few short minutes, he came out to where Ottilia waited with Francis, accompanied by a plump maidservant.

"Miss Bessy will conduct us to the blacksmith's present resting place," he said, with a gesture at the girl, who goggled at Ottilia as she bobbed a curtsy.

"How very kind," Ottilia said instantly, smiling at the maidservant.

Bessy blinked and curtsied again. "Bain't nowt, m'am, if'n you be minded to see him. Though why any'd wish to I can't for the life of me think, what with the stink and all."

"I am sure it will be excessively unpleasant," Ottilia conceded, "but I must steel myself to the task."

Mystified but obliging, the girl led the way around the tavern to the back door, which entered into an area clearly set aside for the living quarters of the family. The deceased was housed in a small room given over to a servant's chamber and temporarily unoccupied. Due, so Bessy informed the assembled company, to the kitchen maid having "loped off in the night" some weeks back and not yet having been replaced.

"Why did she lope off?" demanded Ottilia, instantly intrigued.

Bessy shrugged. "No one don't know for sure, though Mistress thinks as her be got with child."

"By whom? Or is that not known, either?"

A trifle of unease entered Bessy's round features at this, and Ottilia caught the almost imperceptible flicker of the girl's eye towards the mound by the window. She cast a more obvious, and somewhat nervous, glance at Mr. Kinnerton, and a flush entered her cheeks.

"Bain't right, talking of such before the Reverend," she muttered, now fixing her gaze on the floor.

"Indeed, no," said Ottilia at once. "I must thank you, Bessy. We will not detain you further."

She let the girl curtsy herself out of the room before turning to the two gentlemen. "Duggleby without doubt."

Francis frowned. "How do you know?"

"Bessy looked instantly at the body when I asked the question."

Mr. Kinnerton's blue gaze was intent. "You are very observant, ma'am. But how can you be sure this girl knew the truth?"

Ottilia laughed. "My dear sir, servants are privy to all sorts of secrets. The maids in a household cannot hope to hide anything from one another, in particular when it comes to amorous adventures. Besides, I have already ascertained that Duggleby was something of a ladies' man."

"What did I tell you?" cut in her spouse, a species of triumph in his tone. "Believe me, she will know more about this blacksmith than half the village before the day is out."

A ripple of laughter escaped Ottilia at the parson's raised eyebrows. "My husband's confidence is a little overstated perhaps. What I do know is that the shop owner, a Mr. Uddington, is said to have lost his wife to an amour with Duggleby."

Mr. Kinnerton looked across at the misshapen sheet. "An unlikely Lothario, one would have thought, from the look of the fellow."

"Oh, he was undoubtedly a brute," agreed Ottilia. "But that does not preclude his being unnaturally attractive to the opposite sex. Certain females have a preference for the rough male, do you not find?"

"I do not," stated the vicar flatly. "But I cannot pretend to an intimate knowledge of the sex."

"You may take it from me she is right," Francis put in. "But should we not pursue the business of the hour? I understand you are pressed for time, Kinnerton."

With obvious reluctance, the vicar moved towards the corpse, reached for a corner of the sheet, and twitched it away, causing a sudden ascent of a cloud of flies. Ottilia noted the wrinkle at his nose and the distaste in his features.

"I daresay his condition has deteriorated since you saw him last night."

Kinnerton nodded, putting a hand over his nose and mouth and moving aside to give her access. Ottilia moved in, casting a quick look at her spouse, who had whipped out his pocket handkerchief and had it firmly in place against the noxious smells that permeated the chamber more completely. She hoped it was not too horrible a reminder of what he had endured last year. He caught her glance, however, and clearly noted the question in her mind, for he shook his head and gestured for her to attend to what she must.

The mattress had been set aside, and the corpse lay directly on the wooden slats. It was cold to the touch despite the warmth of the day, and the still damp and dirty clothes clung to the softened limbs, for rigor had already passed. Ottilia noted the onset of discolouration turning the slack face faintly green. She reached out and lifted each lid of the blacksmith's closed eyes and found one of interest.

Becoming aware of Francis at her elbow, she nodded towards the eye.

"The pupil is dilated."

"What does that mean?"

"Bleeding into the brain."

Bending to that side, Ottilia looked into the man's ear. A trickle of dried dark red liquid emanated from within. She checked the other ear but found none.

"Now for the skull."

Her fingers felt along the base, moving gently towards the side indicated by the pupil and the fluid from the ear. She found what she was seeking easily enough.

"Ah, there it is."

"What is it?"

"A depression. It is very distinct." She probed a little more, closing her eyes to increase her sense of touch. The sensation of two edges came to her.

"The skull is cracked. The poor man was definitely struck. He will have had a severe blood clot."

"Enough to kill him?"

"Oh yes. If the blood has nowhere to escape, it will pool under the skull and compress the brain. He was probably dead well before the roof fell in on him."

*   *   *

As Ottilia preceded the two gentlemen out of the tavern's back door, she instantly noted a party approaching with the clear intention of entering via the same place. One was a man of middle years attired in a grizzled wig, who, with a hand at one elbow, was supporting the doddering steps of a spindly legged old gentleman, and bringing up the rear came a burly young fellow sporting the long coat, slouch hat, and staff that marked him for a constable.

From behind, she heard the vicar's muttered words. "Just in time, for here is Meldreth."

"The doctor, you mean?" asked Francis.

"Then his companion must be Lord Henbury," Ottilia guessed, recalling the catalogue of local gentry put forward by her new friends of the Blue Pig coffee room.

The elderly gentleman apparently caught his name, for he peered across in a myopic fashion.

"Hey? Hey? Who's that? Trespassing, are you? Nosy villagers, I'll be bound."

"Shades of your godmother," murmured Francis close to Ottilia's ear.

She was obliged to bite down upon a spurt of laughter, but she wasted no time on her questioner, instead turning to Kinnerton.

"Will you do the honours, sir?"

The parson stepped forward and performed the introductions, not without some repetition for the benefit of Lord Henbury's deficient hearing. He was obliged to call upon the doctor to explain his own status, what time Francis took opportunity to vent his frustration.

"If I'd had an inkling we would run into another such cantankerous deaf adder, nothing on this earth would have induced me to consent to your coming to this cursed village."

"Maddening, is it not?" Ottilia returned, desperately covering the gurgle that escaped her with an unconvincing cough.

Francis eyed her balefully. "If you don't take care, my girl, I will abandon you to the wretched fellow, who will hamper you more than somewhat, if I am any judge."

Before Ottilia had a chance to respond to this, the Reverend Kinnerton was at her elbow.

"Forgive me, ma'am, but I must go. I have an appointment with Staxton and his boys."

Ottilia instantly held out her hand. "Of course, and thank you. Your help has been invaluable."

Kinnerton bowed over her hand, and with a brief word of farewell to the rest of the company, he was gone. Ottilia turned her attention to the doctor, knowing better than to make any attempt to explain her presence to Lord Henbury.

"I understand you believe the victim to have been struck on the back of the head with a hammer," she said.

"I'm sure of it," Meldreth returned, looking a good deal surprised. "I can only wish I had been more circumspect when I spoke of it."

"Yes, we understand the tapster heard you," Francis put in.

The doctor grimaced. "Will has one of the longest tongues in the village, and that is saying something."

Ottilia laughed. "I rather gathered as much. I can't think Witherley differs in that respect from any other village, however."

"No, it is endemic to the life, more's the pity."

"Oh, to all life, doctor, do you not think? Find me the person who is not given to gossip of his neighbour on occasion and you will show me a saint."

This had the unfortunate effect of rousing Lord Henbury. "Saint? Saint? Balderdash! Fellow was a downright rogue. I'd not have him shoe my horse for a fortune. Can't now, since the fellow's dead. Not that I set any store by all this talk of murder."

Ottilia raised her voice. "Oh, he was most certainly murdered, sir. There can be no doubt of that."

This statement was productive of a sudden silence. Lord

Henbury looked positively affronted. The constable goggled, his jaw dropping open. And Meldreth regarded her with a startled frown.

Suppressing her inevitable amusement, Ottilia raised her brows at the latter. "You noted the depression in the skull, of course. Which was cracked, I think you will agree. And the dilation in the left eye, taken with the liquid from the ear on that side, together suggest a severe hematoma, do you not think? I cannot suppose the poor man long survived the blow that felled him."

She had deliberately kept her tone low, feeling the less Lord Henbury heard the quicker matters might be despatched. He had a hand to his ear, and his indignant look was now accompanied by a spattering of "Hey? Hey?" as he struggled to grasp what had been said. But the doctor's frown had given way to a lurking smile and a twinkle in the eye.

"So that is what you are doing here. Is it your common practise to examine dead bodies, Lady Francis?"

Ottilia automatically put a hand out to Francis as she felt him poker up beside her, and she smiled at the doctor. "Not invariably. But my brother is also a doctor, and I have had occasion to assist at more than one postmortem."

The doctor let out a laugh. "Extraordinary, ma'am."

"Is it not?" said Ottilia in the friendliest of tones. "I was dreadfully nauseous at first, but that soon wore off when Patrick began to explain the science of his findings."

She was interrupted.

"What's that? What's the woman saying?"

To Ottilia's relief, Meldreth took it upon himself to relay her words to his lordship, sensibly confining himself to the briefest disclosure of the evidence supplied by the body.

"In a moment, my lord, I will show you what has been found."

"One thing I cannot tell is the time of death," Ottilia added quickly in a lowered tone.

"Difficult at any point," agreed Meldreth. "Almost impossible at this juncture."

"Yet you saw him after they brought him out last night, did you not?"

He nodded. "It was gone eleven by then, and as far as I could tell, he had been dead for a couple of hours. Stiffening had barely begun, but the discolouration on the underside of his body was already tending to purple. As a rough guide, I must put the hour at about eight or nine."

A connection struck Ottilia. "What time did the storm break?"

The doctor's brows shot up. "Good God, ma'am, but you have a head on your shoulders!"

Beside her, Francis gave a short laugh. "You will find my wife remarkably acute, sir. Do the times match?"

"Perfectly," nodded Meldreth. "I had just supped when the first lightning gave warning. The heavens opened shortly thereafter."

An explosive shout from Lord Henbury cut through this interesting development. "Hey? What's that you say? Opened him up, have you? Found anything?"

The doctor turned, raising his voice and speaking with remarkable patience. "We are talking of the time of death, my lord."

"Well, what the deuce has it to do with her, hey? Who is the woman?"

"This is Lady Francis Fanshawe, my lord. The vicar presented her, if you remember. She has been examining the body."

Lord Henbury turned his choleric eye upon Ottilia. "Think it's a peep show, hey? The man's dead. Don't need silly females gawping at him!"

Noting her spouse's gathering frown, Ottilia put a staying hand on his arm and dropped her voice as she addressed the doctor.

"I must leave you to explain my advent, sir, though I fear his lordship will be horribly shocked. You, too, perhaps?"

Meldreth smiled. "On the contrary, Lady Francis. I am rather astonished at your level of interest in anatomy."

"Dear me. Do you credit us females with wishing to know nothing beyond the frivolous?"

He laughed. "Not if I am to judge by Lady Ferrensby, whose brain is as good as any man's. Nor, I may add, by Miss Beeleigh. She is renowned for poking—I mean, interesting herself—"

"Poking her nose into matters better suited to the male of the species? Yes, I gathered as much from her discourse. But you cannot accuse Mrs. Radlett of being other than feminine."

"No, indeed," he agreed, laughing. "I see you have the measure of our little community already."

Ottilia could not answer, for Lord Henbury was making noises indicative of his impatience which became too vociferous to be ignored.

"Damme, I won't have it! All this talk of murder. Who the devil would want to murder the blacksmith, I'd like to know? Don't make sense. Besides, roof fell in on him."

"True, my lord, but—"

Meldreth got no further, for Francis intervened, his voice redolent with scorn and raised more in annoyance, Ottilia suspected, than simply to be heard.

"My dear sir, if that is all you know, you have been told less than the truth. It is not merely a matter of the body's condition. There is more, if you will take the trouble to examine the smithy."

"What do you mean, Lord Francis?" asked the doctor. "I intend to take Lord Henbury there shortly, but I cannot say I noticed anything untoward myself."

To Ottilia's delight, her spouse instantly gave an enthusiastic account of their visit to the blacksmith's forge and what he had spotted there.

"None with the slightest degree of common sense could suppose that beam came down only with the storm," he finished. "It has been hacked through. Someone wanted to be very sure the roof fell in."

"Balderdash," snapped the elderly justice of the peace, apparently having had no difficulty in hearing what was said. "Wouldn't hold up in a court of law. And if the matter is brought before me, I shall dismiss it out of hand."

Seeing her spouse's cheeks darken with unaccustomed ire, Ottilia risked all on a single throw.

"Oh, surely not, my lord," she said pleasantly, pronouncing her words distinctly and at a level generally reserved for distance. "I cannot believe you would suffer an innocent female to be harmed in this cause."

Lord Henbury stared at her as if she was out of her senses. "Hey? What the deuce are you talking of, woman?"

"I am talking of Mrs. Dale."

"Dale, hey? You don't mean that flibberty little thing Lady Ferrensby brought here? What's she got to do with it?"

"The villagers are blaming her, my Lord Henbury. They say she is responsible for Duggleby's death."

"Hey? Hey?" Henbury blinked confusedly and fastened his gaze upon the doctor. "That so, Meldreth?"

"Yes, my lord. It is indeed so. Mrs. Dale was stoned by the village boys last night in retribution."

"Stoned? Stoned? Never heard such flummery. Why should anyone do that?"

"Because," said the doctor patiently, "they think she killed Duggleby by witchcraft."

Lord Henbury stared at him for a moment in silence. Then he exploded.

"Mad! Mad as March hares, the lot of them. Well, I won't have it." He turned on the luckless constable. "What the deuce are you doing standing there, Pilton? Do your duty, man. Arrest them! Throw them into the lock-up."

The constable blinked confusedly. "What, them boys, my lord? Or did you mean—?"

"You cannot expect the poor man to arrest half the village," Ottilia cut in, prompted to action again. "And I believe Reverend Kinnerton is dealing with the boys."

"I'll not have it, I tell you."

Ottilia pointedly ignored her husband, whose anger, by his shaking shoulders, had given way to an emotion far more contagious.

"No one could expect it of you, sir. But would it not be a far better solution to demonstrate conclusively that some other party had done the deed?"

Lord Henbury looked struck, but he entered a caveat. "How is that to be done?"

"I believe, Lord Henbury, you are about to examine the body."

"Ha! Yes, that's right." The old man turned on Meldreth. "What the devil are you waiting for, Meldreth? Get on, do. Lead me to the fellow's remains."

The doctor, to his credit, did no more than cast up his eyes before turning for the door. But Ottilia put out a hand to detain his lordship.

"After that, Lord Henbury, my husband will go with you to the smithy and show you the very beam of which he has just been telling you."

The old man threw a glance at Francis and nodded in a pleased way, just as if he had not previously refused to entertain the notion of discovering anything amiss at the forge.

"Capital! Wait there for me, young fellow. Won't be more than a jiffy. Now, Meldreth, I'm with you. Pilton, wait here!"

The constable, who had made to follow, fell back with a sigh. Her interest aroused, Ottilia waited only until the two gentlemen had vanished into the house before bestowing one of her friendly smiles upon the man.

"You are the village constable?"

The fellow started. Turning, he snatched off his slouch hat and touched his forelock. "Aye, m'am. Pilton be the name, m'am."

"Were you well acquainted with Duggleby, Mr. Pilton?"

A flush spread across the young man's face at being thus addressed. Ottilia hid her satisfaction and waited.

"Not to say well, m'am, being as I be over towards Atherstone way. Nor I've nowt by way of business with him, having no horse."

"I see. Yet you knew him, as you must know all in the village, holding such an important post."

The young man's chest swelled a touch, and his chin went up. "Aye, 'tis true as I'd to keep tally of who came and went. Not as we be great folk for travelling like."

"Just so," agreed Ottilia and urged his attention back to the matter at hand. "What did you think of Duggleby? I have heard he could be a difficult man at times."

Pilton nodded, pursing his lips. "He'd a temper on him, m'am, that's a fact. Nor he didn't like none argufying with him."

"Was it anyone in particular who argued with him?"

The constable chewed his lower lip. "Not as you'd say argue. 'Cepting Farmer Staxton. Fit to argufy with anyone for nowt, he be." He brightened suddenly. "Then there be Tisbury over to Cock."

Ottilia's ears pricked up. "Indeed? I understood Tisbury and Duggleby were friends."

"Aye, that they be right enough. Only old Jeremiah Wagstaff, as is Mrs. Tisbury's dad, he goes for to crack a joke agin Duggleby like he do one an' all and no one don't take no mind."

"But Duggleby did mind, I surmise," Francis put in.

"Like a bear he minded, sir," agreed the constable, turning with obvious relief to talk to a fellow male. "Said as he'd haul off an' poke Pa Wagstaff in the eye if'n he didn't shut it, and danged if the old man bain't more'n seventy!"

Pilton then became a trifle crimson about the gills, casting an apologetic look at Ottilia. She smiled encouragingly.

"What was the joke?"

The constable's colour intensified, and he threw an imploring look at Francis, who gave her a questioning glance. Suspecting some sort of amorous innuendo, Ottilia returned an infinitesimal nod.

"Come, Pilton, you need not be shy," said Francis. "Her ladyship is more than seven, and she will not take offence."

Clearing his throat, the constable kept his eyes firmly on the less intimidating male, and his voice was gruff. "Well, see, it be this way, sir. Duggleby were ranting as how he be as good a man nor any who set foot in the Pig, and Pa Wagstaff said as how Duggleby had ought to go a-courting the witch widow if'n he'd a mind to set himself up a gentleman. Duggleby said as how he weren't courting no one for as he be a married man, and Pa said as how that bain't stopped him afore."

"And Duggleby took it ill?" Francis suggested.

"Sore as a gumboil he be. And Mrs. Tisbury got mad an' shrieks on hubby to protect her pa. And Tisbury yells his head off at Duggleby, and before you knows it, the two on 'em be at it hammer and tongs."

"Fisticuffs?"

Pilton's eyes were alight with the age-old male love of watching a pitched battle, and he forgot Ottilia's presence in his enthusiasm.

"Bain't never nothing like it, sir. Place was full an' all, and the two on 'em heaving and shoving like giants and crashing the furniture. And then Mrs. Tisbury sets up a screech for the breakages and yells at the men to lay hold on both. But none didn't pay no mind, what with old Pa Wagstaff cackling into his pipe and everyone shouting odds on one or t'other."

Ottilia, following the tale with a mind crackling with conjecture and a lively image of the scene, was grateful to Francis for asking the question in her head, fearing Pilton would cease his enlivening tale if she intervened.

"Odds? You mean they were laying wagers upon the outcome?"

"Aye, sir. An' old Pa Wagstaff egging them on."

"I hardly dare ask what was the outcome."

Pilton's features registered disappointment. "It come to nothing in the end, for Mrs. Tisbury up and seized one of the brasses off the wall and dashed Duggleby's head."

"Ah. He fell senseless, I suppose?"

"Aye." The constable nodded. "Likewise Tisbury, for her served him just the same, no matter he be her husband. They do say as neither spoke a word to t'other nigh a sennight after."

Ottilia caught Francis's questioning eye and at last spoke out. "When did this happen, Mr. Pilton?"

The constable started, and a bashful look came over his features as he became once more alert to her presence. He squeezed his hat in one nervous hand.

"It were near a month gone, m'am."

Ottilia digested this. "But lately Tisbury and the blacksmith have returned to their former friendly relations?"

Pilton looked dubious, his embarrassment dissipating in interest. "I wouldn't say as how it be forgot. I seen both on 'em scowl one at t'other if'n any mentioned about it."

"You mean there were those who dared?"

"Oh, don't tell me," uttered Francis, grinning. "Pa Wagstaff?"

"Aye, sir. But Pakefield had his say on it once or twice. Nor Mr. Uddington didn't scruple to speak his piece."

Both men having their own reasons to throw jibes, no doubt, thought Ottilia. She sought to clarify a point.

"Do you know if Pakefield and Uddington directed their comments at Duggleby rather than Tisbury?"

The constable considered this. "I'd say as Mr. Uddington

did. But Pakefield has took a powerful dislike to Tisbury, being as the Cock do better nor the Pig."

This piece of information tallied nicely with what Ottilia had already learned. She also recalled the interesting piece of information offered by Mrs. Radlett concerning Uddington's wife and the blacksmith. It began to seem that a number of persons had an interest in pointing the finger elsewhere. How convenient to have Cassie the witch so neatly to hand.

Chapter 6

For the first few moments after Ottilia stepped through the portal of the unremarkable emporium serving the general needs of Witherley's inhabitants, she made a play of examining its wares, while she took stock of its owner.

Mr. Uddington was a man with a shock of white hair, worn tied back at the nape of his neck, which perhaps made him appear older than his years. He did not come forward immediately upon the tinkle of the bell above the door signalling Ottilia's entrance, and she wondered if, like Lord Henbury, he was hard of hearing.

She moved into the shop, casting her eye over the shelves, which were stacked to bursting, and the two large counters boasting a collection of drawers beneath and a plethora of goods on top, juxtaposed one against another with little heed as to type or symmetry. Mr. Uddington's head was bent over a large ledger set on a sloping desk at which he was seated, perched upon a high stool.

Ottilia forbore to draw attention to herself, preferring to

shift quietly along the nearest counter while she surreptitiously took the merchant in. Her eye fell cursorily upon an open tray of coloured gloves, a collection of quill pens, several fancy knots of ribbon spilling from a casket, and a selection of brooch pins in a glass case.

Meanwhile she had time to take in that Mr. Uddington was a lanky specimen, rather on the lines of Pakefield at the Blue Pig, but without the latter's dour aspect. This man had an air of gentility, and Ottilia immediately surmised he had come down in the world and found himself betwixt and between in the limited society of Witherley.

Before she had a chance to pursue this thought, Mr. Uddington suddenly looked up, as at some untoward movement. He saw Ottilia and instantly set down his pen.

"Oh, I beg your pardon, ma'am. I did not hear the bell."

"It makes no matter," she said and waited as he slipped off the stool and came forward, peering at her over the top of a pair of gold pince-nez.

"How may I serve you, ma'am?"

It was then evidently borne in upon him that he was addressing a stranger, for he lifted his head sharply, surveying her instead through the glass of his spectacles. A look of gratification spread across his rather pasty complexion.

"Oh! You will be Lady Francis Fanshawe. Or am I wrong?"

Ottilia laughed. "Dear me. My fame goes before me, does it, Mr. Uddington?"

A sad little smile turned up the corners of the man's mouth, thinned by age—or sorrow perhaps?

"Nothing occurs in this village but that everyone is instantly aware of it, my lady."

"I can readily believe it." Giving him a smile, she added, "You will have heard, then, that we are stranded and in the expectation of having to remain for a day or two."

"I had so heard, my lady." The pince-nez came down, and Mr. Uddington regarded her over the top of them, like a schoolmaster with an errant pupil. "Also that you are taking an interest in the unfortunate demise of our blacksmith."

Ottilia raised her brows, and her tone was cool. "You do not approve?"

He gave an unconvincing shrug. "It is not my place to question your ladyship's actions."

"Yet you wonder at my interference."

Uddington pursed his lips. "Since you press me, my lady, I must confess that I do."

Ottilia brought out her big guns. "Then you possibly have not yet been apprised, Mr. Uddington, of Lord Henbury's having placed his confidence in my ability to track down the murderer."

That this was paltering with the truth she did not allow to weigh with her. She had decided on her tactics in a brief colloquy with her spouse before he left her at Uddington's door, having escorted her thither while the doctor and Lord Henbury had gone on ahead towards the smithy, with Pilton in tow.

"You're going to regret having involved Henbury," Francis had said the moment the others were out of earshot. "He'll drive you as demented as your godmother did."

"Yes, but we need him," Ottilia returned. "He has the only real authority."

Francis cocked an eyebrow. "If you are hoping he will grant you carte blanche as I did, my love, I fear you are doomed to disappointment."

Ottilia could not but agree. "Yet if he is seen to be involved, I may very well persuade those I wish to question that his lordship has sanctioned my activities."

Her husband's smile was wry. "Yes, I've no doubt you will take whatever unscrupulous measures you wish to get your own way."

Seized by a qualm of conscience, Ottilia set her hands

against his chest. "Your indulgence will be rewarded, Fan, I promise you."

He covered her hands with his own. "I'm delighted to know it, but I am obliged to confess I shall find it a wrench to walk away myself at this juncture."

"Ah, now that you have discovered your own investigative powers?" she teased.

"Precisely. If I thought I could pit my wits against yours, I might well set a challenge to beat you at your own game."

"Might you indeed?"

He laughed. "If, I said. But as I have no confidence in my ability to outthink your fearsome intelligence, my Lady Fan, I prefer to work with you rather than against you. Besides, together we may do the job faster and remove the sooner from a place I am speedily coming to loathe."

"I fully sympathise," said Ottilia, choosing the part of prudence. Yet she lost no time in turning it to good account, becoming brisk. "By the by, while you are showing that detestable old man your ingenious find, don't forget the rope. Oh, and it occurred to me there might be advantage in raking through the ash in the forge."

"What for?"

"The remains of a hammer, perhaps?"

Francis stared. "You can't suppose the murderer was so idiotic as to try to burn the thing?"

"Even the cleverest people can be amazingly stupid, do you not find?" countered Ottilia.

Her spouse laughed. "Very well. But is he so clever?"

"Oh, without doubt. What sort of mind does it take, do you think, to plan a revenge with intent to ensure that any number of persons have motive enough to be guilty, in addition to throwing general suspicion upon a single individual?"

That Uddington's was such a mind Ottilia could readily believe. The crease at his brows as he weighed her announcement spoke of intelligence enough to read between the lines. Not that she supposed he would commit the social solecism of gainsaying her. She made haste to turn the subject into innocuous channels.

"But I have not come into your shop on that account, Mr. Uddington. Whether our groom will have the opportunity to bring us any luggage remains a question, and I have need of one or two necessities which I hope you may be able to supply."

The man's evident suspicion abated not one jot, but he allowed himself to be deflected, asking for specifics and then going behind his big counter to delve into a deep drawer. Pushing aside a couple of boxes, he made space on the counter's surface and proceeded to lay out a number of articles for Ottilia's inspection.

She took time to sift through a selection of combs and scented bars of soap, at the same time approving the tooth powder and toothbrushes and asking to see what might be had by way of night attire.

While Mr. Uddington rummaged for the latter, taking, to Ottilia's satisfaction, some little time to uproot nightshirts and nightgowns from the recesses of his drawers, she felt safe enough to resume discussion of pertinent matters.

"Are you by any chance handy with a hammer, Mr. Uddington?" she asked, wading knee deep immediately.

He was bending at the time, but he shot upright, startled into losing his pince-nez. Ottilia leaned across and deftly caught them as they fell off, holding them out. Uddington's hand shook as he took the spectacles, but instead of replacing them on his nose, he folded them and set them down on the counter, placing both hands either side with his fingers pressed heavily into the wood.

"Is that an accusation, my lady?"

His tone was harsh, and the skin of his cheeks had gone a chalky grey. Ottilia kept her voice even.

"Should it be one?"

Naked, his eyes showed the puffy sag of suffering underneath and the cold glint of residual enmity within.

"Oh, I don't doubt you've been told the whole. I'll not deny my distaste for the man. But hatred enough to kill? And in such a fashion? No, I'd not swing for Duggleby."

Ottilia waited to see if he would develop this theme, but he said nothing more, setting the ball firmly in her court. He was not going to prove an easy witness. She chose to throw him off the scent altogether.

"I hear you are taking up a collection for the widow."

His frown reappeared. "I've nothing against the woman. The opposite, if anything."

"You feel for her as the other injured party?" suggested Ottilia.

Uddington looked down and appeared to notice the stiffness of his fingers. With a look of distaste, he relaxed them. Then he picked up the pince-nez and slipped them into place on his nose. The earlier mildness of manner returned as he regarded Ottilia over the top of them again.

"Bertha Duggleby had more to complain of than I. My wife's desertion saved me from further humiliation. Bertha was obliged to put up with whatever came. She had not the means to take such a step."

"Whereas your wife had such means?"

The shopkeeper nodded. "My father-in-law took care of her. He has the means."

"He is a merchant?" Ottilia guessed, adding as he nodded again, "And well to do, I take it?"

"Uddington set us up with this shop."

"Uddington?" Startled, Ottilia stared at him. Enlightenment dawned. "Ah, I begin to see. You took his name when you married beneath you. Who are you really?"

For the first time, a hint of bitterness crept into the false Uddington's features. "I am nobody, my lady. Oh, don't pity me. I am content to have it so."

Ottilia let it lie. She had a feeling there was more to be discovered here, but it would not do to probe too fiercely at this juncture. She tried a different tack.

"I take it your true identity is not generally known."

"If you mean, do the local gentry recognise me, no," he said calmly.

"And I was given no hint of any mystery concerning your past," Ottilia mused, although in fact there had not been time for any detailed discussion of the subject, but Uddington did not know that. "I cannot think it would have been left out."

"Not if you were informed of my wife's infidelity with Duggleby."

Ottilia eyed him, searching for the erstwhile betraying signs. "You are remarkably sanguine on the subject, sir."

"It was a long time ago."

"Yet the desire for revenge, I have heard it said, burns no less fierily for the passing years. Indeed, it can be the more dangerous for growing cold."

Mr. Uddington said nothing. Instead, he indicated the items Ottilia had picked out. "Will you be requiring anything else, my lady?"

"Yes," Ottilia said tartly. "A response to my first question. Are you capable of wielding a hammer?"

Once again, the corners of Mr. Uddington's lips were uplifted in that slight acidic smile. "I am no longer a young man, your ladyship. I call upon the locals to attend to all that sort of thing."

Balked, Ottilia wondered how next to proceed. Before she could decide, the entrance bell tinkled and her new friends of the coffee room stepped into the shop. They greeted her without surprise, and Ottilia instantly suspected she had been observed entering the establishment. She could only be glad she'd had opportunity to tackle Uddington ahead of their arrival.

Ottilia waved briefly and turned back to the shopkeeper with a smile.

"I will take one each of the nightshirts and gowns, if you please. And perhaps you will be kind enough to wrap everything up and have it conveyed to the Blue Pig? My husband will settle up with you presently."

The shopkeeper's defiant manner had disappeared upon the entrance of new customers, and Ottilia was treated to a spurious urbanity.

"As your ladyship pleases."

She was quick to note the ironic inflexion and flashed him a straight look before turning to Mrs. Radlett, who was hovering at her elbow.

"I thought I saw you come in here, Lady Francis," said the latter breathlessly. "I see dear Mr. Uddington has been able to supply your needs."

"Indeed, yes."

"Take it that means you'll be staying," came from Miss Beeleigh, brusque as ever. "Good thing if you are, for Hannah is already chivvying the maid to make ready her best bedchamber."

Ottilia laughed. "Is she indeed? Then we had better not disappoint her."

Mr. Netherburn, who had remained near the door perforce as the ladies crowded in, now threw out one of his flourishes, one hand swirling as he bowed in Ottilia's direction.

"Too kind, too kind, dear ma'am. But I can assure you poor Hannah will look after you splendidly."

"She's not much else to do," snapped Miss Beeleigh, "so I should think she'd better."

With firmness, Ottilia cut into what promised to be a prolonged discussion.

"We are not fastidious, I assure you. But I must not keep you, Mr. Uddington. You have been most helpful, and I thank you."

A suspicious frown came at her from over the merchant's spectacles, and Ottilia met it with a bland look. Before she could make a move to leave, however, Miss Beeleigh addressed the man.

"Hope the storm didn't bring any of your roof tiles down again, Uddington."

A glint showed in Uddington's eye, but his voice retained the same servile tone. "I do not anticipate it, ma'am. The journeyman did an excellent job."

"I hope so. Can't have you toiling up and down that dreadful ladder of yours at your time of life."

Even as Ottilia's ears pricked up, she saw the merchant's features pinch, paling a little.

"Gracious, no!" exclaimed Mrs. Radlett. "We do not want you breaking your neck, Uddington."

"Bad enough losing Duggleby," pursued Miss Beeleigh. "Not that he had half your efficiency, Uddington, I'll say that much."

Ottilia was convinced this must be disingenuous. Had Miss Beeleigh an ambition to turn investigator? She had intended to expose the fact that Uddington owned a ladder high enough to reach the smithy roof.

His deferent manner unmatched by the coldness in his eyes, Uddington was bowing. "I am flattered, Miss Beeleigh."

"No, no, dear fellow, she is perfectly in the right," Mr. Netherburn chimed in. "I dare not think how we would fare without you, Uddington."

"No, indeed," gushed Mrs. Radlett. "It is enough that dear Mrs. Uddington has passed away."

When? The thought leapt into Ottilia's startled mind. In the ensuing silence, a chill entered the atmosphere. Clearly realising her faux pas, the widow flushed, clapping a hand to her mouth. Miss Beeleigh threw her an admonishing look, and Mr. Netherburn emitted a delicate cough.

Uddington stiffened, but he did not speak. When did the errant wife die? Had it been a recent event, thus prompting a long-awaited revenge? Glancing at the man, Ottilia perceived the same closed look she had before observed and conceived an alternative plan to an outright question.

"Well, I have everything I need for the present. I will leave you ladies to conduct your own purchases."

Without pausing for an answer, she went past them, putting out a hand towards Horace Netherburn.

"My dear sir, may I trouble you to escort me back to the inn? My husband would not like me to be wandering around the village unattended."

This was perfectly true, although Ottilia guiltily reflected she would have no compunction in doing just that should it prove expedient. But she knew there could be but one answer from Mr. Netherburn.

True to form, he made an elaborate leg, expressing his immediate willingness to be of service, and opened the door for her. Ottilia passed through as the bell tinkled, inwardly chuckling at having spiked the guns of the two women. If they'd had no intention of buying anything, they now had no choice but to make a play at least of inspecting Uddington's goods.

Outside the shop, she tucked her hand into Netherburn's offered arm and adopted a confiding air. "I was hoping for a moment to talk to you privately, Mr. Netherburn."

An apprehensive expression creased his lined features as he looked down at her. "Indeed, ma'am?"

Ottilia smiled at him. "Do not look so troubled, sir. I merely wished for a point of information which I believe you may be able to provide."

His face cleared, and a trifle of self-importance made him step out more boldly. "If I may be of assistance to you, Lady Francis, you have only to say the word."

Nothing loath, Ottilia waded in. "When did Mrs. Uddington die?"

The arm in which her hand was resting jerked, and Netherburn turned startled eyes upon her. "Why do you wish to know?"

"Is it a secret?" she countered.

"No, no, only we do not like to talk of it. When the woman

has been disgraced, one could not expect Uddington to accept condolences he must deem hypocritical."

"So when did she die, Mr. Netherburn?" pursued Ottilia.

"A little over three months ago. At least that is when we heard the news."

"Did Mr. Uddington attend the funeral?"

Netherburn's sallow cheeks took on a trifle of colour. "No, but it is said that Duggleby did."

Ottilia drew in a sharp breath. "It is said? By whom?"

"How can one know how such news originates?" protested the gentleman, just as if his contribution did not add to the spread of this and any other gossip.

Ottilia refrained from pointing this out, instead murmuring what he might take for agreement if he chose, before resuming her catechism.

"Is it known whether Duggleby was absent from the village at the time of the funeral?"

Mr. Netherburn gave a fervent nod. "Indeed, yes, which is what makes it peculiarly troublesome if one wishes to disbelieve the rumours. The fellow claimed he had gone to Coventry to fetch in a fresh set of rods for nail-making, but one is forced to wonder why he chose exactly that time to do it."

Indeed, Ottilia thought. They had taken a shorter path across the green, Mr. Netherburn having assured her that the grass had been well dried by the sun that had been shining all day, and they were by now approaching the Blue Pig. As Ottilia was digesting the information supplied by her escort, she did not at first do more than note the presence of a gig standing to one side of the house just before the archway. The driver, who had alighted, was talking to someone largely obscured by his bulk, but the booted legs Ottilia could just see became abruptly familiar. At the instant she realised it was Francis, she recognised the tilt of the driver's head. Ryde!

A wave of consternation went through her. Had the groom arrived to fetch them? Would Francis insist upon their departure? Just when she was getting somewhere!

*   *   *

The bed, despite its utilitarian proportions, was remarkably comfortable. Francis, clad not in the new coarse cotton nightshirt thoughtfully provided by his wife but in one of his own made up in fine lawn, was sitting against the banked pillows, partaking of a nightcap of brandy.

"This liquor is quite tolerable," he said, watching the rhythmic stroke of Tillie's hairbrush as she plied it energetically through the soft brown waves that reached partway down her back. His fingers itched to caress them, but he knew Tillie's attention was still concentrated upon the puzzle of the blacksmith's murder.

"Then at least I need not trouble my head about the satisfaction of your palate," she responded, looking round as she spoke.

The mischievous gleam he loved was in her eye, and Francis could not resist.

"It's not the only satisfaction I crave."

A delicious thread of colour raced into her cheeks, visible in the light of the candelabrum she'd set upon the dressing table.

"Francis!"

He grinned and turned the subject. "Other than this Uddington fellow, whom have you in your mind?"

She had looked away, and Francis hid a smile at having made her conscious. As ever, she recovered herself swiftly. It was one of the skills he admired in Tillie, that she was not easily put out of countenance, and then only briefly.

"Oh, Uddington is by no means the only one with a grudge against the blacksmith."

Francis agreed. "Tisbury, by Pilton's account, for one."

"Yes, and his wife, Molly."

"Why so?"

"On account of losing her kitchen maid to his amorous activities, of course."

"I was forgetting that," Francis said, musing as he took a sip of the golden liquid in his glass. "What about his wife? Duggleby's, I mean."

"Bertha? Yes, I think we must include her. And unlikely as it seems, I cannot ignore Evelina Radlett's dog."

He had been regaled with this tale, among others, but Francis was dubious.

"Does a female plot to kill someone because she suspects he beat her dog?"

Tillie's characteristic laugh sounded. "It does sound unlikely. But her friend was obliged to shoot it, remember, and as she expressed it to me, she is convinced Duggleby as good as killed her Toby."

Francis thought this over and entered a caveat. "But didn't you envision a type of mind with cunning enough to conceive of using that witch girl as a scapegoat?"

He had not yet met the widow Radlett for himself, but Tillie's lively description had given him a pretty good notion of the sort of woman she was.

His wife was regarding him with her brows raised. "You are becoming exceptionally adept, my dearest. I cannot be other than relieved you opted to work in tandem rather than against me."

Francis laughed out. "In that case, I am tempted to take to myself the find Pilton made in the smithy, if only I had not been brought up to be truthful."

An expectant gleam lit her eyes. "A find? Why did you not tell me before? What was it?"

"I was distracted by Ryde's arrival, to tell the truth."

"But what has been found? The rope?"

The impatient note was marked, and Francis was conscious of a twinge of something akin to jealousy. Ridiculous. As if he craved his wife's attentions. He hastened to answer.

"Not the rope. The hammer."

Tillie shuffled round on her stool to face him. "Not the very one used?"

"We think it probable."

"But where was it? Not in the forge itself?"

Francis resisted the urge to tease. "Yes, my clever one, it was just where you suggested, buried in the embers."

"Was it burnt?"

"The handle had burned away, but the head is only minimally damaged."

Tillie was silent for a space, running her hand absently across the bristles of her hairbrush in a way that Francis found distinctly unsettling.

"What are you thinking?"

"That this murderer is too clever not to have known the fire could not burn long enough to melt the head. Could there be some other reason for throwing the hammer in the fire?"

A memory hit Francis. "What about this? Had the metal not been partially eroded, Meldreth said he might have found traces of blood, skin, and hair upon the hammer."

Tillie's head shot up. "Dear me, Fan, but that is genius!" Mischief leapt into her face, and Francis's heart warmed. "Either I am growing slow or your quickness is accelerating."

"Wretch!"

Seizing a pillow from her side of the bed, he threw it at her. She caught it deftly, planted a kiss on its smooth covering, and threw it back. Francis batted it away as it threatened to upset his glass, but he softened the rejection by raising his brandy in a silent toast.

Tillie smiled at him and turned back on the stool to resume her interrupted labours with the hairbrush.

For a few moments, Francis sipped in silence, running over the discussion in his mind in a bid to distract himself from the sensuous sight of his wife's ministrations upon her hair.

He suspected it would fall to his lot to interview the landlord of the Cock and Bottle, while Tillie tackled the wife. He hoped she would prime him first, for he had little dependence upon his ability to think on his feet without some prompting. Tillie was a natural at gaining the confidence of her fellows. Indeed, Francis suspected it was owing to her handling of Mrs. Pakefield that the landlady had placed her best bedchamber at their disposal.

It was admittedly clean, of a good size, and adequately furnished, if with little attention to taste and fashion. The walls were whitewashed, the bed-curtains a faded and aged brocade, the woodwork polished but plain. In a word, it was not at all in the class of accommodation to which Francis was accustomed.

Not that he was unable to rough it, as he had hastily assured his darling wife when she expressed anxious doubts. He had not spent years at soldiering without learning to forgo luxury and make do. But he was not fooled for a moment, well aware that Tillie's conscience was plaguing her.

Francis had instantly seen through her spurious welcome of Ryde when she'd come upon them outside the Blue Pig. If he was any judge, Tillie had been altogether vexed to see the groom, fearing she would be obliged to depart from Witherley, her investigations unresolved.

"I am not so hard-hearted," he had whispered in her ear, secure in the knowledge that he had already made his arrangements with the groom.

The relief in his bride's face had made it all worthwhile at the time. But Francis was beginning to have doubts. He had not liked the sound of her conversation with the shopkeeper.

"Do you rate Uddington as your primary suspect?"

The hairbrush stilled. "He has the means at his disposal to have carried it out, and he has motive enough."

Francis knew that tone. "But?"

She ran the brush through and set it down, turning to look at him again, a troubled crease between her brows.

"He struck me as too honourable a man."

Francis emitted a derisive sound. "Too high-minded to kill?"

"No, he might do that. But to point the finger at Cassie

Dale? He is not a man who fears death. I think he would expect to pay his dues, had he done it."

"But you can't discount him, Tillie. From what you've told me, the other possibilities are negligible. Uddington is all you have."

Tillie's gaze was steady. "So was your brother all I had, to begin with."

"Point taken."

Discomfort at the memories sent Francis back to sipping at his glass. The evidence against the marquis had been overwhelming, but not for a moment had Tillie thought of abandoning the hunt for another suspect, indifferent to any danger to herself. Only now she was his bride, beloved and too precious to risk. A sliver of regret attacked him. Why had he not taken advantage of Ryde's arrangements?

The groom had driven up just as he was returning from the smithy, having endured a trying half hour demonstrating his find of the hacked-off beam to the vexatious Lord Henbury. He'd been in a mood to shake the dust of Witherley from his heels, but Ryde had brought disappointing news.

"Williams fears it will take several days to get that axletree mended, m'lord."

After an abortive ride to Atherstone, the coachman had found a blacksmith at Nuneaton. It appeared the coach must limp at a snail's pace to the smithy there, where the body must be removed from its moorings in order to get at the offending part.

"If the blacksmith can't do it himself, and he won't know until he sees it, he may have to send for a new tree from the coachmakers at Coventry."

Francis had cursed fluently, but when Ryde told him of the rooms booked at a hostelry at Nuneaton, he had weighed the notion and rejected it.

"We will remain here, Ryde. Since we must wait in any event, I cannot have her ladyship chafing elsewhere with nothing to occupy her while events in this village are in train."

Upon the groom's astonished look, Francis had briefly enlightened him as to the current state of affairs. Ryde's dour disapproval amused rather than angered him.

"You may as well accustom yourself, Ryde. I have a suspicion this may not be the last incident of this nature in which your new mistress interests herself."

He then expressed his relief that the groom had brought their luggage and asked him to have it conveyed to a bedchamber, once he had arranged with the Pakefields for the Fanshawes to stay.

"There will be no difficulty, for I imagine our remaining here is not unexpected. Then you had best go back to Williams and let him know where we are. Tell him to come for us when the coach is ready. There is little point in your kicking your heels there either, so I suggest you stay at Nuneaton tonight and rejoin us tomorrow. And hire the gig for the duration. We may need it."

Now Francis repented a little of his hasty decision as a riffle of unease disturbed him.

He saw that as he was ruminating, Tillie had left off her dressing gown and doused the candles in the candelabrum. The chamber was now illumined only by the single candles in holders at either side of the bed. In the lesser light, his wife's slim body as she moved towards the bed, clad only in her nightgown, was sinuous and alluring.

Francis was gripped with a sharp attack of dread. As she slipped in beside him, he set down his glass. Turning, he took hold of Tillie and pulled her close.

"I wish you will take care, my darling. I fear you may have made of this man Uddington a dangerous enemy."

Chapter 7

Plagued by nightmares, Cassie had slept badly. In between bouts of restless dreaming, she had begun to feel her bruises. Yesterday she had kept to her cottage, Mr. Kinnerton's instruction in mind, and not entirely because Tabby was as stolid as a gaoler in refusing to let her venture forth.

Towards evening yesterday, Sam had returned from reconnoitring to gather news. Cassie was relieved to see through the window his burly form approaching, but when he entered the cottage, his broad-featured face was eager. It appeared there was a stranger in the village who was going about questioning everyone, and had even gone to take a look at Duggleby's body.

"By all accounts, this here Lady Francis is acting for Justice Henbury," said Sam. "Not as I'd take notice of nothing Will says, only I met Doctor Meldreth and he said it an' all."

Cassie eyed him, stirred by a memory. "A woman with a gaze that might read into your very mind?"

Sam glanced at Tabitha and came frowning back to Cassie. "How am I to answer that, Miss Cassie?"

Drawing a breath, Cassie tried to reassemble the picture of the woman she'd met at the smithy. "I cannot otherwise describe her. She is not handsome, I think." Struggling, she tried to find words that might help. "High cheekbones. A painter might make much of her face, though I cannot. But the eyes, Sam. A gaze so clear one might drown in it, if there were not so much kindness in her voice."

Tabitha clucked her irritation. "As if poor Sam could tell who you meant by such a tangle. And I've no notion who it is, neither."

"No, for I met her in the smithy," said Cassie, turning on her. "You wouldn't come in."

"And I'd be a deal happier if you hadn't gone in," Tabby retorted unabashed. "But why did you think it's the same as Sam spoke of?"

"Because she said she would help me. She said she would find out the truth. And I believed her."

"Seems as she's doing it," said Sam, "if as it's the same female."

"Whom has she questioned?"

Sam shrugged. "I can't tell that, Miss Cassie. But what I do know is that there Reverend rung a peal over Farmer Staxton's boys."

Something clutched in Cassie's chest. "For throwing stones at me?"

"Aye. Seems as Mr. Kinnerton ain't nowise as quiet as he makes out."

"I hope he thundered at 'em," said Tabby vengefully.

Sam shook his head. "He spoke quiet-like, as I heard. But what he said made 'em squirm like they'd beetles in their breeches."

Cassie could not imagine what words could accomplish such a feat, but as Sam had no exact knowledge of just what had been said, he was unable to enlighten her. When she asked from whom he had his information, he said it had come from Staxton himself.

"He were laughing fit to bust hisself, saying he was wishful as he'd thought of speaking so to his sons years back, for no amount of birching had served to curb them boys."

Astonished and incredulous, Cassie wished she might speak to Mr. Kinnerton herself to find out just what had occurred. Never had anyone, not even Lady Ferrensby, taken on her enemies. And how could it be that the gently spoken man who had given her succour should prove so stalwart a champion?

Yet these reassurances failed to appease the demons of the night. It was hard to believe, in the loneliness endemic to the curse of her unnatural skill, that there could be any permanence of peace in her turbulent life.

But the morning brought a resurgence of hope when Mr. Kinnerton's housekeeper appeared at her door. She was a willowy dame, with a manner as redoubtable as it was forthright. She had come, commanded by her master, she said, to enquire as to Mrs. Dale's health.

Cassie could have wept. She invited the woman inside and bade Tabby make them both a cup of the precious tea reserved for special occasions. Lady Ferrensby kept her caddy supplied, but Cassie, hating the charity upon which she was forced to depend, took care to eke out the tea that she might not be too much beholden.

"You serve a kind master, Mrs. Winkleigh."

The woman flushed. "Yes, and I'll stay and serve him whether he likes it or no."

Intrigued, Cassie eyed her. "Why should he not like it?"

Mrs. Winkleigh sniffed, shaking out her petticoats as she took one of the chairs opposite to where Cassie was seated on the other side of the table.

"Well, he don't dislike it. Only when I complained of the place being small and stuffy, as anyone might who came from the Kinnerton family home—not that I mind, I was only saying—all Master Aidan said was that I needn't stay if

I didn't wish to." She sniffed again. "I speedily put him in his place, you may be sure."

Astonished at anyone having the temerity to put the Reverend Kinnerton in his place, Cassie demanded enlightenment.

"I vowed I wasn't going to leave him to reduce himself to skin and bone again like he did in that nasty heathen place he insisted on going to. As if he didn't know already, for I'd no more approval of that than had his mama."

"Which heathen place?"

"Africa, ma'am. Flying in the face of his family's wishes, but would he listen?"

Cassie rose from her chair and crossed to look out of the window, staring over the stream towards the distant spire of the church across the green, as if she might see into the vicarage and look upon Aidan Kinnerton himself.

"I think it is admirable in him to have taken such a step."

"Admirable? To go off into little better than a jungle and nearly get himself killed by a pack of savages?"

Cassie turned, startled. "Surely not."

"Oh yes, ma'am. Spears and all is what he faced, for he wrote as much in the one letter that came. Then we heard nothing more, and his poor mama was convinced he was dead. Which he nigh all was. It was like a skeleton walked into the house!"

Cassie recalled the image she had seen, superimposed on the parson's present features. She looked at the housekeeper, and a stray thought intruded into her head, together with an image of a small boy held in this woman's arms. A younger version, but there was no doubt it was Mrs. Winkleigh.

"You were his nurse."

The housekeeper blinked. "That's right, ma'am. But how did you—?" Realisation sparked in her face. "Oh."

Cassie smiled tightly. "Yes, that is why they call me a witch."

"Witch? Fiddle-faddle, ma'am, if you'll pardon me," said Mrs. Winkleigh, reviving fast. "You ain't no more a witch than Master Aidan is an angel come down to earth, and that's a fact. But you're right, ma'am. I was his nurse, and I promised her ladyship as I'd take care of him, and take care of him I will. Or I'll answer to his family and the Almighty himself."

"Her ladyship?" echoed Cassie, fastening on the salient point in this diatribe.

"Lady Kinnerton, ma'am. She's Master Aidan's mother."

"He is titled?"

"Not he. There's three older brothers, and his lordship is a viscount." Consternation entered the woman's features. "Now don't you go saying I told you, ma'am, for he don't like it known."

Cassie's head was reeling. If this was so, her suspicion of her patroness's intentions concerning the vicar must be unfounded. Not even Lady Ferrensby could suppose the son of a viscount might stoop so low.

"Does Lady Ferrensby know?" she blurted before she could stop herself. "No, that is foolish, of course she must know."

"Oh, she knows all right. She and my lady fixed it up between them to my way of thinking. My Lady Kinnerton being wishful to stop any thought of Master Aidan going away again, and this being a small parish which wouldn't put no undue strain on his health."

"Except that circumstances have so arranged themselves that he will be lucky not to suffer an instant relapse," said Cassie, feeling the bitterness of her curse all over again. How many people was she destined to destroy?

"Be that as it may," came in a bustling tone from the housekeeper, "it wouldn't suit Master Aidan to be idle, no matter his mama's wishes. Not that me and Croy won't have our work cut out, neither."

"Croy?"

"Master Aidan's groom, ma'am. He's away, fetching more of the master's trunks. And some of her ladyship's unwanted curtains and such, for the vicarage is bare as a mousehole. Hasn't been inhabited for months, by the state of it. But Croy and me'll soon set all to rights. And find some work for the locals into the bargain. I fancy I could use a couple of helpful village girls, and Croy might do with a lad, too."

"Then you could give work to Duggleby's daughter," said Cassie eagerly, seizing on this. "The boy is too young yet, I think, but they are bound to need employment. Tabby says Mr. Uddington is taking up a collection, but that will scarcely last them."

Mrs. Winkleigh pursed her lips. "Is the girl any good, do you know, ma'am?"

Incurably truthful, Cassie shook her head. "I hardly know her. But you may teach her, may you not, Mrs. Winkleigh?"

The housekeeper looked dubious, but as Tabby came in at that moment with the tea, she was not obliged to answer. Cassie thanked her maid and took her own seat with a new determination. Here was an opportunity to make amends, if in a small way, and she would not lightly let it go. She sipped the tea, which had, as it always did, the effect of reviving her spirits.

"Let me take you to see the Duggleby girl, Mrs. Winkleigh. Then you may judge for yourself."

It did not take many minutes to traverse the narrow pathway that ran along the little row of cottages. As they reached the bridge, Cassie pointed to the ruined smithy.

"The house lies just beyond. We must go around the back, for I fear the lane on this side by the river is blocked with debris."

Accordingly, both women crossed the lane and went to one side of the forge's courtyard, at which point Cassie advised Mrs. Winkleigh to lift her skirts. But before they could step onto the overlong grass, another female came around the corner, and Cassie recognised under a straw bonnet the sharp-angled features of Molly Tisbury.

Cassie halted, her heart sinking, for she knew the landlady of the Cock and Bottle to be one of her severest critics. Beside her, the vicar's housekeeper stopped, too. She had evidently seen the woman.

"Seems as we aren't the first visitors this morning."

The Tisbury dame was already within hailing distance, and she glared as she looked up. "What be you wanting here? Come to gloat, have you?"

Coming up, she paused before them, taking in Mrs. Winkleigh from her head to her heels. Cassie backed a step but saw the housekeeper stand her ground, her back stiffening.

"And who might you be, my fine lady?" came rudely from Molly Tisbury.

"I might ask you the same question, madam," returned the other, her tone arctic. "Since you ask, my name is Winkleigh, and I am housekeeper to the Reverend Kinnerton."

This piece of information was received with a snort. "Him, eh? And I see as you be as hoodwinked as he, seeing as you be hand in glove with the witch."

Mrs. Winkleigh, to Cassie's admiration, did not rise to this. Instead, she pulled herself up to her full height and looked down at the other woman with disdain.

"Will you be good enough to let us pass, madam?"

Molly Tisbury put her hands to her hips and remained squarely in front of them, a pointing finger snaking towards Cassie.

"I'll not let her pass, not if her've thought to badger poor Bertha Duggleby."

"You are insolent, woman. Don't think as you can browbeat me, for I won't stand for it. Now get out of my way!"

Molly Tisbury's jaw dropped open, and Cassie moved in closer, hurt lending vibrancy to her voice.

"Pray don't quarrel on my account. Molly, I am trying to help. Mrs. Winkleigh has work for a maid, and I thought—"

"You thought!" cut in Molly, her tone vicious. "It be you thinking as killed Duggleby. No one don't need your thoughts round here. Better nor far as her ladyship bain't brung you next or nigh Witherley. Who be next, eh? Who be you seeing in yon visions next?"

The woman was spitting foam, and Cassie shrank back, only half aware that Mrs. Winkleigh's hands were out flat against the creature's shoulders, holding her off.

"That's enough, you hear me? Get back or, so help me, I'll slap your ugly face for you!"

Cassie heard a growl issuing from the other woman's throat as she seized Mrs. Winkleigh's wrists, trying to wrench those restraining hands away. Her heart was hammering as Cassie felt the first swirling fog of a picture forming in her mind. She lifted her hands to her head, desperate and afraid.

"No," she muttered breathlessly. "Please, no."

From somewhere outside her immediate concentration, she heard a calm voice drive into the hubbub.

"What in the world is the matter here?"

Turning automatically, Cassie discovered the strange female who had spoken to her in the smithy on the previous day.

"Is it the invariable custom of this village for females to quarrel in the open street?" pursued this lady, a laugh in her voice that did more to pour oil on these troubled waters than might another raised voice. "Come, come, ladies. I must beg you to release one another. There can surely be no occasion for such violence."

These words acted powerfully on Mrs. Winkleigh at least, for she let go of Molly and pulled back, dusting off her hands. The Tisbury woman was slower to react, but she ceased her struggles upon being released, and her gaze shifted towards the newcomer.

"Are you quite well, Mrs. Dale?" said the latter, reaching out a hand.

Cassie took it and held it, relieved to feel the fog in her brain dissipating.

"Thank you," she gasped, and a memory stirred. "You are Lady Fan."

The other woman smiled. "I am indeed." Then her gaze shifted back to the erstwhile antagonists.

Molly's frown reappeared. "Lady Fan, is it? You be her as seen the body. You be asking all manner of questions."

Lady Francis inclined her head, and Cassie noted the keen glance that raked Molly's face.

"That is so. And you, I think, are Mrs. Tisbury. Am I right?"

Molly gaped. "Aye, but how you knowed it I can't tell. Be you another witch?"

A light laugh escaped the newcomer. "I am merely observant, Mrs. Tisbury. And I have yet to learn that there are any witches in Witherley."

Cassie's heart leapt, but Molly scowled.

"Like that, is it? You be on her's side."

"I am on no one's side," came tartly from Lady Fan, "unless it be the side of truth."

She turned her attention to Mrs. Winkleigh, who was, Cassie realised, appraising Lady Fan with a critical eye.

"You, I fear, have the advantage of me."

Cassie made haste to make the housekeeper known, but Mrs. Winkleigh's slightly suspicious air did not abate one jot.

"I've heard about you from the master, ma'am," she said bluntly. "I'll not deny I was hard put to believe any lady'd poke her nose into such matters."

"Poke her nose, aye," burst from Molly Tisbury. "Poking into my life her be, making the likes of Pilton tell on me."

Lady Fan's bland gaze turned on the woman. "Is there something of import to tell, Mrs. Tisbury?"

To Cassie's amazement, Molly blenched a trifle, closing her lips tight shut. Lady Fan eyed her levelly for a moment and then turned back to Mrs. Winkleigh.

"I take it you disapprove of my interesting myself in these matters?"

"Ain't my place to do so, ma'am," said the housekeeper. "Nor I didn't say that."

"True, but you implied it. Never mind. I shall hope to prove myself in due course."

"Prove? What be you a-going to prove, as if'n it bain't known?" Molly had recovered herself more swiftly than Cassie could have wished, for the woman pointed a bony finger at her. "Her it be as done for Duggleby. Bain't need of no questions."

Once more the woman came under the beam of Lady Fan's level regard. "I'm afraid I disagree, Mrs. Tisbury. But you need not suppose my interest is solely in you. I am questioning everyone who may have had a grudge against this man Duggleby, and I gather there are a number of persons in this category besides yourself."

Molly's black eyes snapped fire. "Who told you as I've a grudge agin him?"

Lady Fan merely smiled and refocused her attention on Cassie. "I was coming to visit you, Mrs. Dale."

Cassie stared. "Me?"

"Why not?"

"Because people don't." Then she remembered Mrs. Winkleigh and put out an apologetic hand. "You came for your master, though you have been kind."

Molly Tisbury exploded again. "Kind! Foolhardy more like." She turned on the stranger. "Be it Hannah who told agin me? You be staying at Pig, bain't you? It be Hannah, bain't it?"

Lady Fan's brows rose. "Dear me, Mrs. Tisbury, you will make me believe there is certainly something to be found out. In which case, I hope you will be willing to talk with me in the not too distant future."

"Talk with you? So as you can poke that nose of yourn more deep? Not I, Lady Fan. Nor it bain't no use talking, seeing as you be sided with her."

A toss of her head in Cassie's direction made the latter wince.

"I hope you will think better of that decision, Mrs. Tisbury," said Lady Fan, her tone perfectly calm. "I should hate to be obliged to call upon young Pilton to bring you to me for questioning."

A gasp from Mrs. Winkleigh hardly took Cassie's attention, her eyes fully taken up with the staggered expression in Molly's face. She could not help a rise of satisfaction to see the woman confounded.

For a full minute the look held, and then with a grunt, Molly wrenched her eyes away and pushed past Lady Fan, heading for the bridge.

Mrs. Winkleigh looked after her and then gave a grunt of her own. "Good riddance! Ask who's next, would she? Wouldn't surprise me if she was, horrid creature."

Lady Fan made no comment on this, instead looking at Cassie. "I don't wish to detain you. Were you perhaps on your way to visit Bertha Duggleby?"

Cassie blinked at her. "How did you know?"

The other smiled. "As I told the delightful Mrs. Tisbury, it is merely a trick of looking. Your position here and your encounter with Molly leads me to suppose it, that is all."

Mrs. Winkleigh gave a gruff laugh. "That's what the master said. You look and listen. He said he noticed it particular, for he has to do the same himself."

"Then I am sure he is very good at his job," returned Lady Fan.

Cassie had made a deduction on her own account. "You wish to see Bertha Duggleby yourself."

Lady Fan's clear gaze had something of a tease in it. "We may yet make a true witch of you, Mrs. Dale."

No one ever teased Cassie. It gave her an odd feeling of

companionship—something to which she was almost a stranger. On impulse, she gave a rare smile.

"Come with us, pray."

The blacksmith's widow looked gaunt and ill, and her greeting was lacklustre. It did not seem to Ottilia that she showed any hostility towards Mrs. Dale, which was surprising. When she was asked whether the house had suffered in the fire, she looked blank.

"Bain't close enough to the forge. 'Cepting if'n the flames had took hold and jumped the gap, like Tisbury said."

"Tisbury suggested this?" Ottilia asked at once.

"Said as how they would've if'n the storm bain't come."

"But the storm did come," protested Mrs. Dale, in that intense way she had. "I told Duggleby it would come. I warned him. I said the storm would bring the roof down."

Bertha Duggleby eyed Cassie Dale in a dull way, but she said nothing. Before Ottilia had a chance to take this up, however, Mrs. Winkleigh intervened.

"I've need of a girl at the vicarage, Mrs. Duggleby. I hear you've a daughter who might do."

For the first time, a hint of animation entered the widow's look and voice.

"My Jenny? You be wishful to take my Jenny?"

Mrs. Winkleigh backtracked a little. "Provided she's a willing worker."

"Her be a good girl, m'am," said Mrs. Duggleby, almost eager, rising from her seat in the neat room obviously kept for visitors and meant for a parlour, if a house this size could be said to have one. "Her be willing, all right. I'll fetch her."

With which, the widow dragged herself to the door and disappeared through it. Ottilia looked at the housekeeper.

"I trust she may be found satisfactory, Mrs. Winkleigh. I daresay you may find it hard to repudiate her after this."

Mrs. Dale stretched out her hands to the woman. "Oh,

take her, take her, I beg you! And when Bertha is forced to leave this house, perhaps you may have Jenny to live in the vicarage."

Mrs. Winkleigh frowned. "Not so fast, Mrs. Dale. She's to prove herself first. I'm sorry for the woman, but I'll not keep the girl from charity."

Ottilia noted the tragic look in Cassie Dale's eyes and wondered how it was the creature had grown so very unworldly. It was clearly not given to her to recognise how the housekeeper's own work must suffer should she be burdened with inefficient help. As well not have anyone at all.

But when Bertha Duggleby returned with her daughter, a strapping child of perhaps thirteen years of age, it was evident to Ottilia there was no need for concern. Intelligence showed in her eyes and in the deference she accorded her prospective employer, although she looked a trifle askance at Cassie Dale.

Mrs. Winkleigh appeared to have judged the girl in much the same light, for she lost no time.

"I tell you what, young Jenny. You come with me to the vicarage this moment, and I'll show you what I need. If you think you can manage it, we'll make our arrangements then and there."

Jenny dropped a curtsy. "Bain't afeared of hard work, m'am. I been helping Ma to make nails for the forge nor five year or more."

Which evidently satisfied Mrs. Winkleigh. While the departure of the housekeeper with the girl was in train, Ottilia took time to wonder at the coming fate of Mrs. Duggleby. A new blacksmith would no doubt be installed in due course, and she could only suppose the local community would take responsibility for the widow, if she was destitute. Which, according to Miss Beeleigh, remained a question.

As soon as the business concerning her daughter was concluded, there was an instant deflation of the little animation

that had illumined Bertha Duggleby momentarily. Ottilia
tried a throw to revive her.

"Well, there is one of your troubles on the way out, Mrs.
Duggleby."

The woman raised her head, the dull gaze training on
her visitor. "Bain't nowt but a drop. There be the boy to
think on."

"How old is he?"

"No more'n six. He be learning his pa's trade, but the
forge be gone now. Bain't no call for 'prentices round here,
not at six year."

Cassie Dale's eyes filled. "He will be cared for, Bertha, I
promise you. Lady Ferrensby will see to it."

The widow nodded, but the gloom of her bearing turned
sour. "Like him it be to leave all to her ladyship. Provide for
his family? Not he. Bain't his way."

Ottilia pounced on this. "But your husband was in a very
good way of business, by all accounts, Mrs. Duggleby. I gather
he was not dependent merely on this village, but took his
customers from miles around."

Bertha Duggleby looked across at Ottilia, and there was
sudden venom in her gaze. "Bain't saying as the forge'd done
bad. Bain't saying as he'd not kept a roof over our heads, nor
food on the table, neither. Only where be the new gown he
promised me nor five year? Where be the schooling as he
boasted all around for his own boy? I tell you where. On
the backs of his string of ladyloves be where. Perfumes and
toys and neck-handkerchiefs and I don't know what more
besides. My new gown, for all I know. If'n there be a pot of
gold hid like he boasted, bain't hid here."

"Pot of gold?" Ottilia repeated, stemming the onslaught.

Bertha shrugged. "Gold guineas, he said. I bain't seen 'em.
Nor I bain't seen no goods bought for this household as had
ought to be if'n he'd seen half such wealth."

Cassie was looking distressed, but Ottilia wasted no time

in idle commiserations, though there was little doubt the woman had been hard done by.

"When did he tell you about this gold, Mrs. Duggleby?"

The brief fire had died, returning the widow to apathy. She barely made the effort to shrug. "It be nigh three month he've been boasting of it. Never believed him at first."

The precise period of time caught at Ottilia's interest. Did it not tally with the death of Mrs. Uddington? She filed it away in her mind.

"When did you begin to believe in this gold, Mrs. Duggleby?"

"Don't know as I did. Not 'til he said as he caught me looking for it and beat me."

A wave of sympathy for the woman came over Ottilia, and she glanced at Cassie Dale, expecting to see horror in her face. Instead she found only pity. A surprising creature, Mrs. Dale.

"I fear you were unfortunate in your husband, Mrs. Duggleby. Did you dislike him? Hate him perhaps?"

Bertha's eyes burned briefly at Ottilia. "Enough for to kill?"

"No," Ottilia said, keeping her gaze steady on the woman's face. "I daresay you might have killed him for the money. But not for hate."

To her surprise, the widow nodded. "Aye. But not the forge. I'd never burn the forge."

Satisfied, Ottilia rose. "Thank you, Mrs. Duggleby. You have been most helpful."

Cassie got up, too, but she was looking puzzled. "Is that all?"

Ottilia smiled. "I think so." Then a thought occurred to her. "Stay! Mrs. Duggleby, did you know your husband was carrying on with Molly Tisbury's kitchen maid?" She heard Cassie's shocked gasp and smiled at the widow, who had not turned a hair. "You have been quite frank with me, Bertha, so I do not scruple to ask you such a question."

"She be with child, I heard," said Mrs. Duggleby, her voice back to the dull monotone of their early conversation.

"Yes, she decamped in the night."

Bertha nodded. "Likely her've got a few of them gold guineas."

"If they exist."

"Aye."

Ottilia took a chance. "And Mrs. Uddington is dead."

Bertha jumped in her seat. That got through, thought Ottilia with satisfaction. The woman's eyes were wide as she stared up at her visitor.

"What is it you mean, Lady Fan?" asked Cassie Dale in a hushed tone, her gaze going from one to the other.

Ottilia did not take her eyes off the widow. "Bertha knows what I mean. It was the first betrayal, was it not, Bertha? That was the one that hurt. Did you think he meant to set you aside? He could not have done so, you know. Mrs. Uddington was disgraced. Duggleby could not have married her."

At last the woman spoke, her voice hoarse with dread. "I thought as he'd kill me. Poison so's none'd know. He wanted her bad, I know that. If I be gone, he'd have her."

Disgust rose in Ottilia, and she went across to lay a hand on the widow's shoulder. "Did he tell you so?"

She nodded numbly. "Aye."

"You poor creature. It was an empty threat, Bertha. More boasting, I suspect. You must be relieved to be rid of him."

At that, the woman's features crumpled and she burst into noisy sobs. Cassie Dale ran across and knelt at her feet, catching the creature into her arms and holding her tightly. Through the cries came words, only just coherent.

"Hate him? No. Loved him, I did, spite of all. Aye. Bain't nowt but a fool, me."

Ottilia waited until Cassie pulled back and caught her gaze.

"I will await you outside," she said softly and quietly let herself out of the parlour.

*   *   *

"Why did you push her so? Is it not enough that she is bereaved?"

Cassie Dale's tone was reproachful, and Ottilia turned to look at her as they made their way around the back of the forge.

"If we are to find out who is responsible for Duggleby's death, my dear Mrs. Dale, we cannot afford to leave any stone unturned."

The dark eyes scanned her face, searchingly, as if their owner could not fathom what she saw. "You can't think Bertha murdered her own husband?"

"I'm afraid it is all too possible. Violence within families is far more likely than outside of it. And there is the matter of the gold." She smiled at the girl. "However, I am inclined to think Bertha is innocent. But that does not mean I am right."

"You hold by this theory of Doctor Meldreth, then? That the poor man was hit with a hammer?"

Ottilia raised her brows. "Well, he was certainly not killed by any supernatural means."

A flush mantled the girl's cheek, and she looked away. "I thought it was the roof falling on him, until Sam told me otherwise."

"No. That was a deliberate blind to hide the truth, as was the fire."

Mrs. Dale halted in the smithy courtyard and turned to look at her, a plea in her dark eyes. "Then it was not my fault? I did not cause it to happen?"

"Of course you did not," Ottilia said, catching at the creature's thin shoulders. "I wish you will rid yourself of any shadow of blame."

The girl drew a shaky breath. "I wish I might. Yet even could I do so, the rest of the village will not."

Ottilia released her, a sharp note entering her voice. "No,

because our killer chose his time well. He took advantage of your warning."

Shock leapt in Mrs. Dale's eyes. It was plain this notion had not previously occurred to her. "Deliberately? To set the villagers on to hound me?"

"Yes," said Ottilia frankly, believing the more she understood, the less she would fear. "You were a convenient scapegoat."

Pain crossed the girl's vision, and the tragic look returned. "Cruel! But it was ever so."

Ottilia frowned. "What do you mean?"

Cassie shivered. "Even my siblings used my propensity to see things, even if I had not. They used to tell my father that their mischief had been foretold, as if they had no control of it. As if I made them do it."

Small wonder the poor girl was so chafed. "What you need, my dear, is someone to guard you from such cruelties."

"I have Tabitha and Sam."

"Your servants?"

"My maid and her husband."

It was plain to Ottilia that Mrs. Dale had little understanding of her meaning. She probed a little. "I daresay your own late husband was of help, too."

Something flashed in Cassie's eyes. She glanced away and back again, and Ottilia thought she saw a rapid change of emotions cross her features—shock, fear, and dismay.

Before she could enquire into the meaning of this extraordinary response, a hail from the bridge took her attention.

"Mrs. Dale!"

She turned to see the Reverend Kinnerton coming towards them. He spied her at the same instant.

"How do you do, Lady Francis?"

"I am well, I thank you, sir."

Ottilia was amused to note that her answer had barely been acknowledged, for the pastor had his attention almost wholly on Cassie Dale. She in her turn was staring at him, a telltale blush creeping into her cheeks. Romance in the wind already? So much for the fond hopes of Horace Netherburn!

Meanwhile, Mr. Kinnerton had reached them.

"I was fortunate to catch Mrs. Winkleigh on her way to the vicarage with the blacksmith's daughter," he said, speaking exclusively to Cassie Dale. "I am glad to find you are not alone. How are your bruises? Are you a little recovered?"

A tentative little smile wavered on the girl's lips. "Yes."

He frowned. "Forgive me, but you don't look it. You are regrettably pale, and there are blue smudges under your eyes."

Mrs. Dale's fingers went to the spot as if to cover the blotches. "I did not sleep well."

"Nightmares?"

The girl let out a gasp. "How did you know?"

Kinnerton smiled, and his tone was gentle. "I have them myself on occasion."

Highly entertained, Ottilia forbore to make any teasing comment, though several rose to her mind. Francis had mentioned the vicar had been obliged to abandon his missionary work due to severe sickness, and perhaps he yet suffered from the aftermath. He clearly had a strong empathy with the passions of this little "witch." Then Mrs. Dale's expressive eyes changed to question.

"Sam told me you spoke to Staxton's boys to excellent effect. Pray tell me what you said."

A gleam of amusement entered the blue eyes. "Oh, I merely asked them to think carefully about what sins each of them had committed so that I could decide just how many stones should be thrown at them in retribution."

Ottilia was amused, perhaps more by the sheer amazement in Mrs. Dale's face. "Ingenious, sir. Did they oblige you?"

He laughed, although he barely glanced at her. "No, indeed. But I bade them not to abandon the notion, for I would be keeping a suitable store of weapons in my pocket for the purpose at any time they felt able to answer the question."

Cassie Dale's expression altered. "You will not do so, will you?"

"Of course not. But I am in hopes they will not guess that. Besides, I will be at pains to regard them with interest and pat my pockets whenever I catch sight of them in the village."

At last Mrs. Dale smiled, and the transformation astonished Ottilia. She looked at once younger and lighter of heart. Mr. Kinnerton's bright gaze showed his admiration. An excellent development, for Ottilia might count him an ally.

"I have been trying to persuade Mrs. Dale of her innocence in the matter of Duggleby's death."

Cassie's eyes remained on Kinnerton's face, and she put out a hand which he automatically took and held.

"Lady Fan says I have been used. She says they took my vision for a signal and killed Duggleby in a way that would make the villagers blame me. I believe it. It is not the first time I have been made scapegoat for the sins of others."

The words were delivered in a rush, a note of panic underneath that Ottilia was quick to detect. She could not but approve the parson's studied response, for all that it was delivered in a tone that verged perilously on a caress.

"Hush, Mrs. Dale. Do not upset yourself. Is it not better to know your enemies for what they are than to hold your own talent suspect?"

"Talent! Would it were one."

"But it is," he insisted. "There is no saying but that the smithy roof would have come down in any event. What you saw was used, but that does not change the fact that you saw it."

"You believe in such things, Mr. Kinnerton?" asked Ottilia, firmly entering the lists.

He seemed to become only now fully conscious of her presence. Releasing Mrs. Dale's hands, he stepped back, a dull colour creeping up his neck.

"I have reason to, Lady Francis."

"Indeed?"

"Or at least to keep an open mind," he amended, throwing an apologetic glance at Cassie Dale, who was frowning deeply. "The abilities of some of the African natives were hard to dispute."

"Ah yes, my husband told me you had been a missionary."

He looked vexed, as if he did not wish this side of his ministry to be talked of. But he reckoned without Cassie Dale. Her eyes shining, she reached out to him again, but Ottilia noted he did not this time take her hand.

"It was a wonderful thing to do, as I said to Mrs. Winkleigh when she told me of it," said Cassie.

At this, a rueful grin drove the vexation from his face. "I'll wager she did not agree with you."

Cassie laughed, and her whole countenance lightened again. "No, indeed. She disliked it excessively."

"I am aware. My mother also."

"Yes, so she said."

His brows lifted. "I perceive I have been thoroughly exposed by my old nurse."

Cassie laughed again. "Utterly. But I'm glad."

Growing a trifle impatient, for all the entertainment of witnessing a budding love affair, Ottilia put an end to this exchange.

"What sort of abilities, sir, did you witness in Africa?"

A crease appeared between his brows, and it was plain his time there had not been uniformly happy.

"On occasion I could swear one or other of these individuals was telepathic. And though I could not approve their pagan rites, their witch doctors appeared to have quite remarkable powers."

"What sort of powers?" Ottilia asked, glancing at Cassie, who was rapt.

"They could heal—though I suspect that was more a matter of persuading the sick to heal themselves. But, like you,

Mrs. Dale, there were instances of visions of events which subsequently came to pass."

"You did not think that someone took care, like our present murderer, to ensure that they came to pass?"

He shook his head. "Perhaps once or twice. But on the whole, I have to say I was convinced."

Intrigued, Ottilia turned to Cassie Dale. "Should you object to explaining how these visions come to you?"

Cassie shivered, and Ottilia found herself the recipient of a distinctly unfriendly look from Mr. Kinnerton. She ignored it, holding Cassie's gaze. The girl's eyes deepened with a species of concentrated pain, but she did not look away.

"It is like a fog to begin with, swirling in my head. Then the pictures form." She shivered and Ottilia wondered at it briefly. "They don't come immediately, and not in any great detail, and not perhaps in order. They are more like flashes than a sequence of events." She put her hands together, twisting her fingers. "But in my mind I know. I know the meaning. I know what will happen. Or what has happened."

"And it is that which panics you?" Ottilia guessed.

She nodded, her tongue darting at her lips in a gesture infinitely more telling than her words.

It proved too much for the Reverend Kinnerton. He caught her unquiet hands and held them fast. "Don't fear it, Cassie! It is a God-given gift. Let it be. Let it be and it cannot hurt you."

As Cassie gazed into the gentleman's eyes, Ottilia began to feel decidedly de trop. She was saved from having to decide whether to efface herself, however, by a sudden shout from the direction of the bridge.

"Reverend! Miss Cassie!"

The effect was felt by all, turning as one towards the shout. Ottilia beheld a burly fellow beckoning with urgency.

"It is Sam! What is it, Sam?"

As Ottilia hurried with the others towards the bridge, the

echo of the man's shout reiterated in her mind. Miss Cassie? Abruptly, she recalled Mrs. Dale's odd reaction when she had mentioned her dead husband. The suspicion raced through her mind and was tucked away for future examination as the present crisis was laid bare.

"It's Molly Tisbury, Reverend," announced the man Sam. "She's gone clean out of her mind, to my way of thinking."

"What has happened?" The sharp note showed another side to the vicar.

"She's attacking Hannah Pakefield, sir. The two of 'em are fighting like cats, and no one can pull 'em apart."

Only now did Ottilia take in the running figures, coming from every direction and racing hell-for-leather towards the Blue Pig.

Chapter 8

As Aidan pelted down the lane, keeping pace with Sam Hawes but outstripping the ladies within a matter of yards, his eyes scanned the hurrying villagers, and he recognised several of the flying figures. Will and Tisbury from the Cock and Bottle, closely followed by Farmer Staxton. He half expected to see old Pa Wagstaff hobbling along, but a glance towards the cobbled courtyard of the Blue Pig told him the aged jokesmith was already in situ, leaning on a thick staff.

As he neared, Aidan caught the sounds of the altercation, along with shouts from the gathering onlookers. When he was able to take in the scene, he saw the huge oaken door of the inn standing ajar and discovered the fight had tumbled out onto the cobbles.

A circle was forming, and he could just see the battling females clutched together in a heaving, screaming mass. There was a roar from the crowd, and Aidan clearly heard the senile cracked voice of Molly Tisbury's father, egging her on.

"Go to it, girl! Her've nowt to gainsay you. Give 'er one in the breadbasket!"

Whether the Tisbury woman heard him was a moot point, for the grunts and yells coming from her own throat had likely made her deaf to anything outside her immediate attention.

As he arrived at the scene, a little out of breath, Aidan recognised Lord Francis Fanshawe standing at the ready, poised to intervene. A little apart stood a lanky man, staggering with a hand to his brow, an expression of horror upon his countenance. And hard by, making quite as much noise as those of lesser status, was the pair of females Aidan had so far seen only at a distance, but of whom he had heard much from Lady Ferrensby.

Wasting no time, Aidan looked to see if Hawes had kept up and found him panting just behind.

"Help Lord Francis, Sam," he ordered tersely and pushed through to the front of the circle. He threw up a hand to attract Fanshawe's attention and raised his voice to pulpit pitch, bellowing across the throng.

"Lord Francis!" His lordship looked quickly across, and their eyes met. "Take the one, while I secure the other."

Without waiting for agreement, he scanned the watchers for the landlord of the Cock and Bottle, who had reached the scene a bare moment before him. Tisbury was found to be standing a little in front of his fellows, his jaw sagging and his eyes following the two women's staggering motions as they cannoned backward and forward across the cobbles.

"Tisbury!" Aidan yelled, running across. "Don't stand like a stock, man! Help me stop this!"

Thus adjured, the landlord came to himself with a bang and nodded, shifting alongside Aidan as he looked for an opening. Lord Francis and Sam Hawes were similarly circling as the quarries threw each other to and fro, neither giving an inch.

Aidan had not previously encountered Mrs. Pakefield, who looked to be the more bulky and robust. She was largely

was quickly recaptured by the farmer and her hus-
ut her fists flailed wildly, and Aidan wondered briefly
oth was sufficient to save him from attack.

have shown yourself not one degree less badly be-
han Staxton's boys, Mrs. Tisbury," he retorted levelly.
nts, I should summon Pilton and have the two of you
into the lock-up for disturbing the peace."

wouldn't never, Reverend!" gasped Tabitha Hawes,
an caught the glee in her features as he glanced at her.
e he could answer, an interruption occurred. He had
n the presence of Cassie Dale, but she erupted sud-
t of the circle, running towards the Tisbury woman.
y, beware! You are in danger!"

e ensuing silence, the Cock and Bottle's landlady
eatures abruptly blanched towards Mrs. Dale, a look
error in her eyes. She backed a step, clearly without
what she did.

Dale," Aidan began, low-voiced, intent on prevent-
er confrontation.

olly's stupefaction was short-lived. Recovering, she
into verbal attack. "You hear? You hear the witch?
reatening me now!"

o, Molly, you mistake," cried Cassie. "I am trying
ou. Only listen to me! I can see it clear. How could
to tell you of it?"

e telling her nowt!" shouted Tisbury, foolishly re-
hold and striding forward. "I'll not have my wife
by your witching spells! You shut your mouth, if
ind to live!"

y!" Aidan stepped between them. "How dare you?
tter foolish threats before witnesses? If this is your
an, you may find yourself hanging for Duggleby's

shrank a trifle but did not back down. "I never
gleby. I never touched him." His hand shot out,

on the defensive, using her ample form to shove hard at the skinnier Mrs. Tisbury and prevent her from moving out of range by clutching the hair on either side of her attacker's head.

Molly Tisbury's fingers were thus free to pummel, gouge, and slap even as she shrieked in pain, and her opponent's grunts and cries showed she was making her mark.

Intent upon his task, Aidan was vaguely aware of the commentary coming from all sides.

"This is terrible! Will no one stop them?" A shrill screech in genteel tones.

"Get her down! Her's bigger nor you, her've to fall harder."

"Use your feet, girl! Don't you know owt?"

At which, Molly Tisbury pulled roughly back and aimed a wild kick at her rival's legs. It fell wide and gave Hannah Pakefield an opportunity to duck her head and butt at the other's face.

A shriek from the Tisbury female showed she had found her mark, and blood started to stream from the woman's nose.

Leaving Aidan flat, the frenzied Tisbury belted over to the lanky fellow hovering at the edge of the action, who Aidan had earlier noticed. Tisbury seized the man by the coat lapels.

"Can't you do owt with your devil wife, you great lummock!"

"Tisbury!" Aidan roared, incensed at this desertion.

At that instant, Lord Francis ran in on the fight and seized hold of the nearest shoulders, which proved to be those of Hannah Pakefield. Aidan immediately grabbed at Molly Tisbury as Sam Hawes joined Lord Francis. To Aidan's relief, Tisbury hurried back to his aid, seizing his wife by an upper arm.

"Is that Hannah's husband?" Aidan asked him, holding fast to his quarry. "Why is he not helping us?"

"For as he bain't nowt but a noddy, is why," retorted Tisbury, adding fiercely, "Shut it, will you?"

This was to his spouse, Aidan supposed, but he wasted no words himself. It was by no means easy to hold the combatants, despite having two men to each woman, both still screaming abuse at one another, the Tisbury female apparently oblivious to the blood now dripping down her chin and onto her clothes.

"We'll hold while you tug her off," Lord Francis barked at Aidan.

But a voice cut in before he could act on this command.

"Don't pull, man! Got to get Hannah's fingers out of the creature's hair first."

One of the ladies had joined them, the tall female with a mannish air, who had taken one of Mrs. Pakefield's arms in a grip that effectively stopped its motion.

"Quite right, Miss Beeleigh," came the calm tones of Lady Francis, as she appeared suddenly into the fray.

The other woman released one of her hands and grasped at the clutching fingers. "Let go, Hannah, let go!"

But the Pakefield female, though her motions had perforce ceased, appeared to have lost her senses. Her shock-filled eyes were fixed upon the other's snarling visage.

Momentarily uncertain, Aidan looked from Miss Beeleigh to Lady Francis.

"Prise her fingers off, Tillie!"

The instruction came from Lord Francis, and Aidan saw his lady's fingers reach towards Mrs. Pakefield's and take hold of them. Gently, she spoke again.

"Hannah, my dear, you must let go."

At this, a haunted look entered Mrs. Pakefield's face, and in an involuntary motion, she opened her fingers. Quickly, her hands were pulled back and the combatants dragged well away from one another.

"Tisbury, take your wife under the arms and hold her still," Aidan panted, trying to keep the wriggling, cursing bundle under his hand from escaping. "Staxton, help him!"

At this command, the tavern's ʜ his hold, instead slipping his arms u and holding her strongly around th

"Shut it, Molly, do," he growled

Farmer Staxton appeared at Aiᵈ Reverend."

A burly arm appeared, and a ha holding so that Aidan was able to last. He moved in between the two nah Pakefield, supported now by Hawes, Aidan could see she was n she looked to be in a fair way to spouse, clearly a helpless individuᵃ a hand to his head, his face a pictᵘ

Aidan stood his ground, ready of the late opponents show any siᵍ fight. But by this time, Molly ᵀ duced in response to her husbaⁿ had ceased her struggles and shru She had apparently discovered h

"I be bleeding! Her've broke

"Her've not, neither. Tamest plained her ancient progenitor.

"You shut it, Pa! Tisbury, he

"Hush, now, Molly. You scrᵃ

Which was true enough, Aᵎ ing back at the other woman's ʜ not neglect his duty.

"You have come by your dᵉ coolly. "Is this a sample of the ᵈ parishioners? I take leave to inf will not be tolerated. Underst

"Do you think I care for Molly shrieked, bursting ou hold. "Bain't one of Staxton's

She band, b if his cˡ

"You haved t

"By rig thrown

"You and Aid

Befor forgotte denly ou

"Moll

In th turned fᵉ of utter t realizing

"Mrs. ing furth

But M launched Her be tʰ

"No, ᵣ to warn y I bear not

"You b leasing hi scared sill you've a ⁿ

"Tisbu Will you u temper, m murder."

Tisbury killed Dug

accusing. "It were her! Her be the witch, bain't her? Now her've seen visions of Molly, her said. Her ought to be burned afore her've a chance to kill us all!"

With which, he turned and grabbed his wife by the wrist, dragging her away towards the green. Aidan watched them go, aware of the crowd hovering, half anxious to follow and half afraid to miss anything. Out of the corner of his eyes, he saw Cassie Dale start in pursuit.

Without thought, he strode after her and seized her by the arm.

"Stay!"

She turned her lustrous dark eyes upon him, and Aidan read the despair within. He smiled at her briefly but did not release his grip.

Then he turned to the onlookers. "About your business, all of you. The show is over."

A high-pitched cackling sounded over the mutters that broke out, and Aidan turned irritable eyes upon the ancient hobbling towards him as the rest of the company began to drift away.

On his feet, Pa Wagstaff proved a slight old fellow, small like his daughter, though he had lost the wiry strength he must have had in youth.

"You be a mighty big man with words, Reverend," he commented. "But how be you hoping to keep 'em from set-ting up faggots and tying that there missie to the stake? More of they than you, I'm thinking."

Aidan looked down into the crabbed and gleeful features. "Since your comments have proved less than helpful, Mr. Wagstaff, I don't propose to burden you with my plans."

The ancient took a moment to digest this. Then he grinned toothlessly up at Aidan. "You be stumped, Reverend. Reckon they've got more plans nor you."

With which, he cackled again and made off with a sur-prising turn of speed.

Aidan was forced to admit, if only to himself, that the wretched fellow was in the right of it. He stared after him for a moment and only came to a remembrance of his surroundings when Mrs. Dale drew his attention.

"Aidan, you are hurting my arm."

With an oath, he released her, turning his gaze quickly towards her. A hesitant little smile hovered on her lips.

"You are upset," she said. "I know because you were gripping me so tightly."

He was conscious of a flush of warmth in his chest, but it was overborne by an immediate feeling of guilt.

"I beg your pardon. You are right. Wagstaff made me excessively angry. I hope you did not take his words to heart."

She drew in a shuddering breath. "Is it just words? Do you think they truly mean to use me so?"

Something twisted in Aidan's gut, and he grasped her shoulders.

"They will not get the opportunity, I promise you that. No one will be allowed to harm you."

Her lips parted as she stared at him, such a mixture of hope and fear in her expressive eyes that Aidan was hard put to it not to draw her close that he might demonstrate his assertion with a more tangible proof than his words could afford.

Conscious, he looked about and discovered that the courtyard was deserted, apart from Tabitha Hawes, standing off at a discreet distance and pointedly looking another way. Hannah Pakefield had evidently been taken inside, accompanied by the rest of the gentry.

On impulse, Aidan jerked his head towards the still open door. "Let us go in. I think we can all do with a little peace and quiet."

She made no demur but turned in that direction and walked beside him.

"I do fear for Molly," she said, and Aidan noted the little shiver that shook her. "The vision was vile."

* * *

Ottilia was glad to have been relieved of the necessity to minister to Hannah Pakefield's hurts, that task having been taken over by Miss Beeleigh, with the doubtful assistance of the widow Radlett and the Blue Pig's overworked maid, who had been despatched to fetch lint and salves while the rest of the party repaired to the coffee room. It left Ottilia free, once the necessary introductions had been effected, since Francis had not previously met these women, to put her attention on recent events.

In a low-voiced conversation with her husband, she was able to furnish him with an unvarnished account of her visit to Bertha Duggleby.

"Then you think she is innocent?"

"Yes, but that is mere conjecture on my part. There can be no doubt she was in the perfect position to do all that was necessary to bring about her husband's death."

"But not," Francis suggested, "to shift the blame onto Cassie Dale?"

"Just so."

"After the encounter outside, I am much inclined to place my wager on Molly Tisbury."

Ottilia shook her head. "You will lose."

A crease appeared between his brows. "With that temperament? The woman is a shrew."

"True, but her temper is too quick. Can you truly conceive of Molly planning anything? No, she is the type to charge in without premeditation."

"Granted, but having hit Duggleby with the hammer in a fit of temper, isn't it conceivable she was capable of working out how to conceal the crime?"

A little laugh escaped Ottilia. "I submit she is far more likely to have fled the place screaming. But you are right. We cannot dismiss her." She sighed as the inevitable thought occurred. "Which means I must tackle her direct."

"Leave it for tomorrow," Francis suggested. "She may have cooled by then."

Further discussion was cut off by the entrance of Patty, the Blue Pig's maid of work, bearing a tray of accoutrements to aid in the succour of her mistress. As she was closely followed by the vicar and Cassie Dale, further private conversation became impossible.

Glancing at them both, Ottilia divined a certain consciousness in the Reverend Kinnerton. She looked to Mrs. Dale to see if she was similarly affected, but Cassie's eyes had gone instantly to where Hannah Pakefield was seated, hissing in breaths as Miss Beeleigh began to dab at her wounds with a piece of lint dipped in some sort of solution in a glass dish. Mrs. Radlett's exclamations being punctuated with the lamentations of the maid, there was a considerable commotion in that side of the room.

Francis rose to greet Kinnerton. "My dear fellow, you must stand in crying need of a restorative. And, I may add, so do I. Pakefield!"

The landlord, who had proved of little use throughout the drama, was hovering helplessly on the fringe of the little group about his wife. He turned at Francis's peremptory call.

"Bestir yourself, Pakefield. We are all gasping here. Mrs. Dale? Would you care for wine?"

It took several moments to sort out exactly what was required by all parties. To make matters worse, Mr. Netherburn entered the coffee room in the midst of the discussion. Having missed all the excitement, he was immediately regaled with a garbled version of events by Mrs. Radlett, punctuated with terse corrections from Miss Beeleigh, still engaged upon her mission of nursing the afflicted landlady.

Ottilia caught Francis's glance, and he cast up his eyes and bodily removed the landlord, taking the parson with him. There could be no doubt he would reappear in due course, having bullied the bemused Pakefield into supplying the needs of the assembled company.

Turning her attention to Cassie Dale, Ottilia was a trifle alarmed to see her staring at an empty chair on the other side of the round table from where Ottilia was seated. She did not hesitate.

"What is it, Mrs. Dale?"

Cassie's large eyes were deeply distressed, and her face registered her horror. She raised a shaking hand and pointed her finger at the chair.

"I see Molly there."

A sliver of impatience almost overtook Ottilia. She overcame it with difficulty, forcing herself to speak with all her usual calm.

"Whatever you see, my dear, it is but a fantasy."

The dark eyes turned on her, fierce in their intensity. "Fantasy? I only wish it were! Do you think I wish to see such things? Do you think it gives me a macabre pleasure to talk of them?"

"I did not say so," said Ottilia coolly, rising from her seat and starting around the table.

Cassie threw up both hands in a gesture of protest. "Don't try to humour me! You cannot know what it is like to be cursed as I am. Are you in my head? How do you dare to belittle what I see?"

Ottilia saw nothing for it but to backtrack. She would get nowhere by further antagonising the girl.

"I make you my apologies, Mrs. Dale. I had no intention of upsetting you."

The girl's lips worked a little, but the fire died out of her eyes.

"I daresay you mean well," she uttered grudgingly. "I know you do. But if you could see it!"

The last was an agonised plea. Aware that everyone in the room had stopped speaking and turned to stare, Ottilia threw up a hand to enjoin their continued silence and gentled her tone.

"Tell me, Cassie."

Mrs. Dale's eyes left hers, flitting aimlessly to and fro. She began to shiver, and her features gave evidence of the dismay her thoughts engendered.

"It began when I met her this morning," she said, speaking in rapid tones, her breath catching here and there. "I felt the fog begin, but it passed without revealing what lay inside. With the fighting, it came back. Then I saw it." She brought her fingers to her mouth where they trembled against her lip. "Molly, sitting there, unmoving. In her neck—something vile." The vileness of the something was in her eyes.

"What was it, Cassie? What was in her neck?"

Cassie threw her head up, fear in the look she cast at Ottilia.

"I don't know. I cannot see. It is sunken in. A knife? A dart?"

"Is she bleeding?"

Cassie looked confused. "She should be, should she not? There is a trickle, I think." She threw her hands over her face, and her voice came muffled. "Oh, it is vile! Horrible! I cannot bear to see it!"

There was movement in the doorway, and Ottilia looked to find the Reverend Kinnerton standing in the aperture, his face naked and forgotten. Compassion, and something more.

Before he could act, another figure pushed through from behind him.

"Begging your pardon, Reverend, but I must get through."

Mr. Kinnerton stepped to one side automatically, and the woman Ottilia had seen with Cassie at the smithy came bustling inside. The vicar's features returned to his normal expression, and Ottilia was relieved for his sake that the exposure of his state of mind had been unremarked by the rest of the persons in the room, whose attention had been all on Mrs. Dale.

One glance revealed their various reactions. While Hannah Pakefield's blank look showed she had taken in nothing of this macabre vision, Miss Beeleigh's features expressed both disgust and disbelief. Mrs. Radlett was wreathed in that sort of suppressed delight that accompanies the contemplation of horrific ideas, although Mr. Netherburn looked perturbed and confused. The maid Patty was staring, openmouthed with shock.

The newcomer, a matronly figure whom Ottilia took to be the maid Tabitha, appeared unmoved as she headed directly for her charge and put an arm about her shoulders.

"Come on, Miss Cassie. Let me take you home."

Unresisting, the girl allowed herself to be shepherded from the room, not even sparing a look for the Reverend Kinnerton. Ottilia could not but wonder at the potential of a union which promised to be fraught with periodic tensions. Or would the vicar prove even more adept at handling the creature than her maid had been?

The departure of Mrs. Dale had the effect of releasing stopped tongues. Mrs. Radlett, her eyes big with anticipation, came over to Ottilia's table. But before she could speak, Miss Beeleigh was bending over the landlady.

"You should lie down upon your bed, Hannah. Can you get up?"

Mrs. Pakefield was dishevelled, but the fright had left her face, and she looked merely dejected. She rose carefully, holding on to the table.

"Poor dear Hannah," mourned Mrs. Radlett. "Shall I help you to bed?"

She made no real attempt to be of service, merely flapping her hands in a hopeless kind of way. Not much to Ottilia's surprise, Miss Beeleigh vetoed this suggestion.

"Not you, Evelina. Horace, give Hannah your arm. You may escort her to the door of her room. Patty, you run ahead and make the bed ready for your mistress."

The maid dropped a curtsy and tripped out of the room with more haste than dignity, and Ottilia guessed she was still reeling from Cassie's revelation. Obedient, but without abating one jot of his habitual gallant air, Mr. Netherburn took charge of the landlady and led her to the door. Here Mr. Kinnerton detained them.

"Are you feeling a little recovered?"

Hannah nodded bleakly. "I wouldn't have done it, Reverend. Not if Molly hadn't flown at me."

To his credit, the vicar smiled at her. "I gathered as much. Take care of yourself."

Mrs. Pakefield nodded wearily and allowed herself to be led from the room. The widow Radlett immediately gave tongue.

"Oh, how could Cassie Dale have thought of such a thing? It very nearly brought on my palpitations. Horrible! Do you suppose it might come to pass, Lady Francis?"

This last was uttered with a look of such avid anticipation Ottilia was hard put to it to refrain from a cutting rejoinder. She was saved having to reply by Miss Beeleigh.

"Never mind that now, Evelina." She came across to Ottilia, her face grim. "Wanted to be rid of Hannah, for I've found out what set Molly off."

Ottilia had a pretty good notion herself, but she raised her brows.

"Have you indeed?"

The other nodded. "Seems she'd heard you'd been told some rigmarole of a quarrel between Tisbury and Duggleby. What's more, rumour has it you're one to find out everything about everybody."

Ottilia had already surmised that they had been overheard when Pilton told his tale. She was fairly sure she knew which ears were listening at the time, but she made no mention of it.

"This was yesterday, I take it?"

Miss Beeleigh nodded. "Put Molly into a foul temper."

"Yes," Ottilia agreed. "She was less than pleasant when we met her coming from Bertha Duggleby's home."

"Ah." The other nodded. "Must've been then she took the idea into her head that Hannah had been feeding you tales about her."

Undoubtedly, from Ottilia's memory of the conversation. She chose not to reveal as much, however. "Well, I did say I wanted to talk to her."

"Which I'll be bound she didn't take to."

"No, indeed. I was obliged to threaten to send Pilton to fetch her to me for questioning."

A bark of laughter escaped Miss Beeleigh's lips. "No wonder she panicked. Seems she came here directly and accused Hannah of speaking ill of her and Tisbury."

"Oh yes," threw in Mrs. Radlett, nodding vigorously enough to shake her golden curls. "Molly said she knew Hannah was jealous of her, which of course is quite true."

"They quarrelled?" asked Ottilia.

"Dreadfully. Hannah says Molly threw all manner of insults at her, but she was in such a state she couldn't recall the half of them."

"Don't matter, Evelina," snapped Miss Beeleigh, taking up the tale again. "That's irrelevant. What's important is Hannah protesting she'd no reason for jealousy and boasting of her privileged association with the most important visitor Witherley has seen in a twelvemonth. Seeing Molly purple with envy, the misguided cloth head then announced she'd not scrupled to tell Lady Francis what she thought of Molly. At which, Molly flew at her."

The ridiculous nature of the quarrel excited Ottilia's amusement, but it was overborne by the reflection that her brief discussion with the Tisbury female had been instrumental in causing the altercation. She felt doubly culpable in that she had made little real progress in uncovering the murderer.

At this moment, Francis, whom she had not even noticed reentering the room, set a cup of coffee down before her. She smiled up at him, grateful to be spared the necessity of responding immediately.

By the time Francis had distributed the contents of the tray held by the landlord, who still looked to be in a state of bemusement, Ottilia had gathered herself and was able to speak with all her usual calm.

"I was going to leave the interview until tomorrow, but perhaps I had best see Molly sooner rather than later."

"You'll get nothing out of her today," stated Miss Beeleigh positively. With a sidelong glance at the vicar, who had remained noticeably silent, she added, "Can't think Cassie Dale has helped the situation, either."

Ottilia saw Mr. Kinnerton's blue gaze flash as he looked up from studying the dark-coloured liquid in the tankard supplied to him by Francis. Her husband, not having been in the room to hear what Cassie said, glanced across at her with a questioning frown.

"Mrs. Dale has had an unfortunate vision concerning Molly Tisbury," Ottilia said briefly, with a look intending him to understand that she would relate the details presently.

"Mrs. Dale is in a highly nervous condition," stated the parson evenly, but the edge of anger was evident.

"Take leave to point out, Kinnerton, that it's habitual with her," returned Miss Beeleigh flatly.

"Is that surprising, in the circumstances? Did you not hear the threat Tisbury made?"

"Pooh!" scoffed the spinster. "So much hot air! Set up a stake in this day and age? Wouldn't dare."

The blue eyes flashed again. "You think not? You think because we are allegedly civilised there cannot be a swift descent to an ancient barbarism?"

"Not so ancient," put in Francis, echoing Ottilia's thought. "The last witch burnings must be less than a hundred years ago. What is more, it is not much over five years since our justices ended the practise of female murderers being burned at the stake."

A shocked silence greeted this reminder, and Mrs. Radlett shuddered, whipping out a pocket-handkerchief and applying it to her eyes.

"For shame, Francis," said Ottilia reproachfully. "Poor Mrs. Radlett will be imagining that the creatures were burned alive, but it is not so. They were in general hung or strangled before the faggots were set on fire."

"As if that made it better," exploded the Reverend Kinnerton. "I tell you, ma'am, I have seen true natives living in conditions of near savagery, but not one of them was ever guilty of the petty cruelties I have here witnessed. They were simple people, and their punishments were harsh. But they did not indulge in a warfare of fear and persecution."

He stopped, drawing in his fangs with an effort, Ottilia thought. Then he set down his half-empty tankard and gave a formal little bow.

"You will excuse me, I beg. I have duties in the parish."

In a moment, he was gone from the coffee room, leaving behind him an atmosphere of embarrassed silence. It was broken by the widow Radlett.

"Well! Anyone would suppose it was our fault the villagers have taken against Cassie Dale."

Her affronted tone very nearly overset Ottilia, who had been silently applauding the vicar's vehement championship. But her amusement was short-lived.

Entering almost immediately upon Mr. Kinnerton's departure came Horace Netherburn, looking perturbed.

"What in the world shall we do about Hannah?" he uttered without preamble, addressing himself as of instinct to Miss Beeleigh as unacknowledged leader of his little set.

She frowned. "What's to do, Horace?"

He waved an agitated hand. "I tried to make her see reason, but I could make no headway."

"What has she done, Mr. Netherburn?" asked Ottilia.

"Nothing. At least not yet. But she swears this is the last straw and she will be revenged on Molly Tisbury."

Chapter 9

Francis watched the landlord Tisbury pacing back and forth in his own cellar, whither he'd been run to earth. The afternoon was far advanced, for the aftermath of the fight had delayed the serving of a repast, and the trio of gentry had proved not to recognise when their presence might be dispensed with. But Tillie had been adamant that the interviews with the Tisbury couple must not be delayed.

Overbearing all opposition from the tapster Will, Francis had accordingly insisted on speaking with the landlord and suborned the maid Bessy into leading him to the wine cellar below the main rooms of the Cock and Bottle.

"I'm minded to slay that witch with my own bare hands," raged Tisbury, hitting his fist against one of the huge barrels resting on its shelf.

"For pity's sake, man," uttered Francis, exasperated. "Set your mind to the matter at hand. We know Mrs. Dale is not responsible for Duggleby's death. Therefore it is nonsensical to set any store by these ravings of danger."

Tisbury turned, fixing Francis with a choleric eye from

within his veined countenance, richly dark in the dim lantern light that did little to render the cavernous cellar anything other than eerily shadowed.

"Danger? Nowt to speak on if it be only that. But it be death for my Molly, for Will heard it with his own ears."

A chill went through Francis as he mentally reviewed the persons present in the coffee room of the Blue Pig when Cassie Dale had spoken of her vision. He had been absent himself, but Ottilia would remember precisely. But the tapster had been nowhere near the place. Had he not followed his master across the green? Curbing his tongue on the itch to refute Tisbury, he eyed the man narrowly.

"What precisely did Will hear?"

Tisbury spat on the floor. "Enough to say as the witch seen her dead, as like nor Duggleby as makes no matter."

"Eavesdropping was he?"

The landlord glared. "Will's my eyes and ears if'n I'm otherwhere."

"Your spy, you mean."

"If'n it be needed, aye."

Francis let it go. There was little to be gained by antagonising the man. Remembering his wife's methods, he tried what a soft approach might achieve.

"I sympathise with your wrath, my dear fellow. You have had much to vex you."

"Aye." But the glare turned suspicious. "Not as I be guessing who telled you."

Francis did not enlighten him, preserving an enigmatic silence.

The fellow was frowning. "What be said then? Nowt to please me, I'll be bound."

Francis struck. "Will you tell me what was the cause of your quarrel with Duggleby?"

Tisbury's head came up, and his eyes went from side to side. "Bain't true as I quarrelled with the man."

"Come, Tisbury, don't be shy. Your father-in-law provoked some sort of altercation, did he not? A month since, I believe."

A snorting laugh was surprised out of the man. "That? That were nowt. Aye, we come to blows, but bain't no bad blood betwixt him and me. Boys together we be, me and Duggleby."

"Yet even the best of friends may turn to hatred, if there is reason enough," Francis returned, offering up one of Tillie's dictums.

"Aye, but there were nowt betwixt us two," insisted the landlord, his features darkening again. "Nor there don't need to be, for no one bain't done for Duggleby 'cepting the witch."

"Then how do you account for the hammer blow to his head? And what of the crossbeam which had been hacked in two to ensure the roof must fall? There is no magic in these facts, Tisbury. This is the work of mortal man."

It was plain from the shock in the landlord's eyes that the crossbeam came as news to him. He began to bluster. "Bain't me as done it. Nor I wouldn't go for to smash his head from behind. A fair fight or nowt."

Francis was inclined to believe him, but he refrained from saying so. Better the fellow did not think himself safe from suspicion.

"I fear you must expect to be questioned, as will be every man in the village who had any sort of disagreement with Duggleby. You would do better to produce evidence that proves you could not have done it."

Fright showed in the sag of the fellow's shoulders and a hopeless look in his eye. "Nowt I can show."

"Then who else disliked the man enough to kill him?"

Tisbury shrugged. "None as I can think on." His eye brightened suddenly. "That there Mrs. Dale could've made all look like another done it for to put Pilton off the scent."

Francis gave an inward groan. They were back to that, were they?

"How, pray?"

But Tisbury had an answer to that.

"Witchcraft. A witch, bain't her?"

Ottilia, interviewing the wife in the woman's own parlour, fared little better. Molly Tisbury was still in a fury,
and it took all of Ottilia's ingenuity to persuade her to talk
of anything but the iniquities of Hannah Pakefield.

"Bad as the witch her be," Molly raged, one hand touching gingerly at the swelling about her nose.

She had cleaned off the blood and changed her clothes, but
it appeared the age-old remedy of putting a key down Molly's
back had failed and Tisbury had been obliged to call in Doctor Meldreth to stop the bleeding. Her voice was nasal, owing
to the linen plugs stuffed into her nostrils, though they did
nothing to lessen the virulence of her speech.

"What did Hannah say to you to make you so angry?"
asked Ottilia, feeling she would get nowhere until the
woman had vented her spleen.

"Bain't what her said to me, but what her said to you,
'Lady Fan,' " Molly threw at her, laying violent emphasis on
the nickname.

"But Hannah said very little to me about you, Molly," Ottilia told her calmly, choosing to use the promising weapon
of intimacy.

"Oh? Oh? And bain't her said as she'd telled you agin me
so's you be thinking I be a bad 'un?"

"Nothing of the sort."

"You be knowing from Pilton as I banged Duggleby and
Tisbury both that night as they took and fought like boys,"
pursued Molly unheeding. "And bain't you going for to
think as I banged Duggleby with that there hammer?"

"Nothing Hannah said to me could make me think that,"
said Ottilia evasively.

The woman's piggy little eyes sharpened. "But her said

summat agin me, nor you wouldn't take and fright me with Pilton. Her've got you in her's house. What's to stop her telling all and more?"

Ottilia's senses went on full alert. "All what, Molly?"

The woman's countenance, already deeply coloured from her injury, reddened still more. Her eyes shifted away, and her shoulders twitched.

"Nowt."

"Oh, come now, Molly," Ottilia said gently. "What was it? Were you a target of Duggleby's roving eye perhaps? Was your husband jealous?"

Molly snarled. "Nowt to speak on. If'n Duggleby set to flirting now and now, what of it? Tisbury knowed it were nowt."

"Did he indeed?"

"Aye, he did," snapped the woman crossly. "Nor you don't need to look at me like as if'n I lied."

Ottilia smiled. "It is a little difficult, Molly. I know about your kitchen maid, you see."

Shock leapt into the creature's eyes. "That fussock? Her've gone and good riddance."

"I gather she ran off during the night. Duggleby was responsible for her condition." Deliberately, Ottilia made it a statement rather than a question.

For a moment the Tisbury woman held her spleen, but the venom would not be contained. "Couldn't keep his hands off, Duggleby couldn't. Nor he wouldn't even when Tisbury told him. Bain't first one of my girls he ruined, neither. Took and done it with my housemaid afore Bessy, and her've gone and all. I telled him I wouldn't stand for it, not again. But he bain't one to care weren't Duggleby."

"What did you do?" Almost hushed, Ottilia hoped the woman's concentration was too much on her own wrongs to remember she was being questioned.

"Telled Bertha."

"Why did you not do so upon the first occasion?"

"For as her be my friend."

This matter-of-fact-pronouncement served to raise Molly's stock in Ottilia's eyes, but she pursued her nevertheless.

"But this time you did so. How did Bertha take it?"

Molly looked merely sulky now. "Laughed in my face her did. Don't mean nowt to Bertha seemingly. Said as if'n her cared nowt for Mrs. Uddington, her've nowt to think on for a kitchen maid. Nor I don't blame her."

Molly fell silent, and Ottilia contemplated her next move. If she was not mistaken, the creature was softened up. Might it be politic to throw in a different topic?

"Tell me about the watered wine, Molly. Was not your husband accused by Mrs. Radlett?"

The woman's head shot up, and the familiar gleam of fury was in her eyes.

"Not her. Her never said it. Nor her couldn't tell, neither. It were t'other one as come over highty-tighty. Rung a peal over Tisbury as the whole village bain't heard nor Domesday. Nor it weren't watered, not one bit. A fair man be Tisbury, and her've no call to say different. Likely as that Mrs. Radlett done it herself, for to hide as her've drunk it."

Shock ripped through Ottilia, and she spoke without thinking. "You mean she drinks in secret?"

Molly shrugged. "Bain't as I'd know. Though wouldn't be first time as her've been walking round the village looking hangdog, like as if'n her'd drunk too much the night afore."

"Looking hangdog how?"

"Grey-faced like, and heavy at the eyes."

Which could be drink. But the widow Radlett showed no sign of the hardened drinker's red-veined nose and cheeks. Could there be another, even more harmful, addiction? But it seemed Molly had not completed her disclosures.

"Bain't saying as she've got no reason. Any'd take to drink if'n they'd to put up with her."

"Miss Beeleigh?"

"Aye. T'other one's well under her's thumb. Nor it won't

be the way of Uddington when his wife up and left him, if'n Mrs. Radlett be set on leaving that Beeleigh for to wed Mr. Netherburn."

"In what way?" asked Ottilia, almost holding her breath.

"Miss Beeleigh don't forget and forgive."

"Whereas you think Mr. Uddington did?"

Molly snuffed a snorting breath through her mouth. "He've done nowt yet."

Had he not? But Ottilia did not put the question. She had no intention of revealing Uddington to be at the top of her list of suspects.

Her initial animosity towards Molly Tisbury had dissipated. She was conscious of a sliver of pity for the creature, locked as she was in a cocoon of bitterness. What was more, Ottilia entertained a lively suspicion concerning Cassie Dale's unfortunate prediction. On impulse, she leaned forward.

"I wish you will take care, Molly. Not that I suppose there is anything in Mrs. Dale's visions, but—"

She got no further. Molly Tisbury leapt from her chair, eyes blazing.

"You and all, Lady Fan? Bain't enough as the witch have put her curse on me!"

"That is not what I—"

"Her've marked me for the devil, bain't her? Her've said as how I've nowt to hope for more in this life. What'll I do? What'll I do? Hide in the cellar all day and night?"

Ottilia wished fervently that she had held her tongue, but there was nothing to be gained by that. Rising from her chair, she tried to stem the flow.

"Calm yourself, Molly. I meant nothing of the kind."

"You be on her's side! I said it afore. You be on her's side, Lady Fan."

"And I told you I am on no side but that of truth. Molly—"

"Go! You bain't welcome here. Her've got you, just like Hannah Pakefield. You be one with the devil, too, bain't you, Lady Fan?"

She was shrieking now, and Ottilia despaired of getting through to her. Turning, she headed for the door and paused there, looking back.

Molly was breathing fast, one hand at her thin bosom, her eyes as wild with fear as were those of Cassie Dale with passion. In some ways, Ottilia thought ruefully, they were two of a kind.

Ottilia lifted a hand in farewell. "Be careful, Molly. Don't go out alone."

Feeling defeated, she quietly left the parlour.

In the full flood of oratory, the parson was impressive. The whole village appeared to have crowded into the church to attend Duggleby's funeral, women as well as children, despite the prevailing custom of confining mourners to the male sex. Finding that Lady Ferrensby had the intention of going, according to the widow Radlett and her friend, who were both also in attendance, Ottilia felt justified in presenting an appearance herself.

She had wanted to be there, primarily for the purpose of taking stock of how certain individuals conducted themselves. The aged and highly decorated dark wooden pews reserved for the gentry at the front were conveniently placed, being set sideways to the nave, whereas the rest of the congregation faced the altar. Dressed in the most sober gown she had with her, of dull bronze silk, unadorned beyond a frill or two and made high to the throat, Ottilia was able to observe without fear of drawing attention.

Within minutes of the start of the service, she felt doubly relieved when she noticed that Cassie Dale had crept into the tiny minstrel's gallery at the back. She was aware that Mr. Kinnerton had advised Cassie to stay away, since the story of yesterday's vision had swarmed across the village like a malignant hive of bees. Ottilia had her own suspicion of where to lay the blame for this, having done a mental review of the persons present in the coffee room yesterday when Cassie revealed the horrid picture. The notion Francis had put forward of Will the tapster eavesdropping from outside she dismissed. He had no need to do so, if Will himself had an informant who had been present in person.

Thank heavens none of the villagers were likely to catch sight of Cassie peeping from behind the wooden bars below the rail up there! She dreaded to think of the consequences should the girl be spotted. Ottilia strongly suspected Mrs. Dale had disregarded the vicar's advice rather for his sake than Duggleby's. In Cassie's place, she would have been as much tempted to witness Mr. Kinnerton in action.

Nor could Cassie be disappointed. So far from the quiet gentleman one had come to know in day-to-day contact, the vicar proved, in his official capacity, to have a magnetic presence, both vocally and otherwise. He had developed a trick of looking round the congregation in silence before a pertinent clause, and then delivering the words in ringing accents of emphasis that echoed around the vaulted ceiling.

"Jesus said, Thou shalt do no murder."

Judging from the expressions on the faces of the villagers, which ranged from stunned to terrified, his oratory was supremely effective. Then softly, he continued:

"And Jesus said, Thou shalt love thy neighbour as thyself."

The shuffling of many feet followed this, as well as sliding glances from one to another as if to register which neighbour might be next in line for a swift exit to heaven. There was more in the same vein, but Ottilia's attention wandered as the vicar took time to elaborate on these quotations from the Bible in his sermon.

Her eyes travelled first to Uddington, whom she found to be preparing for the funeral when she had visited his premises yesterday. The merchant was not in the front when she and Francis entered to the tinkling of the shop bell, and the sound of hammering greeted them as the tinkles died away.

"Uddington?" Francis called. "Shop, ho!"

Abruptly the noise stopped. There was a soft clunk, and then footsteps in the back. A door in the panelling opened, and the snowy head of the shopkeeper appeared, dipping so he could look over his half spectacles to discover the identity of his visitors.

"Good day, Mr. Uddington," said Ottilia pleasantly.

The merchant pokered up at once, hesitating in the doorway. "To what am I indebted for the honour, my lady?"

Ottilia felt her spouse stiffen as alarmingly as Uddington himself.

"If you are minded to take that tone, fellow, it will be the worse for you."

Uddington gave an ironic bow. "As your lordship pleases."

Francis's teeth came together with a snap, and Ottilia thought it prudent to intervene.

"I am sorry to incommode you, Mr. Uddington. I gather you are occupied?"

He came towards them into the shop. "I am putting the lid on Duggleby's coffin, ma'am, if that interests you."

Despite herself, a little shiver shook Ottilia, and she was obliged to struggle to maintain her sangfroid. Not that the body, which she had examined in detail, had the power to unnerve her. It was rather the macabre twist of fate that found Uddington, still under suspicion of bludgeoning the fellow to death, attending to the needs of Duggleby's cadaver in order to send it to a final resting place.

"I did not realise you were responsible for such tasks," Ottilia managed to say as coolly as she could.

Uddington peered at her over the top of his spectacles, his pale eyes steady. "It is not unusual for the proprietor of a shop such as this to include the performance of undertaker in his duties to the local populace."

Glancing at her spouse, Ottilia saw a grim look in his features. His tone was biting. "It is, however, a trifle bizarre, in the circumstances."

The merchant's lips tightened. "Because your good 'Lady Fan,' as I hear it, chooses to number me among those held to be accountable for Duggleby's death."

"Possibly held to be accountable," Francis corrected flatly.

Acid entered Uddington's voice. "The distinction escapes me, my lord, for it fails to alter the insult."

By this time, Ottilia had recovered herself, but she chose not to respond to this. Instead, she said coolly, "Will you be so good, Mr. Uddington, as to show us where you keep your ladder?"

A startled look leapt into the merchant's features, and his animosity visibly deepened, though he said nothing of it. "It is out the back."

Francis threw out a hand. "Lead on, sir." He glanced at Ottilia. "After you, my love."

This time Uddington was determined not to be interrupted by any more unwelcome visitors. Crossing first to the front door, he shot a bolt at its top before leading the way through to his back premises. Following him down a narrow corridor, Ottilia took opportunity to glance past an open door into the room behind, where the plain dark wood coffin containing Duggleby's remains was resting on a pair of trestles.

When they exited by the back door, it was immediately apparent that Uddington was not the only person to have access to his ladder. It lay on its side, tucked neatly against the back wall. Anyone might have taken it at any time.

"Is it always kept here?" Francis asked, and Ottilia saw him take stock of its inordinate length.

Uddington nodded. "It's too long for the shed."

"How would you know if it had been used by another?" Francis asked, his mind clearly jumping with Ottilia's conclusions.

"I wouldn't," came sourly from the merchant. "All the village knows it is here. Most have the courtesy to ask if they wish to use it."

"But others don't?" Francis surmised.

"I have found it missing on occasion. As long as it is returned, I have nothing against it."

"I suppose it is too much to ask if you noticed it missing at any time before Duggleby was killed?" Ottilia cut in.

Uddington sagged a little. "Believe me, my lady, if I had I would have notified you before this."

She eyed him with interest. "Why? What should make you suppose I was interested in a ladder?"

He shrugged in his customary fashion. "It was not a conjecture. I heard of Lord Francis's discovery at the smithy, as did the whole village, I make no doubt."

"And you made the connection."

"I could hardly fail to do so since Miss Beeleigh made it her business to mention my ladder's existence," he retorted, the acid note strong.

"Just so," Ottilia agreed, adding, "It looks excessively heavy."

She gestured towards the ladder and threw a questioning glance at her husband. Francis bent to test the truth of this. Going to the centre, he took hold of the wooden bars to either side and lifted. Ottilia saw the muscle strain under his coat sleeves. The ladder came up a foot or two, and then Francis set it down without comment.

Ottilia raised her brows. "Could one person carry it?"

"A strong man might, with difficulty."

She glanced at Uddington, but he offered nothing by way of embellishment. "Well, I think we have seen enough."

Back in the shop, Ottilia adopted a tone of deliberate friendliness. "You have been most cooperative, Mr. Uddington, and I thank you."

He had made for the front door with alacrity and was engaged in drawing back the bolt. Completing his task, he turned and gave a tiny ironic bow.

"There is little point in my refusing to assist you."

"And every gain."

He chose not to answer this directly, head high as he regarded her through the lens of his spectacles. "Was there anything else, my lady?"

Ottilia adopted the lightest of tones. "Why yes, Mr. Uddington. Since the whole village appears to make free with your ladder, am I to take it you possess the only one long enough to reach the beams of the smithy roof?"

"The only one in the centre of the village, yes. The thatcher has one even longer, but he lives a half mile outside."

"Too far to carry, or to risk being seen," Francis suggested.

A derisive look entered the merchant's features. "None would quibble at the sight of my ladder being carried anywhere in the village."

Francis's brows snapped together. "How convenient."

Ottilia looked at her spouse. "It might be worth a general question at the Cock."

He nodded. "I'll set Ryde onto it."

"No mention of the ladder, mind," she warned once they were safely outside and out of earshot of the merchant. "We don't want to alert the murderer. Let Ryde merely enquire if anyone was wakeful the night before Duggleby died."

"You suppose the preparations to the roof must have been done then?"

"Don't you? Any earlier and someone might have noticed."

Light dawned in her spouse's face. "And the ladder couldn't have been taken during the day. But will it suffice you to know merely that someone was awake?"

"Yes, for once I have them, I will drag out just what I wish to know."

Francis had laughed. "I'll wager you will, unscrupulous wretch that you are."

Regarding Uddington in the church now, where he sat in a side pew with the men who had acted as pallbearers, Ottilia recalled how eager he had been to see them off the premises. Yet he was, had he only known, rapidly shifting down her list of possible suspects, particularly since his ladder was freely available to anyone in the village.

Her eyes refocused on the congregation as Ottilia tuned in once again to the vicar's voice.

"And why," the Reverend Kinnerton was saying, "beholdest thou the mote that is in thy brother's eye, but perceivest not the beam that is in thine own eye?"

With which, the villagers once again looked sideways at one another. Never mind motes and beams, Ottilia thought. What price suspicion? Could it be that one of these had borrowed Uddington's ladder? Could Uddington have slept through such a theft? One could not drag or carry a ladder of that size without a deal of noise.

Francis had reckoned that it would take a strong man, or perhaps two. Tisbury or Farmer Staxton perhaps? Her eyes ran over the party from the Cock and Bottle, all of whom looked to have donned their Sunday best for the occasion.

Molly Tisbury, still sporting a bruised and swollen nose along with puffed-up eyes, had partially concealed the dismaying picture under a black veil that fell from a poke bonnet. She was done up fine in black bombazine, frilled and beribboned. She was fidgety, Ottilia noted, her eyes tending to dart around, and little shivers shaking her frame now and then. One could scarcely blame her, with the shadow of Cassie's vision hanging over her head.

Her husband was also in black, his breeches and countrified frock coat straining a little over his beefy frame. He was flanked by Will the tapster, who had donned a dark coat for the occasion over his working clothes. On Molly's other side sat Bessy the maid, her apron discarded and a black shawl covering her blue cotton gown, and wearing a discontented expression under the regulation mobcap.

For this last, young Patty of the Blue Pig was to blame, as Ottilia knew. The Pakefields' maid was seated on the other side of the aisle and well back from the front benches since Hannah, disfigured from yesterday's contretemps, had chosen to steer well clear of the Tisburys. Patty's nose was in the air, her quarrel with Bessy doubtless in the forefront of her mind.

After yesterday's catfight, there had been little opportunity to glean much more than had been extracted in the interviews with the Tisburys and Uddington. Ryde's probing having yielded results, however, Ottilia had ventured towards the back premises of the Cock this morning, hunting down the chambermaid. She had come upon the two girls engaged in all-out warfare. Unlike their respective mistresses, they were at least confining themselves to words, albeit noisy and vituperative.

"You shan't say as you be promised," Patty was shouting as Ottilia came around the corner of the house, "for I know as Will bain't said as much."

Bessy came back strongly, both words and attitude almost a carbon copy of Molly, her mistress. "Oh? Oh? And how be you knowing what he say or don't say? Fly on the wall, be you? Spider more like, I be thinking. Aye, and with poison in all them eyes as you be seeing with what you hadn't ought."

"If'n you mean as I seen you a-kissing of my Will," snapped Patty, arms akimbo and red in her freckled face, "you be right for once."

"Your Will, is it? I'd like fine to see his ring on your finger, that I would. Nor I won't nor Domesday."

"Nor you won't see it on yours, neither, not if I know it you won't."

Bessy's red cheeks suffused even more at this, and Ottilia thought it prudent to intervene.

"Dear me, children. Will you come to blows over a fellow who is clearly not fit for either of you?"

Both maids whipped around to confront her, and two angry faces struggled hopelessly to recover a semblance of demure servitude. Ottilia smiled at them equally.

"A man who would play you off one against the other is not worth fighting over, my dears."

Bessy glanced at Patty, who steadfastly refused to meet her gaze.

Instead she lifted her chin at Ottilia. "Bain't nowt, m'am. What be you wanting?"

"I came to find Bessy. But since you are here, Patty, I also have a question for you."

"Aye?"

There was insolence both in the tone and the questioning look, but Ottilia forbore to comment upon this.

"Do you happen to know, Patty, how it was that the village came to hear about Mrs. Dale's latest vision?"

If the girl's cheeks had been flushed before, they now became positively crimson. Quick fright showed in her eyes and was swiftly followed by fury.

"Who be saying as I told it?"

"Did you?"

Patty fisted her hands on her hips, glaring. "Never said owt to no one."

Ottilia kept her gaze steady on Patty's face, although she could see Bessy's eyes growing round with apprehension as her fingers fiddled with her apron. Guilt at having passed on the ghoulish tale? Or at having eavesdropped on her own account?

"No one at all?" Ottilia prompted.

Patty's gaze dropped, and one leather-shod toe scuffed at the turf. A mutter barely reached Ottilia's ears.

"I might've said it to Will."

Ottilia sighed with satisfaction. "Ah, I see."

The girl's eyes came up, fierce now as they turned on Bessy. "But none other, so help me. Bain't knowing if'n Will told it, but if'n he did, I know who be passing it along."

Ottilia watched Bessy's cheeks suffuse. "Oh? Oh? Meaning me, I suppose? Bain't me as said owt, you fussock! Not as Will bain't told me, for as he would, seeing as I be his sweetheart."

"That you bain't," Patty began, squaring up again.

"Peace!" said Ottilia sharply, stepping between them. "That will do, the both of you. If neither of you know the fellow well enough to realise how long-tongued is your Will, then I can only say that you are one as moon-eyed as the other."

Neither maid appeared to relish this comment, but each continued to glare at the other, though both refrained from taking issue with Ottilia. She became brisk.

"Now then, Patty, run along, if you please. I want a word with Bessy. In private."

For a moment it seemed as if the girl would refuse to leave the field to her rival. But Ottilia's calm stare had its effect, and she went off with lagging steps, looking back a couple of times as if she suspected herself to be under discussion. In fact Ottilia's mind was on matters far other than lovelorn rivalry.

"Bessy," she began at once, "I want you to cast your mind back to the night before the blacksmith Duggleby died."

The maid blinked, plainly mystified by this turn. "The night afore?"

"Just so."

A frown creased the girl's plump forehead. "Sunday night, you mean?"

"Yes, Sunday night," Ottilia said patiently. "I understand you were wakeful. Do you remember?"

Bessy grimaced. "Aye, I do, m'am, for as I woke and couldn't sleep no more for an age."

"And you heard something?"

The girl nodded. "Aye, summat I did, nor I can't rightly say what it be."

"At what time was this, do you know?"

Bessy's round-eyed look screwed instead into concentration. "Bain't like as it be more'n two of the clock, m'am, though the village were quiet-like."

Ottilia dropped lightly into the tone of easy camaraderie

she found so useful with the lower orders. "What did you hear, Bessy?"

"Voice a-cursing," said Bessy promptly. "Nor it bain't the master coughing and cursing as he do of a nighttime when he wakes too full of ale. Out of doors it be."

Ottilia did not speak, merely eyeing the girl in a considering way that she knew would have its effect. Sure enough, in a moment Bessy piped up again, embellishing her tale.

"Grunting and cursing it be. Bain't none too long, passing behind the house it be." The girl's brows drew together. "There were a thump. Loud it be, for as I dessay that be what woke me."

"Thank you, Bessy, that is most helpful," said Ottilia, satisfied.

Bessy frowned. "I don't know that, m'am, for as it bain't told you owt."

Ottilia smiled. "Ah, but it has, Bessy."

The girl looked interested, but Ottilia did not enlighten her further. She was tempted to bid Bessy not to throw her heart away on Will the tapster, but she refrained, having no faith in the power of words to dissuade any maiden sighing for love. Although if the truth be told, Ottilia suspected that this vying for the fellow's attentions with Patty might be the glue that held her affections so firmly attached.

Besides, it was scarcely part of her function to be interfering with the love tangles of the locals. She had other fish to fry. And the first task was to discover if her suspicion was correct.

"One thing more, Bessy."

"Aye, m'am?"

"You remember you kindly showed me the place where Duggleby's body lay, that first day?"

A wary look crept into the plump cheeks, and Ottilia instantly knew she had guessed right. Bessy was having difficulty meeting her gaze. Ottilia softened her tone.

"There is no need to look so guilty, my dear. Your curiosity was natural, and I don't blame you for listening."

"I never—"

Ottilia put up a warning finger. "Don't lie to me, Bessy. I am perfectly sure Mr. Pilton did not talk of his conversation with us, and yet your master and mistress knew he had told us of the fight between your master and the blacksmith."

Bessy's round cheeks were growing pink, and she began to look shamefaced, dropping her gaze to the ground as she muttered her defence.

"Thought as they had ought to know."

"I understand. But the unfortunate result of your speaking out, Bessy, was to make Mrs Tisbury upset and suspicious, which helped to build the quarrel between your mistress and Mrs. Pakefield. Do you see?"

The girl nodded, her expression now troubled. Ottilia thought she had said enough. Bessy seemed a trifle more inclined to listen to her conscience than Patty, whose indiscretion was likely more damaging. Besides, Ottilia could not forget her own culpability in that quarrel. She smiled at the girl.

"Thank you again for your help, Bessy."

With which, Ottilia left her and betook herself to one of the little row of cottages situated on this side of the brook, just opposite the ruined forge across the water.

It took a few moments for her knock at the door to be answered. She heard halting steps within. The door opened, and an elderly fellow squinted up at her, holding the doorjamb for support.

"Good day to you, Mr. Wagstaff."

One of his uncouth cackles sounded. "If'n it bain't the Lady Fan. Come for as to ask if I done for Duggleby now, have you?"

Ottilia smiled. "I will ask, if you wish to tell me."

"Bain't no sense in asking. If'n I had, I'd say nowt on it to you."

"Very true," Ottilia agreed coolly. "As it happens, I have not come for that."

Mr. Wagstaff reached up a finger yellowed from tobacco and scratched his ear. "Nor you bain't took to visions, neither, like that there Mrs. Dale. Not if I know it."

Ottilia sighed. "I am sorry your daughter has been obliged to hear about that."

The old man snorted. "If'n my Moll be daft enough to think on such drivel, more fool her. Take no account of such meself."

"Well, you should," Ottilia said tartly.

The rheumy eyes sharpened. "Aye? And for why?"

"Oh, not for anything Mrs. Dale might do, for she is no witch."

"Bain't no need to tell me so. Her've no more magic in her than the man in the moon."

"Just so. But there is a murderer at large, Mr. Wagstaff. One who has already used Mrs. Dale's earlier vision to his advantage."

For an instant, a startled frown drew the old man's sparse eyebrows together. Then he let out a cackle. "Daft you be, my Lady Fan, if'n you think as how any be wishful to be doing my daughter like Duggleby. A fool her be right enough, but her bain't a bad 'un. Duggleby now, he've a basinful of enemies, nor there bain't many as be sorry as he've gone."

It was plain to Ottilia that the fellow belonged to that ilk of person who made up his mind and would not be shifted. She changed tack.

"Which brings me to the matter at hand, Mr. Wagstaff. I understand you were awake in the night hours on the night before Duggleby was killed."

The ancient eyes narrowed again. "Aye. Told that man of yourn last night."

"Just so. But you did not tell him whether you heard anything."

"Like as?"

"Anything out of the ordinary. I am not talking of sounds in the night that you might expect. Did it seem to you, for example, that anyone was abroad in the early hours?"

Mr. Wagstaff was grinning. "Fellows making for the fields like? 'Course I heard 'em. Staxton and his boys be on the farm afore dawn, and half the village be shakin' a leg by five or thereabouts."

Ottilia did not allow herself to be irritated by this display of superiority. "Yes, but I am talking of earlier than that. Around two of the clock perhaps?"

"How be as I know? Might've been asleep."

This time Ottilia did not trouble to reply. She merely looked at the man and waited. Aware that he was inclined to take a contrary view as a matter of course, she was yet hopeful that the notion might jog something in his memory, if he was permitted to think for a moment rather than feeling prompted to scorn at her expense.

He champed on an invisible bit for a while, eyeing her in a suspenseful way, like a bird hopeful of crumbs. Then he sniffed, and once again a bony finger scratched at an ear.

"Might've heard summat."

Ottilia raised her brows, refusing to be drawn. Was that respect dawning in his eye? He slumped a little, leaning against the doorjamb.

"Bain't as I can say what time it be, mind," he said at length on a warning note. "But footsteps be a-dragging one time."

"Ah."

Brightening at this little show of interest, the ancient resumed. "Nowt more'n that and a-passing close."

"In which direction?"

"T'wards the bridge," said Wagstaff, who then looked surprised, as if he had not intended to say as much.

Ottilia kept her eyes steady on his face. "Anything else?"

His brows snapped together. "Breathin', heavy-like."

It was plain he had little understanding of how these

extra details came to be in his memory. Intelligent as he was, Ottilia reflected, he lacked the capacity to observe his fellow man. Too busy exercising his wit at the expense of others, no doubt. Ottilia had often had occasion to note that people were apt to dismiss their ability to recall things, when in fact they invariably had a perfect picture of events available, if they were but given the opportunity to examine it.

She probed a little. "I don't suppose there was a thump? Or cursing?"

But Mr. Wagstaff had shot his bolt. "Nowt more I can tell you, my Lady Fan."

Despite the clear irony of the appellation, Ottilia gave him a friendly smile. "It makes no matter. What you have told me is enough."

He gave his characteristic high-pitched laugh. "Who be it, then? Who done for Duggleby?"

Ottilia had given Wagstaff a noncommittal answer then, she remembered, her attention now returning to the church, where the congregation had bowed their heads in prayer. A hymn was next sung, and although she joined in, she took a moment to look across at Lady Ferrensby, to whom she had been briefly presented before the service began.

The great lady of the village was correctly attired in black, if in a fashion somewhat outdated, but she wore no veil, and her strong but attractive features were clear in sight where she stood for the hymn. Ottilia had learned from Mrs. Radlett that young Lord Ferrensby was rarely to be found at his seat, being an active member of parliament and much given to sporting pursuits. It was therefore left to his mother to oversee the workings of the estate, including the activities of Witherley village.

As Ottilia surveyed the woman, something in the set of Lady Ferrensby's features reminded her of Cassie Dale. Abruptly she recalled the oddity of Cassie's conduct yesterday. It had been put out of her head by subsequent events, but now she recalled in detail how the girl had looked when she had spoken of Mr. Dale. A suspicion darted into Ottilia's head, and she could not forbear glancing up to the minstrel's gallery. But there was no sign of the earlier peeping figure. Ottilia looked back at Lady Ferrensby. Was Cassie Dale merely a protégée? Or was there more to this relationship than met the eye?

Chapter 10

Hustled by an irate Tabitha, Cassie hurried her steps along the road leading away from the church and back towards the green.

"High and low I searched for you, Miss Cassie. I've been worried sick."

"You need not have been," Cassie snapped. "Anyone must suppose me to be a moonling, the way you carry on, Tabby. I was well hidden."

"Hidden? Yes, so well hidden that your face was the first thing I see when I finally thought of going into the church. I wouldn't have done neither, only it suddenly come to me you'd be in the very place you'd been told not to go."

Cassie pulled tighter on the concealing shawl she'd worn about her head and shoulders and stepped up her pace still more, as if she might shake off her maid along with the words she did not wish to hear.

"Must you rush so?" protested Tabitha, panting a little. "I'm puffed enough with tramping up them little stairs to fetch you off that there gallery, thank you very much."

"It is your own fault," Cassie said low-voiced. "I did not ask you to come."

"No, you give me the slip like the naughty girl you always was."

Cassie halted abruptly, turning on her maid as the fire leapt into her bosom. "I am not a child, Tabby! I wish you will stop treating me as one. It is my life, God help me, and I will make my own decisions."

Tabitha's lips tightened, and Cassie saw the hurt in her eyes. Her heart softened, but she fought against the urge to back down. Had it not been for Aidan Kinnerton, she felt she might well have given in. The pastor was the first person ever to speak to her as if she had a mind of her own. His manner towards her made her feel comfortable and normal— almost unknown in the catalogue of her days. She had been drawn to the service partly out of the nagging sense of guilt under which she laboured, but Cassie was honest enough to know that by far the major attraction had been Aidan Kinnerton. She had wanted to see how he conducted himself when he addressed the villagers for the first time, and under such difficult circumstances. Well, let her not cavil. She had wanted to see him, to watch him, to drink him in. And she had not been disappointed.

She had walked on as these thoughts teemed in her head, but at length Tabitha's silence beside her nagged into her conscience. She groped for the maid's hand and held it tightly.

"I did not mean to carp at you, Tabby. Forgive me."

Tabitha's fingers squeezed hard. "Nor I, Miss Cassie." A sigh escaped her. "I wish I might forget as I had charge of you when you were nobbut a little slip of a thing."

Cassie's heart swelled. "I owe you a great deal."

"No, you don't," Tabby argued gruffly. "Couldn't help myself growing too fond, and that's a fact. Such a passionate little soul you were then, Miss Cassie, and you ain't changed a bit."

A wild laugh was drawn from Cassie. "Passionate? And have I not cause, Tabby?"

"All I know is it's in your nature, and it ain't never going to be no different, no matter what anyone says."

Except that she was different. Or at least she felt different in the company of Aidan Kinnerton. How well he spoke, with a voice as strong and courageous as his heart. How odd to think of him thus, when in ordinary life he was so extremely gentle and softly spoken. If only it were possible . . .

But here Cassie's thoughts suffered a check. The impossibility struck her anew, and resolutely she thrust down the yearning. She must not think of it. Lady Ferrensby might scheme, but Cassie would die before she brought shame upon the kindest man she had ever encountered.

"Mrs. Hawes!"

The call was tentative, but Cassie halted as Tabitha did, looking round. A youthful girl, pale cheeked and nervous under a mobcap, was hovering at a little distance. She looked vaguely familiar, and her plain gown of grey cotton topped with an apron marked her for one of the maids abounding in the village, this being the chief source of paid employment for young girls hereabouts. Everyone needed a maid, although Cassie could not immediately recall whom this one served.

It was plain Tabitha had no such difficulty. "Young Alice, is it? What do you want with me, girl?"

Alice twisted her hands together, glancing apprehensively at Cassie. "It be private-like."

Tabitha grunted but beckoned her over. "If it's about Mrs. Dale, which I'll be bound it is, you'd best come right out with it before her. I can't abide secrets."

The girl ventured a little closer, her eyes going from one to the other. "If'n you say so, Mrs. Hawes, only bain't wishful to say owt as Mrs. Dale won't like."

Cassie sighed. "You may say what you wish, Alice. There

is very little said in this village concerning me that is not displeasing."

Alice dropped a curtsy but addressed herself exclusively to Tabitha. "It be this way, Mrs. Hawes."

Tabitha stopped her. "Just a minute. Why aren't you at the funeral?"

"Miss Beeleigh sent me to mind the Duggleby boy, seeing as her told Mrs. Duggleby as it be too harsh to make him go, he being no more'n six year. Only Jenny be back now and I've to make the dinner."

"So what is it you wanted to tell me?"

Alice cast another of her nervous looks at Cassie and twisted her fingers again. "I were with Miss Beeleigh afore the funeral, a-carrying the basket for Uddington's, when her be up to Cock."

Cassie's stomach clenched. She knew Miss Beeleigh obeyed no niceties of social custom, should she feel the need to flout them. It would not be the first time, as Sam had often reported, that this redoubtable lady felt it incumbent upon her to stalk into the tavern and ring a peal over the inhabitants. She could not forbear asking.

"What did she say to them all?"

The maid looked even more apprehensive, and Tabitha had to apply a spur.

"Go on, girl."

Alice took a deep breath. "Miss Beeleigh were saying as her'd heard as there be fool talk of stakes and burning. Her said as her hoped as her wouldn't hear more of that, nor no more fool talk of witchery, nor her wouldn't stop at calling in Pilton, neither. Her said if'n any fool were ready to have his head blown off, her were ready with her musket."

Tabitha hissed in a breath. "Why can't she leave well alone?"

"Trying to help Mrs. Dale her be," protested Alice defensively.

"Yes, and are you going to stand there and tell me the likes

of Tisbury and Staxton, not to say that maundering old Wagstaff, ain't talked back at her?"

Pink tinged the girl's cheeks. "Well, that be why I thought
as I ought to warn you, Mrs. Hawes. Mr. Tisbury come back
like a lion he did. Said as how Miss Beeleigh hadn't no say
over the village. Nor she bain't to bring her musket up to
Cock for as he'd have Pilton on her instead."

"And what had Miss Beeleigh to say to that?" demanded
Tabitha in that tone Cassie knew of old which signalled a rise
of fury.

Alice went pink again, looking shamefaced. "You know
as how her be, if'n any speak agin her. Give him snuff, did
Miss Beeleigh. Said if'n Mr. Tisbury weren't a nodcock he'd
see as it were foolishness to do owt with that there Lady Fan
about the village. Said as Lady Fan be looking to have someone's head, and not just for doing Duggleby, and if'n Mr.
Tisbury bain't careful, her'd have his."

Tabitha was frowning. "What did she mean—and not
just for doing Duggleby?"

"That be Mr. Wagstaff's question and all. Miss Beeleigh
said as how that there Lady Fan were all for Mrs. Dale, like
a champion. And Mr. Wagstaff come back and said as all the
world be knowing that. But Miss Beeleigh ups and says for
all of her, it be no surprise if'n all the world bain't saying as
Lady Fan be a witch and all, for as Witherley be full of nin-
compoops."

For a moment Tabitha did not speak. Cassie felt both surprised and gratified to find Miss Beeleigh had taken up the
cudgels in her defence in this way. It was wholly unexpected,
for she hardly knew the woman, having had very little con-
verse with her and her friends. Mr. Netherburn had been
kind enough to visit her on occasion, but Cassie had formed
the belief that the two ladies did not approve of her, for although they were pleasant enough when she had met them
at the Blue Pig, neither had gone out of their way to make a
friend of the outcast Cassie knew herself to be.

"Well, Alice, I suppose I must thank you," Tabitha said, her tone gruff.

The maid flushed, and her eyes registered disappointment as they flicked over to Cassie. "I only said it for to warn Mrs. Dale to take care. Mr. Tisbury be wild over it. And Miss Beeleigh said to me after as there be no knowing what might happen. But Miss Beeleigh said as her be on the lookout for trouble."

With which assurance, Alice glanced again at Cassie, dropped another curtsy, and sped off in the direction of Miss Beeleigh's house, which lay at a little distance past the Blue Pig.

"We'll go home and bolt the door," said Tabitha firmly. "But I know one thing. We'd best have Sam fetch down Lady Francis to the cottage tomorrow morning, so's she can hear all that."

Since it was not incumbent upon her to attend at the graveside, Ottilia left this duty to Francis and waited for the congregation to file out before taking a leisurely look around the church. It was of early date, one of these squat little stone buildings, with arched bays down either side of the nave containing memorials and a few crudely carved figures, plus a charmingly simple rose window on the east wall behind the altar.

Among the commemorative plaques set into the walls, she was interested to discover several village names, in addition to the plethora of departed Ferrensbys. The Pakefields looked to have come down in the world, while Miss Beeleigh's family were clearly long-term tenants and Mr. Netherburn was seen to be a widower. How convenient for the widow Radlett, if she could manage to snare him.

"You did not fancy the graveside, either, Lady Francis?"

Startled, Ottilia turned to find the woman behind her, as if her thoughts had conjured her. She was correctly attired in black for the occasion, but the unlikely golden curls still rioted under a very fussy bonnet. There was, however, a wary look in her eyes, and Ottilia wondered at it. She gave no sign, merely smiling in a friendly way.

"I cannot feel it is my place to follow the coffin."

Mrs. Radlett gave a little shiver. "I do so hate the sight of that empty hole. It seems so final somehow."

"We are fortunate perhaps in being female, in that we are not obliged to attend such affairs if we don't wish to do so."

"No, and thank heavens for it. Though Alethea was insistent we should put in an appearance in the church."

Ottilia noted this peculiarity on Miss Beeleigh's part with interest. "Indeed? She felt it as a duty?"

"Oh, Alethea must always partake of what is afoot, you must know." A brittle laugh tinkled out of the widow's mouth. "She is forever stigmatising me for a gossip, but at least I do not take it upon myself to interfere in the villagers' lives. Nor to tell them what they should or should not do. She can be very fierce with them."

Ottilia digested this in silence for a moment. Then she gestured to one of the plaques. "I see that the Beeleighs have been here for a long time. Perhaps Miss Beeleigh cherishes a sense of responsibility on that account?"

"As to that, it may well be so," said Evelina grudgingly. "If only she would not be so very . . ." She faded out, looking a trifle guilty.

"Dictatorial?" suggested Ottilia, a hint of mischief in her voice.

The widow sighed out a breath of half laughter. "It is too bad of me to speak ill of her, when she has been so very good to me."

"My dear Mrs. Radlett, even those we cherish most may on occasion drive us to distraction. It would be foolish to pretend otherwise."

Evelina fell to nodding, setting her chins in motion. "Very true indeed. Why, only the other day, I declare I could readily have killed——!" She broke off, throwing a hand to her mouth, horrified eyes peeping over the top of it.

Ottilia had to laugh. "Dear me, Mrs. Radlett. It comes to something when the simplest remark may be misinterpreted merely because of events. What did Miss Beeleigh do to warrant this murderous inclination on your part?"

A faint little gurgle was heard behind the hand, and the popping eyes softened into laughter, albeit briefly. Then the widow set the hand instead to one side of her mouth and leaned forward in a confidential way. In a bid to encourage her, Ottilia followed suit.

"She made my tisane the other night, for she insisted I was looking peaky. And I am very nearly sure she put laudanum in it, and I cannot bear the stuff. It makes me feel horrid the next day."

Now thoroughly on the alert, Ottilia did not hesitate. "And did you? Feel horrid, I mean?"

"Oh, dreadful. My head was fuzzy, and I could not think. I had to go to bed in the end, which was why I heard nothing of what had occurred at the smithy until the next morning."

Ottilia eyed the woman with no little degree of suspicion in her mind. Was not this a little too pat? Could Mrs. Radlett have got wind of the queries made at the Cock about the night before Duggleby's death? If so, why should she seek to throw her friend into question? Or was it a ploy designed to assure Ottilia that she had been hors de combat and therefore unable to have carried out the necessary preparations in the smithy?

How much of what had been discovered about that night had she discussed with Miss Beeleigh? They both knew of the hacked beam and that a ladder had been in use. Ottilia found it hard to believe that the widow Radlett had put two and two together for herself. Was she afraid of being accused?

"Shall we walk together to the Blue Pig?" Ottilia suggested pleasantly. "I daresay Miss Beeleigh and Mr. Netherburn will join us there."

Mrs. Radlett fell in with alacrity as Ottilia set off down the aisle, but she entered a caveat nonetheless. "Will not Lord Francis expect to find you here?"

"Oh no. I told him I might wander back on my own."

The sun hit brightly as they exited the church, and Ottilia put up a hand to shade her eyes. A few of the villagers had begun to filter back towards the green, so it seemed safe to assume that the graveside ceremony was nearly at an end.

"Have you yet formed any opinion as to who did the deed, Lady Francis?"

Ottilia had a feeling that Mrs. Radlett had been longing to ask this question. Whether she did so out of curiosity or for a purpose of her own was a moot point.

"I'm afraid it is not near as simple as I had hoped. There are many factors to be taken into account, and far too many people who cherished a grudge against the blacksmith."

"Yes, but you cannot think anyone who had a grudge could be guilty of such a horrid thing," uttered the widow on a note of near panic.

So that was it. She had remembered that Ottilia was privy to the details about her dog. No doubt, had she had the forethought to imagine herself to be potentially suspect, she would have refrained from speaking of it. If she supposed she could thus easily be let off the hook, however, she was mistaken.

"Dear me, no, Mrs. Radlett. But one must always look for a motive. It is unfortunate that Duggleby was a man uniformly disliked by his fellows. It makes for a very wide field indeed."

Ottilia glanced at the widow as she spoke and was almost betrayed into a laugh. The creature's face had fallen mightily, and she looked decidedly out of countenance.

"I must say I shall be glad of a cup of coffee," Ottilia said pleasantly, strolling gently on just as if nothing untoward had occurred. "I do hope Hannah is sufficiently recovered by now to be able to resume her duties as hostess."

Mrs. Radlett appeared to have difficulty in putting words together. "Oh. Yes, I am sure. Or, no. She may have stayed for the burial, for the sake of appearances, you know. But Patty must have returned by now."

"Patty, of course. A girl much given to throwing her tongue about, I fear."

"Oh, they all do so," said the widow in a tetchy tone. "Though young Alice is a good child on the whole."

"Alice?"

"Alethea's maid of work. Poor child, she tries so very hard to please."

Yes, Ottilia could well imagine that Miss Beeleigh made an exacting mistress. Any maid of hers must be crushed beyond bearing, unless she were of the ilk of Patty or Bessy. Evelina's "good child" epithet argued otherwise.

By the time they reached the Blue Pig, Mrs. Radlett appeared to have recovered somewhat from her erstwhile confusion. She entered with Ottilia and sank down into one of the coffee room chairs with a sigh of relief, putting a hand to her bosom.

"I fear the walk has tired you, Mrs. Radlett," said Ottilia, moving to pick up the brass handbell on the table.

The widow nodded. "It is my heart. I am not strong, you know."

Another ploy to plead innocence? Ottilia replied suitably and was glad to see Patty enter the room.

"Coffee, if you please, Patty. Or would you prefer tea, Mrs. Radlett?"

"If it is not too much trouble," replied the other, glancing apprehensively at the maid.

Patty tossed her head. "No trouble. Cook only got dinner to prepare, after all."

Ottilia sighed as the door closed with a snap behind her. "That girl wants manners as well as discretion."

Mrs. Radlett's glance came swiftly in her direction. "Discretion?"

"I am afraid so. We have Patty to thank for the world being apprised of Cassie Dale's latest vision. Not to mention poor Molly Tisbury. She is terrified, of course."

A shudder shook the widow's frame. "I am not surprised. It terrifies me, and I am not even the supposed victim."

But was she the victim's intended assailant? A pity Cassie's visions did not encompass the action of the deed as well as the aftermath, Ottilia reflected, sighing. It would make her task so much easier.

By the time her husband entered the coffee room, Ottilia was heartily wishing Mrs. Radlett otherwhere. Had she said anything to the purpose, it might have been worth the pain of endurance, but the widow confined herself to a long and excessively dull history of her late husband's prolonged and lingering illness, which had dissipated the little fortune he had on medical assistance. While sympathetic, Ottilia could drum up no enthusiasm for a tale uniformly depressing, and she hailed the advent of Mr. Netherburn and Miss Beeleigh with unqualified relief.

Hardly had the newcomers had time to drink the regulatory cup of coffee, however, when Francis came in, accompanied, to Ottilia's surprise and gratification, by Lady Ferrensby.

Before anyone else could say anything, Mrs. Radlett was off.

"Dear Lady Ferrensby! Gracious, is it you indeed? I thought you would come, for I felt sure you must wish to take advantage of the opportunity to increase your so brief acquaintance with Lady Francis."

The lady moved gracefully into the room and extended a hand to Ottilia, who had risen upon seeing her.

"Very true, Mrs. Radlett," came drily from her mouth in a low and musical voice. A keen hazel gaze met Ottilia's. "I am a trifle tardy, Lady Francis, and I fear my welcome comes too late to be of the least use. From what I hear, I imagine you have already developed an ardent distaste for Witherley."

Ottilia laughed. "Not in the least, ma'am. My husband will vouch for it that I have come by my deserts, for I blundered in out of sheer curiosity."

The business of making space for the lady to sit down, along with the general greetings and murmurings over the funeral, gave Ottilia the opportunity to appraise the patroness of the village more closely than she had been able to do in the church.

She saw a mature but handsome countenance, topped off with luxuriant locks just silvering along the temples and caught under a feathered black bonnet. Her air of assurance spoke volumes, and her greeting had impressed with a mix of common sense and humour. Here at least Ottilia might hope for an intelligent and unbiased appraisal of events.

It was plain the widow Radlett was anxious to make one of the gathering, for she did not hesitate to enter upon a matter for conversation.

"What do you think of your new man, Lady Ferrensby? The vicar, I mean. I thought he did very well indeed, did not you?"

The lady's brows rose. "Kinnerton? Oh, I think he will do."

Mrs. Radlett's face fell. "Is that all?"

Lady Ferrensby smiled. "My dear Mrs. Radlett, you cannot expect me to pronounce in public upon the poor fellow's opening performance without speaking to him first upon the matter. But if it will make you happy, let me assure you I think he has shown himself to be an estimable young man."

"Oh, indeed," agreed the widow, nodding frantically. "Such a tower of strength as he has been in these dark days."

"Yes, to Cassie Dale," came on a scoffing note from Miss Beeleigh. She ignored Mr. Netherburn's pointed cough, and did not wait for anyone's response to this, but lost no time in frustrating her friend's design. "Come, Evelina. No need for us to stay and do the pretty."

"Oh, but I—"

"Evelina! Her ladyship don't want us cluttering up the place. Here to talk to the Fanshawes."

She glanced at Lady Ferrensby as she spoke, but the latter made no effort to gainsay her despite a pleading look from the widow. She sat in elegant silence, evidently placing trust in Miss Beeleigh's ability to prise her reluctant companion from the room.

Seeing no help was forthcoming from that quarter, Mrs. Radlett next cast her gaze upon Mr. Netherburn, whose greeting of the newcomer had been more than ordinarily elaborate. But the redoubtable Miss Beeleigh was quick to block this silent appeal.

"You, too, Horace. Make yourself useful and escort us."

There could be but one answer to this, and words of farewell being kept to a minimum, it was not many minutes before Ottilia and Francis were alone with Lady Ferrensby.

"Wine, ma'am?" offered Francis, moving to pick up the handbell.

The lady waved a hand. "I want nothing, I thank you." Her gaze came across to Ottilia, who had taken a seat opposite. "Would you both dine with me tomorrow evening, Lady Francis?"

Ottilia lifted her brows. "Dear me, ma'am, is that why you came?"

A flicker of amusement showed in the hazel gaze. "Ostensibly."

Behind her Francis laughed and came to take a chair. "We thank you, ma'am. A kind thought, but such subterfuge is unnecessary. How can we serve you?"

Lady Ferrensby looked at him. "I should very much appreciate an account of your activities. Preferably unvarnished."

Her eye left Francis upon the last phrase, and Ottilia responded to an unspoken question. "I daresay you may have been given a much garbled version."

"Undoubtedly."

The dry note was pronounced, and Ottilia warmed to the woman. "Then I think we may untangle things a little." She put up a warning finger. "However, I cannot say I am at all sanguine about any possible conclusion at this stage."

Lady Ferrensby nodded. "That is understood." She smiled, catching Francis's eye. "You may be interested to learn that I am acquainted with Justice Ingham."

Ottilia jumped, casting an apprehensive glance at Francis, for Sir Thomas Ingham, the Bow Street Justice, had been very much involved in last year's events, and she knew her spouse hated such reminders.

But he was laughing. "I'll wager he sang my wife's praises."

"He was indeed voluble on the subject," confirmed her ladyship. "He gave me to understand that Mrs. Draycott, as I believe she was then, was instrumental in uncovering the truth."

"Instrumental? He did not know the half of it."

"Come, Fan," Ottilia protested, warmth rising to her cheeks, "pray don't exaggerate."

The look he threw her was intense. "If anything, I am understating the case, and you know it."

Ottilia let out an exasperated breath and turned to Lady Ferrensby. "Pray don't allow my husband's enthusiasm to raise your hopes too high, ma'am. I am by no means certain of a happy outcome in this case. There are far too many factors to be taken into account, and I cannot promise to unravel them satisfactorily."

Lady Ferrensby's intelligent gaze was compelling, with a gleam in its depth that was once again oddly reminiscent of Cassie Dale. Ottilia became doubly convinced there was something here to discover.

"Believe me, Lady Francis, I will be grateful for any light you may shed on the business, since I am forced to accept that Duggleby was indeed murdered. Until this occurrence, I had entertained the hope that Cassie—Mrs. Dale, I

mean—might settle into some promise of normality. But it
seems—"

She broke off, making, as Ottilia surmised, an attempt to
recover her former pose of calm insouciance. Was it a pose?
Or was she merely disturbed by present events?

"For that matter," Lady Ferrensby resumed, "it is distressing for everyone to be placed under suspicion of wrongdo-
ing." A sudden smile lightened her countenance. "And it
will hardly surprise you to learn of my lack of confidence in
Henbury."

Ottilia was obliged to laugh, while Francis emitted a derisive snort.

"The man's a nightmare. For my money, he will do little
but hamper the investigation."

"But we need him," Ottilia reminded him. She gave
Lady Ferrensby a rueful look. "I fear I have used him shame-
lessly, making pretence of his having asked me to institute
enquiries."

"Well, if anyone protests, you may say with truth that I
have asked you," said Lady Ferrensby tartly. "And it is no boast
to say that you will make more headway using my name."

"Excellent. Then it only remains to provide you with the
explanation you seek. But a moment of caution first."

She got up and went to the door. Glancing back into the
room, she put a finger to her lips and abruptly turned the
handle and jerked the door open. The hall was empty. Satisfied, she returned to her chair and noted Lady Ferrensby's
raised brows.

"I have discovered that young Patty rivals Bessy at the
Cock in a mutual penchant for Will the tapster. Patty is apt
to pass on anything of interest she may hear in this place."

"Such as the details of Cassie's last vision, I surmise?"

"Just so. We will, if you please, conduct our conversation
in lowered tones."

This being agreed, Ottilia proceeded to lay out as much

as she felt pertinent of what she had discovered to date, including her reading of Duggleby's character captured from what had been said by various members of the community. She left Francis to describe what had been found at the forge but spoke of Uddington's ladder and the possibility of someone having used it the night before.

"Then you are saying the murder was premeditated?" asked Lady Ferrensby, losing a little of her coolness of manner and looking a trifle upset.

"Things point that way, but I cannot be sure. One cannot rule out the possibility of the murder having been done first."

A little sigh escaped the lady. "You're right about Duggleby, at all events. The man was dissolute and a brute. If it were not for the manner of his death, the village would be well rid of him."

"So I gather," Ottilia agreed. "Though I fear the Tisburys are only one degree less repellent."

"Oh, Tisbury is not a bad fellow," said Lady Ferrensby, regaining a little of her earlier light manner.

"No, and I think I believe his version of his fight with the blacksmith," cut in Francis. "But that wife of his is another matter."

Lady Ferrensby nodded. "A termagant is Molly."

"And much to blame for her husband's temper, I imagine."

"That is so, Lord Francis, but not as much as her wretched father."

"Pa Wagstaff?"

Lady Ferrensby threw her eyes heavenwards. "Jeremiah fancies himself a wit and does not scruple to use the privilege of his years to exercise it at the expense of his unfortunate son-in-law, who is barred from taking any form of revenge. The result, I'm afraid, is that Tisbury takes it out on others."

Ottilia digested this. "Which suggests, if Tisbury did the deed, that it was in a moment of aberration."

"But he claims he would never have hit Duggleby from behind," objected Francis, "and I am inclined to believe him."

"In addition," said Ottilia, "do we deem him levelheaded enough to cover his tracks by bringing down the roof and starting a fire?"

"He does not lack intelligence," Francis said. "Though he is hardly in Uddington's league." His head turned. "What of him, Lady Ferrensby? Is he the kind of man to murder?"

A tiny pause drew Ottilia's attention. Then the woman shrugged eloquently. "How in the world can one know? He had reason enough, of course."

Ottilia eyed her with new interest. "His wife died recently, and it seems Duggleby may have attended the funeral."

The lady's brows drew sharply together. "You mean Uddington has held thoughts of revenge and waited his moment?"

Ottilia did not reply, confident that Lady Ferrensby would answer her own question. She glanced at Francis and gave an infinitesimal shake of her head. She noted from his narrowed gaze that he understood she wished him to keep silent.

At length Lady Ferrensby put her hands together and raised her fingers to her lips, letting her breath go. Then she dropped her clasped hands to the table and looked across at Ottilia.

"His is a sad case. He sold his heritage for gold, I'm afraid."

"And took his father-in-law's name. Yes, he told me as much. But he would not tell me his real identity."

Lady Ferrensby looked a little dismayed. "It is of trifling significance."

Ottilia's senses came alive. Was there something personal here? She did not speak, letting the silence work its way into the other lady's conscience. Lady Ferrensby unclasped her hands, and one set of gloved fingers drummed upon the table for a space. Becoming aware seemingly, she looked down, ceased to fidget, and splayed her fingers. An impatient exclamation escaped her.

"Oh, why dissemble? The fellow was a connection of my late husband."

"Ah, I see."

"Distantly," added the other on a sharp note.

"Far enough distant to allow for impartiality?" asked Ottilia straightly.

Lady Ferrensby's eyes flashed and sank again quickly. She gave a defeated shrug. "If you mean to imply that it will trouble me to find him out a murderer, then your answer is obvious."

Ottilia felt it politic to steer clear of this issue. "I take it that is why Uddington was able to set up his business in Witherley?"

Lady Ferrensby nodded. "I was but a bride at the time, but my husband wrote to Uddington senior to suggest it."

"Was that wise?" Francis broke in. "If the fellow had dropped out of his proper sphere, did it not present a difficulty to Lord Ferrensby to have him so close since he might not acknowledge him?"

The question was productive of another sigh. "I believe he felt it. But they say blood is thicker than water. We are all apt to make such errors on the altar of family loyalty."

Ottilia's ears pricked up again. Family? Was this a reference to Cassie Dale? Had Lady Ferrensby followed her husband's example of generosity and compassion? If so, what had befallen Cassie to make it necessary to hide her true identity?

Francis was still frowning, and Ottilia cast him a questioning glance. One eyebrow rose, and he turned back to Lady Ferrensby.

"Forgive my bluntness, ma'am, but Uddington's attitude seems to me highly suspect. So much so I was moved to warn my wife against having made a dangerous enemy."

"Dangerous?" repeated the other lady, startled.

"How else would you describe a killer? Especially if he feels he may be cornered."

Watching closely, Ottilia thought she read an instant of panic in Lady Ferrensby's eyes. Then it was veiled.

"What will you do if the murder is brought home to Uddington?" pursued Francis relentlessly.

"I do not know, Lord Francis," returned Lady Ferrensby on a tart note. "Nor do I propose to burden myself with the question unless it becomes necessary to do so."

"Then let us hope the blame will be found to lie elsewhere," said Ottilia soothingly. "There are, of course, other persons with reason to dislike Duggleby."

"Half the village, no doubt," snapped the other, her eyes sparking.

Ottilia said nothing, merely allowing her gaze to remain steady upon Lady Ferrensby's face. Francis, having cast a frustrated look at his wife, sat back.

In a moment or two, the heightened colour in Lady Ferrensby's cheeks died down. "I am more dismayed by all this than I had supposed." She gave a tiny smile. "I don't know what I expected. Perhaps that you had drawn a useful conclusion and found out some stranger was responsible."

Ottilia gave her a sympathetic smile. "I fear it rarely is a stranger."

"Count yourself fortunate," cut in Francis, an edge to his voice. "I was obliged to suspect my own brother."

A tiny gasp issued from Lady Ferrensby's throat. "Yes, I know. I beg your pardon, Lord Francis."

He shrugged, and Ottilia read his discomfort. She changed the subject. "What is your opinion of Bertha Duggleby, ma'am?"

"A sadly downtrodden creature," said the other at once. "I can't imagine she would have the strength, never mind the will, to raise a hand against her husband. You suspect her, then?"

The eager note did not escape Ottilia. It was plain that any other name than Uddington was acceptable to the great lady of the village. In the circumstances, Ottilia could not blame her.

"One must invariably look askance upon those closest to the victim," she said, with an apologetic glance at her husband as he winced. "In this case, there is a possible reason why Bertha might dispose of her husband."

"Which is?"

"Duggleby boasted to her of being in possession of a pot of gold, as she phrases it." She smiled at Lady Ferrensby's expression. "Yes, I was quite as sceptical. But it occurs to me the blacksmith might have been remembered in Mrs. Uddington's will."

"Gracious heavens!" Her ladyship was frowning. "It's true, as you said, that he is rumoured to have gone to the funeral."

"Or perhaps he was summoned to a reading of the will. He would not, I surmise, bruit the matter abroad for fear of Uddington coming to hear of it."

"Indeed, no." Lady Ferrensby gave a little shiver. "How macabre it all is!"

"And too close for comfort?" put in Francis, his tone rigid with the memories of last year. "I know just how you feel, ma'am."

"Thank you, Lord Francis. I must admit it comes as a shock to think there are several persons who might have wanted the dratted fellow dead."

"Just so," sighed Ottilia. "Suspicion must fall upon anyone with a grudge against the blacksmith. Including, ridiculous as it may seem, the widow Radlett."

A disbelieving laugh was surprised out of Lady Ferrensby. "Evelina? You are not serious? Why in the world would she want to murder Duggleby?"

"Revenge," said Ottilia stonily. "She believes Duggleby killed her dog. Or at least that he beat the animal half to death so that it had to be shot."

Lady Ferrensby stared. "Yes, but—I mean, I know of that, of course, but . . ." Her voice died, her imagination evidently boggling at the notion.

"You are thinking she could not have cut the beam, brought down the roof, and started the fire," said Ottilia in a matter-of-fact tone. "That is true. But someone might have done it for her."

"Once she had struck the man with a hammer," said Francis.

"Just so."

Lady Ferrensby was shaking her head. "No, this is fantastic. Who would she ask? Netherburn? At his age, the fellow is incapable of climbing a ladder. Nor is he discreet."

"Not Netherburn," Ottilia agreed. "But what of Uddington? Or, come to that, Miss Beeleigh?"

"Alethea Beeleigh? Now you are being absurd."

"Well, she told me she could replace a wheel on a coach," pursued Ottilia imperturbably. "It is not beyond the bounds of probability that she could climb a ladder and hack at a beam."

"Unlikely, I submit," put in Francis. "A difficult task, not to be undertaken without considerable risk."

"But if Mrs. Radlett came to her friend for help, having hit Duggleby over the head," said Ottilia blandly, recalling the curious intimacy she had noticed at their first meeting in the coffee room, "I cannot think Miss Beeleigh would refuse to aid her."

Francis nodded. "Granted, but she need not do the job herself. There are men enough in the village, and I daresay a fat purse would serve to keep some fellow's mouth firmly shut."

Lady Ferrensby's glance had gone from one to the other of them, Ottilia noted, although she had said nothing. But this proved too much for her.

"Fiddle! No, no, stop. This must be nonsense."

Ottilia was obliged to laugh. "Yes, I think it probably is. But we cannot afford to disregard the flimsiest of possibilities."

A shudder of relief went through Lady Ferrensby. "Then you are not serious. Thank heavens! I was beginning to think either I was mad, or you were."

A sharply ironic glance came at Ottilia from her husband's eyes, and she had to bite back an unseemly giggle. Just so was he apt to stigmatise her when she indulged in unorthodox actions, if only in jest. There was an opportunity here that was not to be ignored, however.

"Speaking of Evelina Radlett, has it ever seemed to you, Lady Ferrensby, that she may be a secret drinker?"

A blank stare was directed upon her. "What in the world makes you ask such a thing?"

"There was a complaint about watered wine. Molly Tisbury defended her husband's integrity on the matter and instead suggested Mrs. Radlett had added water herself for the purpose of concealing her own depredations upon the bottle."

Lady Ferrensby frowned. "It has never come to my attention, if that is so. And I am quite sure Tisbury does not water the wine. Who complained? Miss Beeleigh?"

Ottilia nodded. "Yes, it was spoken of the first day I met the ladies."

"Then I'll wager it was indeed Evelina, but not on her own account."

"Whose, then?"

"Netherburn's. If she entertained him when Alethea was absent, she would be at pains to conceal it. Miss Beeleigh tolerates the fellow, but Evelina knows she highly disapproves of the possibility of a nuptial between herself and Horace."

"Yes, I had noticed." Then the grogginess to which Molly had alluded could safely be attributed to laudanum. But this thought she kept to herself.

Lady Ferrensby was drumming her fingers on the tabletop again, her brows lowering.

"What is the matter, ma'am?"

"I simply can't imagine what put it into your head that Evelina Radlett could possibly have done the murder. Even with the aid of another. The whole notion is fantastic."

Ottilia had no answer to this. It was clearly not given to Lady Ferrensby to look beneath the apparency for a deeper significance. Evelina had today shown a remarkable ability to point up what she felt might stand against her. She did not consider herself beyond suspicion, that much was clear.

"But that notion opens up another possibility," said Francis suddenly, interrupting her train of thought. "Remember you said if Molly had done it, then it had been in a fit of temper?"

"Yes?"

"The same may be said of Tisbury, if his wife came to him upon the occasion."

Ottilia started. "How right you are, Fan!" She saw Lady Ferrensby was looking puzzled. "Francis is suggesting Tisbury might have hacked at the beam and started the fire in a bid to protect his wife."

"Not only that," pursued her husband eagerly. "Which of the villagers are the most assiduous in castigating Cassie Dale for a witch and blaming her for Duggleby's death?"

Struck, Ottilia stared at him. "Molly, of course."

"And Tisbury follows her lead."

Lady Ferrensby was frowning again. "But you said positively, Lord Francis, that you did not believe Tisbury had done it."

"Not the murder, no. But his loyalty to his wife is strong. I can believe him capable of a cover-up. Indeed, I would lay money on it." He turned eagerly back to Ottilia. "Tillie, I'll wager we have our murderer."

*   *   *

Sleep had eluded Ottilia until the small hours. Or she felt it so, striving not to toss and turn for fear of disturbing Francis. No matter which way she looked at it, she could not refute the arguments in favour of labelling the Tisbury couple: Molly as murderer, her husband accessory after the fact.

Not that she was opposed to the theory Francis had put forward. Indeed, she would be glad to think the mystery solved. But a nagging doubt could not be suppressed.

The only motive Ottilia had found for Molly to be enraged with the blacksmith was the matter of his getting the kitchen maid with child. Was it enough to make her take a hammer to his head? According to Molly's own account, she had taken her measures by informing Bertha Duggleby. But Bertha had dismissed the matter without interest. Could that have sent Molly into one of her fits of temper? Did she seek out the blacksmith and confront him? Then, when his back was turned, seize a hammer and strike him?

Ottilia had insisted on holding back from taking any action that night. To accuse with as little to go on as Francis's supposition was just the error she might expect from Lord Henbury. Too much remained unexplained.

Molly, if it had been her act, had not gone to the smithy with the intention of harming Duggleby. But if she had, it would be in character to throw the hammer used into the forge in hopes of being rid of it. But had there been opportunity to do the deed? Meldreth thought Duggleby had died around eight or nine, at which time Molly and her husband would presumably be serving customers in the Cock. Time of death was difficult to establish, and it could well have been earlier. Imperative to discover then whether the Tisburys had been absent, alone or together, at any time that evening.

Yet another snag rankled. Was it coincidence that Molly

Tisbury's fit of ungovernable rage overtook her at such a convenient moment? If the act was not premeditated, it had to
be sheer chance that it came to pass a couple of days after
Cassie Dale's vision.

Ottilia was loath to believe in lucky chances. And it was
this little thread, inexplicable by natural means, that was
responsible for the discomfort of the night.

It seemed as if she had hardly closed her eyes when she
was awoken by an unprecedented noise. Starting up in the
curtained bed, she listened, replaying the sound in her head:
the crash of something heavy, followed by a splintering of
lesser sounds.

It had come from below stairs, she thought, as she pushed
aside the curtain and thrust down the bedclothes.

"What's to do?" came sleepily from Francis's side of the
bed.

"Did you not hear it? Something fell downstairs, I think."

He sat up as she got out of bed. "What time is it?"

"I have no notion, but it is light already."

Ottilia found her dressing robe and shrugged it on.

"What are you doing?"

Turning, she found Francis had flung out of the bed and
was sitting on the edge, regarding her.

"Going to see what has happened, of course," she replied,
stuffing her feet into slippers.

He got up quickly. "No, you don't. Not on your own."

"Make haste, then."

She waited while he found his own dressing gown but
went to the door as he was putting it on, an abrupt feeling
of foreboding entering her bosom and lending her impatience.

It did not take her long to negotiate the passage and run
downstairs to the hall, Francis close behind her. She paused
at the bottom of the last flight, looking around.

The place was eerily silent, just as it had been on the day
they first came. It felt an eon ago, and Ottilia remembered

how this same sense of disappearing time had overtaken her last year when she had become involved in the disaster that had precipitated the Polbrook family into a week of unmitigated hell.

"Must have come from the kitchens," Francis suggested, passing her and making for the door to the back premises.

But the ominous sensation that had invaded Ottilia's bosom now struck a chill that led her eyes to the door to the coffee room. Without speaking, almost without willing her feet to walk, she moved towards it.

"Tillie?"

She threw out a hand, but she did not turn. With a calm born of that numbness preceding certain horror, she noticed the tremble of her fingers. Then she reached out and grasped the handle of the door.

Inside the room, the cause of the noise was immediately obvious. Hannah Pakefield was half standing, her bulk thrust against the long table at the back, her hands over her mouth as if to stop a scream. Her eyes, in a countenance white with shock despite the reddened wounds from yesterday's battle, were round and huge, stark with terror.

At her feet lay a heavy wooden tray, its contents scattered around it. Crockery lay broken and crushed, and pooling liquid formed a little lake from which protruded a variety of silver cutlery.

The picture married up with the sounds that had woken Ottilia, but she took this in somewhere in the periphery of her mind, the rest concentrated on what sight it might be that was riveting Hannah's attention.

She let go the door handle and moved into the room, turning in the direction of the landlady's fixed gaze. Her gorge rose, and for a moment she stood transfixed, her brain flying to the horrible vision described by Cassie Dale, which was here brought into being.

Seated on a chair with her head resting on the round table

was Molly Tisbury, her face turned towards the room. Her arm hung loose at her side, and her legs had buckled. Protruding from the whiteness of her neck and stained red at that point was the handle of a kitchen skewer. Her eyes were open, her mouth slack, and she was stone-dead.

Chapter 11

For several heart-stopping moments Francis stared at the spectacle, inevitably thrown back to the hideous day he had discovered his sister-in-law's mangled corpse in her own bed.

Gradually the new picture, with its very different manifestations, impinged itself upon his consciousness, and he forced himself back to the present. The first coherent thought came out of his mouth without benefit of decision.

"Well, that blows my theory out of the water."

Tillie's instant frowning glance brought him to a realisation of the inappropriate nature of this remark, and he hastily pulled himself together.

"Never mind that now. I had best send for Tisbury on the instant."

Tillie caught his wrist as he turned, and he felt the tremble in her fingers.

"Meldreth," she said, an unaccustomed quaver in her voice. "Not Tisbury. Not yet. We must have the doctor before anyone."

He covered her fingers and held them tightly. "Courage, my darling. You are made of sterner stuff than this."

Her clear gaze met his, and she hazarded a tiny smile despite the glistening he saw there. She drew a shaky breath and clutched his supporting hand.

"I will cope, Fan. And you are perfectly right. This throws us back to *point non plus*."

Her voice was strengthening as she spoke, and Francis was struck anew with the fervent admiration that had been his early reaction to the extraordinary woman of whom he now had possession. He drew her briefly close.

"Do you know that I love you more than anything in the world?"

The murmur in her ear was productive of a hiccoughing sob, and Tillie pulled away, her eyes shining and a tremulous smile upon her very kissable lips.

"What a moment to choose to tell me so!"

Francis grinned. "The perfect moment."

Then he let her go, and his soldiering instincts took over.

"To action, my love. You deal with Mrs. Pakefield while I find a messenger. Thank heavens Ryde returned last night," he added, turning for the door.

"Not Ryde," said Tillie quickly, recovering fast. "He won't know where Meldreth lives. Send Pakefield. Or no, better yet, send the girl Patty."

Pausing in the doorway, Francis glanced to where the landlady had sunk noiselessly into the nearest chair, her gaze, now blank, still fastened upon the dead body of her rival.

"Nothing would induce me to send Pakefield," he said in an undervoice. "The fellow is useless. He would likely wander aimlessly all over the green while we waited like idiots."

"Send him to me here instead. He may at least support Hannah."

"Very well. But I will find Ryde, too, for I think we are going to need him."

"Francis, wait!"

He was already in the hall, but he halted and turned back to find Tillie in the doorway, a frown gathering on her forehead.

"One or other of us must be in this room at all times, Fan."

He nodded, instantly appreciating the sense of this. "At least until the authorities—such as they are—have done their part."

She gave a nod and disappeared into the coffee room, the door closing behind her. Francis let out an inward sigh at the thought of what lay before them, remembering again the complications that had piled up on him the previous year. Resolutely he turned and made for the nether regions of the Blue Pig.

Ottilia crossed to where Hannah Pakefield was seated and laid a hand on the woman's shoulder.

"Hannah, my dear, look at me."

The peremptory tone had its effect. The landlady's head turned, and her eyes, near as soulless as those of Molly's corpse, came to rest on Ottilia's face. She was clearly incapable of speech.

"There is nothing to be done for her," Ottilia said gently. "You could not have changed anything."

Hannah's gaze rolled back to the dead woman, and a shudder passed through her. Weakly, she began to weep, and Ottilia was relieved to find the woman's capacity for feeling had returned. Reaching for one of the landlady's cold hands, she held it without speaking, letting the easing of the shock take its toll.

Hannah's hand lay slackly in Ottilia's fingers as her tears gathered and fell, a slight sobbing gasp intervening with each breath. Ottilia moved so that she shielded the landlady's eyes from the gruesome sight and waited. At length she felt the blood returning a measure of warmth to Hannah's hand and felt it safe to speak again and hope to be understood.

"Your husband will be here presently, Hannah. I think it best you retire to your own parlour."

Mrs. Pakefield's head moved, and she wafted a vague hand in the direction of the fallen tray and its wrecked contents.

"Must clean up."

"Later," said Ottilia firmly. "Are you able to stand?"

Hannah made a motion upwards but failed to lift her bulk from the chair. Hopelessly she sank down again, casting a glance up at Ottilia in which apology and despair were mingled.

A riffle of urgency chafed Ottilia, and she began to wonder where in the world Pakefield could be and whether Francis had managed to make him understand that his presence was required.

It was imperative she make an examination prior to Meldreth's arrival so that neither one could be influenced by the opinion of the other. Her brother Patrick's dictum had been that no two doctors should work together on the preliminary examination of a corpse to avoid accusations of collusion. She was no expert, but she hoped she knew enough to be able to answer the inevitable questions that must arise. In particular from the woman's husband. Ottilia shuddered to think of the consequences when Tisbury discovered his wife's death to be an exact copy of the vision expounded by Cassie Dale.

This thought so worked upon her imagination that Ottilia dropped Hannah's hand and made for the door. It opened before she reached it, and Francis came quickly in, the landlord's lanky form behind him.

"Francis, thank heavens!"

Before she could say more, Francis pulled at the landlord, dragging him inside. "See to your wife, man! Take her away and give her a brandy."

He was watching the fellow cross the room, and Ottilia was obliged to catch his attention.

"Francis, where is Ryde?"

Her spouse's glance came back to her, a frown leaping to his brow as her altered tone got through to him. "In the stables, harnessing the gig. Why?"

Ottilia caught his arm, only half aware of the convulsive nature of her grip.

"Leave the gig. He must go instantly to Cassie Dale's cottage. He may find that without difficulty if you tell him. He must wake Sam Hawes and have him bolt every door in the place. Neither Sam nor Tabitha must leave Cassie alone for an instant."

Francis's frown intensified, but he was already ahead of her. "You think Tisbury will act against her?"

"I am certain of it. Don't you see how closely this killing resembles the vision I told you of?"

Francis glanced back at the dead woman seated so bizarrely at the round table. Shock was in his gaze as he turned back.

"I had not taken it in."

"Because you did not hear her say it. We need Kinnerton, Fan. Let Ryde go directly to the vicarage once he has been to Cassie's cottage. He may tell him the truth and bring him back here."

"Would it not be better to despatch him directly to Mrs. Dale?"

"No, for his calling demands his presence here first. Then at least we may reassure Tisbury that everything needful has been done."

Her husband's brow quirked. "Are you mad, Tillie? The man will go off at half cock like a loaded pistol!"

"Yes. But we must make every effort. Has Patty gone to get the doctor?"

"Yes, and for my money, when she returns, we had best send her off again for Henbury and Pilton and be done with it."

"Let Meldreth do so. It is his responsibility."

Francis gave a curt nod. "I'll find Ryde."

He was gone from the room in an instant, and Ottilia turned her attention to the Pakefields.

It took several precious moments to induce the landlord, his wits predictably slowed by this latest disaster, to do anything other than stare owlishly at Molly Tisbury's body. But at last Ottilia, by dint of a combination of hectoring and persuasion, managed to be rid of them both. Drawing a steadying breath, she went to the table to make a preliminary examination of the corpse.

W atching Doctor Meldreth's methodical approach, Ottilia was reminded irresistibly of her brother. Not for nothing had she dwelled with Patrick and his family since the tragically early demise of her first husband in the American wars. Finding insufficient distraction in the care of her two young nephews, Ottilia had insinuated herself into her brother's surgery. Her first desire to keep at bay the memories that were apt to plunge her into melancholy had soon given way to intrigue and interest.

Patrick had allowed her to assist him and begun—in a bid to give her thoughts a different direction, Ottilia suspected—to initiate her into the mysteries of his profession. She had grown rapidly enthused, absorbing this new knowledge like a sponge.

On Meldreth's arrival at the Blue Pig, Ottilia had retreated to the bedchamber to dress as swiftly as she might, leaving Francis bullying Pakefield into organising the provision of some sort of breakfast. She had then returned to the coffee room to find the doctor's attention concentrated upon the area of Molly's neck where the skewer had penetrated, bending this way and that as he examined it closely.

He glanced up, saying without preamble, "The gullet is perforated, but I should have expected a deal more blood."

Ottilia felt a riffle of anticipation. Was he leaping to the same conclusion she had?

"More than a trickle, certainly," she agreed, moving to join him. "Much debris will have spilled into the chest, but inevitably it must have oozed from the wound."

The doctor was peering into Molly's face. "Pupils are well dilated, but both, which tells us nothing more than that she is dead."

He was studying the face with what Ottilia thought to be a critical eye. Her excitement mounted. "What is it, Doctor Meldreth?"

He glanced at her. "She is too pale. She has been dead some hours, for rigor has set into the limbs."

"Can you estimate the time of death? I find it exceptionally difficult to judge."

"Six or seven hours, I should say. At what time did you find her?"

"About a half hour since, I think, and it is after seven now, for I checked when I was upstairs."

Meldreth pursed his lips. "Four hours in this room at the least, I surmise. She may have been killed an hour or so earlier."

"Around one or two in the morning?"

"Or as early as midnight. Though why Molly Tisbury should be abroad at such an hour, I cannot think."

Ottilia eyed him, certain she had guessed aright. "You said she was too pale."

"In the face, yes."

"Which means the blood has not sunk and pooled where her cheek is lying."

His brows rose. "Quite so. From which we deduce?"

The tone was rather like a teacher to his pupil, but Ottilia was too eager to care. "She was not killed here. And the skewer was inserted after death."

Meldreth smiled. "Well done, Lady Francis. Did you look elsewhere for another wound?"

She nodded, unable to prevent herself from casting a swift

glance at the woman's back. Meldreth took the direction and shifted his position so that he might examine the bent over back more closely. Ottilia saw him reach out to touch at a point to the left of Molly's spine.

"Bloodstains. This looks like a stab wound."

"There is another in the front," Ottilia said, forgetful of her resolve to allow the doctor to make his own judgements without her assistance. Gratified to see him immediately move around and drop down to try and see what she had seen, Ottilia added, "I think she was struck twice."

Meldreth rose. "There is a deal of blood around her bosom. A collapsed lung, I suspect. The heart will have given out somewhat rapidly."

Ottilia went towards the table, hardly aware of her own eagerness. "Or her lungs and chest could have bled profusely, cascading blood into the chest cavity. In which case, she will have died painfully, fighting for her breath."

Meldreth stared at her. "There is that possibility. Only a postmortem will confirm which it was."

"And the state of the naked body," Ottilia pointed out. "If there is a large degree of colouring to the skin around the lower ribs—"

"Then we may assume your theory is correct," he finished, a look on his face of growing respect. "You have indeed learned well, ma'am."

Ottilia smiled. "That is a worthwhile encomium, and I thank you. But look at this, if you please," she added, dropping to her haunches and lifting the curtain of petticoats to expose Molly's feet.

She found Meldreth beside her. "What have you found?"

Ottilia pointed to the heels. "Mud and grass on her shoes, do you see? They are badly scuffed, too. And here."

She pulled the petticoats round to show a deep rim of discolouration along the hem, and the linen had small rips. The stains, green and brown, continued for some way up the back of the skirts, lightening as they went.

Ottilia stood up. "She was dragged across the green."

"The cobbles, too," suggested Meldreth. "The wonder is no one heard it."

"Perhaps someone did," said Ottilia. "They might not recognise the sound for what it was."

The doctor shifted out into the room, rubbing his chin. "But how did the killer get into the Blue Pig? Pakefield is assiduous in locking up, for fear of thieves."

Ottilia was still looking down at Molly, but she glanced round. "Yes, it is possibly the one thing at which he demonstrates efficiency. And unfortunately it is the one thing that stands against Hannah."

Meldreth looked startled. "Mrs. Pakefield? Good God, are you suggesting she did the deed?"

Ottilia shook her head. "I am fairly certain she did not. But this is her coffee room. She was heard to mutter of revenge after the fight with Molly on Wednesday, and she was present when Cassie Dale had her vision. Take these facts together with the locked front door and I guarantee Lord Henbury will have Pilton arrest her inside five minutes!"

Meldreth gave a bark of laughter, which he changed rapidly to a cough, casting an apologetic look at the deceased.

"Well reasoned, Lady Francis. Though it seems to me a foolhardy act to recreate this vision in her own house, if Hannah Pakefield was indeed responsible."

"Just so. Besides arguing a mind rather more convoluted than I fear poor Hannah possesses."

At this moment they were interrupted by the entrance of Francis, accompanied by the vicar. Kinnerton came quickly into the room, took one look at the body settled so conveniently into the posture of Cassie's vision, and blanched horribly.

He was hatless and out of breath, and his hands rose to his head where his fingers ran into his hair and held there.

"No," he whispered hoarsely. "No! Who has done this? Who could be so cruel?"

Ottilia exchanged an eloquent look with her spouse and was relieved to see Francis take a hand to the man's elbow.

"Steady, Kinnerton. Sit down. I'll get you a brandy."

But the parson's hands came down, and he waved the offer away, his legs apparently firm. The bright blue gaze swung around to Ottilia.

"Who did it? Has Tisbury been told?"

"Not yet," said Francis, answering for her, and staying close, a wary eye on Kinnerton's profile. "We thought it better to fetch Meldreth first."

The vicar nodded, and Ottilia took a step towards him, half extending a tentative hand, as she uttered words she hoped might comfort.

"I sent to warn Sam Hawes. They will have secured the doors, and neither he nor Tabitha will leave Cassie, I assure you."

The vicar's breath left his throat in a bang, and he nodded. "That was well thought of. Thank you."

"As for who did it," pursued Ottilia, "I fear it may be some time before we can tell."

Francis looked from her to Meldreth, a frown creasing his brow. "What of your findings? Does Meldreth concur?"

The doctor took this before Ottilia could answer. "We are at one on the premise that the deed was done elsewhere."

"Then it was deliberate," said Kinnerton, a bitter note in his voice. "Is there no end to the petty cruelties of this village?"

"A trifle more than petty," Francis cut in, his tone severe.

Kinnerton shook his head, throwing a hand into the air. "I meant the manner of posing the body in this way."

"It is all of a piece," said Ottilia coolly. "It is less a cruelty, I fear, than a case of expedience."

Kinnerton erupted. "Expedience! To what purpose? Lord knows I did not take to Mrs. Tisbury, but what possible motive could anyone have to kill her?"

Ottilia drew a breath. "None whatsoever."

"What?" exclaimed the doctor. "But there must be a reason."

"There is," said Ottilia doggedly. "I disliked the creature excessively, but I must pity the circumstance of her murder."

"So must we all," put in Francis, "but why so particularly?"

Ottilia looked at each questioning face, lingering a little on the distress already evident in Mr. Kinnerton.

"Because," she said with resolution, "I very much fear Molly Tisbury has been sacrificed on the altar of incriminating Cassie Dale."

Leaving Ryde to guard the body, Francis had managed to persuade his wife to repair to their chamber to eat a breakfast which could have better been described as a picnic. Pakefield having proved utterly insensible to the needs of his guests, Francis had been obliged to rely upon the services of the maid.

"I had the girl Patty bring the tray in here, since one can scarcely partake of food in the coffee room. I understand the cook is prostrate, and the maid has done the best she can."

He plied Tillie with a plateful of cold pork and buttered a couple of slices of bread for her.

"Eat," he ordered tersely. "You will collapse if you are obliged to deal with Tisbury and the rest on an empty stomach."

Ottilia laughed. "To tell you the truth, I am more dismayed at the notion of Henbury descending upon me."

"Lord, if I hadn't forgotten him," groaned Francis, providing himself with a more substantial plate of similar fare to that he had presented to his wife.

"Did you think to ask Patty to bring coffee?" asked Tillie, swallowing down a mouthful of pork.

"Do you think I could forget?" he retorted, being fully conversant with her propensity to drink the beverage upon every possible occasion. "I am convinced you are addicted to the stuff. It will be here presently."

Tillie nodded, giving no more attention to his comment than a brief grimace. "It was good of Doctor Meldreth to take on the horrid task of informing Tisbury."

To Francis it was a matter of the fellow's duty, but he refrained from saying so. "It is a good thing Kinnerton elected not to go with him."

"Indeed. Besides, I doubt anyone could have kept him from racing off to Cassie Dale's cottage."

Francis had to laugh. "Besotted!" He threw a teasing look at his wife. "What is it about these murderous affairs that brings out the romance in a fellow, Tillie?"

To his delight, a delicate colour fluctuated in her cheek. "Evidently the malaise is not confined to the male sex."

This piqued his interest briefly. "You think Cassie is similarly *épris*?"

"Oh, entirely—though I fear there is some barrier on her side." He was about to ask what it might be when Tillie returned to the matter at hand. "In any event, Kinnerton is in no mood to hear Tisbury's accusations, which I have no doubt will be voluble. Not to mention violent."

"Undoubtedly," Francis agreed. "Well, his business with Tisbury's wife is done, so we must allow him to indulge his anxiety for Mrs. Dale's welfare."

Tillie nodded. She was wearing her faraway look, he decided. If she had been briefly distracted from the play of events with a reminder of the budding romance in which she had shown an interest, it was plain her thoughts were now otherwhere. He had at least the satisfaction of watching her tuck into her repast with an increasing appetite.

He eyed her covertly, dismayed by the strain in her face. She was a trifle paler than usual, and he suspected she was maintaining her sangfroid with an effort. A telltale muscle twitched now and then in her cheek, and she showed a tendency to avoid his gaze.

"Tillie," he said softly.

Her eyes came up, and the fork stilled on its way to her mouth. He read apprehension in her face and smiled.

"Don't look like that. You're taking this badly."

A little gasping sigh escaped her, and she looked away for a moment. Then her glance came back to him, and he recognised a look she had worn right at the end of the ordeal they had shared last year. He knew what she was going to say before the words came out of her mouth.

"I blame myself."

Wrung, he took refuge in an angered response. "Don't be absurd!"

"But I do," she protested. "That quarrel was my fault, for I set Molly off. She thought Hannah had said something, especially when I threatened her with Pilton."

"What the devil has that to do with anything?"

She waved the fork roughly, and the meat flew off onto the floor.

"Don't you see, Fan? It was the fight with Hannah that fully triggered Cassie's vision, which must have given the murderer the idea."

"Then he must have been looking for an excuse," Francis objected tersely, rising to retrieve the errant morsel and disposing of it on the tray. "You can't take the blame for that."

"And who better than Molly for a victim?" Tillie went on, disregarding this. "Just the creature most likely to set the villagers in a riot."

Francis understood well enough, but he cast about for excuses, anything to take away the agonised expression in that beloved face.

"You are forgetting he used the Blue Pig. That must have been a deliberate attempt to throw suspicion on Hannah Pakefield."

"Oh, a convenient side issue," uttered Tillie, her tone distraught. "The vision was seen in the coffee room; it involved the coffee room. It was meant to set the village onto Cassie."

A knock at the door sent Francis to his feet. "The coffee."
Setting down his platter, he added in a murmur, "If that
wretched girl had not seen fit to bruit the story of the vision
abroad, you could at least confine your suspicions to those
present in the coffee room at the time."

As predicted, Patty was standing outside the door, her
youthful features a combination of nervousness and harass-
ment. She was holding a small tray containing a single cup
and saucer, accompanied by a silver coffeepot, a jug of cream,
and a sugar bowl. A tankard of ale stood alongside.

Francis took it from her and thanked her for her trouble.
Patty dropped a curtsy.

"It's no trouble, sir."

She hurried away, and Francis shut the door, setting the
tray down on the already overburdened table. Then he realised Tillie was staring into space.

Arrested, he watched her. Just so had she looked once or
twice last year when she was making some connection in her
thoughts. Then he had been unwilling to delve, feeling intru-
sive. Now, in the intimacy of marriage, he had no such qualms.

"What is in your mind?"

Her eyes focused upon him, and she reached out for the
coffeepot, suddenly brisk. "That we had best eat quickly. I
want to look for signs outside to see if Molly was dragged in
by the front or the back."

"I telled her not to go, I telled her."
The words, delivered in a hoarse monotone, bore witness to the state of shock that had enveloped the landlord of
the Cock and Bottle. Forcibly removed from the fateful coffee room by Ryde and Meldreth, Tisbury had sunk down onto
the stairs in the Blue Pig's gloomy hallway. Ottilia had come
upon him as she descended and, despite her spouse's protest,
had promptly sat down beside him and taken hold of his
slack hand.

"Why did she go, Tisbury?" she asked gently.

He answered dully, staring before him. "A message it be."

"What sort of message? Was it written or did someone bring it?"

Tisbury's head shook slowly from one side to the other. "Bain't writ. Nor I don't know who brung it."

"What did the message say?"

"I bain't knowing more'n it said for Molly to go by the lock-up. Molly said as all the world be a-going to know once for all as the witch done for Duggleby."

Ottilia's blood chilled. An obvious trap, and the woman had fallen for it.

"But how should Molly think that might benefit her?" she asked, struggling to maintain a casual tone.

Tisbury's broad, ruddy features turned to her, his eyes lacklustre. "Knew as you thought it be her as done for Duggleby."

Ottilia exchanged a quick glance with Francis, standing close by—for fear of the man turning surly with her, Ottilia suspected.

"How could she know that?" he demanded sharply.

Tisbury did not answer. He was still gazing at Ottilia, and a measure of life had begun to return to the fixed stare.

"It be you as said it. Molly done it and come to me after, for as I'd brung the roof down and set a fire going in the smithy."

"Will again!" burst from Francis. "By heavens, but that tapster of yours has a deal to answer for!"

"What do you mean, Lord Francis?" cut in Meldreth.

"He has a pack of females in his train who eavesdrop on his behalf. And one of them is the maid here. She must have had her ear to the door last night and could not wait to run to him with the news." He regarded the bereaved man with a kindling eye. "Is that it, Tisbury? Did Molly have it from Will?"

Tisbury snapped suddenly. "And if'n he bain't said, we

bain't knowing as you be fetching Pilton on my Molly next. Her bain't touched Duggleby, nor I bain't brung down the roof nor set the fire on, neither."

"We know that now," Ottilia said quickly, in an attempt to hold back the tide of his growing anger.

"Now, aye. Now as Molly've took and died, too, at the hands of that cursed witch!"

He was making to rise, his eyes fixed on Ottilia, and Francis hastily gripped her arm and pulled her up from the stair. She found herself behind him.

"Ryde, to me!"

The groom left his post at the coffee room door and flanked Francis, his fists raised.

To Ottilia's relief, the doctor moved in, catching at Tisbury's arm.

"Calm yourself, Tisbury. There will be no fighting in the presence of the dead. Show respect to your wife, man!"

Peeping from behind the protection of her husband's broad back, Ottilia saw the man's high-coloured cheeks deepen to a richer red, and the burgeoning fire in his eyes died down.

"Aye, I'll do none a mischief with Molly laying by." His tone strengthened. "But if'n Pilton nor that there Lord Henbury don't take up that witch, I'll see to her myself."

Ottilia could not let this stand. She pushed past Francis and confronted the man.

"Have a little sense, Tisbury, do. Why in the world should Mrs. Dale call Molly out in the middle of the night? Especially if Molly went to discover something about Mrs. Dale being responsible for Duggleby's death."

But Tisbury was ready for that. "It be a trick, bain't it? A witch her be. Likely her spelled whomsoever brung the message. Then as her've lured Molly out, her've killed her."

"But if she was able to use magic, what need had she to bring Molly out of the Cock?" pursued Ottilia, refusing to despair of making the fellow see reason. "Why not simply make magic to ensure she died in her bed?"

"For as her've had them visions, bain't her? Her've seen as Molly be dead in the Blue Pig. Her tricked her so's her'd do her here like her've seen."

"But Molly was not killed here, Tisbury," Ottilia protested. "Ask Doctor Meldreth if you do not believe me. She was dragged here and put in the position she is in just so that you would think it the mirror of Mrs. Dale's vision. Don't you see? A trick has been played, yes. More than one, perhaps. But it had nothing to do with Mrs. Dale."

She thought for a moment that she might have got through to the man. His jaw hung slack as he stared at her, blinking slowly as if he tried to take in the sense of her words. His eyes swung to Meldreth.

"It's true, Tisbury," said the doctor, to Ottilia's relief. "Molly was killed elsewhere. If the message took her to the lock-up, it's likely that was the place."

For a moment the outcome hung in the balance. Ottilia discovered she was holding her breath and silently let it go, her eyes never leaving the man's face.

It began to work a little, his mouth moving as if speech was struggling to come out. His eyes reddened, glistening, and a trickle of moisture dripped from one nostril. When the voice came at last, it was low, painful with suppressed grief.

"Her said as you be on the witch's side, Molly did. Her said as Lady Fan be one with the devil, too. Now Molly be killed and all. Her be sitting in there with Hannah Pakefield's skewer in her neck!"

His voice rose towards the end, but Francis had not waited. Ottilia was shifted bodily out of the way, and by the time Tisbury reached the end of his accusation, Francis had him by the edges of his brown frock coat.

"You dare speak of my wife in such terms! Lord help me, but if you lay a finger on her, I shall thrash you within an inch of your life!"

"My lord!" Thus Meldreth.

Ottilia saw him close in, trying to wrench Francis's hands from the man's coat. She stepped quickly forward.

"Fan, leave him be, I pray you! He is bereaved. He is not responsible for his words."

Her plea fell on deaf ears. "Then he had better be responsible for his actions," Francis growled.

But he let go, thrusting the man away from him. Tisbury dropped back onto the stair and sat there, dumbly staring at the floor between his knees.

Ottilia seized the opportunity to drag her husband away, whispering urgently.

"As well he is too numb to respond, Fan. I wish you will not take up the cudgels so violently."

The wrath was still in his face as he eyed her, speaking low. "I mean it, Tillie. The fellow is ripe for any violence, and I will not have you become a target for his rage."

"I am sure he speaks only from his grief, Fan."

"Well, so am I not. You keep away from him, do you understand me?"

Ottilia put a finger up to his cheek and stroked it, venturing a smile. "I will do whatever you wish, my dearest one."

A little of his fury seemed to abate, but he took her strongly by the shoulders. "Yes, but will you? I know you, Ottilia. When you become involved in the moment, you are utterly reckless of your own safety."

Ottilia set her hands against his chest. "I promise I will be careful."

He still looked dubious, but there was no further opportunity to thrash the matter out, for the main door to the building burst open, and the elderly little figure of Mr. Wagstaff thrust limping into the hall.

"Where be her? Where be my Moll?"

Francis, ready for any fray, left Tillie and strode forth to take on this ancient progenitor of the deceased woman.

"You've arrived, have you? Let me tell you, Wagstaff, if

you are bent upon supporting your son-in-law in his ridiculous accusations of my wife—"

"My lord, let be!"

He found Meldreth at his side and stopped short. "Let be? After what has been said?"

"Mr. Wagstaff is unlikely to support any such notion, I think you will find."

"Which notion be that, hey?" chimed in the ancient, glaring up into both their faces.

Francis took this without hesitation. "Your son-in-law had the gall to suggest that my wife is in league with the so-called witch."

"Tisbury believes Mrs. Dale is responsible for your daughter's death, Wagstaff," said Meldreth, taking it upon himself to elucidate.

The old man's eyes snapped. "Bain't no witching in Witherley. Daft they be as say so, 'cluding my girl, if'n her be gone and all."

"I am sorry to say she has gone, Wagstaff," returned Meldreth.

Francis watched the confirmation hit the old man squarely. He did not shift from his antagonistic stance, but his eyes narrowed, his face went grey, and his knees wobbled slightly so that he leaned the heavier on his staff.

"Dead, then," he said dully. "As like her ma as nowt to ninepence. Knew as her temper 'ud do for her one day."

Arrested, Francis stared at the man. "Your meaning?"

The rheumy eyes found his, and there was black hatred in their depths. "Bain't no secret. Seen by all the village it be. My Moll scratched her face for her, and her've took revenge. Bain't need to look no further than Hannah Pakefield."

Chapter 12

Francis could not resist a flying glance towards his wife. Tillie had foreseen this outcome, but her anticipation had been for Henbury to make the jump. Her frowning look at the old man Wagstaff told Francis this came as a surprise, but she did not speak. Meldreth took the matter up.

"That is highly unlikely, Wagstaff. It was Hannah who found your daughter this morning."

"That be nowt," argued the old man. "If'n her found her that be no proof as her bain't put Moll there."

"That is true, but—"

"If'n you bain't done it yet," interrupted Wagstaff, "it be time as Pilton be sent for."

"I have already sent the stable boy for both Pilton and Lord Henbury."

A grunt of satisfaction greeted this statement. "Then it be nowt but a moment afore Hannah Pakefield be fetched to lock-up. If'n you be ready, Doctor, I'll take and see my girl now."

"And me," piped up Tisbury, coming alive again.

Francis saw no point in arguing. "Ryde will remain with you, Meldreth." He turned to his groom. "Make sure neither of them touches anything."

Ryde nodded and crossed to enter the coffee room ahead of Meldreth, who preceded the two most nearly concerned with the deceased.

Tillie had shifted out of their way, and as Francis turned, she motioned towards the front door.

"While they are occupied, let us go and see if there are marks to be found."

Francis nodded. "The place will be swarming with villagers in no time. You can hope to find nothing if it has all been trampled."

She looked struck and quickened her pace. Francis opened the front door for her, and she paused on the threshold.

"And then we must make a thorough search of Hannah's chamber."

Shocked, Francis very nearly forgot to follow her out. "What in the world will you look for?"

She did not answer immediately, her eyes travelling across the green. Already there were huddles of villagers, whispering and pointing in the direction of the Blue Pig.

"Not a moment too soon," Francis commented, forgetting he had not received a response to his question.

Tillie headed out across the cobbles, her eyes trained upon the ground. Francis did likewise but could see nothing to suggest a body had been dragged across the area. He joined Tillie.

"Do you see anything?"

"I don't expect to right here. Her shoes were scuffed, but that is unlikely to show on the cobbles."

Francis watched her raise her head and scan the road intervening between the green and the cobbled yard. He glanced across and saw only footprints in the dust, which could have been made by a number of persons who had been to and fro already this morning, including Kinnerton and the doctor.

"Ah, there we are."

Tillie was moving fast, and he followed, his eyes coursing the area for whatever she might have seen. When she halted, he followed the direction of her gaze.

"There, do you see?"

Two grooves led out across the road, directly out of the edge of the green. The grass was a trifle overgrown, and Francis could clearly see a pattern where it had been flattened. He looked towards the lock-up, but the drag did not reach as far.

He automatically moved when Tillie did, following the pattern for a matter of a few feet. Then she halted, carefully examining the grass.

"She was killed here, I think," Tillie said. "Whoever it was must have persuaded her to come this far. Look if there are bloodstains on the grass, Fan. See how it is flattened? She must have fallen on this spot."

There was no shape to be made out, but a small patch of the greensward did indeed look as if something heavy had been laid upon it for a while. Squatting, Francis made a careful examination.

"I can see no blood. There are one or two brown stains, but that might be anything." He wiped at one and lifted the finger to the light. "No, I can't tell."

"Never mind it," Tillie said, turning and retracing her steps back to where the grooves began on the road.

Rising, Francis followed and looked where she pointed.

"The grass must have been wet enough to cause the dirt to turn to mud. See, it fades out quickly."

He followed the line, where the heels of Molly's shoes must have dragged, rapidly drying over the dirt. Then he made a discovery.

"It turns to the side."

"Yes."

Tillie's gaze rose, and she looked towards the side of the Blue Pig, where the archway gave onto the back premises.

"They headed for the stables."

But when Francis accompanied his wife to the archway, he was disappointed to find no further trace of grooves, either on the road or on the gravelled track that led around the side of the building. Following past the stables and all the way to the two back doors, he could see nothing to indicate the passage of a person hauling a body.

"You will not convince Henbury with this," he said grimly.

But Tillie was standing by the door nearest to the side, scrutinising the area around it. She swept a hand in an arc to encompass the yard.

"Do you suppose Hannah's servants are so scrupulous as to sweep the yard on a daily basis?"

Francis's mind jumped, and he cast his eyes down again. Sure enough, there were clear signs of brushstrokes criss-crossing one another.

"Very thorough was our murderer," Tillie said, an echo of the old mischief in her voice.

Awed, Francis agreed. "Indeed. But then how was it he did not think of the grooves or the flattened grass?"

Tillie shrugged. "I daresay the business of arranging the body suitably drove it from his mind."

"Or hers, if it was Hannah."

"It wasn't Hannah."

Francis frowned. "You are very positive."

"Yes, but that does not mean I am confident of proving it."

"And there is still the matter of a key," he pointed out. "I cannot think the servants leave the back doors unlocked."

Tillie's mischievous look reappeared. "Well, we know people are apt to get hold of keys, do we not?"

Which was all too true, keys having figured prominently in the unravelling of the puzzle in his own family last year.

"You suppose someone possessed themselves of the appropriate key beforehand."

"It is possible, you'll admit. It will be easy enough to

discover if one has gone missing. I had best speak to the girl Patty without more ado."

"I thought you wanted to search Hannah's rooms," Francis reminded her.

"Yes, and who better to assist me than the maid. I can question her at the same time."

The paralysing horror that had gripped Cassie was dissipating, giving place to a feeling of violent nausea. She had drunk but two mouthfuls of the tea Tabby had forced upon her, unable to act or think beyond the appalling fact that it had happened again.

The arrival of the Reverend Kinnerton had done nothing at first to mitigate her condition. She recalled only his sitting alongside her at the table and holding her hand. She had been aware of his voice, soothing in tone, but his words had not penetrated the fog in her mind.

Now, as breaks began to filter through the woolly sensation, Cassie realised Aidan had fallen silent. Warmth at her hand brought her eyes down to find it cradled in a comforting clasp. And then the sickness welled up.

Snatching her hand away, she pressed it with the other at her stomach.

"What ails you, Mrs. Dale?"

The tone had a sharpened edge, and Cassie looked up, gasping out her distress. "I am going to be sick!"

Tabitha suddenly came to life, startling Cassie as she leapt from a chair in the background.

"Oh, Lordy! Hang on, Miss Cassie. I'll fetch a basin."

Aidan had risen to his feet. "What can I do?"

"Keep out of the way, sir, if you don't want it all over your shoes."

As Tabby hurried into the kitchen next door, Cassie put her hands to her mouth, pressing tightly as the welling nausea threatened to overwhelm her.

"Here now, take this."

She opened her eyes to find Tabby holding a china basin under her chin. She did not dare release her mouth to seize it. But a pair of strong hands moved in to relieve her of this necessity.

"I will take it. You may be as sick as you wish now, Mrs. Dale."

With a gasp of relief, Cassie took her hands away from her mouth and retched horribly. A little liquid came out, but nothing more, even as the spasms racked her so that she vomited painfully several times more.

"Nothing inside her, that's what," came tersely from Tabby.

"She is recovering a little, I think." This was Aidan again. "Will you fetch a glass of water, if you please, Mrs. Hawes. And a cloth."

The retching at an end, Cassie sat back, her head lolling uncomfortably as the inevitable sequel of faintness attacked her.

"You should be in bed," came on a worried note from the vicar.

Feebly, Cassie shook her head. Speech was as yet beyond her, but at least the dreadful numbness of shock had left her, along with the purge. She closed her eyes.

Presently, a cool sensation passed across her lips and about her brow. Opening her eyes, she discovered Aidan gently applying a dampened cloth to cleanse her face. Gratitude swept through her.

"You are so very kind. Any other man would have retreated."

The bright gaze met hers, close and gentle. "Not at all. Only a monster would leave you at this juncture."

A glass was put to her lips, and he bade her drink. Obedient to the tone of command, though gently delivered, Cassie swallowed a few drops of the blessedly cool liquid. She began to feel a little recovered, and inevitably the memory swept back, and she gave a little cry.

Aidan's brows drew together. "What is it?"

Cassie pushed the glass away, and he set it down. Unthinkingly, as urgency engulfed her, she groped for his hand, and it closed reassuringly about hers.

"I must leave this place!"

He nodded gravely. "Yes, I think you will perhaps be safer at Lady Ferrensby's establishment."

A little sob escaped her as her heart contracted. "Not that. I mean this village. I must leave here altogether. I am too dangerous. None is safe from me."

The hand about hers tightened suddenly, and Aidan's voice became harsh.

"I will not have you talk so. It is not your blame that someone took it into their heads to use what you saw. Lady Francis says it was a deliberate act to copy your vision and use it to incriminate you."

The laceration at her heart did not abate. "So she said of Duggleby. But if I had no vision, none could use it." Her voice thickened, but she was hardly aware of the threat of tears. "I should not have spoken. I should have kept it inside."

"That, perhaps yes," said the parson unexpectedly.

Taken aback, Cassie looked at him, the desire to weep receding. "You are a strange man. You seek to comfort me, and yet you do not refute it when I blame myself."

A little smile lifted the corners of his mouth, and Cassie experienced the oddest leap in her breast.

"We must all recognise the extent of our responsibility. The visions you cannot help. But you have a choice about whether to speak out. You did not know it, but in the event, it turns out to have been unwise."

A helpless laugh escaped Cassie and broke in the middle. "Now you are making too little of it."

"No, I am being truthful."

She regarded him with renewed interest, a glow spreading through her veins.

"I like that in you. My—" She broke off. Her unruly tongue! Too easily she might give it all away. She corrected the slip. "Lady Ferrensby is the same. I can trust her. But she has less patience."

"If that means you are minded to trust me, Cassie, I am glad."

The use of her name on his lips and a particular note in his voice spoke deeply to something inside Cassie, and for a moment she was overjoyed. Then she recalled the peculiar circumstances of her life, and her spirits dropped. Without thought, she withdrew her fingers from his grasp.

"Of course I trust you." Dismayed at the gruffness of her own tone, she looked at him again and tried to smile. "You are a gentle man, Aidan Kinnerton. A gentleman and a gentle man. I will never forget your kindness."

A shadow crossed his face, and Cassie felt the full force of his disappointment through the curse of her overactive sensibilities. If only she were worthy! She would give anything to be able to retract her implied rejection, but she could not. She did not trouble to hide from herself what she had sensed. That Aidan liked her more than a little. As she did him, Lord knew! But Cassie Dale had no business encouraging the attentions of this man. They thought her evil, a witch, but she had more heart than to allow Aidan Kinnerton to cherish false hopes.

He had not spoken again, and his silence reproached her. Cassie cast about for a way through and turned to Tabby, hovering at her shoulder.

"May I please try the tea again?"

Her maid's clucking assent provided a useful interlude, and Cassie was able to turn the subject. Not indeed into a channel any less painful, but at least it had the merit of steering away from matters of the heart.

"Do they blame me? The villagers?"

The vicar rose from his chair, an abstracted frown creasing his forehead.

"As yet there has been no outburst."

His voice was even, but Cassie thought she could detect a modicum of hurt in the faint edge that overlay the apparent calm.

"But you think there may be."

He had retreated to the window and was looking out across the river towards the green. "I dare not suppose otherwise. At present, I imagine Tisbury is too occupied to take action, or he would have done so before this. But I cannot think it will be long before some idiot encourages him to seek revenge upon the only enemy visible to him at the moment."

Cassie eyed him, bleak at heart to note the reduction of warmth in his voice. "I am thankful you do not seek to hide your suspicions from me."

He turned at that, his keen glance piercing across the little room. "I could do you no good thereby."

Cassie looked away, wrung by the implication in his words. "You have already done me good."

He did not speak, and she felt compelled to look at him again. What she saw in his eyes made her lose sight of all caution.

"Aidan, it is not because I don't want you."

His eyes flashed triumph, and he took a step towards her. "Then why, Cassie?"

She drew a shaky breath. "I cannot speak of it. Only trust me. It will not do."

But it was too late. Cassie saw that she had given him hope. For a moment she teetered on the edge of confession, but the thought of his turning from her in disgust would not permit her to speak.

To her relief, Tabitha came in from the kitchen and the moment was lost. She accepted the freshly made tea and, with an attempt at lightness, invited Aidan to partake of a cup.

"Thank you," he said, with a return to a semblance of formality. "And then I must leave you. Such events as these bring duties upon me I cannot avoid."

Her mind flew again to the horrid event. "Have you seen Tisbury?"

"No, I came to you first. But I must do so, and hope to find him less of a potential threat than we have all been led to suppose."

His smile seemed forced, and Cassie suspected he had said as much only to reassure her. She said nothing, but her thoughts inevitably began to turn again upon this immediate problem. Somehow her own potential danger seemed of little importance against the scene just played out in her cottage.

Much to her astonishment, Ottilia's scheme to inspect Hannah's personal effects encountered opposition from Pakefield. He stood stolid and resolute before the door to their private apartments situated on the top floor.

"No one don't go through Hannah's things. Not if I know it, they don't."

Ottilia regarded him with interest, wondering what had roused him from his apathetic state. She opted for an attack direct.

"Why not, Pakefield?"

The gloomy countenance sunk further into sagging hollows. "For as Patty said as Pa Wagstaff is going for to tell Pilton as Hannah been a-murdering of Molly Tisbury."

Reflecting that the sooner she spoke to the all too garrulous Patty the better, Ottilia nodded. "That is true, which is exactly why I wish to check over Hannah's clothing."

The landlord's eyes widened with reproach. "You think it and all."

"No, I don't, Pakefield. But I need to be able to convince Lord Henbury, do you see?"

His unfortunately elongated head shook from side to side. "I see naught. Nor I won't let none meddle with Hannah's things."

Ottilia was tempted to tell him it was a pity he had not shown such backbone at an earlier date when he might have been of some use. At this time, his obduracy could only be a hindrance—just as his slow-witted responses had been before. She strove for patience.

"Let me see Hannah, if you please."

For a moment, she thought he would refuse even this simple request, but after an indecisive pause, he stood aside and allowed her to pass into the room.

It was a parlour of sorts, fashioned out of one of the smaller chambers, and Hannah Pakefield was seated in a comfortable chair set before the empty grate, her head resting on a cushion. Her eyes were closed, and her breath rattled a little in her throat so that Ottilia thought she was asleep. She tiptoed across.

"Hannah?"

The woman's eyes slid open at once, and it was immediately plain that she was somewhat recovered from this morning's ordeal. She spoke, however, with a trifle of breathlessness, and a stray notion voiced at one time by her doctor brother floated into Ottilia's head. Should she have Meldreth check the woman's heart?

"Pakefield don't understand, my lady. I ain't afraid of you looking. I ain't got naught to hide."

Ottilia smiled at her. "I am sure you have not. Pardon me, but may I go through your clothes?"

Hannah nodded and pointed to an inner door. "That's our bedchamber."

"Thank you. Will you send for Patty, if you please?"

At this, the landlady raised her head, a little frown creasing between her brows. "What for?"

"I need a witness, Hannah. My word will not stand on its own."

It was not strictly true, but Ottilia had no wish to stir Pakefield again by revealing her wish to question the maid.

Hannah gave the necessary instruction to her spouse, who did as he was bid and rang the bell. Ottilia thanked Hannah again and made towards the indicated door.

"Mine's the larger commode, ma'am, over by the window."

Ottilia threw a nod over her shoulder and opened the door. Upon entering the bedchamber, she shut the door firmly behind her and paused to survey the room.

It was unexpectedly untidy, with garments strewn across the bed and over the backs of chairs. Both commodes were cluttered on top with all manner of odds and ends, including a candelabrum and a collection of wooden boxes, several open with their contents spilling out. The bed was unmade, and Ottilia guessed this was due to the events of the day. Likely the maid had to attend to breakfast and the chambers of the guests before she had leisure to see to her mistress's wants.

Ottilia crossed to the bed and made a methodical examination of the clothing laid there, not omitting that of Mr. Pakefield, inconceivable as it might be that he could be party to anything as complex as this murder had proved. Just as expected, she found nothing in the least degree incriminating.

She was laying down the last of the items cluttering the second chair when the door opened to admit the maid Patty. She was looking scared, her eyes big in her freckled countenance. She was pretty enough in a countrified way, and Ottilia could well imagine she might attract the likes of Will the tapster.

"Ah, Patty, come in."

The girl bobbed a curtsy, casting an apprehensive glance about the chamber, quite as if she expected something or someone to jump out at her from concealment.

"Help me look through your mistress's commode."

At this, Patty blinked and her mouth dropped open. "Look through the mistress's commode?"

"Yes. Come along."

With hesitant steps the girl crossed the room and came to rest at Ottilia's side as she shifted to the front of the chamber, selecting the larger piece of furniture set on the wall near the window.

"This is it, is it not?"

Patty nodded, and a trifle of puzzlement entered her face. "What be we looking for, m'am?"

Ottilia looked at her. "Bloodstains, Patty."

Horror leapt into the girl's eyes, and Ottilia almost repented of her candour. She was not unhopeful, however, for already a creeping look of excited anticipation was replacing the first shock in Patty's face. Satisfied, Ottilia opened the commode doors and slid out the top tray.

The clothes within were loosely laid, and it was plain to Ottilia's critical eye that Patty's folding lacked precision. Nor was the girl adept at putting the limited space to its best use. She took out the first garment and shook it out. A nightgown.

"There bain't no blood on it, m'am."

Ottilia was almost betrayed into a laugh. "No, I hardly think Mrs. Pakefield would venture forth clad so lightly. Where are the day gowns?"

Patty took the nightgown, bundled it up unceremoniously, and stuffed it back in the tray, which she slammed into place. Bending, she drew out the third tray and pulled forth a cotton chintz, much out of fashion but serviceable.

Ottilia watched the girl shake it out and scrutinise it minutely, then declaring it to be free of bloodstains, set it aside on the bed in a fashion as enthusiastic as it was careless.

Waiting until the girl had delved for the next, Ottilia slipped in her first query.

"I don't suppose you heard anything unusual last night, did you, Patty?"

The maid was busy running her eye down the blue stuff gown she held, but at this she paused and looked at Ottilia, a sudden intentness in her gaze.

"I bain't took no account on it, m'am."

"Then you did hear something?"

Patty appeared reluctant to commit herself. She pursed her lips and then bit the lower one before speaking. "Thought as I were dreaming, m'am."

"Very well, but what did you hear?"

The girl frowned in an effort of concentration, and Ottilia waited for her to find a way to express her thoughts.

"It be like as if an animal come creeping."

"How do you mean?"

Patty's eyes narrowed in thought. "There be a *pad pad pad* what be its paws like. Next there be a scraping, as if'n it be laying on its stomach and pulling of itself."

Ottilia did not allow her burgeoning excitement to show. "Did these sounds go on for long?"

"Can't say, m'am. It be like a dream, in and out of me head."

Ottilia turned back to the commode and lifted out another garment. Following her lead, the maid folded the one she held in the same careless fashion and dropped it on the bed. Satisfied to see her resume her labours, Ottilia asked another apparently casual question.

"Where is your chamber, Patty?"

"In the attic I be, m'am."

"Yes, but where in the attic? Are you by chance situated over the backyard?"

Patty paused again, her hands full, her gaze flying back to Ottilia's face. "Aye."

Her surprise was evident, and Ottilia smiled. "A good guess, Patty, that is all."

The maid looked less than convinced, and Ottilia realised that, despite the most blatant shortcoming of her gossiping tongue, she possessed a degree of intelligence superior to that of her master. She said nothing, however, and went on with the work of checking Hannah's clothing.

They had moved on to aprons by this time, and thence to underclothing. Ottilia went through each drawer, regardless of whether or not the contents were likely to have been worn. Had Hannah been guilty, she could well have hidden a bloodstained gown among her other clothing. But there was nothing to be found, and Ottilia gave a secret sigh of relief. Not that she had for an instant supposed Hannah to be the murderer, but she had to be sure.

"We must next tackle the kitchens, Patty."

"For why?" asked the girl, her initial apprehension utterly past.

"To see if anything has been burned in the fire."

It was plain to Ottilia that the girl now thought she had taken leave of her senses, but she said nothing.

"Shall I put all back first?"

"No, you may do that later."

As they passed through the parlour, Ottilia took a moment to reassure the landlady. "Don't despair, Hannah. I promise you I will do all in my power to dissuade those who may believe you were involved in Molly's death."

Hannah sighed gustily. "Better me than that poor Mrs. Dale. None ain't going to try and burn me."

"I should hope not," snapped Ottilia. "There will be no nonsense of that sort if I can prevent it, my dear. Now then, Patty."

Descending the stairs with the girl close behind, Ottilia stopped abruptly at the top of the last flight. "Patty, had there been a key missing, do you know?"

The girl's jaw dropped open. "How be you a-knowing?"

Ottilia smiled. "A lucky guess. The back door to the yard?"

"Aye."

"When did it go missing?"

Patty started. "It be only last night, m'am."

"Dear me."

"Aye, just last night. The door be already locked when Master went to lock it, but there bain't no key. Master said as the stable boy must have turned it, and he being clumsy, could be as the key fell through the grate and be lost in the cellar."

"Indeed? Which grate?"

"Top of cellar stairs. It be kept on the window ledge above."

Where anyone might have noticed it. How very careless.

"Master be a-going to look for it this morning, only . . . "

"Indeed, one could scarcely expect anyone to remember under the circumstances," Ottilia soothed, but her mind was working swiftly. Someone familiar with the Blue Pig, then. Did that narrow the field?

She was still weighing the personnel of the village in her mind when she and Patty entered the kitchen where the cook was found to have recovered sufficiently to be able to begin her preparations for dinner.

A stout woman with a broad red face, she paused in her work of chopping the fat off a joint and looked up. At the sight of Ottilia, her eyes popped. Ottilia summoned her most soothing manner.

"Pardon me, if you please. I am very sorry to be invading your kitchen."

The woman laid down her chopper and wiped her hands on her well-used apron. "You be welcome, m'am. What be you wanting?"

"To find out if anything was burned in your fire this morning," said Ottilia promptly, noting Patty's eyes trained upon the bloodstained apron.

The cook's glance went directly to the big open range where a blaze was making the room uncomfortably hot. "Only lit the fire nor an hour since, m'am. Nowt be burning in there, for I've still to put the meat on the spit."

"Well, that is a relief," said Ottilia pleasantly. "I don't

suppose there is any outside fire? A wood-burning stove, perhaps?"

Both Patty and the cook eyed Ottilia with unmixed astonishment, and the latter expressed it. "In summer, m'am?"

"To heat water for washing?"

Patty crossed to the open range and pointed out a huge kettle sitting on a makeshift hob. "Cook has it going all day."

"Aye, and keep it filled and all."

Which conveniently disposed of any possibility of Hannah ridding herself of bloodstained clothing. Feeling absurdly pleased, Ottilia thanked the cook and informed Patty she had no further need of her services. The maid bobbed a curtsy, electing to remain in the kitchen, no doubt to regale the cook with an account of her activities.

At the door, Ottilia paused and turned back, fixing the maid with a bright smile. "I almost forgot. I know it is your usual practise, Patty, to pass on anything you may hear to Will at the Cock and Bottle, but did you do so last night?"

A tide of red suffused the girl's freckled cheeks, and she cast her eyes to the floor. The cook's glance went from the maid to Ottilia, dawning respect in her eyes.

"Come, Patty, let me have the truth," said Ottilia gently. "You had your ear to the keyhole when I was talking to Lady Ferrensby, did you not?"

Patty burst into tears. Satisfied, Ottilia watched the cook envelop the girl in a comforting embrace.

"You have been very helpful, Patty, and I thank you," Ottilia pursued in the same soft tone. "But you need to understand that when you betray what has been said in secrecy, there are always consequences."

Patty's sobs redoubled, and Ottilia decided she did not need to point the moral any further. There could be no doubt the maid's own intelligence had told her she was in part responsible for Molly Tisbury's death. An abject lesson. Let her reflect on it and perhaps do less inadvertent harm in the future.

*   *   *

Ottilia could not but be struck by Miss Beeleigh's efficiency. She arrived with Netherburn, announced straitly that Mrs. Radlett was too much distressed by the news to be able to come over just yet, and said that she herself had come with the intention of proving useful.

"Now, Lady Francis, what is the situation here?"

A trifle taken aback, Ottilia, who was in the hall with Francis at the time, gave a necessarily expurgated account of the events of the morning. Miss Beeleigh took it in her stride.

"If Patty is rushed off her feet and Hannah too bowed down to operate, we'll have to make shift for ourselves," she pronounced.

"In that case, the most urgent need is to clean up in the coffee room," said Ottilia. "They are in the process of taking Molly's body now."

Lord Henbury having seen it, Doctor Meldreth had sanctioned its removal from the Blue Pig. Not before time, Ottilia had reflected, for the corpse had deteriorated. Rigor was passing, and the limbs and torso were beginning to sink in a fashion that contorted the poor woman's posture horribly. Even Uddington had blanched a trifle at the sight of the unfortunate Molly. He had arrived at the Blue Pig a short time earlier, presumably dragged thereto by Tisbury and Wagstaff, who accompanied him, along with a couple of stout village men carrying the coffin.

Miss Beeleigh did not turn a hair. Mr. Netherburn was despatched to her house to fetch her maid Alice, who was to be put to work along with the Blue Pig's stable boy to make the coffee room habitable again.

"Send Alice over, Horace, and then remain with Evelina until she feels up to coming across. By then I daresay we may have got the place back into use."

She then declared her intention of bearding the cook in her kitchen, or making the coffee herself if need be, and vanished into the nether regions, what time Mr. Netherburn hurried off on his errand.

Once the coffin cavalcade was on its way to Meldreth's surgery, where the postmortem was to be conducted, the rest of the party, at Francis's suggestion, repaired to the Blue Pig's taproom across the hall, where Ottilia at once ran afoul of Lord Henbury, who had apparently taken the advent of a second murder as a personal insult.

"Damme, I won't have it! What is the place coming to? Corpses littering the village, hey? Mad, the lot of them!"

"I thought it would save time, my lord," said Ottilia, in a bid to stem the flow, "if I made a thorough search of Hannah's clothing."

Henbury glared at her. "Hey? Search her clothing? Who are you to go searching the woman's clothing? What the devil for?"

Thankfully Meldreth chose to cut in at this point. "You will recall the stab wounds, my lord. The perpetrator must have got blood on his or her clothes."

"Perpetrator? That Pakefield woman is the perpetrator. Knew it at once. Pilton will have her under lock and key in no time."

Ottilia cast an exasperated glance at her spouse, who had constituted himself tapster behind the counter and was busy taking tankards of ale off the draught. He threw his eyes heavenwards but could offer no other comfort. Sighing inwardly, Ottilia tried again.

"Before Pilton does his part, my lord, would it not be politic to search for evidence?"

"Evidence? What more evidence do you need? Fighting in the open street one day, and the next, one of the party is sitting in the Blue Pig with a skewer in her neck. Know who to blame. Obvious."

"Nevertheless," Ottilia pursued patiently, "would it not be well to ensure that there is no miscarriage of justice? After all, we have no evidence to support the notion that Hannah

Pakefield also killed Duggleby. Unless you think there are two murderers at large?"

At last Henbury looked a trifle less sure of himself. "Two? Good Gad, never thought of that." He turned to the doctor. "Hey, Meldreth? Could it be the same hand, do you think?"

Doctor Meldreth shot Ottilia a questioning glance, and she briefly nodded. "It would seem unlikely that there is more than one guilty party."

"Ha! In that case, Pilton had best search the house. Probably find ropes and ladders and all sorts of stuff, as well as blood on her clothes." He rounded on Ottilia. "Bloodstains! Found some, did you?"

"I did not," Ottilia replied, relieved to have got this far. "Nor is it likely that Hannah could have burned any blood-stained clothing, for there has been no fire alight until an hour or so ago, and the wood-burning stove is not used at this season."

"Well, I will have Pilton search the whole place from top to bottom."

"Except that you have already set him on guard outside Hannah's chamber, my lord," Meldreth reminded him.

"Well, he need only do that until Hannah is sufficiently recovered from her ordeal to continue her duties," Ottilia suggested. "There are surely enough of us to ensure that she does not leave the Blue Pig, do you not think? I can guarantee she is not going to escape by way of a window. She is far too stout."

This was productive of a bark of loud laughter from Henbury. "Ha! Well, well, I daresay the search can wait. Evidence won't be going anywhere. I'll see Pilton, and then I'll be off to Lady Ferrensby. Best keep her informed."

Thanking Providence for a much needed reprieve, Ottilia bade the man farewell with a lighter heart. Meldreth took his leave after downing the ale thoughtfully provided by Francis, heading for his surgery to begin upon the postmortem.

"A moment to ourselves, thank the Lord," Francis said,

taking a seat on one of the wooden benches, armed with a tankard of his own.

"Indeed," Ottilia agreed, sinking down on another.

The taproom was dingy and dark by comparison with the coffee room, and smelt of stale smoke and ale. Ottilia guessed it was little used, even the few male members of the gentry preferring to take their potations at the more lively Cock and Bottle. But it served the present purpose.

"What about the knife, Tillie?" Francis said abruptly. "Molly was stabbed, remember."

"Well hidden, I suspect."

Francis grunted and then quirked an eyebrow at Ottilia. "What next?"

"The messenger," she said without hesitation. "Someone lured Molly out of the Cock."

He nodded. "But how you are to find out who it was defeats me."

"I have no notion how. But find out I must, for I cannot think that person's life is worth a moment's purchase."

Chapter 13

Their privacy proved momentary, for at the sound of arrivals, Francis went out into the hall to prevent anyone's going into the coffee room. Next moment the widow Radlett, hanging on the arm of a solicitous Mr. Netherburn, came into the taproom. She appeared quite unlike her usual self, and at the urging of her escort, she sat gingerly upon a bench in dismal silence.

Ottilia noted the worried look cast upon the widow by Mr. Netherburn, as he accepted a tankard of ale from Francis, still playing tapster. Returning to the bench, he caught Ottilia's eye and spoke in a hushed tone, as if in the presence of a sickbed.

"Poor Mrs. Radlett is severely overset."

The widow looked up at the sound of her name, and a fluttering sigh escaped her. Her voice was a thread. "Dreadful! It is so very dreadful."

Ottilia eyed her in no little surprise, not to mention suspicion. Under the paint, which had been applied somewhat sketchily, as if the hand that did the honours were full of tremors, the widow's features were pasty with smudges of blue about her eyes.

Intent, Ottilia exchanged her seat for one next to the woman and quietly possessed herself of one of the widow's hands.

"You look a little pale, my dear Mrs. Radlett. You cannot have cherished a fondness for Molly Tisbury, surely?"

"Oh no, not that."

A wan pair of eyes slipped upwards, and Ottilia thought she read there more of fright than dismay. Mrs. Radlett's hand lay slack in her hold, but the fingers quivered.

"What is it, then?"

The widow's lips trembled into shaky speech. "It is all so very horrid. How could Mrs. Dale have known? So exactly like."

"Just so," Ottilia agreed. "Far too exact indeed."

Now there was more than fright. Mrs. Radlett's eyes widened, and she looked upon Ottilia as if at her nemesis.

"What do you mean, Lady Francis?"

Ottilia struck hard. "I mean that poor Molly was placed in a chair in the coffee room in just the position outlined by Cassie Dale, and that a skewer was thrust into her neck."

A whimpering cry escaped the widow. Snatching her hand away, she put the back of it to her mouth. Mr. Netherburn set down his tankard and, casting a reproachful look upon Ottilia, stepped quickly up to the bench and dropped to his haunches before her.

"Do not upset yourself, dear Evelina," he uttered warmly, seizing her free hand and beginning to chafe it with rather more enthusiasm than Ottilia felt was warranted. "Try not to think of it, dear lady."

"Not think of it! Oh, dear God, I shall have nightmares for weeks!"

Ottilia glanced at Francis, and he gave her a questioning look, not without a touch of reproach within it. She kept her gaze bland, and his brows drew together. Devoutly hoping he would realise she had a sufficient purpose, Ottilia pursued the widow with a ruthless hand.

"Oh dear, Mrs. Radlett, I had no intention of distressing you further," she uttered on a spurious note of contrition. "A horrid way to be killed, of course, but in fact Molly was already dead."

The widow's breathless whimpers ceased abruptly. Both she and Mr. Netherburn turned startled faces towards Ottilia. But before either could say anything, Miss Beeleigh spoke from the doorway.

"What the deuce is to do?" She came into the taproom and closed the door, her gaze roving from one to the other. "Evelina?"

Glancing round, Ottilia spied a look almost of revulsion in the widow's face as she stared at her friend. It vanished in a second, and Ottilia was left wondering, had it been still an effect from the deliberate shock of her own words, or was it possible Evelina's reaction had been to Miss Beeleigh?

Whichever it was, the widow sat up straighter and pulled her hand from Mr. Netherburn's grasp. "Nothing to fret over, Alethea. Lady Francis was telling us how Molly died, and I was startled, that is all."

The smooth tones of the woman's voice amazed Ottilia. How had she recovered herself so swiftly? Or was she something of an actress perhaps?

"Coffee room is habitable again," announced Miss Beeleigh, apparently accepting the explanation. She looked around the present accommodation and wrinkled her nose. "Can't say I fancy sitting in the coffee room after what has passed, but anything is better than this fusty taproom. Patty will bring coffee through presently."

"Oh, I shall be glad of it," said Mrs. Radlett, almost in her usual tone. Watching her, Ottilia thought there was yet a telltale quiver in her chin, and the message of her eyes had not fully mended.

Mr. Netherburn had risen, and Miss Beeleigh noted him

picking up his tankard again. "Best bring that with you, Horace. Unless you choose to drink coffee with us? Come along, Evelina."

Obedient to her mentor's instruction, Mrs. Radlett got up—a little shakily, to Ottilia's hawkeyed glance—and made the best of her way out of the taproom, Netherburn following.

Francis was hanging back, and Ottilia caught his fixed regard. She waited for him in the doorway, and his whisper caught her at once.

"You don't suspect her, do you?"

Ottilia looked back, murmuring, "She knows something."

"You drove her pretty hard."

"I meant to. A pity Miss Beeleigh chose that moment to come in." She eyed him. "Did you remark how quickly Mrs. Radlett recovered herself?"

He frowned. "You think she was faking it?"

"Not the upset, no. I think she is faking now, however."

Francis looked across the hall, where Mrs. Radlett was apparently balking at the coffee room door.

"Oh dear, I am almost afraid to enter."

Miss Beeleigh's hand was immediately at her back. "You must steel yourself, Evelina. Can't be deprived of our foremost meeting place or we'll have nowhere to be sociable."

The widow shuddered. "Yes, but it seems so callous."

"Nonsense," said her mentor, giving her a shove into the room. "No use giving way to sensibilities at a time like this."

"I feel quite sick," complained Mrs. Radlett in a voice that would have belied the statement had the earlier episode not occurred.

"We must go in," Ottilia whispered. "Something important may be said."

She darted across, Francis behind her, and entered the coffee room in time to see Miss Beeleigh push the unfortunate woman into the very chair at which the victim had been sitting.

"Sit down and don't think of it."

Ottilia refrained from pointing out the faux pas, hoping the widow would not recall the precise chair Cassie Dale had indicated when talking of her vision. Ottilia was abruptly struck with the recollection herself. How very precise had this murderer been. He had not missed a trick.

Mr. Netherburn, coming in just ahead of Ottilia, looked a trifle askance but said nothing. Ottilia wondered at it. She briefly questioned in her mind whether he had the physical strength to drag the dead weight of a body all that distance. Unlikely, she decided. Besides, where was his motive?

Burdened with a laden tray, Patty followed almost upon Francis's heels, and Ottilia went forward to help the girl lay out the various accoutrements. The earlier reprimand was apparently forgotten, for Patty looked to be on her dignity. Sotto voce under cover of setting out the silver pot and the cream jug while the maid set out the coffee cups, Ottilia asked what was the matter.

"Her've no right," Patty muttered, with a sidelong glance at Miss Beeleigh.

Ottilia had no difficulty in interpreting this cryptic remark. Patty was evidently in a huff that an outsider had taken upon herself the ordering of affairs in the Blue Pig.

"But is it not of use to have a little help from another maid? You cannot do everything."

"Aye, but bain't her right," insisted the maid. "Nor I won't have that flibbertigibbet Alice a-serving of coffee, not in this house I won't."

Had Ottilia not felt so oppressed, she might have been amused by this further evidence of jealousies amongst the village maids. Was Miss Beeleigh's Alice yet another contender for the affections of Will at the Cock?

Miss Beeleigh herself appeared hardly less high in the instep, for the moment Patty left the coffee room, she shouldered her way to the table, ousting Ottilia, and took charge again. She had just begun pouring the coffee when the vicar reappeared.

He was looking strained, Ottilia thought, eyeing him as he made the round of greetings and listened to Mrs. Radlett's expressed dismay. There was a suppressed air about him, as if he fought to maintain his sangfroid. She was just hunting for an innocuous way to ask how he had fared with Cassie Dale when Mr. Netherburn forestalled her, addressing the reverend himself.

"You have been with poor Mrs. Dale? So tragic to have been instrumental in this. Does she feel it unduly?"

Kinnerton's cheeks grew taut, and reserve entered his voice. "One would scarcely expect it to be otherwise."

"No, indeed," chimed in the widow. "Especially when the deed mirrored what she saw in every particular."

Ottilia glanced at Mrs. Radlett, detecting anxiety underneath the apparent calm.

"Mrs. Dale is much distressed at the outcome," said the parson on a repressive note. "As are we all."

"It is perfectly appalling," stated the widow in a dismayed tone that Ottilia took to be genuine.

Kinnerton glanced around the coffee room. "I am astonished all has been set in order again so quickly."

"Ah, but we are indebted to Miss Beeleigh for that," said Ottilia, taking the opportunity to look fully at the latter to gauge her reaction to these references, for she had said little so far of the actual occurrence. "She has loaned her own maid to assist."

Miss Beeleigh's almond eyes met Ottilia's, but they gave nothing away. "Nothing in that. Girl has little else to occupy her. Might as well make herself useful."

Before any could comment on this, the vicar intervened. "Do you need more help? My housekeeper has recently engaged a new maid for the vicarage—"

Miss Beeleigh's nose shot skywards. "Jenny Duggleby?

Surprised at you, Vicar. Have you forgot the girl's father was murdered, too?"

By chance, Ottilia caught another odd change in Mrs. Radlett's face. It showed for only the briefest moment as she stared at her friend, as if struck by a disconcerting thought. It occurred to Ottilia that this show of sympathy towards a mere maid did not ring with what she had previously judged of Miss Beeleigh's character. Was there some hidden reason she did not wish the Duggleby girl to enter the Blue Pig?

Puzzled, Ottilia cast her eyes again towards the widow Radlett and found no trace of the look. She had already realised the creature was adept at concealment. But which was the real Radlett? Could it be that her flustered manner was a blind?

Kinnerton had flushed darkly. "You are right, ma'am. I did not think. One would not wish to thrust her into memories which can only be painful."

Her sympathies stirred for his evident embarrassment, Ottilia smiled at him. "It is as well if no other maid arrives at the Blue Pig, for I fear Patty's nose is already out of joint."

A snort came from Miss Beeleigh. "Stupid girl. Ought to be grateful."

"She has borne much today," Ottilia said excusingly. "And I had rather see her highty-tighty than bowed down under the blows of fate."

A grateful look came her way from the vicar. "Indeed. I must go, for I promised Tisbury to be present at the postmortem to ensure his wife's soul takes a safe exit from this world."

A brief bow and he was gone, leaving a depressed silence behind him.

Ottilia partook of her coffee, keeping a covert eye upon the three visitors until she felt her spouse's interest and glanced at him. He was regarding her with a look of question as if he waited for the direction she chose to take. If only she knew!

She could not readily forget the prominence of this trio in the coffee room upon the fatal day, despite knowing Patty herself had reported the matter elsewhere.

She was startled when Mr. Netherburn broke into the hushed atmosphere.

"You said that Molly was already dead when she was put in this room, Lady Francis. Do you mean she was not killed here?"

The reaction to this could not have been more startling. Miss Beeleigh, who happened to be taking a sip of coffee at the moment, almost choked and was taken with a fit of coughing. The widow Radlett cried out, throwing her hands out in a gesture that nearly upset her cup.

Mr. Netherburn's glance flew from one to the other, his mouth slack and quivering a little. "Oh dear, I did not mean to startle you. But—but is it not what you meant, Lady Francis?"

Ottilia exchanged a glance with her spouse, who was looking decidedly eager. She nodded.

"Yes, it is exactly what I meant." She regarded Miss Beeleigh with interest. It was the first occasion upon which she had been seen to be disconcerted. "Are you quite recovered, ma'am?"

The other gave a nod, applying a pocket-handkerchief to her eyes. Her voice was a trifle husky. "Gave me a nasty turn, Horace. What possessed you to come out with that before Evelina? Bad enough as it is. Poor dear has been knocked to flinders by the whole business."

Ottilia seized on this. "But you seem to have taken it in your stride, ma'am."

Miss Beeleigh shrugged. "I'm a hardy spirit, but I'll admit to being considerably shocked. I might add I am relieved to have been spared a particularly gruesome sight."

"Yes, it was decidedly gruesome," said Francis, with a gleam in his eye as he flashed a look at Ottilia.

She took the point at once. "Where had you your information about the scene, Miss Beeleigh?"

The woman's countenance took on its habitual look of superiority. "The way anyone has it in this village. Can't put your nose outside your own door but the whole populace is aware of it within moments. Everyone is talking of it." She sniffed. "Thought they were exaggerating, of course, but that appears not to be the case."

Ottilia recalled the stragglers on the green when she and Francis had been looking for betraying marks—an activity that had not been reported to Miss Beeleigh apparently, since the fact of the body being killed elsewhere came as such a surprise.

Mr. Netherburn was eyeing the widow with some degree of apology in his face. "I had no intention of upsetting you, dear lady. You must forgive my unruly tongue."

"No, no." Mrs. Radlett waved a vague hand. "An unfortunate reminder, that was all." Her troubled eyes swung round to Ottilia. "I supposed you only meant the poor woman was killed in another fashion, not in another place. But I don't understand. I thought it had been just as Cassie Dale said it."

"Yes, that is what you were supposed to think," Ottilia said lightly. "What we were all supposed to think."

"But it was not so?"

"Far from it. The case is that Molly was enticed from her home by a message. She was killed on the green."

"Oh no." The whisper came through pale lips, the widow's countenance now ashen. "Tricked! Tricked and betrayed."

"Yes." Ottilia did not mince her words, aware that Francis was regarding the three as closely as she was herself. "Her body was dragged out of sight around the back of the Blue Pig."

Mr. Netherburn, looking quite as horrified as the widow,

ventured to complete the picture. "And then brought here to be made to look like Mrs. Dale's vision."

"Just so."

Ottilia could not resist a glance at Miss Beeleigh, who had not spoken throughout this recital. There was a sickened look on her face, and her eyes were narrowed as she caught Ottilia's glance.

"Disgraceful. Can't think who would do such a thing."

"But, why?" cried Mrs. Radlett. "I don't understand. What had Molly done?"

"Nothing at all," said Ottilia, "and that is the tragedy. The poor creature was but a scapegoat, used to fasten the guilt upon Mrs. Dale."

"Horrid! Oh, so horrid!"

Mrs. Radlett's upset was once again extraordinarily vivid, and Ottilia's suspicions revived. As if to underline them, Miss Beeleigh got up.

"Going to get you a tot of brandy, Evelina."

Francis rose swiftly. "I can do that, Miss Beeleigh."

"Stay where you are, man," responded the woman almost on a snap. "Do you think I'm incapable of finding my way to the taproom?"

Upon which note, she stalked from the room, leaving Francis lifting his brows at his wife. Ottilia met the look but lost no time in taking advantage of Miss Beeleigh's absence.

"Pardon me, ma'am, but you seem to be severely dismayed. What part of this business upsets you so?"

The widow's pale cheeks were overlaid with a sheen of faint colour. "It is so very shocking."

"Yes, it is." Ottilia waited, for this was no real answer.

Mrs. Radlett's lips trembled and parted, her eyes darting this way and that. Ottilia essayed an encouraging note.

"Is there something you wish to ask me, ma'am?"

Her glance stilled, meeting Ottilia's. Yet she hesitated, and Ottilia gave her a warm smile.

"Come, ma'am. You will be the better for getting it off your chest."

A little frightened sigh escaped the other. "Is it—is it known who took the message?"

"To Molly, you mean?"

The widow gave a tiny nod. "You said she had a message."

"So Tisbury said, but he did not know who brought it."

The widow's cheeks grew taut, and she spoke tightly, her words only just audible. "It must be found out."

"I heartily agree with you." Ottilia eyed the wan cheeks and the fearful look in the woman's eye. She took the plunge. "Have you any suspicion who it might have been?"

A tinge of pink entered Mrs. Radlett's pale cheeks, and her gaze widened. "I? No, indeed. How should I know such a thing? I have no notion at all."

It was said with alacrity, accompanied by such an expression of dismay as gave the lie to her utterance. She had a very valuable suspicion; Ottilia would stake her oath on it. But there was clearly little hope of getting her to reveal as much.

Then Netherburn chose once again to champion the creature, a flush of ruddy colour inflaming his usually urbane features. "How should she possibly know? I declare, Lady Francis, it is too bad of you!"

Before Ottilia could answer this, her spouse cut in, that familiar edge to his voice as he bristled in her defence.

"She is investigating a murder, Netherburn. Two murders, in fact. No possibility can be overlooked."

Horace Netherburn rose and faced him, thrusting out a jaw. "I daresay, Lord Francis. But to imply that Mrs. Radlett had something to do with this affair—"

"Did I so imply?" put in Ottilia mildly.

He champed a little, reminding her irresistibly of Lord Henbury. At last he sighed out a defeated breath. "Not in so many words, I grant you."

"It makes no matter, Horace," uttered the widow in a stronger tone, instantly giving away the warmer relationship that clearly existed between them. "She must ask. I see that." Her eyes turned again upon Ottilia, showing a resumption of control. "I wish I might help you. But I know nothing, nothing at all."

Ottilia smiled in a friendly way and picked up the coffeepot. "May I refresh your cup, Mrs. Radlett? Coffee has such a calming effect, do you not find?"

The widow looked a trifle disconcerted at the change of subject, but she accepted the offer, and for several moments there was silence as both Mrs. Radlett and Mr. Netherburn, partaking of a cup of coffee to replace his empty tankard, took refuge in the opportunity to diverge from the urgent topic that was occupying every mind.

Netherburn was still standing, and Ottilia was amused to see the elderly gentleman's attempt to overcome his evident discomfort with a pretence of watching the village through the window.

"What is the matter, Evelina?"

Startled, Ottilia turned her head to discover Miss Beeleigh standing in the doorway, a glass in her hand and a frown directed upon her friend. The creature surged towards the widow.

Out of the corner of her eye, Ottilia was surprised to see Mrs. Radlett cringing away, fear in her eyes. By the time Ottilia was able to look at her fully, there was nothing in her demeanour to indicate that this had happened.

"It is nothing, Alethea," she was saying, quite in her usual manner. Her eye turned on the glass. "Is that brandy? Oh, thank you, but the coffee has done much to calm me."

Ottilia was forced to conclude either that she had been mistaken, or that Mrs. Radlett was more of an actress than she had supposed. Was she a little afraid of her friend? Or had she a deal more to hide than Ottilia had thought? At this juncture, the notion of Evelina Radlett in the role of murderer did not appear as far-fetched as Lady Ferrensby had made out.

"Good Gad! What in the world is to do?"

Mr. Netherburn's exclamation, uttered in stronger accents than Ottilia had ever heard him use, took the attention of the whole company.

"What is it, Horace?"

The elderly gentleman was looking out of the window. He turned to Miss Beeleigh but gestured towards the green.

"Pouring out of the Cock, do you see? Half the village, you'd think." He looked out again and dipped his head to one side as if to see better. "I think they're heading for the bridge."

Ottilia's head shot round to find Francis and saw the same thought had entered his mind. He spoke even as she did.

"Cassie Dale!"

Francis went quickly to the window to join Netherburn. "Yes, they are heading for the cottage."

To Ottilia's instant relief, he took immediate charge, turning to face the room again. "You ladies stay here. Netherburn, to the vicarage with you and fetch Mr. Kinnerton on the double."

"Try Doctor Meldreth's surgery first," Ottilia cut in. "The reverend was going to be present at the postmortem."

Mr. Netherburn was already at the door, but he held back a moment to throw a plea to Francis. "Pray hasten, sir! If harm were to come to that poor young girl—"

"Trust me, nothing will happen to her." It was the voice of the soldier, and Ottilia thrilled to hear her spouse in total command. "I will take Pilton and my groom for reinforcements. Now go, man!"

He thrust Netherburn from the room and paused on the threshold, looking back at Ottilia.

"Tillie, find Ryde for me, if you will. I'll get Pilton, for I'm going upstairs for my pistol."

Ottilia was on his heels and through the door, but Miss Beeleigh's voice caught her as Francis took the stairs two at a time.

"Lord Francis!"

He halted on the landing, looking back with an impatient frown.

"I have a musket. Shall I fetch it?"

"No time," he snapped back, once more on the move.

He disappeared from sight, and Ottilia hurried through the back door into the domestic area. She found Miss Beeleigh immediately at her rear.

"I can be home and back in five minutes."

"Leave it to the men," Ottilia said without thinking, intent upon her mission. "By the time you are able to load a musket, all will be over."

"So easily? I fear you are too sanguine, Lady Francis. I take it Tisbury has broken out in his grief. He will not easily be satisfied."

Ottilia paused at the kitchen door and turned back. "My dear Miss Beeleigh, if you are intent upon joining the fray, by all means do so. But for the present, I pray you let me alone to do my part."

With which, she whipped through the door, shutting it in the creature's face. The domestic staff, comprising the cook, Patty, Alice, and the stable boy, were gathered about the kitchen table, quaffing a no doubt much-needed drink. All four gaped at the intruder.

"Where may I find Mr. Ryde, if you please? My husband's groom?" Ottilia looked at the stable lad. "Have you seen him lately?"

"Out back he be," offered the boy.

"Go and tell him to come to his master in the hall—immediately."

This last, uttered with all the authority at Ottilia's command, had the effect of sending the boy scuttling for the back door.

Satisfied, Ottilia looked over the three women.

"There is mischief afoot on the green. I pray you all remain here where you are safe."

She left them on the word, suspecting they would desert in a body the moment her back was turned. She reached the hall in time to see Francis about to leave the premises, with Pilton in tow, armed with his staff.

"Send Ryde after me as soon as may be."

Ottilia's heart lurched as she saw the heavy pistol in his hand. "Pray don't shoot anyone, Fan."

"It is not my intention. But we will be few against many, and I need a deterrent."

"Is it loaded?"

"Don't be absurd! What is the use of an unloaded pistol?"

Ottilia had no chance to respond to this, for the door to the back premises opened behind her and Ryde belted through.

"In good time," Francis hailed him and headed out of the front door, throwing back a parting shot as he went. "Stay here, Ottilia!"

She watched him go, her heart thumping in her chest. Could he be in any real danger? How many were in the mob? What if they should turn violent towards those who sought to prevent them having their way? Francis could get in only one shot before they overwhelmed him. He would have no time to reload.

For several heart-stopping minutes, Ottilia stood frozen to the spot, regret teeming through her. Why had she insisted on coming here? If she should lose Francis, how could she ever live with herself? Bitterly she castigated herself for her selfishness. Never had it crossed her mind she could be sending her beloved into danger. She was little better than the murderer she sought.

Miss Beeleigh's curt tone cut into her chaotic thoughts. "You'd best come and see this."

Ottilia turned her head. "See what?"

Miss Beeleigh, who was standing in the doorway to the coffee room, jerked a thumb over her shoulder.

Hurrying across the hall, Ottilia felt heartily relieved to have suffered an interruption. As she struggled to pull her-

self out of her unaccustomed panic, it came to her belatedly that Miss Beeleigh had opted not, after all, to join the
male element. Had she ever truly intended it, or was it mere
bravado?

There was no time to decide, for as she entered the coffee
room and looked out of the window in obedience to Miss
Beeleigh's encompassing gesture, she was obliged to confront the full horror of the situation.

"Oh, heavens above, they are setting up a stake!"

Chapter 14

Her husband's injunction notwithstanding, Ottilia wasted no time in weighing the advisability of remaining in the Blue Pig. Her mind reeling with shock, she thrust through the hall again and wrenched open the heavy front door.

It had never crossed her mind that the villagers would truly go to these lengths. Had they taken leave of their senses? Her fear for Francis returned tenfold, but her feet raced across the cobbles in tune with the increasing rhythm of her pulse. Straining to see across the green, her darting glance took in a couple of men a little way off the Cock into the common land.

One had hold of a pole which had been set into the ground, while another, perched unsteadily upon a chair, pounded the top of it with a serviceable mallet. Coming from behind the tavern a gaggle of boys were running, burdened with arm-loads of faggots.

Ottilia became aware of Miss Beeleigh panting behind her and wasting precious breath on useless imprecations.

"Imbeciles! Who is that fool banging in the pole? Can't see. Is it Will?"

The tapster? Ottilia was little acquainted with the man, except in his capacity as a beau fought over by the maids. It mattered little. Only one thing was in her mind. To call a halt to these proceedings before mob rule made it impossible to prevent a hideous miscarriage of justice.

As she came within hailing distance of the little group, Ottilia saw that several of those involved had ceased their labours to watch her approach. Which gave her a desperate hope they were not yet wholly given over to the loss of reason.

She shuddered to a stop, one hand at her stomach as she fought for breath. She did not lose sight of her own common sense. Useless to berate them.

"Who—is in charge—here?"

They looked at one another but were prevented from answering by Miss Beeleigh, who chose to do precisely what Ottilia was trying to avoid.

"Have you all run mad? Will, I thought it was you! Foolish fellow, what the deuce do you think you are doing?"

She was addressing the man in possession of the mallet, and the irate tone served only to put up the fellow's back.

"Burning the witch, we be. Afore her does for someone else."

"Is this Tisbury's notion?" pursued Miss Beeleigh, striding up to the stake and laying hold of it. "There's some excuse for the wretched man, but as for the rest of you—"

She got no further, for a furious Will leapt off his chair and pushed her violently away.

"You get off that, missus!"

Ottilia shot forward and grasped his arm, speaking with what calm she could muster. "Are you in charge?"

The tapster turned towards her, and Ottilia noted the red-rimmed eyes and flushed cheeks that told her the man was drink-sodden. But not so far gone that his pride could not be pricked.

"Aye. Master give me the office to make ready for to burn the witch."

Ottilia kept a steady grip upon the fellow's arm, ignoring the muttered oaths emanating from Miss Beeleigh, who was righting herself from a near fall.

"Do you understand, Will, that what you are doing is against the law? It is murder, and you may be hanged for it."

This proved an unfortunate remark, for the tapster's nostrils flared and he shook her off.

"Murder, aye. Bain't yon witch done murder? First Duggleby and now the mistress. If'n Pilton bain't arresting her, it be for the likes of us to finish her for good an' all."

"They are mad," snapped Miss Beeleigh. "See here, Will—"

"Leave it, if you please," said Ottilia so sharply that the other woman was startled enough to desist. She turned back to Will.

"You will not be permitted to do this. Tisbury and his mob will not get to Mrs. Dale." She waved towards the bridge where a dozen or more persons were gathered in an unmoving knot. "They are already stopped, do you see?"

For a brief moment, as all heads turned towards the bridge, Ottilia dared to hope for a propitious outcome. And then Miss Beeleigh ruined all.

"Ha! You see, you craven bullies? Did you think you could ride roughshod over everyone? Fools! Madmen! How dare you? How dare you behave like this?"

With a sinking heart, Ottilia saw the frenzy return to the tapster's eyes. Ignoring both women, he jumped up on his chair again, calling to the loitering boys.

"Bring they faggots! Hold the stake, Dick, whiles I bang it in more."

Miss Beeleigh, red in the face and scowling, came up to Ottilia.

"No use! You'd best come away."

By no means, but Ottilia did not waste her breath saying so. There must be help at hand, if one could only fasten upon the right person.

Thinking furiously, she looked beyond the immediate group, who had resumed their labours, the boys now starting to lay faggots around the base of the stake as Will hammered wildly with his mallet.

Spying a few stragglers standing in the road, apparently forming no part of the action, Ottilia ran her eyes across them and recognised Bessy, the maid from the Cock. She hurried across.

"Bessy! Where is Mr. Wagstaff?"

The girl looked both excited and scared. "Up to the doctor's house, m'am. Said as how he were a-going to watch over the mistress while her be cut up."

Ottilia turned back, looking for Miss Beeleigh. She was standing watching the action, hands on hips, making no further attempt to intervene.

"Miss Beeleigh!"

Her head turned, and she strolled across just as if there were nothing untoward occurring. "What is it, Lady Francis?"

"Pray go to Meldreth's house and find Wagstaff."

The woman's brows rose. "What can he do?"

"He will not countenance this. Fetch him, if you please."

Miss Beeleigh shrugged and began to move off. "If you wish it."

"And hurry, I pray you!"

Thus adjured, the woman picked up her pace. As Ottilia turned to watch her go, she saw the vicar on the road at the far end of the green, haring down in the direction of the bridge. Trotting valiantly some way behind came Mr. Netherburn. Ottilia was tempted to call to him to come to her aid here, but she dared not stop any help arriving at the bridge where by far the bigger part of the trouble was situated.

The rumble of voices from there was growing, and Ottilia guessed they would need all the assistance they could get. She looked across but could not see Francis, nor his acolytes. One or two of the crowd appeared to have made it through, but as her eyes frantically searched towards Cassie's cottage, she saw the burly form of Mrs. Dale's servant Sam Hawes planted squarely ahead of the front door, awaiting them.

Breathing a faint sigh of hope, she looked around again for succour at her end of the proceedings and bethought her suddenly of Mr. Uddington.

Turning, she looked towards his establishment and saw him standing outside his shop door, watching. A flare of anger swept through her. Did he intend to do nothing to prevent this travesty? She raised her voice and waved.

"Mr. Uddington! Mr. Uddington!"

If he heard her, he made no sign, but continued to stand, his gaze fixed upon the growing pile of faggots about the improvised stake. Ottilia ran a little towards him and tried again.

"Mr. Uddington, will you not help me?"

His head turned, and sunlight glinted off his spectacles. But he did not raise his voice or a hand to acknowledge her. A horrid fear coursed through Ottilia. Had she read it wrong? Was it he, after all? Is this what he intended all along?

She began to feel desperate. Was there none here with enough humanity remaining to stop this madness? So be it. She must manage alone.

Turning, she crossed back towards the stake. As she did so, a voice suddenly called out behind her.

"Take care, m'am! They be after you! Run!"

She recognised the shrill tones of Bessy the maid and halted, looking warily about her. She could not see the tapster, but the rest of the group were standing about the stake, watching her. Too late, the hairs on her neck prickled, and she knew someone was behind her.

Before she could turn, a painful grip seized upon both her upper arms. Without thought, Ottilia struggled.

"Let me go! How dare you touch me? Let me go!"

"In league with the witch you be," growled a voice in her ear. "Tisbury said."

Numbing horror entered Ottilia's chest as she recognised the maddened tones of Will the tapster. He was pushing her towards the stake.

"Tie her up!"

A curious sense of unreality overlaid Ottilia's senses. This could not be happening. Somewhere underneath she was aware of stark terror coiled deep inside. But the present numbness made it possible to override it.

She made no further resistance and was vaguely astonished at the steady tone of her voice, which sounded to her own ears distorted and out of true.

"You cannot mean to do this. Do you not know who I am?"

"Witch's 'complice, that's who you be," came the gruff response. "Tie her, I said."

This to the little gathering ahead of them. In the periphery of her mind Ottilia knew the rest were hesitant, and a faint hope grew.

"Don't do it," she uttered in the same strange tone of spurious calm. "He is not himself. He does not mean it."

She felt the outcome hanging in the balance for the space of several seconds. And then the gaggle of boys were grouping round her. Many hands seized her, muttering and chanting.

"Burn the witch. Burn the witch."

Ottilia felt she was dwelling in a dream. As if they played a macabre game, the boys dragged her through hastily shifted faggots to the pole. She had the oddest sensation of watching events unfold from outside herself, and she felt powerless to resist. Before she knew what had happened, her back was hard against the pole, her hands stretched behind it, and she could feel the cruel dig of ropes upon her wrists.

Her thoughts mirrored the sensation of floating, as if the world had slowed down around her.

How had she come to this? Francis would be so angry with her. Had he not told her to stay at the Blue Pig? She would have done better to obey him. How would she satisfactorily explain herself?

And then she caught the whiff of burning. Wonderingly she looked to see if they had indeed set fire to her. Her gaze cast vaguely about, and abruptly she saw it.

Will the tapster was coming from the direction of the Cock and Bottle, a flaming brand held high in his hand.

Reality swept over Ottilia in a wave, and the name engraved on her heart came screaming out of her lips.

The cry did not at first penetrate its meaning into the head of its intended recipient.

His pistol steady in his hand, Francis stood centre to the crowd, Pilton to one side, Ryde at the other. He was eye to eye with Tisbury, who was flanked by Farmer Staxton and others of whose identity Francis was unaware.

So far the barrier had held, reinforced by Pilton's staff and Ryde's rough, bare-handed disposal of those who had ventured to attempt a pass. At least two had been accounted for and were lying in the roadway nursing broken heads. Another was cooling off in the stream, Ryde having heaved him over the side of the bridge. They had lost only two, who slipped past while the defenders were occupied, and Francis was relying upon Sam Hawes to take care of those.

He had tried soft words, but they availed nothing with Tisbury, whose ale-ridden grief knew no bounds. Much of their success at holding the men at bay Francis attributed to the potations they had clearly been imbibing for some hours.

"Francis!"

This time he heard it. His view of the green was necessarily restricted, but he had already noted the activity near the Cock without fully taking in its portent.

He looked across, and for a second or two his mind played him false. How in the world could they have the witch tied there when Cassie Dale was safely in her cottage?

"Francis!"

This time it hit him with the force of a bullet from his own gun. Tillie! They had Tillie!

The scene he had taken in but sparely now imprinted itself upon his inner vision. He could see the stake, the woman tied thereto, and the man with the flaring torch moving in.

Sheer instinct overrode every vestige of shrieking horror, giving way to such rage as he had never felt before, deadly and cold.

Without thought or feeling, he cocked his weapon and moved, and the barrel of his pistol set squarely in the centre of Tisbury's forehead.

"Get out of my way."

For an instant, Tisbury's terror was reflected in his eyes. Then he swiftly backed off, knocking into the men behind.

In the spurious calm of an overlaid control, Francis saw every eye trained upon the gun. He paid no further heed but plowed through the crowd as they parted in haste before him.

As he reached the other side of the bridge, he saw Kinnerton arriving and threw him a brief nod. Then he took off, his heels flying over the grass, a single target in his eye, growing as he neared.

Tillie. His Tillie, fettered like a criminal.

She was quiet now, and Francis knew she waited for him, trusting in his strength. He willed his legs to run faster, instinctively holding his weapon high and tilted towards the heavens.

Within yards of the area, he squeezed the trigger, and the explosion shattered on the air.

Its effect was instantaneous. The entirety of the scene stilled, and Francis took it in as if it were a painting on a wall.

There was Tillie, staked and tied, surrounded by a group of youths and boys. To one side stood Will the tapster, from whose struggling hand the shopkeeper Uddington was wrenching the burning brand. A little way behind came a coterie of persons—Meldreth running, Wagstaff limping, and Miss Beeleigh bringing up the rear.

Reaching the scene, which sprang again to life, Francis pocketed his pistol as he heard the doctor's thunderous voice.

"You villains! What are you about?"

But Francis had no words. Seizing a stout branch from the faggots, he set about any within reach, wielding this new weapon to excellent effect, indiscriminately beating all around the stake at heads and backs and legs even as his victims scrambled, yelping, to tunnel out of reach.

As the circle widened, he became aware of Ryde, similarly armed and doing excellent business on his own account. Without looking, he called out.

"Relieve me here, Meldreth!"

"With the greatest of pleasure," snapped the doctor.

Francis stayed only to see the man pick up a useful weapon on his own account and take over the work, causing those who were not yet nursing bruises to retreat with alacrity.

Throwing away his stick, Francis went to Ottilia, where he discovered Miss Beeleigh already behind her, wrestling with the knots at her wrists.

His heart wrenched as he looked into Tillie's white features and saw the pools of darkness in her normally clear gaze.

"I am with you, my darling," he said swiftly and slid around behind.

Miss Beeleigh gave way as his fingers went directly to the knots. Cursing, he looked to find Ryde.

"Your pocketknife, man. Quickly!"

Without taking his eyes from the watching circle, his groom dived a hand into the recesses of his costume. Darting up, he handed over the instrument and danced back to the edge, inviting anyone who had a mind to come on and take his medicine.

None took up the offer, and Francis had a grim smile for

Ryde's black humour as he cut through the ropes holding
Tillie prisoner.

Released, her knees buckled, but Francis was instantly
there. He caught her and lifted her clear off the ground.

"Thank God," she whispered and sank into his hold.

Francis carried her away towards the Blue Pig, the un-
chained rage now roaring in his chest.

Ottilia sipped at the liquid in the glass thrust unceremoniously into her hands by her irate spouse. The sensation
of icy cold that had entered her limbs began to dissipate, but
the quiver at her fingers threatened to upset the vessel at any
moment.

Carefully she set it down on the coffee room table, uncomfortably aware of the raised voices in the hall beyond the
closed door. From across the table she caught Mrs. Radlett's
anxious gaze.

"Are you a little recovered, Lady Francis?"

Ottilia's lips felt stiff as she attempted a response. "I don't
yet know."

The widow's eye fell upon the glass. "You had best drink
it all up. I should not care to have Lord Francis blame me if
you don't."

A faint laugh escaped Ottilia. "He knows who to blame."

Mrs. Radlett's gaze widened. "Oh no, I am persuaded. If
only you had seen his face as he carried you in here, Lady
Francis. He feared for your life, you know."

Ottilia sucked in a steadying breath. Francis had not yet
rung a peal over her, but his brusqueness had warned her to
expect one. Now that she was able to think a little more
coherently, she could appreciate why he might do so, but a
slight tinge of rebellion remained.

"I don't believe my life was in any real danger. They would
have stopped. Don't you think they would have stopped?"

To her dismay, the widow slowly shook her head. "I wish I might think so."

"But you don't."

A little disconcerted, Ottilia took up her glass again. She was childishly pleased to note the shaking had reduced. A few more sips of brandy served to clear her head a little, and her gaze wandered to the window.

A tiny shudder shook her as she saw the crowd still milling about in the place from which she had so lately been rescued. It had grown in number, and the reason was not far to seek.

"They have abandoned the bridge."

Mrs. Radlett nodded with fervour. "Oh yes. I daresay the spectacle of Lord Francis laying about him proved of more immediate interest. I was outside the Blue Pig, you must know, though I dared not come across."

Ottilia frowned at her. "What happened? After Francis brought me away, I mean."

The widow's eyes lit. "Oh, it was immensely dramatic. Doctor Meldreth, together with your husband's groom and the vicar, threw the faggots far and wide. And Alethea uprooted the pole and—"

"Alethea?" Interrupting without apology, Ottilia gazed at the woman.

The golden ringlets bounced as Mrs. Radlett nodded again. "Yes, and she used it like a battering ram to thrust at the men who had come down from the bridge."

"Miss Beeleigh uprooted the pole?"

"Oh yes. She is immensely strong," averred the widow, not without a touch of pride. "The whole thing became quite chaotic, you must know. Mr. Wagstaff shouted at his son-in-law, and someone called upon Pilton to lock up the culprits. I do believe it was Mr. Uddington, now I think of it."

"Are they locked up?"

"I cannot say, for Lord Francis asked me to remain here

with you, and I could see no more. Alethea will tell us the rest, I daresay."

Before Ottilia had time to digest all this, the door opened and Francis came in, accompanied by Doctor Meldreth. Francis's brown gaze, its wrath thankfully reduced, came directly to Ottilia and raked her face. Then it fell to the glass in her hand, and Francis frowned.

"I am doing my best," Ottilia said, forestalling criticism.

Something flashed in his eyes, and the frown disappeared. His tone, as he spoke, was a deal less harsh than heretofore.

"I've asked Meldreth to look you over."

Ottilia glanced at the doctor and summoned a smile. "I am not hurt, I assure you."

The doctor returned the smile, but his manner became avuncular. "Nevertheless, it is as well to be certain. You may have suffered bruises."

"I am sure I have not," Ottilia said, steadfastly refusing to meet her husband's eye.

There was sympathy in Meldreth's look. "You were roughly used, ma'am." His glance went to her hands. "Your wrists?"

He took the glass from her fingers and set it down. As he took one hand to examine it, Ottilia looked and was chagrined to find reddened weals. She had felt no pain, but the instant the doctor set a gentle touch to the spot, she winced and hissed in a breath.

Without thinking, she looked up at Francis and found him biting his lip, his gaze darkening with some unnamed emotion. Ottilia was obliged to hold her tongue on the words that begged to be uttered. She could not begin upon any defence in this company.

"I will send you a salve to put on the bruises, Lady Francis." Meldreth laid down her hand and raised his brows. "But you have had a trying day, have you not? May I suggest you lie down upon your bed for a while?"

Ottilia balked. "Lie down upon my bed? Doctor Meldreth, I am not an invalid."

He gave her a meaning look. "Shock may be delayed, as I am sure you know."

"Yes, but—"

"Have no fear," came from Francis in the determined tone she knew well. "I'll see she does as you suggest."

A mutinous feeling entered Ottilia's breast, but she was only half aware of flashing a look of it at her spouse. He met it blandly, but she noted the stubborn tilt to his jaw.

"And perhaps a tisane of herbs," Meldreth pursued, "to help you relax."

Ottilia gave him a tight smile. "I am perfectly relaxed, I thank you, and I will drink coffee."

"Coffee is a stimulant."

Closing her lips firmly together, Ottilia refrained from any response. She was by now thoroughly irritated, not least because she was certain Francis would insist upon her carrying out Meldreth's instructions to the letter.

Nor was she mistaken. The doctor made to take his departure within minutes, saying he must send to Lady Ferrensby and return to the task he had interrupted.

Ottilia realised he must be referring to the postmortem on Molly Tisbury.

"Have you found anything yet?"

He nodded. "The lung had indeed collapsed, which at least offers the hope the poor woman suffered only briefly."

"And the weapon?"

"A small knife, easily concealed. I doubt Molly had a notion she'd been stabbed before her life was extinguished."

A choking sound drew Ottilia's attention to Mrs. Radlett across the table. She had her handkerchief to her mouth and was retching.

"You had best have some of my brandy, Mrs. Radlett," Ottilia said, pushing the glass across. "Pardon me, I should not have asked about Molly in front of you."

The widow shook her head and was presently able to raise it. Her eyes were watering, and she swallowed painfully, but there was consternation in her gaze.

"Stabbed?"

"I am afraid so."

Mrs. Radlett shuddered. "Horrible!"

"Yes."

Ottilia did not take her eyes off the woman. Was it an act? In her mind's eye, she pictured the widow Radlett dragging Molly Tisbury's body around the back of the Blue Pig. Had she the strength? Molly had been a small woman, but a dead weight was hard to shift. One need not be fooled by Mrs. Radlett's overt femininity, which did not preclude an ability to act outside that role. Ottilia would not have credited the creature with the wit to think up this devil's plan, but for the skilled acting earlier in the day.

"I think you should take a cup of tea, Mrs. Radlett," said Meldreth. "It has the property of calming the stomach, as coffee does not."

The widow nodded, rising unsteadily from her chair. "I had best beard young Patty in the kitchen."

"If she is there," said Ottilia drily. "I should not be surprised if the whole contingent had not run out to join the fun."

"Fun!"

The exclamation came explosively from Francis, and Ottilia belatedly recalled she had yet to make her peace with him. She had been feeling so much more herself, but the reminder served to pull her down a little. She reached out for the brandy, which the widow had not touched.

"Mrs. Radlett."

The widow checked at the door and turned to Francis.

"If you do find anyone in the kitchen, would you be so kind as to request them to make up a tisane and send it up to my chamber?"

The widow assented with alacrity and vanished through

the door. Meldreth followed her, and Ottilia was left confronting her spouse.

He met her gaze, but his voice was bland. "Shall we go up?"

Ottilia did not speak but rose a little unsteadily. Francis must have seen it, for his hand came instantly to her elbow. The shock of his touch went through Ottilia, and she shivered.

"You do need rest," he said, a gentler note in his voice.

Ottilia's throat thickened unexpectedly, and she did not trust herself to speak. She avoided meeting Francis's eye and began a slow progress towards the door.

"Are you able to manage, Tillie?"

She nodded, sighing out a breath. But Francis paused, bringing her to a halt. Next instant he was before her, still supporting her with one hand. The other reached to her face, and his fingers tilted her chin. Ottilia had perforce to look at him.

"You're weeping."

Ottilia sniffed. "I am not."

His expression softened, and his lips twitched. "Redoubtable as ever." He leaned to swiftly kiss her forehead. "Forgive me! I very nearly lost my temper with you, and that was cruel, after what you had suffered."

Ottilia tried to smile, but it went awry. "I know why, Fan."

"I was crazy with fear, that's why."

"It is the way of relief."

His eyes darkened. "I can't let you stay here, my dearest one. Not after this."

She drew a breath. "As to that, let us discuss it later."

"So that you may have leisure to devise arguments to persuade me? I think not, Tillie."

She allowed herself to be shepherded from the room and said nothing to the purpose as they climbed the stairs, only responding to his frequent queries as to her condition that she was perfectly able to make it to their room.

When they reached the privacy of the chamber, however,

she found she was glad enough to sink down upon the four-poster.

"I am more shaken up than I had realised."

"I am glad you admit as much."

Ottilia looked up at him. "You are angry with me, and I don't blame you."

He shifted his shoulders in that way he had which signified discomfort. "I am not angry with you."

She held his gaze. "I disobeyed your express command, and I am sorry for that. But what would you have had me do, Fan? Every man in the place was gone upon your own errand."

"True, but—"

She rode over him, speaking fast and low. "But I don't mean to excuse myself on that score. When Miss Beeleigh showed me what was happening, I did not pause to think of your injunction, nor anything but the urgent need to stop them."

"I understand so much, Tillie," cut in her spouse. "Pray don't distress yourself."

But Ottilia was not finished. "No, you don't understand, Francis! You suppose it possible for me to consider my own safety at such a time, but it is not. I may be a woman, but no less than you do I seek to act when there is something urgent to be done. You did not hesitate. Why should you imagine I might do less?"

It was not what she had intended to say, but the rush of passion proved too quick for her. Ottilia had not recognised the state of her own mind, nor seen the rebellious spark for what it was. She felt her breath shorten as she stared up at this man into whose keeping she had committed herself— her person and her life. For the first time, she felt a flicker of question at the wisdom of her marriage. The doubt was so unpalatable that she was thrown into speech.

"I was not wrong, was I? I have not been mistaken in you?"

Francis had not attempted a response, only standing above her with mute question in his face, as if he weighed his answer. But at this, a swift frown descended.

"What the devil do you mean, Tillie?"

Ottilia threw out a hand, shaking her head as a fresh threat of tears tightened in her throat.

"I don't know," she uttered, dismayed by the hoarse note. "I spoke unthinkingly."

"Yes, it is a habit with you," he returned gruffly. "But it does not mean you had no thought behind your words."

Ottilia balked at an explanation she dreaded to make. She dropped her gaze to her lap and discovered her hands there, fingers gripped together.

His tone softened. "Tillie, what is amiss? What have I done?"

She shook her head. "Nothing. Everything that is good and true."

The bed creaked as he sat beside her. A strong hand reached to cover her tense fingers. Ottilia stared at his hand, her heart thumping a slow beat that echoed in her head.

"It will never be all roses, Tillie," he said gently. "We cannot honeymoon for the rest of our lives."

A sob wrenched out of her throat, and she turned into him, throwing an arm about his neck as she felt the welcome haven of his embrace close about her. She was permitted to weep silently for the space of several minutes, until her breath calmed and she moved to sit up.

Francis released her and found his pocket-handkerchief. Ottilia took it with a word of thanks and made use of it, struggling to restore herself to her usual sangfroid.

"I have been for too long my own mistress," she ventured, looking to see how he took this. She was relieved to see his quirked eyebrow.

"A poor excuse, Tillie, but let it stand." He reached out a finger to tuck a stray strand of hair back into her cap. "I might likewise justify myself for being protective, not having been obliged to think first of my wife's safety for many a long year."

Ottilia drew a shaky breath. "But I am not a girl, Fan. I am well able to take care of myself."

He frowned a little. "Yes, under normal circumstances."

She took one of his hands and held it between both her own, meeting his gaze. "They were intoxicated. And I very nearly succeeded in bringing that tapster to his senses. Had it not been for Miss Beeleigh—"

She broke off, struck by sudden suspicion. Had it been deliberate? But for the woman's intervention, Ottilia felt certain she would have broken through Will's drink-crazed purpose. Was Miss Beeleigh simply maladroit? Or could there have been a fell intention in the attitude she chose to adopt? There could be no denying that her brusque manner of addressing the men had contributed in no small measure to their ire. Could she have meant them to turn on Ottilia?

"What are you thinking?"

The brief altercation with her husband faded into insignificance as she turned to him. "Fan, have I been blind? Have I missed it altogether?"

Chapter 15

Francis's mind jerked. Was she at that again? He reacted
without thought.

"Oh no, Tillie. Have you learned nothing today? This
cannot go on."

To his instant dismay, she shifted back, away from him.
There was anger in her face, and he braced to withstand it.

"You are not going to hold by your scheme of leaving?
Francis, for heaven's sake!"

He threw himself up from the bed and strode a couple of
restless paces. Why could she not realise how impossible it
was? Had she no inkling of the cold horror he had felt at her
danger? Was his suffering nothing to her? Frustration con-
sumed him as he turned to confront her.

"You want me to let you continue? You expect me to
stand by, after you've been all but sacrificed, while you solve
the mystery for these wretches? They don't deserve it!"

With a sinking heart, he took in the disbelief in her stare.

"You would have me walk away, knowing who will be
blamed if I don't uncover the true murderer?"

He swung away, not looking at her. Yes, he would, if it meant he could rest easy to know she was secure. He grasped at straws.

"Cassie Dale has Kinnerton to protect her. Not to mention Lady Ferrensby."

"But it took you and Ryde and Pilton, not to mention Sam Hawes. And what can Lady Ferrensby do?"

Francis had no answer to that. He was well aware of the difficulty, but nothing mattered, he told himself, except his wife's security. He fell back upon the simple truth.

"I don't want you involved, Tillie. I want you out of here. I want you *safe*."

She got up and came to him, and Francis felt his resolve lessening as she set her hands to his shoulders. He clenched his teeth against the pull of her need.

"I am involved, Fan. Guard me, if you will, but don't ask me to leave."

Almost he gave in, but the thought of that cursed stake and the flaming brand sustained him. He must be firm. Taking her hands from his shoulders, he gripped them hard.

"I'm not asking you. I know your answer already."

Her eyes darkened, and he struggled against a flush of remorse.

"You are commanding me, is that it?"

She tried to pull her hands away, but Francis tightened his grip, obliged to speak almost through his teeth to hold on to his determination.

"Yes, that is it, if you insist upon it. You may risk your life if you choose, but I will not. If that makes me a tyrant, then so be it."

She blanched and stilled, deep reproach showing in her clear gaze.

"You can't mean it, Fan. You haven't thought. How can I go? How can I? Don't you see what must happen next?"

"Yes, too well I see it," he retorted. "I see your beloved face, like Duggleby or Molly, devoid of life!"

Tillie wrenched her hands away. "Not mine! Not mine, Fan. But there will be another murder—unless I can stop it. Whoever took that message to Molly is in mortal danger."

Arrested, Francis stared at her. "You think the killer will strike again? But Cassie Dale has not had another vision."

"And must not. Therein lies my only hope."

She was right. He knew it. Yet in his fear for her, Francis hunted his mind for refutation. Or some other way to defeat the enemy. He found it.

"Leave it to Kinnerton. If anyone can keep that silly girl from blurting out whatever crazy prophecy she thinks up next, he can."

"Then what?" Tillie's clear gaze held steady on his, overlaid with a luminous film that cut him to the heart. "Do you think it will all blow over? Will there be peace in the village while each man eyes his neighbour askance, wondering? While the killer waits, seeking the right moment? No, Fan. There is a mind at work in Witherley that is bent upon destruction. As you love me, don't try to make me act against my conscience, for I cannot. *I cannot.*"

Francis reached out a finger and gently wiped the wet from under her eyes. He smiled. "I am a soldier, Tillie. I know when to recognise defeat."

With a little cry, she almost fell against him, and Francis gathered her close, tucking her head into his chest and holding it as her body trembled in his arms. His heart twisted as he heard her valiant efforts to stifle sobs.

"Hush, my dear one," he murmured, moved beyond endurance. "Since you will have it so, we will see it through."

He offered up a silent oath to keep her from harm, come what may. His Tillie had a soldier's instinct, he reflected. Yet he swore, if his own life depended on it, that she would not be called upon to fulfil a soldier's duty and die for strangers.

*   *   *

Aidan kept a firm hold of Cassie's arm as he escorted her from her cottage towards the Blue Pig. The rumpus had died down, and most of the villagers had retired to the Cock and Bottle, having at last wearied of standing around the little lock-up in which Will the tapster, his closest accomplice, and the Staxton boys had been incarcerated.

Despite this, Aidan took the precaution of borrowing Ryde from Lord Francis to walk ahead while Sam Hawes and his wife brought up the rear.

He was relieved there was no longer any sign of the stake and faggots that had been set up on the green, and he had enjoined Ryde and Sam Hawes to say nothing of them to Cassie.

"Here we are," he said as they passed into the cobbled courtyard. "You will be safe enough here until Lady Ferrensby comes."

Her expressive eyes, enormous in her white countenance, searched his gaze.

"What will you tell her?"

"To take you to her own home," said Aidan without hesitation. "You cannot remain in the cottage. Not with the villagers in this wild mood."

She stepped into the dark interior of the Blue Pig but halted there, her eyes casting about the shadowed hallway. She gave a little shiver.

"I cannot wholly blame them."

"Cassie, we do not live in the Dark Ages. However much you may conceive yourself to be at fault, there is no excuse for them, given over to mob rule as they are."

He turned to beckon Tabitha Hawes inside and guided Cassie towards the coffee room door, throwing it open. Inside he discovered the three companions—Mrs. Radlett, Miss Beeleigh, and Mr. Netherburn—but there was no sign of the Fanshawes.

Miss Beeleigh frowned as Cassie slipped into the room.

"What possessed you to bring the girl here, Vicar? D'you suppose the Blue Pig to be any less open to attack than Mrs. Dale's cottage?"

The widow Radlett looked startled. "Oh, but it must be, Alethea. For one thing, it has a stout door."

Aidan pushed Cassie into a chair. "It has also the advantage of being well populated. Besides, Mrs. Dale will not be here for long."

Mr. Netherburn had risen and now came forward with a gallant bow. "May I order you some refreshment, Mrs. Dale? Coffee perhaps?"

A smile flickered on Cassie's pale features. "To tell you the truth, I am excessively hungry."

"I should think you are," grumbled Tabitha behind her. "You ain't touched a morsel today." She looked at Netherburn. "Never you fret, sir. I'll to the kitchens and fetch her a bite and something to drink."

Netherburn gracefully retreated and Aidan smiled at the maid. "Thank you, Mrs. Hawes. I will remain with Mrs. Dale until you return."

Tabitha nodded and bustled from the room. Aidan was about to ask after the Fanshawes when Mrs. Radlett piped up.

"Poor Lady Francis has gone to lie down upon her bed. She was white as a sheet and no wonder. So horrid for the poor thing!"

Aidan's heart sank as Cassie instantly looked across, consternation in her gaze.

"Why, what happened to her?"

"Mrs. Radlett—" But Aidan was too late.

"They tried to burn her at the stake!" announced the widow in accents so close to ghoulish delight, Aidan wanted to shake her.

His eyes turned swiftly to Cassie, and he saw the predictable shock as she blanched the more. Not much to his surprise, she turned instantly to him, reproach in her tone.

"You said nothing of this."

Aidan shrugged. "I did not wish to frighten you more than I need."

Her eyes grew round with horror. "They meant it for me."

"Afraid so," chimed in Miss Beeleigh in the flat tone nearly habitual to her. "Might as well face it. They're all mad, no doubt about that."

"They were intoxicated," said Mrs. Radlett, almost on a snap.

Mr. Netherburn was shaking his head in a sorrowful fashion. "Terrible. I could not believe my eyes when I saw poor Lady Francis tied up there. And if Uddington had not snatched the firebrand from out of Will's hand, I dread to think what would have happened."

Cassie turned horrified eyes once more upon Aidan. "But why? Why should they hurt Lady Fan?"

"Said she was in league with you," Miss Beeleigh explained. "Or rather, with the witch, as they would have it."

"But that is sheer madness," protested Cassie. "When Lady Fan has been trying to help me."

"Exactly," came from Miss Beeleigh on a curt note. "Trying to help *you*."

Aidan saw the instant look of culpability that overtook Cassie and wished vengefully for a gag. Why could the woman not keep her mouth shut?

"I must see her," Cassie uttered fretfully. "Where is she? Lady Fan, where is she?"

She moved to the door, and Aidan went quickly to her side. "Wait!"

At this moment Mr. Netherburn, who was in a position to see out of the window onto the green, provided a much needed diversion.

"Ah, here is Lady Ferrensby's carriage. She has Henbury with her, I believe."

"Not a moment too soon," muttered Aidan. Time seemed to have grown wings, for it felt an age since the justice of the peace had gone to apprise her ladyship of events.

"I must go out to her."

"And I must go to Lady Fan," Cassie said again, and Aidan saw determination in the tilt of her chin. She looked across at the other three. "You said she went to lie down. Where is her chamber? Speak!"

"One moment, Cassie. Let me fetch Tabitha." A tinge of irritation showed in her eyes, and he added with a quick smile, "To show you the way."

The look turned to eagerness, and to Aidan's relief Tabitha chose that moment to come in, saying the girl Patty would be along presently with a tray.

"Excellent. But will you take Mrs. Dale to see Lady Francis, if you please, Mrs. Hawes." He held open the door for Cassie to go through and leaned close to Tabitha as she passed, murmuring, "Stay with her."

Tabitha nodded, and Aidan watched them start off up the stairs before heading for the front door. By the time he caught up with Lady Ferrensby, she and Lord Henbury had alighted from the carriage and were seen to be in close conversation with Pilton, who was guarding the prisoners in the lock-up.

Lady Ferrensby, to Aidan's grim amusement, hailed him with obvious relief.

"Mr. Kinnerton, thank heavens! I trust you are able to furnish a round tale about what has been going forward here? So far I have been privileged to understand not one word!"

Aidan had to laugh. "You are scarcely to blame, ma'am. Nor dare I suppose you will be inclined to credit the tale."

Her keen gaze met his. "Oh, I think I may. You are not a man to exaggerate, I believe."

He was pleased to think she read him so well. Without bothering to raise his voice for Lord Henbury's ears, he left the man arguing with the constable and drew Lady Ferrensby aside.

"I think you must prepare to be very much shocked, ma'am. Matters are serious indeed."

When he had told her the facts, unvarnished and as briefly as he could outline them, he saw that her ladyship was made of sterner stuff than he had supposed.

"I am more angry than shocked, sir. I have been remiss. I should have taken this matter under charge days ago."

"It is not too late, ma'am. I must beg you to take Mrs. Dale into your household for her safety."

She nodded coolly. "I shall certainly do so. But that is not what I meant." She turned towards the Cock and Bottle. "Come, Mr. Kinnerton. I think we must both take a stand."

Despite Francis's reluctant agreement to allow her to remain, Ottilia felt the truce between them to be uneasy. In a bid to mollify him a little, she had acquiesced in his insistence upon rest, supping the tisane brought up by Patty. Inwardly she chafed, a plethora of questions tumbling in her head to which she needed immediate answers. Under other circumstances, her spouse's jealous guardianship of her person would have thrilled her. But at this moment, it felt restrictive and irksome.

Thus, when a rapid tapping on the door produced Cassie Dale, Ottilia could not but feel a degree of relief.

"Come in, come in, Cassie," she called, forestalling any attempt Francis might make to prevent the girl entering their chamber.

Cassie did not wait for the door to be fully opened, but dived under Francis's arm and sped towards the bed, her dark eyes redolent of shock and remorse.

"What have they done to you?" she burst out, low-voiced. "Oh, it is monstrous. Monstrous! Are you hurt? Pray tell me you are not badly injured!"

"Not in the least," Ottilia assured her, receiving the stretched-out hands into her own as the girl leaned impulsively down towards her. Ottilia released one of her hands and patted the bed. "Sit by me, do, Cassie."

Mrs. Dale's hand gripped hers tightly, but she did as she was bid, her eyes never leaving Ottilia's face.

"I cannot bear it! It should have been me. That is what they wanted."

"And a very good thing they got me instead," said Ottilia firmly.

Glancing past the tragic-eyed girl, she noticed the maid Tabitha hovering in the doorway. Francis was still holding the edge of the door, and looking vexed. Ottilia threw him a look of apology but lost no time in taking advantage of the situation.

"Fan, I am much in need of sustenance. Would you see what can be done, if you please? I am sure we will both be safe enough with Tabitha to guard us."

His gaze narrowed, and he cast a glance at the robust figure of the maid. Then he strolled towards the bed and quirked an eyebrow, quite in his usual fashion.

"I am de trop, is that it?"

Relief flooded Ottilia, and she threw him one of her mischievous looks. "That is it exactly."

His lips twitched. "Then there is nothing for it but to retire gracefully. Mrs. Dale, you have precisely fifteen minutes."

"Francis!"

"Thank you," Cassie said, quite sincerely. "I will not tire her, I promise."

Francis nodded and went to the door. "Mrs. Hawes, you'll remain in the room?"

Reassured on this point, he at last removed himself, and once she had begged the maid to be seated, Ottilia was able to give her attention to Cassie Dale, who demanded an account of her sufferings. Ottilia made as light of the occurrence as she could, but Cassie was not easily satisfied, determined to shoulder the blame.

"Miss Beeleigh said the villagers think you are in league with me, and that it is all my fault because you were trying to help me. And she is right."

"Nothing of the sort," Ottilia retorted. "Miss Beeleigh is a great deal too busy."

"Well, but she did try to stop this from happening, so perhaps I should thank her," said Cassie on a forlorn note.

Ottilia eyed her. Had Miss Beeleigh exaggerated her own part in today's events, when her efforts had hampered Ottilia not a little?

"She tried to stop it? How do you mean?"

Cassie's features blanched. "They have been talking of burning me at the stake for days. Miss Beeleigh heard of it and did what she could to scotch it."

A flurry disturbed Ottilia's pulse. "When?"

"Yesterday, before Duggleby's funeral." Cassie looked round at her maid, who had taken a seat on the dressing stool. "Is that not what Alice said, Tabby?"

"Alice? She is presently here helping Patty," Ottilia said. "Miss Beeleigh sent for her because of all the upset."

Tabitha rose and came to the bed, her frowning gaze steady on Ottilia's face. "What is it, ma'am? You look as if you've a thundercloud gathering over your head."

Ottilia's senses were humming, but she forced a smile. "I am merely weighing one or two notions in my mind, Mrs. Hawes."

Cassie was regarding Ottilia in frowning question. Trying to see what her maid saw? Ottilia summoned every ounce of her customary sangfroid.

"Pray tell me what it was that Alice said."

"Oh, it was horrible—" began Cassie, but the maid Tabitha intervened.

"Best if I tell it, Miss Cassie, for it were to me Alice came."

"Yes, and she did not wish to speak before me, but Tabby made her say it nonetheless. We were on our way back from the church."

"I'd the intention of telling you in any event, ma'am," said Tabitha. "Only with what happened this morning, it went clean out of my head."

Ottilia strove to curb her impatience. "Quite understandable. But pray go on, Mrs. Hawes."

"Well, from what I could understand, it seems Miss Beeleigh took it upon herself to give snuff to any as were in Tisbury's taproom come yesterday morning. She spoke of this stake-burning talk and said as she'd have her musket out on any who took it into their heads to do any such."

"Did she indeed?" murmured Ottilia appreciatively. A tactical move which one could not but admire, even while deprecating its intent.

"That were all very well," said Tabitha grimly, "if Miss Beeleigh hadn't taken it into her head to start on you, my Lady Fan."

Ottilia raised her brows, a little spark of realisation slotting into place like the cogs in a wheel. "How, pray?"

"Warning them folk, if you please, as they hadn't ought to be thinking such foolishness as of you being in league with the witch, for as they'd heard as you were by way of being a champion to Miss Cassie. Nor she didn't scruple to say as the Lady Fan were looking to have someone's head, and if Tisbury weren't careful, you'd have his. I can't give it you word for word, but that's the brunt of it, ma'am."

"It will suffice, I thank you," Ottilia said drily.

Cassie was looking from one to the other of them, puzzlement in her eyes. "But why, Tabby, are you cross about it? I thought to be grateful to Miss Beeleigh for taking the trouble to work on my behalf. No one else in the village has done so."

Tabby Hawes set her arms akimbo, and the ire in her eyes deepened, her face colouring a trifle. "Because none but a nodcock wouldn't think to say such a thing to such folk as the Tisburys and Staxton and their like, for as anyone with any sense in their head would know as it was bound to make them mad as muck and bring on the very thing as it was trying to stop."

"Just so," Ottilia agreed.

But she refrained from pointing out that Miss Beeleigh, so far from being a fool, possessed a staggering intelligence— if only she could be induced to use it for the greater good. Which was, Ottilia feared, past praying for. There was only one person who inspired the woman to charitable deeds, such as she saw them.

Cassie's face had fallen, and Ottilia was not much surprised. She had so few fighting in her corner, it must depress her to be obliged to relinquish this tiny ray of hope. Ottilia made a bid to brighten her.

"Don't look so dismayed, Cassie. After all, you are well supported in Mr. Kinnerton, are you not?"

At mention of his name, a light flared briefly in the girl's face, and then died again. "He has been inexpressibly kind."

"More than that, I think," suggested Ottilia with a meaning look.

Cassie's eyes instantly clouded. "No." Her gaze swung this way and that. "At least—it might be that he wishes— but it cannot be."

Glancing at the maid, Ottilia noted a troubled expression in her face. Deliberately, Ottilia threw the matter into play.

"What do you think, Mrs. Hawes? Have you not noticed a certain warmth in Mr. Kinnerton's regard when he looks at Cassie?"

Tabitha compressed her lips. "It don't matter what I notice, ma'am. She won't pay me no mind."

Cassie leapt up from the bed, confronting her nurse. "Because I know you are in Lady Ferrensby's confidence, Tabby. It is all of a piece! I daresay you knew all along she meant for this to happen."

The maid retreated to the window. "Ain't no manner of use carping at me, Miss Cassie. How should I know what is in her ladyship's mind?"

"Because the two of you are forever making plans for me without my knowledge," cried Cassie, like a thwarted child. "Do you think I cannot tell? Not all my visions are laden with doom, Tabby. Do you think I cannot see the picture that is in Lady Ferrensby's head?"

Her voice had thickened with the hint of tears, and Ottilia swiftly cut in. "Dear Cassie, pray do not upset yourself. If your aunt—or godmother, or whatever she is to you—has such images, they are only a hope for your happiness."

Both visitors were staring at her. Shock and dismay were in Cassie's eyes, but Tabitha's had narrowed with suspicion.

"Her ladyship told you, then, did she?"

Ottilia laughed. "Dear me, no, Tabitha. I am confident Lady Ferrensby would never betray Cassie." Her eyes went to the girl. "What is she to you, Cassie? I feel sure the relationship is close."

"She is my aunt," Cassie uttered, still looking utterly confounded.

"Then you came here under a cloud, I must surmise," said Ottilia calmly, holding out a hand to the girl in invitation.

Walking as if in a dream, Cassie came back to the bed and took her hand. Ottilia drew her down to sit again on its edge.

"Pray don't look so astonished. I assure you it is not second sight. My gift, if you can call it that, lies in an ability to notice things others might not."

Tabitha gave a grunt and resumed her seat on the dressing stool. "How did you guess it, ma'am?"

"Oh, by a number of things," Ottilia said airily, not wishing to upset Cassie with the notion of how easy it had been to make this deduction. "For one thing, in a certain light you have a look of your aunt, Cassie. Then I'm rather afraid I embarrassed you by referring to Mr. Dale." She gentled her tone, holding the girl's hand rather tighter. "There is no such person, is there?"

Cassie sighed. "Aunt Ida chose the name from Armadale."

"That is your real name? Charis Armadale?"

A film of liquid reamed Cassie's eyes, and she looked down. "It is as well I do not use it, for I have disgraced the name."

Ottilia wasted no time on spurious question, going directly to the heart of the matter. "Who was he, Cassie?"

She jumped, her downcast eyes flying up to Ottilia's face. She was taken too much by surprise, Ottilia guessed, to prevaricate.

"Our neighbour." The characteristic passion deepened her voice. "It was wicked of me."

"Wicked of him, too, Cassie."

"You tell her, ma'am," came gruffly from Tabitha Hawes. "I've said it often and often, but will she listen?"

Having formed a fair opinion of the child's depth of self-loathing, Ottilia was not much surprised. That the fellow had not been induced to behave honourably by Cassie told its own tale.

"If he was already married, he was doubly wicked."

Cassie sucked in a rabid breath. "You guessed that, too?"

Ottilia chose not to answer this. "Could the scandal not have been hushed up?"

"That's what I said," groaned Tabitha. "Only the silly wench couldn't keep her tongue."

"How could I?" Cassie uttered wretchedly. "I felt so dreadfully. I knew it was wrong, but he offered me comfort at a time when—when—"

"At a time when you were made unhappy by what you see as an unfortunate talent?"

"Yes."

Ottilia took her other hand and held both of them, looking the girl directly in the face. "And now you believe you are unworthy to deserve Mr. Kinnerton's affections."

Cassie burst into sobs. Ottilia promptly drew her into a comforting embrace. Over the heaving shoulders she saw Tabitha diving a hand into the recesses of her costume. The maid came out with a pocket-handkerchief, but instead of bringing it over to her charge, she applied it to her own wet eyes. A little amused, Ottilia waited for the girl to recover sufficiently to sit up again, and then Ottilia signalled to the maid, who handed over the handkerchief. Ottilia watched Cassie wipe her eyes.

"I believe you do Mr. Kinnerton an injustice, Cassie."

She heaved a sobbing sigh. "Oh, I could not. I admire him greatly."

"Yes, but you do," Ottilia insisted.

The dark eyes surveyed her, registering doubt. "What do you mean, Lady Fan?"

Ottilia smiled. "I think I will allow the gentleman to speak for himself, which I cannot doubt he must do in the very near future."

This prophecy appeared to alarm Cassie Dale so severely that Ottilia was almost betrayed into merriment. But the door opened just then to admit her husband, and one look at Francis's face served to shatter any inclination to laugh.

"Oh, what is it?"

Francis moved into the room and shut the door. "Pilton has found a bloodstained kitchen knife in Hannah Pakefield's commode."

The atmosphere in the taproom of the Cock was subdued, although the place was crowded. Bessy the maid had taken office behind the counter, while Tisbury and his co-horts were sitting in a morose group on the benches around the hearth. The landlord had his head in his hands, elbows on his knees, while Staxton had placed an awkward arm across the fellow's bent shoulders.

No one had troubled to glance up as Aidan led Lady Ferrensby into the room. Then the maid, catching sight of so unusual a spectacle, gave a shriek.

"My lady! Master Tisbury, my lady be here!"

From the immediate reaction all around, it was evident that the exclamation stigmatised but one person. Heads shot up. One after the other, blurry-eyed men surged to their feet, snatching off hats and wiping greasy hands on sweat-stained breeches.

Farmer Staxton looked up, his jaw dropping, and Aidan saw him slap his companion on the back and mutter something into Tisbury's ear. The landlord unfolded his torso, revealing features haggard and red-eyed with weeping. And no doubt a liberal ingestion of ale, came Aidan's cynical thought.

"M'lady?" mumbled Tisbury confusedly.

Lady Ferrensby's hand left Aidan's arm, and she went forward. Wholly ignoring everyone else, she stopped before the landlord, who made a clumsy movement as if to rise and failed.

"Don't get up," said her ladyship.

But beside him, Farmer Staxton shoved a hand under the fellow's arm and tugged him to his feet, holding him there even as Tisbury sagged a little at the knees. It was evidently a momentous thing for the great lady of the village to enter the tavern. There could be no doubt of the high level of respect in which she was held.

"I am sorry for your loss, Tisbury," she said evenly, "which provides some little excuse for your conduct." Then she turned, surveying the remainder of the company. "As for the rest of you, I have only one thing to say. If you are determined on bringing back barbaric practises, let us have the stocks set up, shall we? Then you may all take your turn in them."

Aidan watched with grim satisfaction as the battery of faces turned sheepish, eyes dropping to the floor. Muttering broke out, together with an embarrassed shifting of feet. He saw Staxton swallow hard and open his mouth.

"I'll see to them boys of mine, my lady. I promise you that."

Lady Ferrensby looked him up and down. "And will you see to yourself, Staxton? I understand you made one of the party intent upon raiding Mrs. Dale's cottage and dragging her forth."

Staxton shuffled his feet and wiped his free hand on his breeches. Her ladyship waited, but he did not venture upon a retort. Lady Ferrensby nodded.

"Very good. I see you realise your error. You will do better to comfort your friend than to engage upon criminal pursuits. Yes, I said 'criminal,' Staxton."

This in response to a sudden fearful look as the man's eyes rose swiftly to glance at her briefly.

"I hope to dissuade Lord Francis from pressing charges, since I believe you have all of you acted somewhat out of character. But I cannot promise any of you"—with another slow look around to encompass the whole company—"that you will not find yourselves in the dock at the next Assizes."

A flurry of excited whispering broke out at this, and a couple of men called out to protest that they were not of the party bent upon mayhem. Aidan intervened to scotch this at once.

"None need attempt to escape retribution, for we have witnesses enough to know just who was involved." His tone hardened. "And, I may add, if you stood by while these events were in train and did nothing to help Lady Francis, nor to stop your fellows behaving in this disgraceful fashion, you may well be accused of conspiracy."

This threat caused a mass retreat upon the part of the onlookers, who shifted back, one going so far as to sidle to the door in a bid for freedom.

"Where be you off to, young varmint?" came a senile voice from outside.

Seconds later, the escapee returned, with Pa Wagstaff's fingers attached to his left ear, the old man demonstrating surprising strength. Aidan was obliged to bite down on a laugh as the fellow squealed. Released, he scuttled behind a collection of bodies and dropped out of sight.

Wagstaff's rheumy eyes travelled around the room and discovered Lady Ferrensby. "Giving 'em snuff be you, my lady?"

She moved towards him. "You have my heartfelt condolences, Jeremiah. It's a tragic day for Witherley."

The old man's gaze turned sour. "Aye, so it be, when the whole village be crazed."

"Which is exactly why I am here," said Lady Ferrensby, turning back to the rest. "This must stop, do you understand me? We are in enough trouble as it is, what with Duggleby's murder and now Molly."

Muttering broke out again, and Tisbury spoke up at last. "Bain't no wind of who killed Duggleby, if'n the witch bain't done it. Nor I don't believe as there be another who killed Molly, neither."

Aidan strode up to the man. "You don't know what you're talking about, Tisbury. You may count yourself highly fortunate if your antics today have not driven away the very person who has pledged to get to the bottom of these murders."

At this, Staxton burst in. "If'n it be yon Lady Fan you mean, it be her as said Molly and Tisbury done for Duggleby."

"Nothing of the kind," snapped Lady Ferrensby. "And I should know, for I was present at the Blue Pig yesterday when the matter was spoken of. Be that as it may, take this for a warning. One more trick of this nature and Lord Henbury will have the lot of you taken to Warwick gaol to await the Assizes. I trust I make myself plain."

The murmuring started up again, and a few nods were seen. Lady Ferrensby passed one more glance about the taproom and turned to Aidan.

"Mr. Kinnerton, your arm, if you please."

But before he could escort her out, the sound of pounding footsteps seized the full attention of the taproom, and a murmuring started up. Seconds later, the door burst open and Will the tapster flung into the room, his accomplice and the three Staxton boys crowding in his rear.

Wagstaff lifted his staff, and for a moment Aidan thought he was going to use it to swipe at the newcomers. But his words forestalled any action.

"Be it done?"

Mystified, Aidan was about to demand enlightenment when Tisbury took the floor.

"What be you doing here, Will? Bain't Lord Henbury said as you be for the lock-up nor morning, you and the boys?"

Despite his dishevelled appearance and the grime and dust upon his face and clothes, Will's eyes were blazing with excitement.

"He've let us go, Master, for as Pilton have locked up Hannah Pakefield."

"What?" burst from Lady Ferrensby.

" 'Tis true, my lady. Pilton said as how it be Hannah done for Molly."

With Tillie on the warpath, Francis had no choice but to relax his dictum that she remain in their chamber for the rest of the day. Besides, he was almost as hot against the doddering justice of the peace as was his irate wife. Without any other evidence than this conveniently placed kitchen knife, Henbury had acted.

"It is a plant," Tillie repeated yet again, pitching her voice at a level that the fellow could not fail to hear. "There can be no other explanation."

"Twaddle, woman! Who'd shove the thing in a drawer, except the murderer?"

"Just so, sir. But that does not mean that the murderer was Hannah."

"Hey? Hey? When the body was found in her coffee room? Got the body. Got the weapon. What more do you want?"

"Proof, Lord Henbury. This is proof of nothing save that the body was where it was and the knife was found in Hannah's commode. It does not say who put them there."

The argument was taking place a little way off the old

lock-up, but Lord Henbury's deafness made it unlikely that
the woman inside would not hear what was being said. The
round little building of grey stone gave off a truly depressing
air, the domed stone roof rising directly from the walls and
topped off with an ornamental ball. A stout wooden door,
barred for extra strength with rusty nails, contained one
small rectangle of an opening in the top, and the only other
windows—if one could call them that—comprised a couple
of small slits near the top at either side. The place could
not have been more than six feet in diameter, and Francis
could well imagine the fetid air and stinking condition of
the interior.

To one side of the door sat Pakefield, groaning and leaning a broken and bleeding head against the cold stone in an
attitude of defeat, for he had fought like a tiger to prevent
his wife being incarcerated until Pilton had dealt him a blow
with his long staff. The constable now stood silent sentinel
before the door, the large lock-up key attached to his belt.

Francis, keeping pace with Tillie, had arrived too late to
aid with the landlord's brief rebellion, and they were indebted
to Mrs. Radlett, hopping up and down in intense dismay, for
their information. Miss Beeleigh had elected to assist Tabitha
Hawes to guard Cassie Dale in the Blue Pig, but Patty the
maid was much in evidence, alternately weeping and hectoring at the stolid Pilton.

Tillie had lost no time in going directly to the source of
the trouble, but her efforts had so far met with no success.

"Besides," she pursued, "do you not remember that I
thoroughly searched Hannah's room this morning and found
nothing?"

"Ha! Exactly why I set Pilton to do the same. Can't trust
a woman to do the job properly." He glared at Tillie. "Didn't
find the knife, did you?"

Tillie's gaze met Henbury's with unblinking clarity, but
Francis detected the underlying rage in the tautness at her
cheek.

"I did not find it because it was not there."

"Hey? Hey? What the deuce do you mean, woman? Pilton found the thing in an instant."

"Yes," said Tillie, and Francis could swear she was speaking through her teeth, "because in the meanwhile, someone had put it there to be found."

Although how a person could have done so remained a question. So far as Francis was aware, Hannah Pakefield had been in her own quarters pretty well throughout the day, with Pilton outside, at least until the riot. Had Tillie thought of that?

"Don't know what you're talking about, woman," snapped Henbury. "Know the Pakefield dame did the job. Have it on excellent authority that she said she'd be revenged on the Tisbury woman. Now we have the weapon, case is all sewn up."

Francis watched Tillie's face as she stared at the man. But before she could say anything more, there was an eruption from the Cock across the way. Looking up, Francis saw Kinnerton hurrying across with Lady Ferrensby on his arm, a crowd from the tavern falling in behind. He put out a hand to his wife's arm.

"Rescue," he murmured, nodding towards the approaching group.

Tillie glanced at him and then in the direction he indicated. Relief flooded her features. "Thank heavens!"

"I think you may have to change your tune, Henbury," said Francis, not without a touch of satisfaction.

But Tillie shook her head, her glance flying to Francis's face. "Oh, he won't. Not for Lady Ferrensby. But I have a better notion." With which, she moved a little to meet the new arrivals, calling out, "Mr. Kinnerton! Pray do me the kindness to go and fetch Doctor Meldreth."

"Why do you need Meldreth?" asked Lady Ferrensby as they came up, removing her hand from the vicar's arm.

Tillie did not answer immediately, instead addressing

Kinnerton again. "Pray don't delay. Fetch him as swiftly as you may, if you please. And ask him to bring his bag."

The last request was called after the vicar's retreating form, and he flung up a hand in acknowledgement and hastened away on his errand. By this time, Lady Ferrensby had turned her attention to Lord Henbury, asking for an account of his actions. Nothing loath, the aged justice of the peace launched into a fresh recital of Pilton's findings and the assumptions he had made.

Francis cornered his wife under cover of this discussion.

"Tillie, what is it? What are you planning?"

She looked round. "I am trying to get Hannah out of there, of course."

"But why Meldreth?"

"That you shall see."

An echo of her mischievous look flashed in her eyes briefly, and Francis rejoiced to see it. The contretemps earlier in the day had resulted in a dismaying feeling of distance towards him from his wife, and he'd had ample time to regret some of the things he'd said. Not that he had changed his mind, for her safety was still paramount with him and he determined she would go nowhere without his escort until this murderer was apprehended. But the effect of the argument upon the woman he loved was hard indeed to bear.

"Poor Hannah! Poor Hannah! Oh, Lady Francis, I am sure she did not do it."

The widow Radlett had joined them. Francis noted an oddly intent look in Tillie's eye as she turned her attention to the woman.

"What makes you so certain, Mrs. Radlett?"

Mrs. Radlett's eyes widened, and her jaw dropped open. "But—but you have said as much yourself to Lord Henbury."

Tillie's clear gaze remained fixed upon the creature's face. "Yes, but why do you think her innocent? Have you any reason to suspect someone else?"

An attack direct. Francis held his breath. Into his memory

leapt the instant just before he had been swept up into the argument about going or staying. What had his wife said? Something about having been blind? Had she fastened upon the identity of the murderer? He had missed it, and Tillie had said nothing of it since.

The widow was shaking her head with vehemence, setting the feathers on her bonnet adrift. "Gracious, no! How you do take one up, Lady Francis. Why should you think—? No, no, nothing of the sort."

Running out of steam, she blinked rapidly, looking decidedly upset. Casting a glance at his wife, Francis noted how her clear gaze remained steady on the other lady's face until Mrs. Radlett began to fidget, a delicate colour creeping into her cheeks.

At last Tillie gave one of those reassuring smiles of hers. "Ah well, no doubt I was mistaken." But Francis was pretty sure the widow, as well as he, knew full well she did not truly think so. He was not surprised when Mrs. Radlett found an excuse to remove from the scene.

"Only look how the villagers are jostling. I had best go and warn Mrs. Dale not to venture out of the inn."

Tillie watched her go, and Francis took a step in, speaking in a murmur. "You think she knows something?"

His wife's eyes turned towards him, and he read the answer in her face even before she nodded. "Oh yes. Or she thinks she does and is terrified of discovering that she is right."

Chapter 16

Francis was conscious of a sliver of excitement and was about to ask for further enlightenment when the doctor's name was shouted out and Kinnerton was seen to be returning, Meldreth at his side, carrying his medical bag. They were coming at a fast walk, and Tillie instantly moved to meet them.

The doctor, to his credit, did not bother to interrupt the argument in train between Lady Ferrensby and Lord Henbury, which was affording a deal of entertainment for the onlookers from the tavern.

"Kinnerton has told me the trouble," he said, a trifle out of breath as he reached Tillie's side. "How can I serve you, Lady Francis?"

"Pray will you insist on examining Hannah Pakefield, Doctor Meldreth? I meant to ask you to do so this morning, only in the press of events it slipped my mind."

"Hardly surprising," commented the doctor on a rueful note.

Tillie disregarded this. "I believe that woman has a heart

condition. If she is left in that awful hole, I dread to think of the consequences."

Meldreth's brows flew up. "Indeed, it is the worst possible place for her." He nodded. "Leave it to me."

Francis could not but feel sceptical of anyone succeeding with Lord Henbury where Tillie had failed, not to mention Lady Ferrensby. But it was quickly apparent that Meldreth had an authority that the old man was apt to respect, although he did indeed voice the strongest objections.

"Can't see why you need to check the woman over now," he complained. "Tomorrow will do as well."

"Not if she is ill," the doctor pointed out. "You could not wish her to expire before she has a chance to come up on charges before you."

"Expire? Expire? Only expiring she's going to do is on the rope, old fellow."

"Indeed, but that must be after the trial, my lord. One would not wish to have to explain to the authorities at War-wick that the prisoner was unable to appear because we had not exercised due care and attention."

This argument had a powerful effect upon Lord Henbury. He was, after all, a mere local officer of the law and had no further jurisdiction once he had committed the matter for trial to a higher court. It would scarcely sit well for him to lose an accused murderer prior to her appearance at the Assizes.

Pilton was ordered to unlock the door, a move that roused Pakefield from his stupor. The villagers, who showed a tendency to surge forward, were thrust back by the constable's staff. Lady Ferrensby stood aside with Kinnerton, and Meldreth went into the dark interior of the lock-up, Henbury at his heels. Seeing his wife about to follow, Francis went quickly up to her and seized her arm.

"What are you doing?" he asked sotto voce.

"I am going in."

"No, you don't. Besides, there is scarcely room," he added, poking his head inside.

It was dark, dank, and dismal. In the light from the open doorway, he could see Hannah Pakefield, a sunken heap on the cold stone floor. She was breathing stertorously, air heaving slowly in and out of her chest. Meldreth was already on his haunches beside her, while Lord Henbury, his head thrust forward on his neck like a chicken, was rocking on his spindly legs.

Francis moved back out and pulled Tillie aside. "We are blocking the light."

"Did you see her?"

"She's on the floor. Lord, I believe she is ill! I thought it was one of your tricks."

Tillie was peering around the edge, trying to see inside. "No, I truly am concerned for her. She looked grey this morning, despite the wounds on her face, and her breathing was shallow."

"It's worse now," Francis said frankly. "I hope to God the woman does not die on us."

"If Meldreth gets her out and into her bed, I imagine she will recover presently."

But it was several moments before the doctor emerged, and he was alone. He looked round and selected the vicar.

"Kinnerton, your aid, if you please." Glancing at the shattered landlord of the Blue Pig, he added, "Pakefield, we are bringing Hannah out. Send your maid ahead, if you will. Your wife must be put straight to bed."

There was a flurry of noise and activity as Patty raced off towards the inn, closely followed by several young girls who came out of the crowd, Bessy among them. Kinnerton disappeared inside the black maw of the lock-up along with Meldreth, and Francis pulled Tillie away a little to join Lady Ferrensby.

"We will but hamper the proceedings, my love."

"Quite right, Lord Francis," Lady Ferrensby said, turning at once to Tillie. "Thank goodness you thought of Meldreth. I could make no headway at all with that foolish old martinet."

Tillie sighed. "I'm afraid he has developed the habit of old age where nothing will do but one's own opinion."

"Old age?" scoffed Lady Ferrensby. "Nothing of the sort. The man has been a mule for all the years I have known him. Though I admit his hardness of hearing has made him ten times worse."

When Hannah Pakefield was brought out, obviously upright only by virtue of being closely held between the doctor and the parson, a loud cheer went up from the crowd. Amazed, Francis glanced round.

"Why in the world are they pleased?"

Lady Ferrensby's brows were raised as she surveyed the villagers. "Oh, because Henbury has been bested. You will note, however, that Jeremiah Wagstaff looks less than happy."

Which was true. The ancient stood champing his jaws, leaning heavily on his staff, his eyes vengeful as he watched the cavalcade moving slowly towards the Blue Pig, Pakefield jogging alongside, his eyes fixed upon his wife in her state of semi-collapse.

"Jeremiah knew this was happening, I surmise," pursued Lady Ferrensby. "I daresay he would have told Tisbury and the rest if Will had not forestalled him."

Evidently it would not have suited ill with Pa Wagstaff had Hannah Pakefield died in the lock-up, Francis thought cynically. Tisbury looked merely morose, which was scarcely surprising. But there was no sign of Will the tapster or the boys who had earlier occupied the lock-up, which afforded Francis a moment of grim amusement. No doubt they had made themselves scarce for fear of being put back in to replace the lost Hannah.

His ruminations were interrupted as Tillie's hand slid into the crook of his arm. He glanced down at her.

"Back to the Pig?"

"Yes, for it occurs to me," she said, low-voiced, "that if the knife found its way into Hannah's commode, the back door key may likewise have returned like a homing pigeon to its place on the window ledge."

Ottilia had perforce retired early, urged thereto by her careful spouse. In the privacy of their curtained bed, she felt safe enough from listening ears to rid her mind of the deepening suspicion that was now almost a certainty. Francis was at first incredulous, but as she outlined her reasoning, he slowly became convinced.

"You have done it again, my woman of wonder."

She welcomed his embrace but felt compelled to whisper a caution. "None of it would convince a jury, let alone the villagers. I have not a shred of real proof."

Francis captured her restless hand and held it. "Then how are we to prove it?"

Ottilia drew in a tight breath. "I must find out who took the message to Molly."

"Have you any notion who it might be?"

"One, perhaps."

"And if you find it out, will that be enough?"

"It may save a life. Though I am in hopes any further attempt will be delayed now Cassie has removed from Witherley to Lady Ferrensby's home."

Francis moved a little in the darkness. "You mean if there are no visions, the finger cannot be pointed elsewhere?"

"Just so."

Then a thought exploded in Ottilia's brain, and she sat bolt upright, disarranging the bedclothes. Beside her, Francis pushed up on his elbow.

"What in the world ails you, Tillie?"

She turned, looking back at the dark shape beside her. "You have set off a firecracker in my head, Fan! We have no proof, but we can catch our murderer just the same."

Her night's rest was indifferent, her mind turning on the

morrow and the actions she must take to set her scheme afoot. But since it depended wholly upon the identity of the person who had been suborned into taking a message to Molly, she had first to unravel that mystery.

Awake betimes, Ottilia was anxious to set out the moment she should have broken her fast. She had perforce to wait for her husband, Francis having decreed that she might not set foot outside their bedchamber door without his escort. She chafed while he dressed, and chafed again, once she had swallowed a hasty meal of a single baked egg accompanied by a slice of fresh bread, while her spouse worked his way through a plateful of ham. As it chanced, this little delay afforded an unexpected opportunity to glean a vital piece of information.

Patty sailed into the coffee room where they were partaking of breakfast just when Ottilia decided to broach a second cup by way of distracting herself from the spectacle of her spouse eating at what she considered an unnecessarily leisurely pace. She had discovered the coffeepot had cooled and hailed the maid with relief.

"Patty, thank heavens! Will you fetch a fresh pot of coffee, if you please?"

The girl plonked down the covered silver dish she was carrying, shoving it towards Francis. "Your eggs, sir."

"Eggs as well?" burst from Ottilia before she could stop herself.

Francis looked up. "I'm hungry. Besides, the Lord only knows when we'll get to eat again with what you have planned for today."

Incensed, Ottilia would not trust herself to reply. At a time like this! Desperate for anything to speak of other than food, she caught the maid before she reached the door.

"How is your mistress today, Patty? I meant to ask you before."

Patty's freckles wrinkled across her nose. "Abed her be, and Master says as how he be a-going to send for Doctor

Meldreth, for as her bain't ate nowt nor yesterday when Miss Beeleigh took up a tray to her whiles we were all out on the green."

Ottilia eyed her with interest. "That was kind of Miss Beeleigh."

"Aye, for Cook be rushed off her feet," said the maid, adding with a darkling look, "Not as I be best pleased, as Miss Beeleigh took as if her be mistress in this place."

"With everything at sixes and sevens, and poor Hannah laid up, perhaps it was as well," soothed Ottilia.

Patty tossed her head. "Bain't as I hadn't got all done and dusted without her say-so." A gleam of triumph entered her eyes. "It be me as found the back door key and all, spite of having all to do."

Ottilia's senses prickled, and she saw Francis halt in mid-chew, his fork in the air, his gaze riveted on the maid.

"You found the key?"

The maid shifted her shoulders. "Well, it be on the cellar stair when I went down for to fetch up the joint from the cool room below."

"When?" barked Francis. "When did you find it there?"

Patty jumped at his tone, and Ottilia threw him a repressive look.

"Was it before all the business on the green?" she asked, carefully casual.

The maid's puzzled stare withdrew from Francis and found Ottilia. "Aye, for I be just come up with the joint when you come into the kitchen, m'am."

"You put the key back on the windowsill?" Where Ottilia had indeed found it, when she had gone to look for it there after Hannah was freed from the lock-up.

"Aye, for I meant to tell Master. Only with all the rumpus, I forgot."

"I am not surprised," Ottilia said lightly. "It is a wonder you managed to do so much. Be sure I will tell Hannah how excellently you have coped."

Patty's eye brightened, and as quickly fell again. "If'n it be as Mistress bain't took and hanged."

With which gloomy utterance, she departed. Ottilia found her spouse's gaze on her.

"I remember you saying how much people knew that they didn't know they knew."

Ottilia laughed. "Just so. It is astonishing what is noticed without awareness." Then a stray thought came into her head, and she mused aloud, "I wonder."

"What do you wonder?" came from her spouse, pardonably irritated.

She looked at his plate. "I wonder when you are going to finish that so that we may begin. Do you not realise, Fan, that the matter is pressing?"

The Cock and Bottle not yet having opened its doors, it was left to Francis to rouse the servants and hunt out the maid Bessy. Since he had hastened his breakfast, he was not in the best of moods. Having laid down the law to his wife, however, he could scarcely cavil at her impatience.

If the truth were told, Francis reflected, he was lacking sleep. Tillie had tossed the night away until he had drawn her into his arms and stroked her into quiet. That she was restless and troubled was hardly surprising, for she had set herself a tricky task. In vain had Francis tried to think of an alternative scheme. He could not like the one Tillie had outlined, but for all his furious thought, he could come up with no alternative.

Finding Bessy had not been part of her original intention, but Tillie had not enlightened him as to her reason for the change, and if she did not wish to tell him, he would not ask. Aware of the childishness of this resolve, he was yet unable to overcome it.

Once he had extracted Bessy from the house via the back door, however, Tillie's intent rapidly became clear.

"Do you recall on the night your mistress died seeing anyone about near the Cock? It would have been late, Bessy. Think carefully now."

Bessy frowned in an effort of concentration but then shook her head. "Bain't seen no one, m'am."

"Well, did you hear anything unusual?"

The girl shifted her shoulders and looked away. A sign of discomfort?

"No, m'am."

Francis watched his wife, reading the signs in her clear gaze. She was going to change tack.

"You did not go to bed until late, I think, for you were upset."

Shock leapt in Bessy's eyes, which became riveted on Tillie's face. How in the world came she to guess that? Francis saw her gaze narrow a little and knew she was going to push the maid further.

"Patty came over from the Blue Pig, did she not? She brought news for Will."

The maid's chubby cheeks reddened, and her eyes rimmed with liquid. Words burst out of her mouth. "That fussock! Her've no right. I telled her afore, but her won't listen. Bain't for her to come mewling round here."

"Only she brought such news as turned the house upside down, did she not? And I daresay Will paid you no attention afterwards."

"Bain't as I care," snapped Bessy. "Nor as I'd time for no gossiping, not with the work as I'd to finish."

"No, and nobody could blame you if you were late," said Ottilia gently. "If perhaps you had gone to your room to have a good cry first."

Bessy looked as if she might dissolve again right at this moment, Francis thought.

"Now think carefully, Bessy. When you went to do your chores, was there any unusual sound or sight?"

An echo swept through Francis of the admiration he had

felt for his wife when he had first seen her in action during the drama in his family last year. The moment she had an advantage, she was ruthless in following it up.

Sniffing back the threatening tears, the maid cast her eyes to one side, staring into the middle distance. Francis almost held his breath, his attention riveted on his wife as, with infinite patience, she waited. Could it work? Would not the girl have been too wrapped up in her grudge to notice? But then Francis saw the frown deepen in the maid's face. Was a memory about to spring?

All at once, Bessy's head turned back and she stared at Tillie, surprise in her face. By God, but Tillie was sensational!

"Aye, there do be summat," said the maid. "When I be dousing the fire in the mistress's parlour, it be like tapping on a windowpane."

Someone trying to attract attention? Francis saw the characteristic warm smile spring into Tillie's face.

"Oh, very good, Bessy. Thank you. You did not, I take it, investigate this tapping?"

Bessy shook a regretful head. "No, for as I bain't paying no mind. I'd forgot as I heard it, m'am."

A pity, Francis mused. She might have made a better witness. But Tillie had not quite given up.

"Could you have seen a face at the window perhaps?"

The girl thought for a moment, but even to Francis's mind, it was obvious there was no more to be got from her. He saw a look he recognised in Tillie's face and was astonished at how well he was able to read her. She would not pursue it further. She thanked the girl again.

"Never mind. What you heard will suffice, I believe."

The maid curtsied and scurried back into the house, while Francis searched for words to express all he had felt. Tillie tucked a hand in his arm before he could think of anything. Her tone was brisk.

"The vicarage, I think."

"You want Kinnerton?" asked Francis, surprised.

"Kinnerton? No, indeed. But Mrs. Winkleigh employs Jenny Duggleby."

"The blacksmith's daughter? Why do you want her?"

Francis saw her draw a tight breath, and his hand went to press the fingers resting on his arm.

"What is it, my dear one?" he asked in a softer tone than he had used towards her since yesterday's disagreement. Her clear gaze met his, and his heart tightened.

"Only someone well acquainted with Molly would think to catch her attention by tapping on the window, and there was intimacy between her and the Duggleby household."

"And so?"

"I fear it may be Jenny who was sent to fetch Molly from the Cock and Bottle the other night."

Mrs. Winkleigh was discovered to have become as over-protective of Jenny Duggleby as Francis was of Ottilia. She greeted the visitors politely enough, ushering them into the rather bare room that apparently served Mr. Kinnerton for a parlour. But when asked for the girl, her eyes narrowed and she set her arms akimbo.

"Talk to Jenny, is it? What now, pray, if I may ask, ma'am? Hasn't she been upset enough?"

Ottilia's interest quickened, and she raised her brows. "More recently than by her father's demise?"

The housekeeper blew out her cheeks. "Wouldn't you be, if the fellow who did it turned out to be crazed enough to do it over again? And in brutal fashion, too."

Francis had gone over to the window and was looking out across the vicarage gardens. He turned at this.

"For the Lord's sake, woman! Why do you suppose my wife is here, if not to find the perpetrator?"

Mrs. Winkleigh's willowy frame swayed a trifle, and she clutched a hand to her breast, gazing at Ottilia in horror. "You can't mean to accuse poor Jenny?"

Quick suspicion kindled in Ottilia's mind, and she rapidly revised her first instinct to repudiate this for an absurdity. "Is there some reason why I should?"

A gasp escaped the housekeeper, and her hand left her breast to go instead to her mouth, as if she sought to chide it for letting out incautious words.

Ottilia became sharp. "Mrs. Winkleigh?"

"You'd best speak up at once, if you don't wish me to draw in your master on this matter," Francis said curtly, coming across to flank his wife.

Ottilia said nothing, for his altered attitude towards her was so very welcome. But she could have wished he had kept silent. She did not care to use threats. Yet it had the desired effect.

Mrs. Winkleigh sighed out a defeated breath. "You'd best speak to Jenny. Not that she's in any way to blame."

"But she knows something?"

"I don't know if it has to do with that woman's death," said Mrs. Winkleigh worriedly. "But I can't deny Jenny's been out of sorts since that night. I'll fetch her to you."

She hurried out, and Ottilia turned as Francis spoke, low-toned.

"Is it possible you are wrong, Tillie? You never gave the girl a thought, did you?"

Struck, Ottilia stared at him. "As a potential murderer? Why should she do it? How would it serve, presuming it to have been in revenge for her father's death?"

"If she found out Molly was responsible?"

"Or if she heard from Patty that we thought so," said Ottilia, thinking fast.

It was possible, but it rang false. She had met Jenny Duggleby but the once and had been struck by her intelligence. But to go so far as to mirror the vision?

"And she can't have murdered her own father," Ottilia said, putting her next thought into words.

Francis frowned. "Why not? If she knew of her mother's ill-treatment at his hands? And she would have been well placed to carry out everything needful. If you are willing to suspect the mother, you had as well extend to the daughter."

But Ottilia's instinct argued against it, although she could not fault her spouse's logic. Besides, she was nearly certain she had it right. And with luck, she was about to garner the word of one supremely important witness.

There was time for no more speculation, for a knock at the door preceded the entrance of the girl herself, accompanied by Mrs. Winkleigh.

Francis instantly cocked an eyebrow at Ottilia, and she took it that he was prepared to eject the housekeeper should she wish for it. She gave him a tiny smile and an infinitesimal shake of the head as she went forward.

"Jenny, thank you for coming to talk to me," she said, holding out a hand.

It was immediately apparent that Mrs. Winkleigh had spoken nothing but the truth. The girl's erstwhile assured air had deserted her, and her eyes—were they a trifle reddened from weeping?—had a tendency to wander. In an effort not to meet her gaze, Ottilia decided. Jenny did not take the outstretched hand, nor even look at it. Instead, her hands remained clenched on folds of her apron.

"Come and sit down, my dear."

Ottilia took her gently by one shoulder, drawing her towards a wooden settle where she obliged the girl to sit. Taking her place beside her, she looked up at her husband and the housekeeper.

"Would you object to allowing me to talk with Jenny alone?" She saw refusal in Francis's eye and remembered his intention to keep her in sight at all times. Not unhopeful, given the better atmosphere between them, she threw him a look of appeal. "Just outside the door?"

He hesitated and then nodded. Opening the door, he looked at the housekeeper. "After you."

Mrs. Winkleigh did not move, her eyes going to the girl. "Do you want me to stay, Jenny?"

At this the Duggleby girl looked up. "Bain't no need, m'am."

Relieved, Ottilia waited until the door had closed and they were alone.

"You are troubled, I think, Jenny."

The capped head bobbed in acquiescence, but still Jenny did not look at her. Ottilia opted for tactics designed to shock.

"Has it to do with the night Molly Tisbury was murdered?"

Up went the head, and a groan issued from the girl's throat. But still she volunteered nothing. Ottilia took the bull by the horns.

"Was it you, Jenny, who was asked to take a message to Molly?"

At this, there was a frantic shaking of the head, and out it came at last. "Not me, m'am. But—but I'm afeared as it were Ma."

Ottilia's brain shot into high gear. "You think your mother may have been the messenger? What makes you say so?"

Tears had begun to trickle down Jenny's cheeks, and her voice became hoarse. "Bain't that. Not only."

Then it was Bertha who took the message? But what more? Ottilia prised one of the clenched hands off the girl's apron and held it fast.

"Tell me, Jenny. What is it you fear?"

The girl's tear-drenched gaze turned to meet hers. "I think as Ma done it."

Shock suspended all thought in Ottilia's head for an instant. No, she must not be sidetracked. Although not for a moment had she suspected Bertha's hand in Molly's murder. But why not? The woman had strength enough. Only there was no reason for her to kill Molly unless she had also murdered her own husband. Comprehension made Ottilia tighten her grip on Jenny's closed fist.

"Are you thinking your mother also killed your father? Is that it, Jenny?"

A burst of sobs confirmed it. Jenny retrieved her hand and grasped her apron, throwing it up to her face and weeping into its concealing folds.

Ottilia made no attempt to quiet her, using the moments she must wait for the overwhelming grief to expend itself in furious thought.

Had she missed a trick? She had been so sure she had the answer, but doubt sprang up, throwing her calculations into disarray. Bertha had been a suspect in her husband's death from the start. If it had not been for the evident apathy of her demeanour in the aftermath of Duggleby's death, Ottilia must have counted her at the top of her list. In her experience, a guilty person did not fall into this frame of mind, their deeds weighing too heavy. Rather they took the attitude adopted by Uddington or the Tisburys, ready to attack any who chose to examine their actions.

"What makes you think this, Jenny?" she asked, when the girl's sobs had abated.

The apron had slipped down, and Jenny gave a doleful sniff. "Like a cat on a hot bakestone be Ma. Bain't like her, not even when her found as Pa—" She broke off and swallowed painfully.

Ottilia sought to turn the girl's mind. "When did you notice her behaving like this, Jenny?"

"Nor two days," muttered the girl.

"Since the night of Molly's death, in fact?"

Jenny nodded miserably. "Nor her weren't in the house that night, not 'til late."

"How do you know? Did you hear her go out?"

"Bain't that. Only young Ned be crying and woke me. I

thought nowt to it at first, expecting as Ma'd go in to him, for as he've been having bad dreams. Only he bain't stopped a-crying, so I got up to him—and Ma weren't in her bed."

She ended on a note of panic, and Ottilia was moved to set a hand about her shoulders, which were racked by intermittent shivers.

"Did you wait up for her?"

Jenny's head shook again. "I crooned Ned to sleep again and then went to my bed." Her fingers twisted in her disarranged apron. "I couldn't sleep. I heard Ma come in."

"Do you know what time it was?" asked Ottilia without much hope.

"It be late, I know that."

"You did not go in to your mother?"

Another desolate sob escaped the girl. "I dursn't."

"Why not?" prompted Ottilia. "It is not as if you could have known what had occurred that night."

Jenny sighed a quick breath in and out. "I dursn't for as I thought as Ma were up to smithy, searching."

"For what?"

But here the girl would not be drawn. She kept her eyes averted and did not speak. What did she know of Duggleby's alleged windfall, if anything? She was clearly aware of something, for her silence could not otherwise be explained. Matters were too desperate now for such reticence.

"Was it your father's gold?"

Jenny flinched. "Bain't none."

Ottilia's tone sharpened. "How do you know, Jenny?"

"For as he told me. He were drunk, else he'd have said nowt. He told Ma to spite her."

Or did he? Ottilia was ready to believe the fellow had lied as easily to his daughter as to his wife. But she let it alone for the moment.

"Did you speak of your mother's absence in the morning?"

Jenny shuddered. "How could I? That fretted her be, snapping at Ned and telling him to get out from under her feet. Nor her'd no good word for me, neither. Nor you'd think as her bain't done no cooking ever for her burned they sausages and near set the house afire pulling down the pot of porridge. Half the logs come with it and rolled near full across the kitchen floor."

Evidence of a severely unquiet mind, Ottilia was bound to agree. No wonder Jenny's suspicions had been aroused.

"And then no doubt you heard the news about Molly," she said gently, "and put two and two together to make five."

The girl's eyes, bright with distress, came round to face her. "What be I to think? Nor that bain't all. If'n Ma done for Molly, why'd her do it? Why, if'n her bain't done for Pa?"

A fresh deluge of weeping ended this outburst, and Ottilia absently patted the girl on the back. At least she had judged Jenny's intellect aright, she reflected. It was too much to expect she would make the jump to realising that more was needed by way of evidence than mere supposition. However, there was a great deal here to be checked, and Ottilia resolved to repair at once to the blacksmith's abode.

There was nothing of the lacklustre about Bertha Dugleby today. Jenny had been right. On opening the door and spying Ottilia, she looked horrified and made to shut it in her face. Francis's hand shot out, holding it strongly.

"Stand aside, woman, for we are coming in."

For a moment the blacksmith's widow held fast to the edge of the door, glaring defiance. Then, with a grunt of frustration, she let go and vanished inside the house.

Francis swept through the door, and Ottilia, following more slowly, could hear Bertha's growling protests as she was bodily seized.

"The parlour, Fan," said Ottilia hastily, throwing open the door she remembered from the last occasion.

Her spouse manhandled the woman into the little room and thrust her down into a chair.

"Stay!" he ordered, as if he spoke to a disobedient dog.

Mrs. Duggleby glared resentfully up at him, but she remained where she had been put. Francis released her and straightened up.

Ottilia shut the door and came into the room. She abandoned any notion of requesting her husband to leave her alone with the woman. Not that he would have agreed, as he had made plain on their way here once she had given him the gist of what Jenny told her.

"That settles it. I'm not leaving you alone in a room with a wretch who may have already murdered twice, so don't waste your breath in asking."

In vain had Ottilia argued that she was as certain of her facts as she could be.

"Until your scheme comes to fruition, Tillie, we will take no risks."

The feeling of being unduly restricted had come back, but at this moment she was heartily relieved to have the strong arm of her husband just where it was needed.

She took a chair to one side of where the woman sat, noting that Francis retreated but a pace, his eyes trained upon Bertha's limbs, alert, like the soldier he'd been, to any slight sign of her making a sudden spring.

Ottilia had no wish to cause dissension between mother and daughter, but she was hard put to it to know how to question the woman without giving away the source of her intelligence. She tried a simple approach.

"Bertha, had you heard that someone was sent to Molly Tisbury with a message on the night she was killed?"

There was an immediate effect. The woman's face drained of colour, and her eyes grew round and fearful. Yet she did not open her lips in response.

Ottilia wasted no more time. "Was it you, Bertha?"

For a moment nothing in the creature's aspect changed. Then abruptly she fisted her hands and set them either side of her forehead, tightly shutting her eyes.

"Never meant no harm," came in a low mutter from her lips. "Bain't my doing."

"You mean you did not kill her?"

"Bain't my doing," she said again, beginning to rock back and forth, still holding her head as if it pained her.

Ottilia exchanged a glance with Francis, who was looking decidedly grim. He raised his brows, mouthing, "What now?"

Well might he ask! The woman was distraught. Guilt, yes, but for what offence? It was evident Ottilia would get no direct answer if she continued in this line. She sought for a way to calm the woman, in hopes of loosening her tongue.

"Bertha, have you been searching for your husband's pot of gold?"

The change of subject broke into the concentrated absorption of Bertha's mind, as Ottilia had hoped it would. The fists did not come down, but her eyes opened.

"Why wouldn't I? Bain't as he'd took it with him. If'n it be hid, in smithy is where it be."

She was breathing hard, plainly driven beyond endurance. But by what? Curbing her impatience, Ottilia gentled her tone.

"Where did you look in the smithy?"

The woman's hands, still curled tightly, dropped to her lap. She did not look at her interlocutor, nor at Francis, her gaze swinging this way and that, almost as if she spoke to herself. Too overwrought to be much aware of what was happening?

"All round I looked. In forge itself even. Pulled aside muck and timber. Dragged down his tools. Tried if'n the floor be hollow, if'n he'd dug a hole. Bain't nowt. Bain't nowhere."

"Then it is perhaps safe to assume it does not exist, Bertha."

At this, the woman's countenance turned in Ottilia's direction, fire in her eyes. "It be there! It be there someplace, nor Duggleby wouldn't have beat me for looking if'n it bain't."

Ottilia seized on this. "When did that happen, Bertha? When did he beat you?"

"Night afore." Her tone became vicious. "Dead, and the last I knows of him be his belt across my back."

Startled, Ottilia sought to clarify this. "You did not see him at all after that? Until his body was found?"

"Aye."

"Pardon me, but did he not come to your bed?"

Her mouth twisted, and Ottilia thought she bared her teeth.

"Not he. Left me with my back burning and went off to Cock. Likely he snuggled up along of some new doxy." Her eyes narrowed with anger. "Only I heard him. In the night, I heard him."

"Doing what?"

"In the smithy, do you mean?" asked Francis, cutting in for the first time.

Bertha barely glanced at him. "Aye."

"What was he doing?" Ottilia repeated.

"Hiding that there gold, bain't he?"

"How can you know that?" Francis again, speaking the thought in Ottilia's mind.

"For as I heard the hammering. Up to roof he be, hiding yon gold up there."

Ottilia's eyes leapt to meet those of her husband, and she read the exact same surmise that had flown into her head. Not Duggleby, but the murderer. And Bertha had heard the preparations. Little did the woman realise how her words served to exonerate her. She did not kill her husband—and Ottilia's surmise was correct.

"How could he get up to the roof?" she asked, guessing what was coming.

"Likely he took old Uddington's ladder."

"And put it back again the same night?"

"Aye, afeared as I'd see it and know his game. Not as I seen him Monday, for as he bain't come in. Sent young Ned for to fetch his dinner. Nor I bain't gone next or nigh forge."

"Because of the beating?" Ottilia surmised.

"Aye. But now Duggleby's gone, and the roof is down, and that gold bain't there. It bain't there."

Her fists beat upon her knees, and Ottilia could not but recall how the creature had shown a mere suggestion of this underlying passion on the last occasion, when she had confessed her futile feeling for the wretch who'd betrayed her and his vows. With his loss, however, it appeared her love was rapidly turning to hate.

But there was yet the question of her involvement in the second murder. Ottilia phrased her question carefully.

"What were you promised, Bertha, if you took that message to Molly?"

Chapter 17

Having dined at the Hall upon the previous night, Aidan had timed his visit early on purpose, not wishing Lady Ferrensby to suppose him to be hankering for a second invitation. He had to be back in the village by the afternoon, in any event, to meet with Tisbury and Wagstaff. Meldreth having completed the postmortem and sanctioned a burial, it was time for arrangements to be set in train.

Aidan had come to check that all was well with Cassie, but he was struck by the drawn look in her ladyship's features and did not hesitate to voice his concern.

"Are you quite well, ma'am?"

Lady Ferrensby straightened up, casting a brief glance towards Cassie, whose dark eyes moved to study her at this question.

"Why, do I look out of sorts?"

"You look as if this business is preying upon your mind," said Aidan frankly.

Cassie's features expressed instant dismay. "It is my fault.

Forgive me, pray. Aidan says I should not have spoken of my vision, and he is right."

"I said nothing of the kind. All I said was—"

"You did not phrase it so perhaps, but it was what you meant," Cassie cut in, an undertone of passion reverberating in her voice.

"True, but I never imputed blame to you for these murders."

Lady Ferrensby uttered a short laugh. "It is pointless arguing with her, Kinnerton. If Cassie can find a way to writhe in guilt, she will do so."

Quick anger kindled in Aidan's breast, but he maintained a cool tone. "I believe Mrs. Dale has reason enough to feel haunted."

Cassie's tragic gaze came back to his face. "Lady Ferrensby does not believe that I see these things. She thinks I suffer from an overactive imagination. I only wish it were so."

Aidan smiled at her. "I believe you."

Her lips trembled on a smile, and the dark eyes became luminous. "I know. You are the greatest comfort to me, Aidan."

"I am glad."

At this moment he caught the wry look of amusement in Lady Ferrensby's face, and his cheeks warmed. At least it was not disapprobation. Not that he supposed his intentions required her permission, but since Cassie was in some sort her protégée, it would be politic to court her approval.

He was just wondering if the moment was propitious, when the butler entered to announce another arrival.

"Lord and Lady Francis Fanshawe."

Cassie started oddly, the colour fluctuating in her cheeks. Aidan looked worriedly at her, and by the time his attention turned to the visitors, Lady Ferrensby was already exchanging greetings, her manner gracious and welcoming.

The instant the door closed behind the butler, however, this spurious politeness deserted her, and her hazel eyes abruptly showed a haunted air that was so reminiscent of Cassie that Aidan was startled.

"You are recovered, I hope, Lady Francis?"

Transferring his regard to Lady Fan, as Cassie had it, Aidan noted an energised look about her. She wafted a hand dismissively.

"Oh, I am perfectly well, I thank you, but I have not come for that."

A sudden shift in Lady Ferrensby's face gave evidence of hope. "You have news?"

"Not that precisely," the other responded. "At least, not in the way you mean. But I had to come."

Cassie started forward. "There has not been more trouble? You are not hurt?"

Lady Francis caught Cassie's hands as she reached her. "Nothing of that sort. But it is you I have come to see, Cassie. I need your help."

The dark eyes grew wide, and Aidan was conscious of a burn in his chest.

"Mine? But what can I do?"

Lady Francis seemed to steel herself. "I am sorry to ask it of you, Cassie, but could you bear to have another vision?"

Shock ripped through Aidan's breast. An outrageous request! Unsurprisingly, Cassie was staring at her, blankness in those lustrous, large eyes. Then they darkened. She wrenched her hands away, and her tone as she spoke was husky and vibrant.

"Do you make game of me, Lady Fan? I see what I see. I cannot make a picture appear in my head."

Aidan longed to reach out to her in comfort but perforce held back for he had no right as yet to show protection in company. He had not realised he was staring at Lady Francis until she spoke to him.

"Do not look daggers at me, Mr. Kinnerton."

At which, Aidan caught a fiery glance from Lord Francis,

but he was forestalled from making any comment as his wife turned back to Cassie.

"I am not making game of you, Cassie. Indeed, I am deadly serious. You shall have a vision this afternoon, if you please, and a very specific one."

Lady Ferrensby was regarding the woman with a deep frown. "You mean you want her to pretend?"

"Just so."

A sharp breath left Aidan's chest, and he struggled to contain the flooding fury. He knew it sounded in his voice despite himself.

"You would set her in danger? Merely upon a whim? I should have thought you, Lady Francis, must be the last person to ask it of her after your experience."

At this he came under instant fire from Lord Francis. "Her reason is sufficient, Kinnerton. What, do you suppose her cruel in this? You may count yourselves fortunate I have not removed her from the scene. Which I would have done had not her representations of the need to remain spoken too deeply to be ignored."

Aidan eyed him in frowning silence as he took this in. Then he looked to Lady Francis.

"If I have done you an injustice, ma'am, I offer you my apology." His glance swept back to Lord Francis. "I think your husband must understand my concerns in this for Mrs. Dale's safety."

"Yes, I do," snapped the other man. "But you would do better to hold your fire until you know all."

Before Aidan could respond to this, Lady Ferrensby intervened.

"Gracious me, gentlemen! Is it to be pistols at dawn? Have we not enough on our hands without the two of you coming to blows?"

Aidan tightened his lip upon an unwise retort, noting that Lord Francis did likewise.

"Shall we return to the matter at hand?" came coolly from Lady Francis.

It was fortunate, Aidan felt, that Cassie chose to reenter the lists at this point.

"Why do you wish me to pretend to have a vision?"

"Because I have not a vestige of proof, my dear, and I need to catch our murderer red-handed."

Aidan's mind leapt as fast as Lady Ferrensby's words. "You mean you know who did it?"

Lady Francis drew a visible breath. "I am as certain as I can be at this moment."

"Which is why you are seeking to trap the villain?"

"Indeed, Lady Ferrensby."

"Well, who is it?"

As eager to hear the answer to this as her ladyship, Aidan was instantly disappointed when Lord Francis shook his head.

"She will not tell you, ma'am."

"But she has told you?" Aidan asked shrewdly, and he was surprised to see a sudden grin lighten his lordship's countenance.

"On this occasion, I have been so privileged, yes."

A little smile of appreciation crossed the lips of his spouse, and Aidan was conscious of a twinge of envy. Might he hope for a like felicity? If his suit should prosper, of which he was by no means certain.

He became aware that Lady Ferrensby was eyeing her visitor in some dismay and wondered at it. Then Lady Francis saw it and reached a hand towards her hostess.

"I regret I cannot reassure you at this time. I have learned, from bitter experience, ma'am, that a word out of place may be a word too many."

"But do you suppose any one of us will speak of it?"

For the first time Lady Francis's clear gaze showed a hint of some inner torment. "A young man died because of some incautious words of mine."

"Tillie, are you at that again?" burst from Lord Francis. "It is not so! We all were to blame, if blame there was."

A blind look was in the lady's eyes as they turned towards her husband. She put out a hand, and he took it and gripped it.

"It is not a mistake I intend to repeat, Fan."

There was a silence. Aidan felt unexpectedly moved as he watched Lord Francis set a kiss upon the hand he held, a gesture innocent and yet wholly intimate in that particular instant. Glancing at Cassie by his side, Aidan saw her eyes riveted upon the little drama. As the gentleman released his lady's hand, Cassie cried out.

"It will not happen again, Lady Fan. Only tell me what I must do, and I will do it."

Aidan's heart sank as Lady Francis outlined the details of the charade. Needed it might be, but it hurt him to see Cassie dragged into just such a situation as she ought to avoid. He resolved to ensure her safety, at all costs. And after, he would see to it that there would be no further repercussions from the visions she could not avoid.

Ottilia was not much surprised to discover that Cassie Dale had the makings of an actress. Indeed, she rather suspected the girl was apt to exaggerate her passionate outbursts. Not, Ottilia did her the justice to own, from any conscious will. Likely she had developed the habit in defence against an environment of disbelief and scorn. From such stray remarks as Cassie had let fall, her immediate family had not been sympathetic. It was hardly surprising, in her lonely state, that she strove for greater and greater effects in her conduct.

However it was, no fault was to be found with her required demeanour when she came bursting into the Blue Pig's coffee room, a wild look in her features that appeared wholly natural even to Ottilia's eyes.

"Lady Fan? Where is Lady Fan? I must see her at once!"

All the habitués were present, having arrived in due time, agog for news. The widow Radlett, who did not look as if she had slept well, started violently. Miss Beeleigh's calm demeanour did not desert her, but she looked up with a frown. Most affected was Mr. Netherburn, distinctly ill at ease this afternoon. He rose from his chair and half started towards Cassie.

"Mrs. Dale! What has occurred?"

Francis had been standing by the empty fireplace, leaning his arm along the mantel. He straightened up, gesturing towards Ottilia seated in her favourite chair at the round table, which gave view at the same time of the green and any who entered the room.

"My wife is here, Mrs. Dale. What is amiss?"

Cassie's large eyes fastened upon Ottilia's face. "Lady Fan, help me, pray!"

Ottilia got up at once, moving to catch the girl's hands. "Calm yourself, Mrs. Dale." She drew Cassie to the table as Francis pulled out a chair. "Come, sit. Of course I will help you." She reseated herself, not wishing to lose the advantage of watching the reactions of those present. "Now, my dear, tell me what has happened."

"She's had another of them visions," came gruffly from Tabitha Hawes, who had entered behind Cassie and was hovering in the open doorway.

"Good Gad!" Mr. Netherburn visibly blanched, setting a hand to his chest. "Not another death."

"Oh, it was horrible!" cried Cassie, quite as if she really had seen something. "I went at once, to warn her. Only Tabby would not let me go in to her. So I came to you, Lady Fan, for I don't know what to do."

"Who? Her—who?" came from the widow Radlett in a hoarse tone barely above a whisper.

Ottilia cast a quick glance at the woman and noted her pallid cheeks. Afraid to hear the name? Or had she guessed what was coming?

"Bertha Duggleby."

"*Bertha?*" uttered Mrs. Radlett, shock in her voice.

Of course, Ottilia thought. She had expected the girl Jenny to be named. Taking in the reactions of the other two, Ottilia noted that Mr. Netherburn was looking horrified, while Miss Beeleigh's frown had merely deepened. But it was she who broke the silence following the revelation of the name.

"Not going to tell us you foresaw Bertha's death now, are you? Really, Mrs. Dale, it is too bad." She flicked a look at the maid. "Shut the door, Tabitha. Don't want this getting out to the village."

"No, indeed," agreed Ottilia hastily. "Don't say any more, Cassie, until we are assured there are no listening ears."

"I'll check," said Francis.

He moved swiftly to the door and reopened it, walking out into the hall. There was silence in the coffee room, every eye upon the open doorway. As her spouse made a show of opening the other doors that led into the hall, Ottilia had the chance to take stock again.

Evelina Radlett was severely affected, her breath rattling a little as she drew it in and out. Her features had paled considerably, and there could be no doubt at all that she knew just what this new vision portended. Miss Beeleigh's expression denoted both that smug superiority of hers and disgust, as if she was thoroughly put out by Cassie having yet another vision. The surprise was Mr. Netherburn, who truly looked as if he was about to suffer some sort of spasm. Had he begun to suspect?

Ottilia became aware of Cassie's gaze on her and quickly focused on the girl's face. Cassie's brows flicked upwards in a questioning look, and Ottilia gave her a swift smile of reassurance before calling out in a low tone to her husband, whose figure she glimpsed moving back in the direction of the coffee room.

"Is all well, Francis?"

"It looks all clear. There is no one about."

He came in and shut the door, remaining with his back to it, as if he stood on guard. Ottilia took hold of one of Cassie's hands again.

"Now, Mrs. Dale. What did you see?"

Cassie shuddered artistically, resuming her role. "It was so horrible, Lady Fan. She was in the smithy. Bertha, I mean. There was a rope, and—and—a shadow swinging in the light that came in from the roof."

A swift glance took in the widow's horror, Netherburn's distress, and Miss Beeleigh's growing revulsion. Ottilia remembered to inject the appropriate dismay into her own voice.

"You mean Bertha was hanging from a roof beam?"

Cassie nodded, shivering violently. "I must tell her, must I not?"

"For pity's sake!" burst from Francis, as if goaded. "Have you learned nothing, Mrs. Dale? Did not Kinnerton specifically instruct you not to speak of your visions?"

Ottilia lifted a warning finger as Cassie flung her hands over her face. "Enough, Francis. The girl is distraught."

"His lordship is right, though, my lady," said Tabby gruffly. "She hadn't ought to have said nothing to nobody, not even you."

"Yes, well, it is too late to be thinking of that," said Ottilia firmly. "We must do what we can to minimise the damage." She looked around the room. "At least those of us here may be trusted not to speak of it."

This assurance did not appear to be mirrored in the faces of the trio, despite the widow's fervent nod and Netherburn's rapid, "I shall say nothing, ma'am, believe me." It was left to Miss Beeleigh to express the feelings of the group.

"After all that has passed? Good God, no! Shouldn't dream of spreading such a tale about."

"Just so," said Ottilia, and she turned again to Cassie.

"Mrs. Dale, it is not safe for you to be seen about the village. You had best remain here with us for the time being. Mrs. Hawes, will you be so kind as to fetch Mr. Kinnerton?"

"Oh no," uttered Cassie, rising swiftly, her dismay genuine this time, Ottilia was convinced. "Aidan cannot be disturbed. He is with Tisbury and Wagstaff, arranging Molly's funeral, for he told Lady Ferrensby so this morning."

"Then he will come when he is finished," said Ottilia in a soothing tone. "Mrs. Hawes?"

"Go and fetch him at once, Tabitha," cut in Miss Beeleigh, as if her word carried more weight. "Ain't as if we don't all know the vicar cares more about Cassie Dale's safety than that foolish woman's funeral."

Foolish? Ottilia eyed the creature with unalloyed wonder as Tabitha Hawes exited the room, ignoring Cassie's protests. Foolish Molly had undoubtedly been, but her death had been encompassed in a fashion as macabre as it was undeserving. Was there no pity at all in Miss Beeleigh's heart?

Mr. Netherburn had taken a seat next to the widow, his anxious gaze upon her pallid features. "I wish you will not look so distressed, dear Mrs. Radlett. I am sure the danger has been averted."

Ottilia caught the widow's appalled expression before she managed to overcome it with a pathetic attempt at a smile. Her voice quavered.

"Horace, is it possible—do you suppose Bertha might take her own life?"

"Instead of someone else doing it for her?" cut in Francis with a ruthlessness Ottilia had not expected of him.

She watched to see how Evelina Radlett took this and was scarcely surprised to see tears start in the creature's eyes.

"Determined on setting us all by the ears, are you, Lord Francis?" snapped Miss Beeleigh, bristling in defence of her friend. "For my money, Evelina is in the right of it. No reason at all to suppose the murderer will strike again. All know

Bertha has been a wreck since that scoundrel of a husband got himself killed. Wouldn't surprise me at all if she took means to end her suffering."

Not until she'd found that pot of gold. But Ottilia did not voice the thought, instead glancing at Cassie Dale's now pallid features. Was the girl taking this seriously?

"Don't look so worn, Cassie," she said, unthinkingly using the girl's given name. She realised it even as Miss Beeleigh's sharp-eyed glance hit her, and she hastened to retrieve the slip. "Oh, I do beg your pardon, Mrs. Dale. I am far too free, but you worried me so."

Cassie shook her head. "It makes no matter what you call me." She came to the table, looking down into Ottilia's face. "Is she right? Could Bertha be so unhappy she might—she might—"

Ottilia seized her hand and drew her down to sit again. "Dear Mrs. Dale, if she did, none could blame you."

"But what if she hung herself?" cried Cassie, desperate now.

It was clear to Ottilia that the notion of the vision, despite its being invented, had penetrated Cassie's mind so deeply that she almost believed in it. Did she suppose Bertha Duggleby might take it into her head to do the deed, merely because she heard about it? As hear about it she would, since Francis's excursions in the hall were intended to ensure Patty came out of the kitchens to investigate. By tonight, the tale would be all over the village. Which was precisely what Ottilia wanted.

Cassie's fears were not wholly allayed, although Aidan's representations, as he drove her back to Lady Ferrensby's home, were comforting.

"Don't forget, Cassie, that the whole thing is a concerted plot. Lady Francis meant for the village to know about the vision, which is why you must be safely ensconced at the Hall."

"But I had no vision, Aidan," Cassie protested. "And if Bertha should die because of it—"

"She will not die. We don't know precisely what Lady Francis is planning, but you may be sure she will have taken this into account. There must be a solid reason why she used Bertha in particular."

Cassie looked round at him. The gig was proceeding at a sedate walk, the road to the Hall being pitted with holes since the storm. She could not help being glad of it, for it prolonged this precious time when they were for once alone, Tabitha having been sent, at Lady Fan's request, to find Sam at the cottage and give him certain instructions.

She regarded Aidan's profile with a jerk at her heart and had spoken the thought in her mind before she could stop it.

"You are the kindest of men, Aidan."

He looked round quickly, and Cassie saw a light in his eyes that made her breathless. He pulled up his horse, and the gig came to a halt. Cassie's heart began to beat a little faster.

"Forgive me if I am precipitate," he said, "but I must speak."

Cassie was instantly gripped by conflicting emotions. She had no thought of visions or second sight at this moment, but she knew precisely what Aidan intended. While she longed for him to say the words, she dreaded to hear them. He would offer. And she must refuse him. The knowledge sent her spirits plummeting. No, she could not bear to hear it.

"Don't!" she cried, shifting back a little in the confined space. "Don't say anything, Aidan. It cannot be. I cannot endure to hear the words, though I long to do so. It cannot be, Aidan."

He grasped her hand with his free one, the reins slack in the other. "Why, Cassie? My feelings are not unknown to you. And though I cannot pretend to your talents, I will not insult them and feign to be unaware that you are by no means indifferent to me."

Cassie tried to draw her hand away. "Indifferent? I only wish it were so, for I could be less distressed at the necessity to hurt you."

He would not release her. "But why must it be needful? You are a free woman—"

Cassie felt as if her heart must burst. "Free? Yes, free to join a sisterhood you must despise, were it not for Aunt Ida's generosity."

Perplexity showed in his eyes, and he let her go. "I don't understand you."

She retreated as far as the gig's seat would allow, covering her eyes so she need not see his confusion.

"Are you talking of Lady Ferrensby?"

Cassie dropped her hands and flung them into the air, her feelings threatening to consume her. "Yes, Lady Ferrensby. There, you know it now. She is my aunt."

Aidan's bright blue gaze was fixed upon her, and Cassie could not avoid meeting it. "I wondered if you were in some sort related."

"Then you should also have wondered why she brought you here," cried Cassie, despair engulfing her. "You were carefully chosen, Aidan. I knew it from the first. Oh, she cannot have thought it would come to pass as swiftly, but—"

"Wait!"

Such was Aidan's tone of command that Cassie stopped midsentence. She eyed him, a little frightened by the look of frozen shock in his face. But his voice was even.

"Is this true? She thought me a—what shall I say?—a desirable parti?"

Cassie almost snorted. "A desirable sacrifice, Aidan. Oh, I wish you had taken me in dislike, if only to confound her."

For a moment he did not speak, and shame swept through Cassie. She could not have held her tongue had her life depended on it.

"You say nothing. Can it be you suppose me to be a party to my aunt's matchmaking scheme? I promise you, Aidan, I knew nothing of it. The moment I guessed, I tried to—"

"Cassie, stop!" he cut in sharply, and there was hurt in the blue gaze. "Do you know me so little? We have been acquainted but a matter of days, Cassie, but I feel as if I have known you far longer. It is so for you as well, is it not?"

She could not deny it. "Yes, but I could not blame you for thinking ill of me."

He smiled. A smile of such gentleness that Cassie's heart turned over. "I could never think ill of you, Cassie. Don't you know that?"

For a moment the warmth blossomed in her chest. And then she remembered. With a passionate cry, she thrust her hands out, as if to ward him off.

"But you will, Aidan, you will! You do not know the worst, and I could never cheat you. I would not cheat any man, but—"

One of her flailing hands was caught in a strong grip. "Cassie, nothing you can say will change my feelings towards you. I knew my mind within two days of knowing you."

"Words! Just words, Aidan."

"You prefer deeds?"

Before she could think what he meant, her lips were seized in a kiss so hard and strong that Cassie was shocked into silence. When Aidan released her, she could only stare at him, aware of nothing but the blankness in her head and the thumping in her own chest.

The blue eyes were tender. "There now, Mrs. Dale. Tell me now that you don't believe my words."

Tears sprang to Cassie's eyes, but she ignored them. "I believe you. But you don't know." She drew a shuddering breath. "Aidan, I am not Mrs. Dale. There is no Mr. Dale. There never was. I am a fallen woman."

It was said. Sick with dread, Cassie waited for the inevitable reaction, the disgust in Aidan's face. Instead she saw a rise of compassion there. She felt her hand taken and watched in fascination as he drew it to his lips.

"Let he who is without sin cast the first stone."

Cassie snatched her hand away. "Is this your answer? To preach at me?"

He shook his head. "I am not without sin, Cassie. None of us are. It does not lower you in my eyes." A little smile drew the corners of his mouth upwards. "Besides, I had already guessed as much."

Arrested, Cassie blinked at him. "How? How could you know?"

"Well, not by the use of second sight."

Too bemused to laugh, Cassie stared at him. He let out a sigh.

"I will be frank with you. Setting aside this witch business, your situation was strange. A widow, isolated from her family, who was clearly in some sort indebted to the proprietor of the village. And your retainers never addressed you as Mrs. Dale, but as Miss Cassie. I did not guess your relationship to Lady Ferrensby, although I supposed there must be a connection."

Disbelief wreathed Cassie's mind. "But don't you care? You do not know my sin."

"Nor do I wish to. I will not judge you, Cassie."

Her heart swelled, and she was only vaguely aware of the tears trickling down her cheeks. But she could not let this pass.

"Do you think I could bear such generosity? No, you will hear me out."

He frowned. "I will do so if you wish it, but only when you have consented to be my wife." A sterner tone than she yet had heard entered his voice. "I will not have you take it into your head that there is some sort of divine forgiveness in my offer. I love you, Cassie. You, the creature of passion and insight. You, with your loneliness and your tragic eyes. *You*, Cassie. I don't care what you did, do you understand? I adore you. I want you."

To Cassie's utter astonishment, a little of the darkness that had engulfed her for so long lifted. "Is it possible?"

A very gentle look came into Aidan's face. "Are your visions uniformly unhappy? Can you not foresee an image of sunshine?"

She gave a laugh that cracked in the middle, and her heart was suddenly light.

"I must learn, if you will teach me."

Then she could say nothing at all, for Aidan's lips found hers again, gently this time, and all thought became suspended. Somewhere in the periphery of her mind she was aware of the uncompleted mystery still to be resolved, but her heart softly echoed to fulfilment.

The night was eerie. Despite the ban on any sort of conversation among those waiting in the shadows, Ottilia reflected, there was no such thing as absolute silence.

She could hear breath going in and out, including her own. From nearby came ripplings of water from the ever-flowing brook, with now and then a faint splashing sound to go along with a slithering that perhaps signified the motions of some nocturnal animal searching for a drink.

The moon was well up, casting a convenient gleam of silver to catch the bundle suspended from a rafter in the remains of the smithy roof. Even to Ottilia's eyes, it looked horribly real. God send it would serve its purpose! Assuming the murderer came.

A faint *pitterpat* disturbed her heartbeat on the thought. The trap was laid, but had the perpetrator taken the bait? Had Ottilia been too clever? Was it possible that devious mind could outthink her and refuse to play the game out to the finish? Or was the risk too great not to take advantage of the opportunity?

Ottilia was banking on the fact that the murderer must be awaiting the chance to eliminate Bertha Duggleby. She could bear witness; therefore, she could not be left alive. But to escape detection, the circumstances had to point to Cassie Dale.

If Ottilia had the measure of the creature, the plan must work. If not—no, she dared not think of failure. Not at this juncture.

Francis, sturdy at her back and armed nevertheless, inclined to the belief the murderer would wait a day or so. He might be right, in which case, as she had said, they must lie in wait again tomorrow night.

The thought of going through it all a second time made Ottilia's heart sink. They had been obliged to take a circuitous route around the green to avoid being spotted. Ryde had been sent on ahead, concealing himself in Cassie Dale's cottage with Sam Hawes, primed by his wife to bring an empty portmanteau for the necessary equipment. Anyone must suppose Sam was fetching and carrying for Mrs. Dale, known to be staying with Lady Ferrensby. Ryde and he had smuggled what was needed away. The two of them had done all that was required by the time Francis and Ottilia arrived at the smithy, having made their way around the back of Uddington's shop and the Cock and Bottle, and crossed the stream downriver by way of an old wooden footbridge. It was then left to Francis to arrange the bundle suitably and tie it off on a convenient hook.

Time dragged, and Ottilia tried not to fret. If it were all in vain, she dreaded the uncomfortable drop from tension. Not to mention the hideous realisation that she could have made a mistake.

Then a whisper at her ear alerted her.

"Listen!"

Ottilia strained to hear beyond the sudden thumping in her own chest. A footfall? If so, it was stealthily taken. Like a cat slinking through the night.

Ottilia shivered and felt Francis's hand slide about her from behind.

"Courage!"

His breath caressed her ear as he murmured the word, and Ottilia willed her fast beating heart to silence.

The footsteps were nearer at hand, abruptly sounding stronger on the gravel outside the front of the smithy. Ottilia listened as they padded lightly over the stone flags in the darkened part beyond the moonlit scene.

They came to a stop. Ottilia held her breath. An audible gasp sounded, followed by a grunting curse. Then something fell to the floor with a loud clunk.

"Now!" whispered Francis behind her.

Ottilia stepped around the ruined smithy wall and walked quietly into the gloomy interior.

A figure was standing just inside the roofless smithy, its shocked features, ghostly but visible in the rays of the moon, staring up at the improvised body hanging from the remains of the rafter, its full skirts half concealing a pair of legs— mere stuffed sacking—with shoes on their ends.

Ottilia thrust down upon the wild beating at her heart and spoke as coolly as she could.

"Good evening, Miss Beeleigh."

Chapter 18

The woman jumped, and her head came down, sending her face back into shadow. For a moment she neither moved nor spoke, and Ottilia could only surmise that she was staring directly at her. She shifted a little farther into the smithy, the better to confront the creature.

"You are too late, you know. Poor Bertha."

At that a snort escaped the other woman's lips, and she walked quickly forward into the light, her glance flying up to the suspended figure.

"Do you take me for a fool? You tricked me!"

"Yes," agreed Ottilia coolly. "It was the only way to catch you."

The almond eyes narrowed. "You think you have me? We'll see about that!"

Swiftly she turned and made to speed back the way she had come, but she had taken only two steps when Ryde moved into the aperture behind her, blocking her way. She stopped dead.

"A pox on you!"

Turning again, she looked past Ottilia, who realised at once that Francis had shown himself, his pistol held loosely in his hand.

"A pox on you all!" uttered Miss Beeleigh fiercely. Once more she glanced up at the hanging figure. "What *is* that?"

Ottilia went to the hook and untied the rope, letting the dummy fall. It crashed between them, and Miss Beeleigh gazed down at the stuffed sacking with its ludicrous legs and petticoats.

"Where is Bertha, then?"

"Safely in her home, with Sam Hawes to guard her. We could not be sure, you see, that you would not go there first. Although I expected you to make your preparations here before fetching her upon whatever excuse you had dreamed up."

"What has she brought with her, Ryde?" asked Francis, nodding towards the indistinguishable pile that had evidently fallen from Miss Beeleigh's hands when she saw the body. He moved forward a few paces. "Don't fear to leave your post. I have her covered."

Ryde glanced at the gleam of metal protruding from Francis's hand and bent to examination, holding up the items as he identified them.

"Rope, hammer, nails, cloth. Probably meant to cover her head once she'd delivered the killing blow."

"And then fulfil Cassie's vision by hanging the poor woman's body just as we made it appear," finished Francis.

"Just so," said Ottilia, her gaze fixed on Miss Beeleigh.

The woman's eyes gleamed in the moonlight. "You can't prove anything."

"Hence this subterfuge," Ottilia agreed. "I hardly think it will take much to convince a jury. Besides, we do have some evidence."

"What evidence?" spat the woman.

"Well, since you have failed to silence Bertha, we know

for a start that you persuaded her to fetch Molly out of the Cock. You told her, did you not, that Molly had killed her husband? And that you planned to prove it."

Miss Beeleigh's features remained frozen, and she did not speak. Ottilia sighed inwardly. The woman was not going to admit a single thing.

"Bertha believed it to begin with. But after she had done the deed and went home, she started to think. She knew Molly very well, you see, their husbands being friends for so long. Belatedly, she began to disbelieve what you had said. Then she began to wonder why you, Miss Beeleigh, should take it into your head to play investigator when I was known to be looking into her husband's death. Why had you not spoken to me of your suspicions? Bertha grew afraid. And in the morning, when she heard the news, she knew she had lured the poor woman to her death."

"Pah! A fairy tale," snapped the other. "Why did she not carry this story to you?"

"She was afraid. And with reason. She was an accessory to a murder, for one thing. For another, I don't doubt she feared for her life. If you had slain Molly, you must also have slain Duggleby. What should stop you from killing her, too?"

Miss Beeleigh drew in a sharp breath through her nose. "You've yet to prove I had any hand in either killing."

"It was not only the killings, Miss Beeleigh," said Ottilia, unable to keep a note of reprimand from out of her voice. "What of the work you put in to incite the villagers to turn against Cassie Dale? Once I had entered the picture, you saw it was insufficient to use the visions. You took care to breed violence in the Cock with your warnings, issued in such a way as to ensure rebellion. Just as you did when Will set up his stake and you saw an opportunity to drive me away."

"That was her fault, too?" uttered Francis on an edge of rage.

"Oh yes. She had primed them well. Tabitha Hawes had the full story from Alice."

"You will pay for that," Francis told the woman venge-fully, and the gun in his hand lifted a trifle.

Ottilia threw up a hand to enjoin his silence, for she had not finished. Miss Beeleigh's commanding countenance gave nothing away, but a telltale muscle twitched briefly in her cheek, and the moon's rays showed a glitter at those almond-shaped eyes.

"When you found I had discovered Molly was not killed in the coffee room, you sought to make use of the accusations against Hannah. You took up her tray, did you not, whilst everyone was on the green, including Pilton?"

"The devil!" Francis swore. "That was when she planted the knife in Hannah's commode?"

"The very knife she had used, yes, and perhaps wondered how best to dispose of it." Ottilia drew a shaky breath. "It would not have mattered to you, would it, Miss Beeleigh, if poor Hannah had expired in that lock-up? Lord Henbury would have been satisfied of her guilt."

At last Miss Beeleigh spoke, thrusting up her chin in her peculiarly superior manner. "And how was it I got into the Blue Pig after Pakefield had locked up."

Ottilia was betrayed into a laugh. "Oh, come, Miss Beeleigh, do you take me for a simpleton? The back door key was missing. You gave yourself ample opportunity to slip it back, leaving it on the stair when you chose to supervise the kitchen staff in a brave show of help."

Miss Beeleigh snorted. "Highly inventive, Lady Francis. You have proved nothing to say I committed these deeds. Nor yet why I am held to have done so."

Ottilia tutted. "Dear me, Miss Beeleigh, you must think me remarkably naïve. Pardon me if I speak with candour."

"Say what you like. Makes no difference to me. Poppycock, the whole thing."

"Is it? You are a woman of iron, Miss Beeleigh, but there is one chink in your armour. I saw it from the first, and it has betrayed you."

The woman's face stiffened, and her eyes dared Ottilia to go on, despite her words. "Don't know what you're talking of."

"I think you do. Poor Evelina and her dog."

Francis, who had been watching the swift give-and-take of words, intervened again at this point. "What the devil do you mean, Tillie?"

Ottilia glanced at him. "I daresay you will not credit it, but I'm afraid Miss Beeleigh cherishes a fondness for Evelina Radlett which goes far beyond mere friendship."

"What, you mean—"

He stopped, and Ottilia knew he would not give voice to a possibility that must revolt him. Ottilia did not suffer a like revulsion. Rather, she pitied the woman.

Before she could say more, a new voice entered the fray, quavering a little.

"Don't say you did it for me, Alethea?"

"Mrs. Radlett!"

Ottilia peered into the gloom as Miss Beeleigh turned sharply. She could just make out the shorter and stouter outline, standing a little behind where Ryde still remained, ready to leap should Miss Beeleigh attempt to escape by that route.

"Evelina! What are you doing here?"

Mrs. Radlett, her person enveloped in a dark cloak, moved into the forge, her eyes riveted on her friend. "I followed you."

Miss Beeleigh started towards her, but the widow flinched back, and Miss Beeleigh halted abruptly, pain just visible in her ghostly features.

"You should be asleep."

The widow Radlett's eyes were large in a countenance pale as the silver sheen above. Ottilia could not tell whether it was a trick of the moonlight, but indeed there was matter enough here to dismay the poor creature.

"So I would have been, had I drunk the tisane you made up for me."

"Laudanum?" Ottilia guessed. "Just as she gave you the

night before Duggleby's death, so you would not know she had gone out to make her preparations."

Mrs. Radlett's eyes remained on her friend. "You gave it to me again on the night Molly died. But I spilled it. I saw you from the window, Alethea, making for the smithy. And after, I saw you coming back from the direction of the Blue Pig."

Francis gave a grunt. "You saw her? And said nothing of it?"

"How could I? She is my friend."

"A pretty friend, to be doing away with the blacksmith merely for a dog," snapped Francis.

Little rivulets gleamed upon the widow's cheeks, and Ottilia realised she was weeping.

"Was it that, Alethea? Was it Toby?"

At last Miss Beeleigh's rigid pose relaxed a little, and she put out an unsteady hand. A sighing breath left her lips, and her voice was hoarse.

"You were so very unhappy, my dearest. I could not forgive him."

For a moment no one said a word. Despite all, Ottilia was moved by the note of unutterable tenderness in the woman's voice. So deeply did the two of them seem to hold each other's gaze that Ottilia believed they were in that moment oblivious of the rest of the company.

Then one of Mrs. Radlett's hands came out from beneath her cloak, and she held it towards her friend, a silent invitation. Miss Beeleigh hesitated, and then took the few stumbling steps that brought her close to the other, and Mrs. Radlett sank into the woman's embrace.

The pose held for the space of several seconds. Then a deafening report shattered the silence.

Shock held Ottilia in thrall. In seeming slow motion she saw Miss Beeleigh recoil. Her eyes registered a species of horror. Then they rolled up into her head as she swayed and then crashed to the smithy floor.

Ottilia came out of her stupor to discover the gun in

Mrs. Radlett's hand, its ball spent. She was looking down at the wreck of her friend, her shoulders heaving with silent sobs.

Miss Beeleigh lay crookedly on the ground, her eyes still open, blood streaming from the wound just below her bosom. Evelina Radlett had shot her through the heart.

For the space of several agonising seconds no one moved or spoke. Mesmerised, Francis gazed upon the tableau set before him, unable to think beyond the appalling occurrence.

His eyes lifted from the bleeding corpse to the metal protrusion held in the other woman's hand, which now extended from its former deathly concealment beneath her cloak. The sight dictated action.

"Dear Lord! Ryde, get that thing off her!"

His groom moved to extract the pistol from Mrs. Radlett's nerveless hand.

"It won't go off again, m'lord."

"I know that," Francis said, shock lending impatience to his tone. Without reloading, the gun could not fire again, but he could not endure to see it in the widow's hands.

What the devil were they to do now? Were all Tillie's efforts blasted? With the murderer killed would anyone believe the truth? And how in the world were they to explain away a third corpse to the irascible Lord Henbury?

He glanced at Tillie and found her gaze fixed upon the weapon now in Ryde's possession. As if she felt his regard, her head turned, and in the pale gleam of moonlight he saw the tautness in her face. She spoke before he could formulate a question.

"Francis, we must act! I'll wager few will not have been awakened by that shot. We will have half the village about us in a trice."

Francis's mind leapt, encompassing the myriad complications about to engulf them all. "Lord, yes!"

But Tillie was ahead of him, her quick intelligence already disposing of the problems that were rising in his head.

"The gun, Francis. Put it into Miss Beeleigh's hand."

He was already moving towards Ryde as he spoke. "You want to make it look like suicide?"

Tillie nodded. "Meldreth will not be fooled, but it will serve for the villagers."

Francis saw her shift to the still-frozen figure of the widow Radlett and set an arm about the woman's shoulders. The creature lifted her head at last, staring in a blank fashion at Tillie's face. Her voice was a pitiable plea.

"I could not bear to see her hanged."

Was that all her reason? Francis wanted to scream at the wretch, but Tillie spoke with indescribable kindness.

"Yes, my dear, I understand. Come, don't look any more."

Ryde handed Francis the weapon, and he bent to the corpse, lifting the limp hand and attempting the tricky task of folding its fingers about the butt.

Tillie was shifting the widow away, but despite her injunction, the woman's gaze returned to her friend's body, silent tears seeping down her cheeks.

"Evelina must not be found here," Tillie was saying. "There is not time enough to get her back to her own home. Besides, she cannot be left alone. Ryde, take her to Bertha Duggleby's house."

The groom was instantly at her side, taking hold of Mrs. Radlett's arm.

"You come along with me, ma'am."

The fearful countenance left the sight of the body, its blood gleaming silver under the moon's soft light.

She looked at Ryde, repeating, "I could not bear to see her hanged."

"Go with Ryde, Mrs. Radlett, if you please," Tillie said with firmness. "I will come to fetch you presently."

"You don't want me to stay there, do you, m'lady?" asked the groom.

"No, we need you. Also Sam Hawes."

Francis was looking critically at his handiwork, but he glanced up at this. "Can you trust the Duggleby woman to look after her?"

Ryde was guiding Mrs. Radlett towards the back, from where Tillie had made her entrance.

"Stay, Ryde!" said Tillie quickly. "Thank heavens you mentioned her, Fan, for we need her, too! Ryde, have Mrs. Duggleby wake her daughter Jenny—if she hasn't already come running downstairs, which would scarcely surprise me—and let the child watch over Mrs. Radlett."

Even as she spoke, footsteps sounded from behind the smithy, and the voice of Sam Hawes was heard.

"My lord? What's to do?" He appeared next moment and stopped short at the scene that met his eyes. "Lordy me!"

"Just so," said Tillie. "Ask no questions now, Sam, for we are in urgent need of your help."

"Ryde, get about your business, for the Lord's sake!" Francis urged. "You've had your orders."

"Bring Bertha Duggleby here, Ryde," Tillie called after the groom as he shifted with alacrity, almost dragging Mrs. Radlett with him.

Her pathetic refrain was heard again as she exited the smithy. "*I could not bear to see her hanged.*" A forlorn little litany—as if it could justify firing the shot that killed her friend. Despite the untold complications she had caused, Francis felt a sliver of compassion for the wretch.

Tillie had turned to Sam Hawes. "Sam, run to fetch Doctor Meldreth, if you please. And Mr. Kinnerton. I daresay both or either may already be on their way. Go!"

Sam exited rapidly through the front of the smithy, and Francis heard his footsteps pounding along the lane. They were not, he realised, the only ones. Urgency engulfed him as he turned to Tillie.

"What else? Quick! They're coming!"

Her gaze swept this way and that around the ruin of the

smithy, and Francis was conscious of a wave of impatience. His eye fell on the wreck of Miss Beeleigh.

"I'd best cover her. We don't want all the fools of the village gaping."

Tillie seized his hand as he made to grab the dummy off the floor, thinking to use its skirts for the purpose.

"No! She must lie there. And the trick we used to capture her must be wholly visible."

Francis had bent to the dummy, but he rose again. He looked at his wife to find her eyeing his handiwork with the pistol. He had stuffed it into the slackened hand, simulating the position of the grip.

"Will it serve?"

"I think so. It looks well enough for the untutored eye."

He noted the fretful tone. "You say Meldreth will know it is false?"

Tillie nodded. "He cannot help but do so. The position of entry of the ball into her body will tell him so at once."

Francis moved to look at the corpse from below the feet. He glanced to the hand and saw just what Tillie meant. In order to accomplish her own death, Miss Beeleigh would have had to twist her wrist to an impossible angle.

"You will have to take Meldreth into your confidence."

"I intend to. Also Kinnerton and Lady Ferrensby."

A grim sliver of humour slid into Francis's head. "But not, I take it, Lord Henbury?"

"Heaven forbid!"

The sound of running feet was building. How many? Francis went to his wife and took her by the shoulders.

"Are you enough prepared?"

A smile trembled on her lips. "No, but it makes no matter. If I fail to convince them, I have at least the satisfaction to know that there will be no more murders committed in Witherley."

Francis pulled her to him briefly. Then, as the first steps sounded on the gravel outside, he kissed her swiftly and put her from him, turning at her side to confront the villagers once more.

T hey gathered in the moonlight around the edges of the scene. Tisbury, Staxton, Will the tapster, and others Ottilia did not know. Pa Wagstaff was one of the first to arrive, his cottage but a stone's throw away.

"That Beeleigh, be it?" he said, the moment he took in the identity of the corpse with the now sluggish liquid seeping from the wound in her breast. His gaze moved to the gun in the woman's hand, and he looked up at Ottilia, bright intelligence in his tone. "It be her, then? Her've done for Duggleby and for Molly both?"

"Well reasoned, Mr. Wagstaff."

But the outburst of muttering and exclamation overrode her words.

"Bain't so. How, if her be dead and all?"

"Where be the witch?"

"Bain't Bertha a-lying down there, I be thinking."

"What be that?"

"It be a dummy, fool."

Ottilia waited for it to die down, watching the questioning looks that went from the body on the floor to the dummy, and then again to where Ottilia stood with Francis at her side, his strengthening arm at her back, one hand holding her at the waist. She was glad of it, for though her voice was steady, inwardly she trembled.

"Bertha is safe and well. She will be here at any moment."

"Wait," murmured Francis, jerking his head back towards the village. "More are coming."

Several runners, by the sound of it, Ottilia thought, hoping for Meldreth or the vicar. What was keeping Bertha? Surely Ryde must have settled Evelina Radlett by now? Why was he not back with Bertha? To her relief, the villagers were all craned towards the pounding footsteps, and she dared to hope they were too bemused at this point to pose any threat. But that could not last.

The footsteps closed in, slowing as they hit the gravel outside. Next moment, Sam Hawes entered, bringing with him both the doctor and Mr. Kinnerton. Ottilia breathed more easily. But she lost no time in bearding Meldreth. He must not be allowed to make mention of what to him would be obvious.

"Doctor Meldreth, thank heavens!" Leaving Francis's cradling arm, she went forward as the doctor thrust through the surrounding watchers. "Pray be careful!"

He halted perforce at the edge of the corpse, and his swift gaze went about the smithy, taking in the dummy and the presence of the Fanshawes.

"What the deuce has happened here?"

As he dropped to his haunches by the body, Ottilia quickly went to join him, going down to his level, and infusing meaning into her tone.

"She shot herself, Doctor Meldreth."

Meldreth took one look at the gun in the woman's hand, and his frowning gaze came up to meet Ottilia's. The moonlight gave her the question in his face, and she swiftly put her gloved hand to her lips, passing one finger across them while she stared at him the while. His frown deepened, but she thought he nodded slightly.

"Why did she shoot herself, Lady Francis?"

Ottilia heard the mockery in his tone and sighed out a breath she had not realised she was holding.

"She knew the game was up," came from Francis behind her, holding out a hand to help her to rise.

The doctor got up and confronted him. "What game, my lord?"

"That, sir, I will leave my wife to tell."

Aidan Kinnerton saved Ottilia the trouble as he moved into the inner part of the circle. "Was it she, Lady Francis? Was Miss Beeleigh the murderer?"

At this, the villagers broke out again.

"Bain't so," came from Tisbury. "For why should Miss Beeleigh take and kill Molly?"

"For why should her kill Duggleby, for the matter of that?" demanded Staxton.

"Bain't so," echoed Will the tapster. "It be the witch! Her've had a vision, bain't her?"

Pa Wagstaff's ancient features squirmed up at the man. "There be nowt in that head of yourn, Will. There weren't no vision to that Beeleigh. It be Bertha as were in vision, if'n vision there be."

With which, the ancient screwed his glance back towards Ottilia, the rheumy eyes gleaming in the ghostly white light.

"How clever of you, Mr. Wagstaff," said Ottilia, seizing the opportunity. "There was indeed no vision. I asked Mrs. Dale to pretend she had seen Bertha hanging in the smithy. I knew Miss Beeleigh must take advantage of it."

"Set a trap, eh, Lady Fan?"

"Just so."

There was a fresh outburst of muttering at this, but Tisbury was the first to object. "Bain't so. Why'd Miss Beeleigh want to do for Bertha? For what reason?"

"I be the one to tell you that."

A new voice entered the fray, and Bertha Duggleby emerged from the darkness in the back of the forge with Ryde at her side. There was a concerted gasp from the watchers at this sudden appearance.

"Bertha?"

Shock was in Tisbury's voice, as if he spoke to a phantom. Ottilia could scarcely be surprised, for she had herself been startled despite knowing the woman was coming.

"Aye, it be me. Nor I bain't dead yet."

As Bertha moved into the light, several glances went from her to the dummy on the floor, and Ottilia wondered if indeed one or two of the villagers had supposed it to be real.

Duggleby's widow halted before them all, looking down on the wreck that had been Miss Beeleigh.

"Lie there, aye," she said to it. "If'n you bain't dead, it be me on the rope for sure."

Her gaze came up and passed around the watching faces. There was fear to be seen, and the stirrings of a morbid curiosity. Ottilia could not have hoped for better. Quietly she shifted back to Francis, letting the woman take centre stage.

"A fool I be," came from Bertha in a tone both curt and bitter. "More'n a fool to believe what Miss Beeleigh told me. Her said as Molly done for my man Duggleby. Her said as if'n I do get Molly out from the Cock quiet-like, her be going to show as Molly done it."

"Molly bain't done it!" Tisbury shouted. "Her bain't!"

"No, I knows it now," Bertha said. "Truth be I knowed it after I got Molly and her be a-going to meet Miss Beeleigh."

"What be you saying to her? What lies be you telling?"

"Telled her as it be the witch as done it. Telled her as it be secret, but I seen as Pilton had the witch to lock-up. Telled her not to say nowt to nobody."

Tisbury's features crumpled. "Tricked! Molly was afeared as Lady Fan meant to have her head for Duggleby. Why bain't her said it all to me? Why, Molly?"

Great heaving sobs wrenched out of his throat. Beside him, Farmer Staxton turned and flung his arms about the man, glaring the while at Bertha.

"Good as killed Molly you did, Bertha."

"Aye," was all she said, still on the same bitter note.

Ottilia thought it would be long before the wounds healed. But at this moment, Bertha had done enough. She stepped forward.

"You must remember that Bertha was grieving."

There was no softening in the surrounding faces. To Ottilia's relief, the Reverend Kinnerton stepped in, taking Bertha by the arm.

"I will pray for you, Mrs. Duggleby." His glance took in the rest. "For all of you. But do not lose sight of the truth. Try to remember who began all this. Bertha is a victim of that woman's schemes." He pointed to the corpse.

The aged Wagstaff cut through the murmurs, addressing himself to Ottilia. "Bain't said as why Miss Beeleigh done for Duggleby, Lady Fan."

Ottilia drew a breath. "She had a grudge against him." Before she was called upon to explain the nature of the grudge, she sped on. "She was only waiting her chance to have her revenge. Miss Beeleigh planned it all very carefully. She knew Mrs. Dale had seen a vision of the roof coming down on Duggleby. The night before the storm, Miss Beeleigh borrowed Mr. Uddington's ladder——" She broke off at an exclamation in the crowd and for the first time realised that the merchant was among those present. "Yes, she meant you to be suspect, Mr. Uddington." Several turned to locate the snowy head, and Ottilia resumed swiftly. "But Miss Beeleigh was heard both by Bessy and Mr. Wagstaff."

"That be what you be after?"

"Just so."

"She was also heard by Bertha," put in Francis, taking up the tale and pointing skywards, "when she climbed the ladder and hacked at the crossbeam."

"Only Bertha thought it was her husband," Ottilia told them.

"She probably also tied a rope to the beam and coiled it in the roof," Francis added.

"But she put the ladder back," objected Uddington, and several heads nodded. "How could she get the rope?"

"Easy enough," said Francis. "A thread tied to it would go unnoticed if she pulled it aside and tied it off at the wall. All she had to do was pull on the thread to bring down the rope."

"On the night of the storm," Ottilia resumed, "I think Miss Beeleigh came here under pretext of a job for Duggleby.

There were hammers enough to choose from. She waited for him to turn his back, and then she struck."

Even in the gloom, Ottilia could see that the faces round about were intent. But at this came a chorus of sucked-in breaths and murmurs of dismay. One lone voice, unknown to Ottilia, piped up a protest.

"How be it a woman could deal a blow to kill a man?"

Wagstaff took that one. "Bain't nowt to that. Bain't seen no man here nor strong as Miss Beeleigh, if'n her'd a mind to clout him."

"Nor her bain't one to need no man's help," put in Staxton. "Seen her chopping wood. If'n any got strength for to lug a ladder here and back to Uddington's, it be Miss Beeleigh."

Tisbury, drawing a sleeve across his eyes after his brief bout of weeping, here entered a question. "Be you saying as her fired the forge and all? Why, if'n the storm be coming?"

"I don't think Miss Beeleigh expected the storm to break so quickly," Ottilia answered, relieved to find interest in the workings of the crime had overtaken disbelief. "When she had brought down the beam, most of the rotting timbers came down with it, along with half the tiles. I think she took a burning brand from the forge and set fire to the timbers around Duggleby's body."

"Lucky the storm put out the fire."

"Quite right, Mr. Uddington. If the storm had broken later, the body would have been burned, and it would have been unlikely, if not impossible, for Doctor Meldreth to discover that Duggleby had received a hammer blow."

Meldreth, who was still frowning as he followed the tale, responded to Ottilia's questioning look. "Highly unlikely."

A murmuring broke out as the villagers turned to one another, but the round pulpit tones of Kinnerton rose above it.

"In which case you would, all of you, have hounded an innocent woman with your false accusations of witchery."

A reminder that was greeted with a shuffling of feet and a

few sheepish looks. Tisbury was notably defiant, looking the
parson in the eye, although he refrained from saying anything.
Wagstaff, who seemed to have constituted himself spokes-
man for the group, gestured to the body on the ground.

"What be you going to do with her now, Lady Fan?"

Ottilia breathed more easily. The worst was over. "I will
leave that to Doctor Meldreth."

Upon which, the doctor took charge, calling for volunteers
to carry the corpse back to his surgery. The move to accomplish this had the effect of breaking up the gathering, with
Kinnerton assisting to direct operations since he must of necessity accompany Miss Beeleigh's body to perform his part
following the woman's untimely end.

In the general shift of persons, Ottilia was able to remove
from the limelight at last. She went to Francis, who caught
her hand and held it tightly.

"A brave effort, my love."

She let out a relieved breath. "I could not have managed
it without Bertha."

"Lady Francis?"

Meldreth was at her elbow. A hollow feeling entered her
bosom as she turned to face him. In the rays of the moon
under the open roof, she could see his face more clearly and
read the portent of his stern look.

"Oh dear."

"Indeed," he said, with a faint relaxation of his features,
although he did not quite smile. "This was no suicide, Lady
Francis."

Before Ottilia could say anything, Francis intervened,
roughness in his tone.

"This is neither the time nor the place, Meldreth. No
doubt your investigations in your surgery will yield more
answers than we can give at this moment."

The doctor's glance went from Francis back to Ottilia. "I
take your point. Tomorrow morning? Before Sunday service,
assuming Kinnerton still intends to hold it?"

Ottilia nodded. "Yes, for we need him, too. Also Lady Ferrensby."

Meldreth's lips pursed. "Leave them both to me."

With which, he turned to follow the men who had already left with Miss Beeleigh's body, accompanied by several of the villagers who seemed unwilling to disperse altogether.

Ottilia turned to Francis. "And now for Evelina."

F rancis could not have supposed anything could be more unnerving than the earlier events of the night. But he had not bargained for the necessity to transfer the wretched Mrs. Radlett, in the greatest secrecy, from Bertha Duggleby's abode to that of Mr. Netherburn.

The elderly gentleman's house was situated quite on the other side of the village, one of a row set in front of the church, close to Meldreth's surgery. They had perforce to wait long enough to allow the village to settle into quiet before the cavalcade set off. Which meant that the moonlight was fading and the skies were just beginning to grey over at the horizon.

Huddled in her concealing cloak, with Ottilia's arm about her shoulders, and still in a state of benumbed shock, the widow Radlett was escorted slowly to her destination, with Francis in the lead and the two women flanked by Sam Hawes and Ryde. It was hoped that if they were seen, they would look but a straggling group that none would recognise.

In view of Evelina's condition, the journey was necessarily taken at a snail's pace. Tracking the length of the green, Francis felt it was like the hazardous foray of a scouting party from his army days, interminable and open to enemy fire. Not that one would expect to be shot at in the midst of a country village, but events had become so unpredictable that Francis could not avoid a creeping sensation of eerie apprehension.

He was never more glad to reach his destination until, after knocking gently on the door, he was faced with the sight of Horace Netherburn, clad in his nightshirt, with a dressing gown hastily thrown over it and his nightcap on his wigless head. The fellow's mouth was at half cock, and the expression on his face was one of comical dismay.

"We need your help, Mr. Netherburn," Tillie told him in an urgent undervoice. "Pray let us in."

"I believe the poor man was more shocked by the impropriety of Mrs. Radlett staying in his house overnight than by the horrific events I outlined for him," Ottilia told Lady Ferrensby the following morning, unable to prevent herself from emitting a spurt of laughter.

The great lady of the village looked little amused, her own poise having clearly been shattered at the outcome of the adventure.

"I am not surprised. Horace is a stickler."

Meldreth had spared Ottilia the difficult task of apprising Lady Ferrensby of Miss Beeleigh's death and the circumstances of her guilt in the murders. But it had fallen to Ottilia's lot to pass on the unvarnished truth of what had happened. The meeting was taking place in the Blue Pig's coffee room, where they might be assured of privacy, Ottilia having ascertained that, with the landlady somewhat recovered, Patty had been given a day's holiday after her recent exertions and was not in the house.

"But how will it serve to leave Evelina at Netherburn's?" asked Lady Ferrensby.

"Oh, we cannot leave her there," Ottilia said frankly. "It was the safest place last night, for I dared not risk Patty's wagging tongue here, and the creature could hardly be expected to sleep in Miss Beeleigh's house after what transpired."

"Ah, poor thing," came with a gush of compassion from Cassie Dale, who had arrived with Lady Ferrensby.

At first surprised, Ottilia rather thought she understood when she noted the Reverend Kinnerton choose a seat next to Cassie's and take possession of one of her hands. Highly entertained, Ottilia had sought, by way of faintly raised brows and a flicker of her eyes, to draw this suggestive action to her spouse's attention.

But Francis, whose mood had lightened considerably now that all danger had passed, had his attention on Lady Ferrensby.

"Mark my words," he had warned his wife earlier, when they went to snatch a few hours' sleep in their chamber, "you will not easily secure Lady Ferrensby's complicity in hushing the matter up."

"Then I rely on you to back me to the hilt," Ottilia had retorted. "She sets great store by the example of her deceased husband, so I daresay she is one of those females who respect the opinions of the superior male."

"Unlike some I could mention."

Which had set Ottilia into such a fit of the giggles as afforded them both a much-needed release from the tensions of the evening.

Cassie Dale, however, despite an evident newfound happiness seen in the bloom on her cheek, proved an ally in this respect.

"How dreadfully poor Mrs. Radlett will feel it! The guilt and the grief combined. How will she bear it, I wonder? I wish I could help her."

"Well, you may, if you so choose," said Ottilia, seizing on this. She gave a grimace as her gaze turned back to her ladyship. "I'm afraid I have committed you in your absence, Lady Ferrensby. I think it will seem most natural for you to take Evelina back to the Hall for a time."

"Do you indeed?"

The tart tone did not deter Ottilia. "Yes, I do."

"Yes, and so do I," uttered Cassie on a passionate note. "Where else is the poor thing to stay?"

"Poor thing?" Lady Ferrensby's brows went up. "So poor a thing that she turns a gun upon her friend and benefactor?"

"Yes," agreed Meldreth heavily. "There is no getting away from the fact that Mrs. Radlett has committed a murder."

"You might call it a mercy killing," cut in Francis loyally.

"I might call it anything I please," retorted Lady Ferrensby acidly, "but that does not alter the facts."

Ottilia sighed. "What would you, ma'am? The culprit has been discovered. Bertha Duggleby's confession has persuaded the villagers to believe our version of events. What will it profit you, or indeed anyone, to pursue Evelina Radlett to the limit of the law?"

Meldreth was nodding, but he entered a caveat. "Although you know as well as I, Lady Francis, that one such killing may blind a person to the evil of their deed."

"There is such a thing as compassion, Meldreth," came sharply from the Reverend Kinnerton. "A sinner may recant. And I am persuaded Mrs. Radlett is not a true murderer."

"But suppose she were to kill again?" argued the doctor. "Only look at Miss Beeleigh."

"Miss Beeleigh was a very different creature," stated Ottilia flatly. "One might almost call her insane."

"Oh, come now," protested Lady Ferrensby.

"She is right, you know," Francis broke in sharply. "Can you truly count it the act of a sane woman to murder for such a reason as she did? And then to do so again, merely for the purpose of incriminating Mrs. Dale? Not to mention her extraordinary conduct in life. What sort of female goes about mending coach wheels and chopping wood?"

Lady Ferrensby shifted uncomfortably. "Merely because she had odd habits does not make her deranged. Eccentric, certainly, but—"

"You are missing the point, Lady Ferrensby," said Ottilia calmly.

The cool gaze looked across at her. "Well?"

"Figure to yourself, ma'am. Evelina's dog is beaten almost to death. Alethea Beeleigh is obliged to watch the woman she cares for most in the world weeping her heart out as she nurses the animal through the night. In compassion, Alethea ends its suffering, perhaps wishing she was instead aiming her gun at Duggleby."

"Well, that is natural enough," said the reverend.

"Yes, Mr. Kinnerton. But a normal mind, distressed by these events, would be prompted to take issue there and then with the fellow. Alethea does not do this. Instead, she dreams up an elaborate plot in order to destroy him utterly."

"I grant you that," conceded Lady Ferrensby. "But how must Evelina Radlett have been driven to do as she did?"

"Driven, yes," cried Cassie. "She could not have intended it."

"I believe Evelina was driven by fear," Ottilia said. "Indeed, it was her conduct on the day Molly was found that made me certain we had Miss Beeleigh to thank for these killings."

Lady Ferrensby was frowning. "How so? And why in the world could you not have voiced your suspicions?"

"Because of ears glued to the walls," snapped Francis. "She told you as much yesterday."

"Very well, but what made you suspect?"

"Oh, I suspected them both days since," Ottilia confessed. "But I dismissed the notion on account of the dog. It seemed just as far-fetched to me, ma'am, as it does to you. I thought it had been Evelina who committed the deed, and Alethea was merely guilty of a cover-up. But Evelina was transparently dismayed on the day of Molly's death. As she told us last night, she had seen too much. When Miss Beeleigh objected to Jenny Duggleby being sent for to help here, Evelina thought it meant that Jenny had taken the message to Molly. She also looked fearfully at Alethea, which alerted me more than anything else."

There was silence for a moment, but then Mr. Kinnerton spoke up, his question a surprise. "Forgive me, Lady Francis, but is it not possible that Mrs. Radlett shot her friend to prevent the truth coming out?"

"I thought of that last night," said Francis, "but Miss

Beeleigh as good as confessed when she was confronted by her friend."

"Besides," Ottilia pursued, "to be candid, I could not suppose Evelina capable, either of planning for the roof to fall in or of incriminating Cassie. Her intelligence is by no means on the order of Miss Beeleigh's, which was frankly awesome."

"That at least is true."

Lady Ferrensby sounded despondent, and Ottilia could not blame her.

"Moreover, Evelina is far too squeamish to have contemplated the necessary actions to dispose of Molly."

"She was not too squeamish to pull the trigger on her friend," Meldreth pointed out.

"Oh, she did not even think it through. If you question her when she is in a better frame of mind, I daresay you will discover that the gun she took was Miss Beeleigh's and that she knew it was always kept loaded. I suspect she thought only of trying to prevent Bertha Duggleby from being killed. When she found us there and Miss Beeleigh accused, Evelina believed there was only one thing she could do for her friend. All she would say afterwards is that she could not bear to see Miss Beeleigh hanged."

Cassie was openly weeping, and Mr. Kinnerton had his arm about her. Even Lady Ferrensby's expression had softened, and Ottilia thought her handsome countenance looked positively hagged. She felt sorry for the woman, left to deal with the aftermath of this terrible week.

"With reluctance," said Doctor Meldreth, "I am forced to condone your decision, Lady Francis." He looked to the village's patroness. "My lady?"

Lady Ferrensby heaved a gusty sigh. "It appears I have little choice."

Cassie clapped her hands. "You will not regret it, ma'am, I promise you. Aidan and I will take care of the poor woman, you will see."

Ottilia raised her brows, but her question was forestalled by Francis. "Do we take it felicitations are in order, Kinnerton?"

Both parties flushed, and the vicar cleared his throat. "It is scarcely the moment, but yes. Cassie has consented to be my wife."

The congratulations took a little time, and Ottilia, having said her piece, took the chance to change her seat for one next to Lady Ferrensby. The latter eyed her with suspicion, and Ottilia had to laugh.

"Pray don't look at me as at a scorpion, ma'am."

"Your sting is quite as deadly," retorted her ladyship, but a gleam entered her eye, and she set a hand on one of Ottilia's. "I am decidedly ungrateful, am I not? Without you, I cannot think how we would have fared." She sighed again, shaking her head. "Alas for Witherley!"

"Come, ma'am, the village will recover. People are amazingly resilient, don't you find? They will each find their way to cope. Those with a personal tragedy will have the hardest time of it, but even they will learn to live again."

Lady Ferrensby gave a wan smile. "You are right, of course. If it were not for the weight of this business with Evelina Radlett—" She broke off, frowning. "And if that was not bad enough, you must needs set us a potential scandal by placing her with Horace Netherburn, of all things!"

Ottilia smiled but hastened to reassure her. "You need have no fear on that score. Alice was fetched early this morning to attend her, and we will say that Evelina sought refuge with Mr. Netherburn in the early hours when she heard of Miss Beeleigh's demise."

Lady Ferrensby fairly glared. "If you imagine anyone will believe that for one moment, you must have windmills in your head."

"Yes, my husband is apt to say the same."

"I am not in the least surprised."

A gurgle escaped Ottilia. "But I wish you will not fret,

ma'am. I am persuaded Mr. Netherburn will do the honourable thing and take Evelina off your hands within a sennight."

As Ottilia relayed this passage to her spouse when they were at last at liberty, Francis looked at her with horror.

"Do you tell me this cursed village is about to be engulfed by a spate of weddings?"

"Well, two perhaps."

"Two too many," Francis said flatly. "Where the devil is Ryde? I will send him straight off to discover when that wretched carriage is going to be ready."

Ottilia sipped at her coffee, a fresh pot having been supplied by Hannah Pakefield, once more upon her feet and pathetically grateful.

"I think I will suggest to Mr. Netherburn that he hold his wedding breakfast here," she said, heedless of the exasperated snort that escaped her spouse. "Poor Hannah is going to be one patron short as of now."

"Not at all," said Francis. "Don't forget that Cassie, shortly to become Mrs. Kinnerton, is pledged to take care of Evelina Radlett. Severally or together, the four of them should amply supply Hannah's shortage."

"Yes, and now I think of it," Ottilia agreed eagerly, "there is no Molly to fret poor Hannah with her jealousies, so I daresay she may open her doors to lesser men. I will suggest to her that she court Mr. Uddington's custom."

She took another serene sip of her coffee before she noticed an alarming look of frowning indignation in the features of her husband. Her brows rose as she stared at him.

"What?"

"If you imagine, my Lady Fan, that you are going to remain one moment longer than is necessary in this Godforsaken village, merely so that you may go about rearranging the lives of the inhabitants—"

Ottilia broke in without ceremony. "Nothing of the sort. Merely an idle whim, my dearest love. You may remove me at any time you choose."

He regarded her with an eye quite as scorpion-like as that of Lady Ferrensby earlier. "You are not, then, planning anything further?"

"Not in the least."

"Such as helping Bertha Duggleby to search for this fictitious pot of gold?"

"You know, I believe it does exist," said Ottilia cheerfully. "I daresay she will tear the place down brick by brick, and I hope she finds it."

"Or ridding Cassie Dale of this tendency to have visions?"

"Kinnerton will do that, though I daresay she will be far too fearful of consequences to divulge a word if she does have them."

"Nor attending these pestilential weddings," pursued her spouse doggedly.

The word threw Ottilia's mind out of kilter. An abrupt desire to weep caught in her throat, and she could not speak. She stared helplessly at Francis and saw his expression alter. Concern leapt in his eyes, and he rose swiftly from his chair and came around the table.

"What is amiss, my darling?"

Ottilia felt the stinging tears and tried to sniff them back, swallowing on her thickened throat. Francis seized her, catching her up from the chair and pulling her into the safe haven of his arms. Ottilia clung, gulping down the rising sobs.

"My love, my dear one, what in the world is the matter?"

The murmur in her ear served only to make things worse. Unable to help herself, she wept briefly into his shoulder, hiccoughing on her breath as she tried desperately to say what was in her heart.

"Oh, Fan, I love you so."

Finding her voice at last, she drew away a little, gazing

up into his beloved features. His dark eyes were tender, but puzzlement warred a little with dismay.

"Is that why you are weeping?"

Ottilia's breath shuddered in her chest. "No. It is because I never want to go through that again."

He drew her head back into his shoulder and held her so. "Nor I," he said feelingly. "I will never forget the moment when I realised it was you tied to that infernal stake."

Ottilia jerked her head up. "No! I don't mean that. I care nothing for that."

Francis was frowning now. "What then? I don't understand you."

She drew an unsteady breath, and her hands came up to rest against his chest. "I never want to doubt again. Not for an instant. I could not bear to think we had made a mistake to marry."

For a moment he said nothing. Then, to her incredulity, he let out a laugh, and she read relief in it. "Is that all?"

"All?"

Francis shifted back and caught her hands, holding them hard. "My darling Tillie, for all your brilliant mind, you are a hopeless idealist."

A little of the darkness she had been harbouring these several days began to lift. "How so?"

His smile was tender as he released her hands, instead using his fingers to wipe the straying wetness from her cheeks. "Do you imagine we can possibly get through a marriage without doubting its wisdom? Either of us?"

"I want to, Fan," she uttered on a desperate note.

Francis kissed her. "Then try. For my part, I am prepared to doubt with all the power at my disposal." Then he grinned. "Don't look so crestfallen, my dear one. The joy of it is the repeated realisation that marrying you is the wisest thing I could have done."

She sighed, a little comforted. "Even if I should involve myself in another such imbroglio?"

Francis's eyes narrowed. "If you ever dare to so much as whisper any such intention—"

Upon which Ottilia thought it prudent to demonstrate her affection in a fashion that must prevent her darling Fan from completing whatever dire threat he had been about to utter.

About the Author

An avid reader from an early age, Elizabeth Bailey grew up in colonial Africa under unconventional parentage and with theatre in the blood. Back in England, she trod the boards until discovering her true métier as a writer, when she fulfilled an early addiction to Heyer by launching into historical romance with Harlequin Mills & Boon, and fuelled her writing with a secondary career teaching and directing drama.

Now retired from teaching, and with eighteen romances published, she has switched to crime. Elizabeth still occasionally directs plays for a local group where she lives in West Sussex, England. She also finds time to assess novels and run a blog with tips to help new writers improve. For more information, go to elizabethbailey.co.uk.